A Time to Love Again. . .

"When I'm with Dan, it seems so right," Liz told Kate one evening. "But when I leave him, I feel as though it's wrong, Kate. It's only been a little over a year since Bill—"

"I know," Kate said, shaking her head wisely. "But I'll tell *you*, Liz, just as I have to keep telling myself, that it's all in the past." She was quiet for a moment. "We can't bring them back. And we're here. . .with so many years ahead of us."

Liz looked at her, her eyes filling with excitement. "I *knew* it. You and Adam."

Kate nodded, her eyes dreamy.

Liz threw her arms around her. "How exciting. When?"

"Next month. And I want you and Jenny to be there. At Finisterre. . .I won't pretend, Liz. It's going to be a wonderful kind of life. . .No more remodeling last year's suit. . .no more quick lunches at Walgreen's counter. . ."

"You are in love with him, aren't you, Kate?" Liz asked softly.

"Oh, Liz. . .I didn't think it could ever happen to me again. . ."

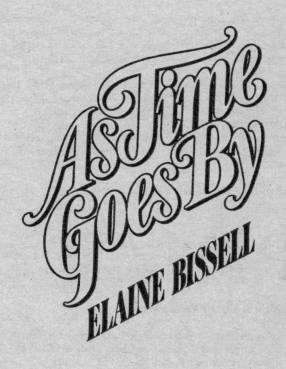

As Time Goes By

ELAINE BISSELL

PUBLISHED BY POCKET BOOKS NEW YORK

Distributed in Canada by PaperJacks Ltd., a Licensee
of the trademarks of Simon & Schuster, a division of
Gulf+Western Corporation.

To my three daughters

The radio announcement in Chapter 25 is excerpted from "This Is George Hicks Speaking," published in *A Treasury of Great Reporting*, Fireside Books, copyright © 1962 by Simon & Schuster, All Rights Reserved. Broadcast by George Hicks, American Broadcasting Company, Inc., D-Day, June 6, 1944. All Rights Reserved by American Broadcasting Company, Inc.

Another *Original* publication of POCKET BOOKS

POCKET BOOKS, a Simon & Schuster division of
GULF & WESTERN CORPORATION
1230 Avenue of the Americas, New York, N.Y. 10020
In Canada distributed by PaperJacks Ltd.,
330 Steelcase Road, Markham, Ontario.

ISBN: 0-671-42043-7

First Pocket Books printing September, 1983

10 9 8 7 6 5 4 3 2 1

POCKET and colophon are registered trademarks
of Simon & Schuster, Inc.

Printed in Canada

Chapter 1

IT WAS SNOWING. Not heavily. Not in long thick flakes that drift down over a sleeping city to shroud it in a ghostly white silence like the snows of January or February. It scurried around the deserted street corners of Lower Manhattan, gusting upward into the dim light of the lampposts in thin, icy plumes, demonic phantoms, fleeing through the night.

It was bitterly cold for that early in the month, the first Saturday night in December of 1941, but Liz Starrett, huddling in the front seat of the green Nash coupe, felt nothing but the agonizing pain that had her doubled over, her head pushing against the dashboard while her sister-in-law, Jeanne Starrett, guided the car through the heavy Times Square traffic.

Neither young woman was conscious of the festive air in the brightly lit area. People flowed from the theater and movie houses, hurrying in taxis or on foot toward the warmth and conviviality of bars and nightclubs; others ran down steps into subways or clambered onto buses. They stood in crushing groups at corners, laughing and impatiently waiting to dash through the honking traffic, their voices lost in the rush and rumble of taxis and autos, the clang and clatter of trolley cars and trucks. But the green Nash pushed relentlessly on, past the moving ribbon of light high above Times Square that announced that the British had renewed the tank battle at Tobruk, that John L. Lewis had won his fight for the mine workers, and that only fifteen more shopping days remained until Christmas.

Though Broadway glittered like daylight, blazing under the brilliance of theater marquee lights and flashing neon signs, neither Jeanne nor Liz glanced to either side as the car finally gained speed. Breaking clear of the traffic jams and throngs of hurrying pedestrians, it shot ahead and screeched around the corner to head south on Seventh Avenue.

"Hang on, Liz," Jeanne said, her gray eyes squinting into

1

the sudden half darkness of the avenue. "We're almost there."

· "I'm not going to make it, Jeanne," Liz cried out despairingly. "The hemorrhaging is getting worse."

"No, honey, you're going to make it, and the baby, too. They'll probably do a cesarean," she said, reaching out to squeeze Liz's arm. "Just another few blocks, Liz," she pleaded. "You're going to make it. I promise you!"

At the hospital Liz was lifted onto a stretcher and rushed up to the maternity floor. Jeanne watched for a moment, then parked the car and walked the half block back along the darkened street to the entrance, carrying Liz's small overnight bag, her pretty face weary but relieved.

When she reached the seventh floor, she looked around for a moment. The lights were turned low and the nurses' station was empty. The only person in sight was an attractive young woman with dark gold hair and striking features sitting in a wheelchair. She was wearing street clothes, and the tweed coat slung across her lap almost hid her swollen abdomen.

"Are you with the pretty blonde woman?" she asked, her smile warm with sympathy as Jeanne slowly unbuttoned her heavy coat.

"On a stretcher?" Jeanne said.

The young woman nodded. "I think they rushed her right into a delivery room," she said, then smiled again. "I heard the nurse say the name Starrett."

"My sister-in-law," Jeanne said, watching nervously along the corridor.

"Here." The young woman held out a package of cigarettes. "Have one. It will calm you down." As they lit their cigarettes, they were silent for a moment. "She'll be all right. She has the same doctor I have, and he's one of the best in New York."

"And you—?" Jeanne asked, her eyes worried.

"Oh, I'm fine. Pains still fifteen minutes apart. I've been hounding the doctor for the past few weeks because the baby's about three weeks past its due date, so when your sister-in-law was just brought in, he shouted at me as he ran down the corridor, 'For once, Kate, I'm glad you're late.'" Suddenly she put her hand out and touched Jeanne's arm. "I'm sure she's going to be all right. As soon as the nurse comes back to the station here, you can ask her how everything is."

* * *

Seven floors below, a young woman was standing at the high counterlike desk while a nun, all in white, bent over a printed form, her quill pen scratching loudly through the silence of the empty marble lobby. As she gritted her teeth against the uncontrollable pain that was peaking, the young woman held her breath, then let it out in small silent gasps so the nun wouldn't hear her.

"Your name, please?" Sister Rita-Marie asked, head still bent.

"Jenny MacKenzie." She forced the pain from her voice.

"No, dear, your husband's name." The nun looked up with a reproving smile. It was obvious that the young woman had been drinking. She could smell the liquor, and the pupils of her large brown eyes were dilated.

"You asked for *my* name," Jenny said stubbornly.

"Well, that's your husband's." The nun's smile had vanished.

Jenny paused for a moment, swallowed hard, and looked away. "Mrs. . . . Alan MacKenzie."

"Your age?"

"Twenty-two."

"Date of birth?"

"August eighteenth, 1919."

"The names of your parents?"

"I have no parents." Jenny tensed, felt the familiar rise of anger.

"Even deceased parents, dear." Sister Rita-Marie looked up with a sympathetic smile.

"Not even dead ones."

Their eyes held for a moment, Jenny's defiant, the nun's confused behind the rimless glasses.

"But—"

"Just write down that I was born on a bench in Grand Central Station," Jenny said, the words slurred but filled with rage. "At least that's where somebody found me. On August eighteenth."

Sister Rita-Marie gazed at her, seeing a small triangular-shaped face, a mass of tousled dark hair, the small mouth set, eyes filled with anger. "Your adopted parents, then."

"Guess again?" Jenny almost laughed. "No, I served out my time at the orphanage right to my eighteenth birthday." She gripped the edge of the high desk again and gasped with a wave of pain. "Do you think I could go up to wherever the hell it is I'm supposed to go?"

"Well, your husband . . . ?" The nun looked toward the revolving glass doors. "Is he parking the car?"

Jenny laughed aloud. "My husband is about five thousand miles away, at a place called Hickam Field in Hawaii. He's an Air Corps pilot." She leaned closer, waiting to see the shock on the nun's face, *wanting* to see it in her pain and anger. "But frankly, Sister, it's not very important. I didn't get married because I wanted to. I got married because I was pregnant."

Sister Rita-Marie stepped back as though she had been slapped. She picked up the telephone. "I'll call for someone to take you up to the maternity floor."

Jenny Smith had grown up in a grim, dark, red-brick orphanage on Manhattan's West Side. Once, when she was eight, she was almost adopted by a couple from Glen Cove, until they discovered she had been found as a newborn on a bench in Grand Central Station.

The only other really significant event in her years at the orphanage was the day she was taken to a movie about gangsters, big-city graft, a crusading newspaper editor, and a flippant but courageous girl reporter. That was when Jenny decided that she wanted to be a reporter, a desire that became an obsession.

At eighteen, when she was free to leave the orphanage, she carefully planned her strategy. She began to make the rounds of all the many newspapers in New York, finally concentrating on one. She hounded Henry Wilkens Fremont, the day city editor of the *Daily World-Dispatch,* until in desperation he gave her a job as a "copy boy." She hunted the city for human interest stories in her spare time, writing them in her little apartment, and then putting them on his desk the following day. Most of them went into the wastebasket. But when she had been there for six months, he finally published her first story, and under her by-line, and when she had been there for a year, she was moved up to reporter at $17.50 a week, the first female on the City Room staff. She made four dollars a week less than the lowest paid male reporter on the staff, but still it was a triumph. Life had become even more exciting than she had dreamed.

She had everything she wanted. Men were low on her list of important matters. She had never become serious about any

4

of the men she dated until she met Alan MacKenzie, an Army Air Corps pilot from Massachusetts, who was stationed at Mitchell Field on Long Island.

It was easy to drift into an affair with Alan. He was clever and good looking and desperately in love with her. She was twenty-one and curious and deeply attracted to him. One night after an Air Corps dance she let him come into her apartment when he brought her home, insisting he could only stay for half an hour.

"I thought I had everything I wanted, the way I wanted it," he murmured into her hair, breathing her fragrance as they stood in the darkness of her living room. "But I can't get you off of my mind." Half-heartedly she tried to pull away as he caressed her.

"Alan, I have to think," she pleaded as he kissed her neck and then her mouth, a deep and searching kiss that left her trembling. "No—please—" But she felt her strength flow into him, felt her body melt into his, and as he picked her up and carried her into the bedroom she wound her arms about his neck and buried her face against him.

In the dark of the bedroom he slowly undressed her until at last she stood before him, tiny and perfect, her skin like marble in the bands of light from the streetlamps shining through the windows. They lay down on the bed, their hands caressing each other, his swift and sure, lighting tiny fires and releasing wild currents until her body glowed. He was a skilled lover, leading her with the rhythm of his body and hands and lips until he brought her to an aching, throbbing pitch of desire. He took her then with a driving force and she gave herself completely, losing all conscious control. For moments she swirled in the darkness. There was a rush of sensations and she gasped, held on to him, cried out softly as the piercing pleasure shuddered through her over and over again.

Reality returned slowly. The silence of the bedroom enfolded them. And she coiled her leg across his, fingers tracing the wonder of his eyes and mouth. "I love you, Jenny," he murmured and held her as they slept, just the first of many nights, but the beginning of the end for her.

When Jenny discovered that she was pregnant, she wept bitter, angry tears. All the joy of the weeks and months before went up in the smoke of her dreams. They were married at City Hall, Alan making no secret of his elation. Because of a rule at the newspaper against pregnant women

5

or women with children, she was released from her job, and her bitterness deepened. Then Alan was transferred to Hawaii, promising to send for her after the baby was born, promising he'd make her happy, painting pretty pictures of their future, a future she didn't want.

She didn't want Hawaii, she didn't want Alan, and she didn't want a baby. She only wanted her job back, the sound of the roaring printing presses, the smell of the dust in the City Room, the clatter of typewriters and teletype machines, and Henry Fremont's gruff voice muttering down onto the pile of copy on his desk. "Nice job, Smith, on that milk fund fraud."

"Christopher? Is that the name you said earlier, Mrs. MacKenzie? You want to name him Christopher?" The voice was coming to her through layers of fog. She opened her eyes for a moment, but everything was white, and there were blinding lights over her head, people in white masks leaning over her, the smell of ether, and pain . . . so much pain. All she wanted to do was sleep.

"Go away," she moaned.

"There," a voice said, a deep voice. "We're all through with her here. Take her to her room and let her sleep."

"Sleep . . ." she moaned. "Sleep . . ."

Chapter 2

"GOOD AFTERNOON, MRS. Gray. I'm Sister Mary-Clare."

Kate glanced up from the nursing baby in her arms. A cheerful round-faced young nun, all in white and wearing a surgical mask, stood in the door of the hospital room, an exquisite arrangement of red roses in her hands.

"How beautiful," Kate said, keeping her voice just above a whisper so that the sleeping patient in the next bed wouldn't be wakened.

"Oh, that's all right, Mrs. Gray," the nun said in a normal voice. "She'll be out for another hour or so." She put the vase on the bureau. "Shall I read the card?" Kate nodded. "'Congratulations and love. Margaret and Justin Wheeler.'" She looked up, smiling. "Relatives?"

Kate's eyes clouded for only an instant. "No, the man I worked for and his wife. They're very close friends."

The nun walked to her bed. "I understand you've written out a cable to be sent to your husband? I'll take care of it now for you, if you'd like me to."

"Oh, thank you," Kate said, gesturing to a piece of paper on the bedside table. "It's there, if you can read my writing."

"I'd better read it back to you," the nun said. "'Joanna Thompson Gray, healthy, beautiful, and six pounds two ounces, arrived 12:35 this morning. Doctor says we can join you in Hawaii in April. Love, Kate.'" She looked up. "Where do you want it sent?"

Kate reached into the top drawer of the bedside table with her free hand, pulled out an envelope, and handed it to the nun. "Philip's address in Pearl Harbor is on the back of this envelope, Sister."

The nun walked to the door. She paused there a moment, then suddenly nodded, her eyes smiling over the mask. "Oh, of course. Your husband must be in the Navy. I've heard of Pearl Harbor."

Kate nodded. "He's an officer on the USS *West Virginia.*" For a moment his face was vivid in her mind, lean and tanned, his gray eyes beneath the billed cap searching hers, his fine figure straight and tall in the snowy Navy whites.

"Well, for your sake I hope the months between now and April go quickly," the nun said softly as she went out the door.

Kate smiled, her wide green eyes growing soft with memories. And as the baby stirred in her arms she held her close and looked down at her. She *was* beautiful. Even the nurses had said so. "None of the wrinkles and redness most newborns have," Miss Lee had said, laughing, when she had first put the baby into Kate's arms. "That's the first thing mothers look for, after counting the arms and legs."

The first thing mothers look for. Was that what her own mother had done? Kate wondered as she gently touched the petal-soft cheek of her child. For a moment she closed her eyes, forcing her memory back . . . far back. Could she really remember her mother? Or had Mrs. Hosmer told her about her so many times, described her so often, that Kate just thought she remembered her . . . lovely and slender, with Kate's wide green eyes, gold-flecked, standing in her studio in the paint-daubed smock, the easel in front of her, looking off through the windows at the golden beach stretching down to the sea, painting her endless seascapes, until Katy's father came home each night from the university where he taught. He was always so quiet while her mother chattered brightly, on and on.

Mrs. Hosmer took care of her and her mother. A big round woman in a white uniform, she would sometimes softly close her mother's bedroom door and say, "Your mother's not feeling well today, darling, so we'll play outside."

When her mother "didn't feel well," Katy's father would stay at the big house in San Francisco for days at a time and not come to the beach house, saying he'd had evening lectures.

She was shy with her father, and as time went on and her mother became more ill and reclusive, Katy missed him, missed having someone close and loving, someone who cared about her. And though they rode their horses along the beach and he told her stories of early California and her ancestors, she always felt a strain, his preoccupation, an estrangement.

One bright sunny morning when she was only five, watching from her bedroom window, she saw Mrs. Hosmer slowly walk down the beach to the high tide mark and pick up a robe—her mother's robe. She ran from the house and down the beach, shrieking, "Mama, Mama, Mama!" But Mrs. Hosmer caught hold of her, swung her up in her arms, and held her to her breast, then carried her into the house, where she called James Thompson at the university. Somehow, in her five-year-old wisdom, Katy understood her mother had taken her own life.

When Kate was graduated from the Berkeley campus, she left immediately for New York, where she got a job with Wheeler, Byfield, and Mason as a copywriter. Her father had remarried and there was little to keep her in San Francisco. She never quite trusted men, and held herself rather aloof from Philip Gray when she met him at a party, as she had from other men she had dated. Philip was stationed at the Norfolk naval base. He fell deeply in love with her the moment he met her and traveled to New York to see her each free weekend he had.

He was tall and fine looking with sharp, clean-cut features, a serious young man with strong persuasions and ideals. Within weeks she knew she was in love with him, in a way she had never dreamed possible, and six months after their first meeting they were married at New York's City Hall, then left for a honeymoon on Cape Cod in a beautiful old inn overlooking the ocean and beach, right at the edge of Provincetown.

They walked on the beach the evening they arrived, then at dusk climbed the stairs to their room, where windows faced the ocean and a fire in the fireplace took the chill from the cool autumn night. They drank champagne from slender wine glasses in the soft light from the fire, then he carried their glasses to the bedside table, put them down, and turned and opened his arms.

Gently he pulled her down to the bed, slipped the filmy gown from her shoulders, and kissed her, his lips trailing down her neck and across her breasts.

"I love you," she whispered.

With the words, all the pent-up desires and needs they had achingly known since their first meeting suddenly blazed into reality. The release was shattering. His hands were gentle at first, then demanding and sure, and she rose to his touch, grasping at each pulsing second, moaning as she moved beneath him. He pressed within her, deeper and deeper, penetrating to a core that throbbed with urgency, and then for a brief moment there was exquisite pain, but the explosion of passion lifted her beyond the pain to where the burst of sensations came. For a long, long moment they clung to each other in absolute stillness, then sank back, floating, dreamy, a part of the earth again. The fire crackled softly and he looked down at her, gently pushing the damp hair from her brow.

"I think I've always been waiting for you," he said.

Kate stayed on at her job in New York, and they spent the weekends together either there or in Norfolk. Her pregnancy was something they both wanted, and it came as no surprise several months later. They agreed that she would leave the advertising agency and move to Norfolk, but then his orders had come to proceed to Pearl Harbor.

"Okay," Philip had said. "A change of plans then. Just as soon as the doctor says you can travel, you and the baby will come to Hawaii." He was pulling on the jacket of his dark blue uniform with the gold buttons while they stood in the pretty living room of their apartment in the pink dawn. The orders were waiting in Norfolk.

"Dr. Chase said April or May if everything goes well," Kate said.

He had pulled her to him and held her close. "Everything's going to go fine," he had reassured her, knowing she was fighting the tears, forcing her voice to stay calm. He held her closer, wanting her to know how desperately he loved her, how much she meant to him.

"Philip—" she had faltered.

"Just seven months from now, Katy," he had whispered into her hair, breathing the fragrance, pulling away a little to look down into the striking face with its high cheekbones and wide green eyes, the dark gold hair sweeping back from her brow. He had kissed her, a long and tender kiss, then picked up his bags and walked out of the apartment.

The door to her room was suddenly flung open and a white-masked nurse cheerfully bustled in and over to her bed, pulling Kate into the present again.

"Back to the nursery," Miss Lee sang out, taking the sleeping baby from Kate's arms and hurrying out into the hospital corridor.

Drowsily slipping down on her pillow, Kate closed her eyes. She was more tired than she realized. She'd wait until evening to call Justin and Margaret Wheeler to thank them for the roses and tell them she'd be ready for visitors on Monday. And she would write Philip her daily letter when she woke from a little nap.

Chapter 3

ELIZABETH STARRETT FELT as though she were underwater, fighting her way upward. Her feet seemed caught, impossibly tangled in something below, preventing her from reaching the surface. She stopped struggling and felt the pain. It was a dull pain, one that seemed to be floating somewhere outside of her.

She opened her eyes slowly and saw the white ceiling above, then the white walls, then two big windows at the end of the room and a leaden winter sky beyond. She was stretched flat and tried to move. But the pain sharpened, leaping knifelike across her abdomen.

It was slowly coming back to her . . . the delivery room with the blazing lights overhead, white-gowned figures with skull-like caps and masks over their faces. She was terrified when they wheeled her in and shifted her to the delivery table. She was bleeding heavily.

"It's all right, Elizabeth." Dr. Nealson's voice had been soft but reassuring behind the white mask. "Everything's going to be fine." He was holding her hand and peering down at her above the white mask, his gray eyes warm behind horn-rimmed glasses. "Now I'm going to briefly explain what we're going to do." Only vaguely conscious of other voices and figures moving about, she had clutched his hand as he went on. "We're going to do a cesarean section. First your Navy doctors and then I hoped that by confining you to bed these past months—well, we'd hoped we could avoid this. I'd wanted to get you into your eighth month at least, but unfortunately there's been this premature separation of the placenta, and we're going to have to take the baby."

All she remembered after that was another masked figure above her head, holding something over her face and telling her to start counting from one hundred backward.

"One hundred, ninety-nine, ninety-eight, ninety-seven, ninety-six . . . ninety . . . five . . ."

Someone was gently shaking her, trying to wake her up. But she was too far away. Then slowly, slowly she opened her eyes and heard someone say, "It's a little girl, Mrs. Starrett, and she's . . ." But it began to fade again, and she smelled the ether as she slipped back onto a soft cloud, away from the harsh lights and loud voices.

Now, though, she was wide awake. A little girl, the woman's voice had said. She felt a soft surge of excitement. Moving her head, she looked at the sleeping figure in the bed next to her and smiled but was glad the other patient was asleep. She wanted these moments alone, just for a while, to think about Bill.

She had seen him again for the first time in so many years at the beach, the summer of 1940, on a hot July day. When she was a little girl growing up in the Rectory in Larchmont, she had played with his younger sister, Jeanne. But then as she and Jeanne had grown older they had gone their separate ways. Liz wasn't allowed to date boys, wasn't permitted to go to dances or movies, and Jeanne, a sparkling redhead, had come to the Rectory less and less and then finally not at all. Even Liz's brother, Frank, and Bill Starrett, who were friends, had begun to see little of each other as they grew older. Liz's father, Dr. Oldingham, discouraged what he called disreputable friendships, and his wife, Ellen, meekly agreed. Frank, when still in high school, had run away.

She had been flattered when Bill slumped down on one elbow next to her at the beach, but frightened when he persisted in a date. Her father would never approve. Bill had just graduated from Annapolis, a good looking young man with an engaging smile and personality, whose parents belonged to the fast-moving shore clubs set.

"I can't go out, Bill," she said miserably. "My father is very strict. He won't allow it. And I have to be truthful. He doesn't approve of your family."

"Then I'll come to your house and we'll sit in the parlor and talk."

And he did. For the twenty-one days remaining from his thirty-day leave, he sat each evening in the Rectory parlor, confounding even her father with his persistence and winning her timid little mother completely. Within six months they were married and went directly to the small house he had rented near the naval base in Newport.

"I'm going to assume," he said as he held her close in the darkened bedroom, "that you don't know very much about all this." He slowly led her over to the bed and sat her down. His voice was soft and he kissed her with gentleness. "I don't want to frighten you, and I want you to feel that marriage is something wonderful, something beautiful between two people, between us."

Lifting her eyes to his, she whispered, "I'm not afraid, Bill. Not with you."

"Then get undressed," he said, kissing the tip of her nose, "and get into bed, and I'll come back in just a few moments."

He left her there, closing the door behind him. She quickly undressed and put on the white silk nightgown Jeanne had given her, then slipped into the bed. Soon he returned and in the half darkness stripped off his clothes and lay down beside her. She touched the dogtags swinging against his chest, and as he gathered her in his arms she whispered that she loved him, over and over.

"Make love to me, Bill."

He kissed her softly, then with a deeper urgency as his hands whispered over her body, lifting off the gown and cupping her small breasts, then trailing down to her thighs and gently pushing her legs apart, stopping each few moments to assure himself that she wasn't frightened. With hands like fire and agonizingly sure, he brought her to a pitch where she grasped him and pulled him to her, moaning that she loved him, moving beneath him until he pressed into her and caught her with the rhythm of his own body. She gasped softly as the first spasm of passion flooded upward like liquid fire; then, matching the wild pulsing of his motion, she cried out as something leaped within her, rushed past the brief stab of pain, and filled her with a singing radiance. For long moments she clung to him, feeling a delicious heat spread down through her limbs, and she felt his hands once more, gently cradling her until she slept, never stirring from his arms, her face buried against his chest.

By the middle of the summer she knew she was pregnant. The baby was due in February, and they were both elated. She told him as they walked along the beach one early evening, hand in hand, letting the incoming surf wash across their bare feet, watching the sunset turn sailboats on the horizon into ships of gold.

"You're everything I ever wanted while I was growing up," she told him breathlessly as he caught her up in his arms and

14

ran along the beach with her. "And now this, Bill. I wanted us to have a baby right away, and it's all coming true, just the way I dreamed."

Slowly he put her down and looked into the blue eyes, large and fringed with dark, long lashes. She was lovely, her skin like porcelain, her hair a pale gold.

"It's time you had everything you want, Liz," he said, holding her close, feeling his love for her pound in his chest.

But within months the Navy doctors discovered an abnormality, the ovum implanted down low near the cervix rather than above in the lining of the upper part of the uterus. They confined her to bed, and when Bill's orders to proceed to Hawaii came, he took her to Jeanne's apartment in Manhattan, promising her that when she and the baby could travel, they would join him at Pearl Harbor. The moment he left, she started counting the days.

"We're going to move you, Mrs. Starrett," a nurse said as she and an aide hurried into the room.

"Why?" Liz asked with some bewilderment as they lifted her onto the stretcher and briskly tucked the sheet in all around her, just as the patient in the other bed began to stir.

"Well, who can say about these orders they give around here?" the nurse answered cheerfully as she pushed the stretcher across the room. While easing it through the door, she called out over her shoulder, "Oh, say there now, did we wake you up? Sorry, Mrs. O'Dell."

The fourth bed in the large room, on one side and nearest the door, was empty. In the bed closer to the window, Jenny MacKenzie, half raised on one elbow, looked at the two young women in the beds opposite her just as Miss Shelby and an aide shifted the patient with pale blonde hair from a stretcher over onto the sheet and tucked her in. Seeing all that she cared to see, she slid down on the pillow.

"Not that it matters particularly," Kate Gray said as she pulled herself to a half sitting position against her pillows in the bed nearer to the door, "but why have we all been moved in here?" She looked across at the other two women, then at the nurse.

"Well, you just never know why they do these things," Miss Shelby said as she bustled about tucking sheets and plumping pillows, but Kate thought she sounded too brisk and cheerful. There was a false note somewhere, she decided,

15

just as the door swung open and a tall nun walked swiftly into the room, her starched white robes making a swishing sound, the heavy black cross swinging against the front of her habit.

"Good afternoon, ladies," she said in a low, compelling voice. "I'm Mother Frances, the Superior of the Order here." Miss Shelby and the aide stopped as though frozen to the spot, their heads at attention, as Mother Frances moved to the foot of Liz Starrett's bed and stood there, a faint smile on her strong face.

"I wish there were another time and some other way of telling you three young women what I have to tell you," she said, a low warning in her voice. Kate sat sharply forward as the Superior looked at her. "You must be Mrs. Gray? I asked Miss Shelby not to connect your little radio until after I talked to you. She told me you had brought one with you. And I'd rather you hear this news from me than from a strange voice coming out of that little speaker." She paused and took a long, shuddering breath. "The Japanese bombed military installations in the Hawaiian Islands this morning."

No one in the room moved. Silence gripped each of them, then Liz gasped and Mother Frances moved to her side and clasped her hand, the motion saying far more than words could.

"We don't know too much. The reports are confused and confusing. But we've heard that Pearl Harbor and Hickam Field were both hit."

Kate gripped her hands together to keep them from trembling. She looked from one face to another, seeing deep concern in the faces of the nurses and the Superior, a swift and terrible fear in the eyes of the young woman in the bed next to her. But as her gaze moved to the patient in the bed across from them, she was startled to see no expression at all other than surprise, then a quickly veiled look as Jenny MacKenzie calmly lit a cigarette.

"Sister Rita-Marie at the admitting desk was quick to inform me that your husbands are all military officers stationed in the Honolulu area. I decided it was best to put you in a room together so that you wouldn't have to be in the two-bed rooms with patients whose husbands will be visiting them. And I felt, too, that you share something . . . and will be sharing something in the days ahead as we . . . wait for more news." She looked down at Liz. "Mrs. Starrett, your sister-in-law called and is on her way to the hospital. She should be here at any moment." Looking at Kate and Jenny, she said, "Is there anyone, a relative, friends, anyone we can call for you?"

Jenny simply shook her head and tapped the ashes of her cigarette into a drinking glass beside her. "No, but someone could bring me an ashtray," she said in a flat voice.

Only the faint tightening of her lips betrayed the thoughts behind Mother Frances' expression as she turned from Jenny and looked at Kate.

"No . . . no, thank you, Mother Frances," Kate said. "I have no relatives here. But I'll call some close friends. Later." She tried to smile, shook her head a little. "I . . . I'm just trying to grasp what it means at the moment."

"Of course." Mother Frances smiled, then turned to Miss Shelby. "Would you connect Mrs. Gray's radio now, Miss Shelby. I think they'll want to be listening to the news broadcasts."

As Miss Shelby bent down to put the radio plug in the socket, Mother Frances walked to the door and turned.

"If there is anything at all we can do for you, please don't hesitate to ask. And my prayers are with you."

Chapter 4

JENNY LOOKED DOWN at the small face in the crook of her arm where the nurse had unceremoniously placed the baby. Dark silky curls crowned his head, and she recognized his nose as her own, slightly tipped at the end. But the mouth was Alan's, wide and with the promise of generous laughter. Chalk another one up for Alan, she thought as she quickly lifted the baby and pushed him into the arms of the nurse standing next to the bed holding a nursing bottle.

"Sorry," Jenny said. "Feeding him is your department."

"It's the rule of the hospital, Mrs. MacKenzie," Miss Lee said. "Mothers who are not breast-feeding their babies still must give them their bottles, except for those at two and six a.m."

"That may be the hospital's rule, Miss Lee," Jenny said, sliding down beneath the sheet and turning on her side toward the window. "But it's not mine."

For a long moment Miss Lee watched her, then she strode from the room muttering, "I'll have to report this to Mrs. Harrison."

Kate and Liz saw Jenny's shoulders shrug beneath the sheet. They glanced at each other uneasily, then Kate looked back at the nursing Joanna, and Liz, flat on her back, turned up the volume slightly on Kate's small radio on the table between them. They were both tense and pale. Neither had slept much the night before, refusing sleeping pills, talking through the evening and into the night, and keeping the radio tuned to an all-night news station. But they had learned little in the way of new information. Reports were conflicting, with rumors that the battleships *Oklahoma* and *West Virginia* had been damaged or sunk at Pearl Harbor, and that three hundred and fifty aircraft had been destroyed on the ground.

They were puzzled by Jenny's behavior, and had been from the moment on Sunday when they had all been brought to this

18

one large room. But the events of the past twenty-four hours and their own tragic involvement turned their attention from the covered figure in the bed opposite them to the small radio when they heard a voice announce a special bulletin. "Oh, quick, Liz, turn it up, please," Kate said.

". . . and the Army and Navy were ordered onto a full war footing by President Roosevelt, who will address a joint session of Congress at noon today. It is expected he will then ask for a declaration of a formal state of war, and that Congress, shocked and angered by the Japanese attacks, will vote for any steps he requests, including a declaration of war on the entire Axis . . ."

"Mrs. MacKenzie?" A thin, gray-haired nurse with a clipped British accent was striding across the floor to Jenny's bed as Kate and Liz looked up. Jenny turned slowly onto her back and glanced up at the woman.

"I am Mrs. Harrison, the floor supervisor here on the day shift."

"Good," Jenny said. "I've been asking for some kind of pill for this pain I'm having. Could you do something about it?"

Mrs. Harrison lifted the record from the foot of Jenny's bed and glanced at it. "According to this, you've had more medication than is good for you already. You've done nothing but sleep since your baby was born." For a brief moment there was a conciliatory tone in her voice. "Now, under the circumstances of yesterday afternoon, we felt we could stretch a point and—"

"Please don't stretch any points for me, Mrs. Harrison," Jenny said, starting to turn over again, but the nurse lightly grasped her wrist.

"Mrs. MacKenzie, Miss Lee informed you of the regulations on this floor. Whether you are nursing your child or not, you must take over his feeding."

"And what do you propose to do if I refuse?"

There was a pause. "I shall have to report it to Mother Frances." Her face had hardened.

"And what will Mother Frances do? Have me put in jail?"

Kate watched with fascination. This small, pretty young woman, who looked like a child without makeup and in the shapeless hospital gown, was obviously deeply troubled about something—something beyond the news of the bombing of Pearl Harbor. For a moment the young woman in the bed and the nurse stared at each other, then Mrs. Harrison turned and walked to the door, where she stopped.

"Just today we lost several interns and doctors and seven of our nurses. They rushed to sign up in the military medical corps of both the Army and Navy. The staff is already dreadfully overworked. And we are certain to lose more in the days ahead. Many things are going to have to change here, and quite drastically, just as they have in much of the world. Maternity cases will not be able to stay for the full ten days that is now required." She started out the door, then stopped again. "Babies are born in the air raid shelters back in London. When I was working there during the night bombings of the blitzkrieg, I helped deliver them. I even delivered some myself in the underground where I was stationed. The women were splendid—"

"Well now, girls," Jenny said with a hard laugh. "We missed our big chance in the subway."

Tight-lipped and angry, Mrs. Harrison swept past the remark. "But here you are, fussed over and pampered, just as though there were nothing happening in the world, as though there were no war going on over there. And now finally your own country—"

"Hey, you, wait a minute!"

Jenny was up and on her knees at the edge of the bed, a small bundle of fury, eyes blazing and one hand pointing at the gray-haired nurse. "Just who the hell are you, telling us we don't know there's a war going on? You listen to me, lady, if anybody knows, it's the three of us here. You may have delivered babies in the underground in London, and you may have seen a lot, all of it bad, but we don't need anyone telling us what it's all about. Because I've been listening to the two of them over there—" She pointed to Kate and Liz who were staring at her in shock. "And you know what? I don't even know them. But I feel as though they're me. *Me!* Because we've been there together, and we know what it's like to look ahead and wonder where the hell we're going, and how we're going to put our lives back together again if our husbands don't ever come back—"

"Don't!" Liz cried out as Kate slowly shook her head.

"And what are you doing here, anyway? Why aren't you in England where the going's pretty damned rough at this point?"

Carolyn Harrison pushed the door open as though to leave and stopped again, her back to the room. There was a long pause.

"I came here with a shipload of children from London, to

get them away from the bombing. We turned them over to the Red Cross when we arrived in New York, and the Red Cross placed them with families here who will take care of them until the war is over." Slowly she looked around at Jenny, who was sitting back on her heels. "I'm sorry, Mrs. MacKenzie," she said in a low, barely audible voice. "I guess we sometimes forget what others are feeling. Perhaps too much happens to us sometimes, making us forget others. I . . . I volunteered to bring the children across, because I . . . I had to get away. My son was killed at Dunkirk. Just eighteen months ago. He was waiting with the others on the breakwater at the harbor, and they saw a troopship and swam out to it, but just as they were climbing up the sides, the ship was hit by shells. He was just twenty-four. His father was killed in the First World War."

She left the room. As the door closed behind her there was utter silence.

"Oh, my God!" Jenny sank slowly back on the bed.

"You couldn't have known," Liz said softly, urgently.

"When will I learn?" Jenny said, shaking her head back and forth. Then she looked up, and said in a small, subdued voice, "Somehow, before I leave, I'll tell her I'm sorry."

"I don't think you'll have to," Kate said. "I'm sure she knows."

For a long while the room was quiet; music flowed softly from the radio and the sound of a match scratched as Kate lit a cigarette. She looked over at Jenny, who was leaning against the head of the bed. "Want one?"

"Thanks."

Kate tossed the package of cigarettes across to her, then said, "Keep them. I have a carton."

Slowly lighting her cigarette, Jenny tried to smile, and leaning back, said, "Well, all we need is a fourth for bridge."

Chapter 5

THAT WAS WHEN the bond among the three began to form.

Often in the next eight days Kate wondered if they would have been drawn to each other if they had met under other circumstances. "Probably not," she wrote Philip. She had continued her daily letters to him, never permitting herself to believe he was anything but safe. She had even written a letter to Bill Starrett for Liz, with Liz still under doctor's orders not to sit up.

"We're so different really," she said in Philip's letter. "So we probably wouldn't have been at the same place at the same time. Oh, I might have met Liz at a naval base, of course, at one of the officers' wives teas or Bundles for Britain meetings. But we're just not anything alike, and it would probably have simply been a passing acquaintance. She's very conservative in her thinking—"

She paused, smiling. She could just see Philip's smile at that asinine remark and hear him say, "My lovely slay-the-dragon wife, out battering her head against middle-class walls on behalf of the impoverished and unskilled working class." A one-woman vigilante of intellectual dissent, Philip called her. She looked at the sleeping Liz and wrote, "But I would have missed so much. She's an adorable, rather childlike creature with large trusting eyes and a completely sweet and wonderful nature, without being sticky about it. Now, the other one—"

She looked over at Jenny, sitting up cross-legged on her bed and devouring a copy of the *World-Dispatch* while surrounded by a strewn mess of five or six other newspapers. "Jenny is most unpredictable," she wrote. "Bright, very talented, I suspect, a stormy personality, the kind you wouldn't want as an enemy but would cherish as a friend. She defies most hospital rules, constantly jumping out of bed to get things—whenever the nurses aren't around, of course.

But she's been a godsend for both of us. Liz is going through hell with the baby just hanging on to life by a thread. And although Jenny's own situation about her husband and the baby is a mystery, she's kept our spirits up daily. We've only seen her baby once. Since then she hasn't allowed them to bring him near her. All she's told us is that her husband, Alan, is a pilot, transferred from Mitchell Field to Hickam, and that she became pregnant and married him because of her pregnancy. She was dismissed from her job as a reporter on the *World-Dispatch* when they discovered she was going to have a baby, and she loved that job more than life itself.

"I thank God for someone like Justin. There simply aren't enough men like him in the business world. He's told me my job is waiting for me. Now that our plans are changed, until the war is over, my dearest, I will go back to Wheeler, Byfield, and Mason as soon as I feel able. The next time I write, your beautiful little daughter and I will be safely at home in our apartment. We are besieged by rumors and unconfirmed reports, and censorship has only permitted the vaguest information, but I feel certain you are safe and well. Love, your Kate."

Kate became aware that the radio news broadcast was about Pearl Harbor and slowly raised her head from the letter. ". . . a battleship of the *Pennsylvania* class, the USS *Arizona* was sunk . . ."

As Liz gasped, Jenny jumped out of her bed and ran to her while Kate quickly snapped the radio off. "It doesn't mean anything, Liz," Kate insisted. "You have to remember, the ships were moored right there at Ford Island. He would have easily gotten off. Or he may have even been ashore for the weekend."

"I know, I know," Liz moaned as tears ran down her face. "I'm sorry. But it just came as such a shock, a report straight from Secretary Knox, not a rumor, but real." She was twisting her hands, and she sounded on the edge of hysteria. "He was there, Jenny," she said, putting her hands on either side of Jenny's face and forcing her to look in her eyes. "Secretary Knox flew there and saw everything. He flew to Hawaii earlier this week."

"Okay, he saw everything, and he didn't say a word in his report about casualties, so that probably means everyone, or at least mostly everyone, got off the ship."

"Yes," Liz said, suddenly pausing a moment. "That's right. He didn't say anything about casualties." She lay back on the pillow and looked up at the ceiling. "I . . . I *feel* Bill is all right," she murmured. "Someone like Bill couldn't be . . . anything but alive. He's just that kind of person, you see."

Jenny walked slowly back to her bed and crawled up into it, then looked across at Kate. For a moment, as their eyes held, each saw doubt. Then they looked away.

As she turned her head Liz said in a small voice, "Please turn the radio back on, Kate. We might hear more news. Good news this time. Maybe it will be good news."

The door to the corridor was standing open, and Kate and Jenny, fully dressed, were standing on either side of Liz, who sat in a wheelchair. Liz's face was flushed with excitement.

"They're going to let me hold her today, just for a moment, of course. But at least this means she's going to be all right, that most of the danger is gone. Now if I'd just hear that Bill is all right—" She reached out and clasped their hands. "That all three of them are safe—then I couldn't want another thing in this world." Her face was drawn, but her eyes were clear.

Kate stooped to kiss her cheek. "After you bring the baby home in a week or two, what then?"

Liz's face clouded for a moment. "Well, I'll go back to Larchmont, until—until Bill comes back to the States."

Kate started to say something more to Liz but changed her mind. "Margaret Wheeler is waiting down in the lobby to take Joanna and me home."

At that moment Miss Shelby came to the door, a big smile on her face. "Well, I guess you girls won't mind seeing the last of us today." She stepped behind the wheelchair, and as she started to push it Jenny quickly leaned down and held Liz close for a moment.

"If I had to be in a hospital, I couldn't have chosen better roommates," Jenny said, trying to laugh to hide the tremble in her voice. "And I thought I was going to hate you both that first day."

They laughed shakily. Then, taking hold of Liz's hand and starting to walk, Kate said, "We'll walk you as far as the nursery, as long as we're all headed there anyway."

But Jenny held back, and Kate turned around. "Coming, Jenny?"

"You two go ahead," she said with a small wave. "I—I'll wait here for a little."

They watched her, concerned. She had been quiet all morning.

"The babies will be ready to leave. Mrs. Harrison said three o'clock." Kate held her hand out, then dropped it as Jenny turned away.

"I don't want to go just this minute."

Kate hesitated for a moment as Miss Shelby and Liz watched. Then she walked over to Jenny and hugged her. "Be good to yourself, Jenny," she said cautiously. "You have a beautiful new little guy in your life."

Jenny stiffened for a moment, then turned away as Kate returned to the door, where she half raised her hand. "Let's keep in touch?"

Jenny nodded. "Sure . . . I'll call you both soon."

Long after the echo of their footsteps was gone, Jenny slowly wheeled and looked around the room. Finally she walked over to one of the windows and, leaning on the sill, looked up at the sky.

". . . keep in touch," she murmured. Then, sinking to her knees, she put her head down on the sill and wept.

Jenny walked slowly over to the living room window and looked down into the street. The Western Union boy was just running down the steps of the old brownstone. As he hurried across the sidewalk to his bicycle he quickly buttoned the jacket of his dark greenish-brown uniform against the bitter cold and then rode toward the corner. He couldn't have been more than thirteen or fourteen, Jenny thought, thin almost to the point of emaciation, eyes watering from the cold wind, hands chapped and red as he handed her the telegram.

She almost laughed as she watched his bike round the corner. She had given him a dime, tipped him a dime to deliver a message telling her her husband was dead. Her mouth was twisted in a grimace as she turned away from the window and stared at the yellow piece of paper on the table beside the door in the small foyer. All the way across the small living room it seemed to mock her. "The War Department regrets to inform you. . . ."

She felt so empty. As though she were dead too. She had *known* when she opened the door and saw the boy standing there with the yellow envelope in his hand. She stared at the small peaked face, saw how he dropped his eyes, and she knew what the message in the envelope would say. She wanted to tell him that he could look at her, that he didn't have to be embarrassed, that she wasn't going to weep or cry out. He knew before she knew that her husband was dead,

25

and he was ashamed because he knew before she did, uncomfortable because he knew at all. She knew he wanted to run back down the staircase, but she simply kept on staring at the yellow envelope in his hand, outstretched toward her, the skin on his thumb chafed.

Finally she had taken it, then muttered something to him about waiting for a tip. And when she came back to the door from her purse on the desk, he was pushing the scuffed toe of his shoe into a worn spot on the hallway carpet. As she shoved the dime into his hand he mumbled something and glanced at her, his eyes stricken.

"It's all right," she said, surprised at the strange sound of her own voice, high and unnatural, and realized she was trying to reassure him. She held the envelope up for a moment. "I know what's in it. And it's all right—"

Suddenly she closed the door and leaned against it. What does he care? she thought, soundlessly pounding her fist against the door panel. All he wants to do is run down the stairs and get away.

Finally she opened the envelope, stared at the taped strips of printed words across the piece of paper. She held it in her hand for a long, long time, then let it flutter down onto the small foyer table and walked to the window, where she watched the Western Union boy disappear from her life.

For weeks she had been waiting in a kind of limbo, not knowing if Alan was alive or dead. The newspapers had at first published confused and confusing communiques from Pearl Harbor, then settled down to carefully censored reports, and released names of wounded, missing-in-action, and dead only after the nearest of kin had been informed. She knew that Hickam Field had been badly damaged, even suspected that it had been virtually destroyed, including most of the planes stationed there, while they were on the ground or trying to get into the air.

Poor Alan, she thought as something caught in her throat and began to ache. He had loved it so, loved flying, loved the danger, the howling of the engines and the feel of the wind, the reaching up to touch the sky, sweeping above the clouds, then soaring weightlessly against the fathomless blue. He had loved it more than life itself.

Slowly she sat down, hunched on the edge of the chair. She felt nothing, only an emptiness. I still want what I wanted before, she thought, my life the way it was before I met Alan—no, not before I met Alan, but before the baby. I want what I can't have, what they took away from me. And now Alan's gone, everything's gone.

She looked toward the closed bedroom door, where the baby lay sleeping, then suddenly turned, buried her face against the soft arm of the chair, and sobbed.

"I got here as quickly as I could," Margaret Wheeler said, hurrying into Kate's apartment. She pulled off her gloves and threw her fur coat down on a chair in the foyer, then folded Kate in her arms and held her. She felt the slim figure quiver, heard the soft whispery sobs, and held her closer, but dropped her arms as Kate turned and walked slowly into the long, pretty living room where wintry late-afternoon sunlight fell like quiet sorrow through the windows. How beautiful she is, Margaret thought, following her, as Kate sat on the cushioned window seat and looked down onto the small park across the way. The heavy gray satin of her robe gleamed dully in the winter light as she wearily pushed back the dark gold hair from her face. For a long moment there was silence, then she spoke as Margaret quietly sat next to her.

"That was the place he always stopped to wave," Kate said. Margaret followed her gaze down to the corner of the black iron fence around the little park. She heard the tight control in Kate's voice, the hesitation, the husky edge of unshed tears. "And it's like an image, against my eyelids—" She stopped for a moment, fighting for control again. "Like when you stare at the sun too long, then look away and an image is frozen there. I . . . can see him so clearly."

Margaret Wheeler reached over and clasped Kate's hand. The soft lines in Margaret's face had deepened as she fought back tears. Kate slowly turned her head and looked at her, suddenly finding comfort in the warm brown eyes and softly waved silver head bent close in sympathy.

"I sent his father a cable. He's a Navy commander with the Atlantic Fleet. Philip's mother died when he was just ten." There was a pause. "I called you because I wanted someone here who had known Philip, who had loved him—"

"Oh, we *did*, my dear," Margaret said with gentleness, her hands tightening on Kate's as she heard her voice break. "We did."

Kate looked down into the park again, and when she spoke it was in a whisper. "I can't believe he's gone. He was so alive, so real. He always stood there and waved, tall and straight and with that wonderful smile. . . . There was no

27

question he'd come back. People like Philip always come back." They were silent again for a long moment.

"He's still here, in Joanna, Kate," Margaret said.

Kate slowly nodded. "After a while I can begin to believe that, Margaret. Right now—"

"I know," Margaret said quickly, softly, pressing Kate's hands again. "It's too soon. But as time goes on, you'll see."

"Thank God I have her," Kate whispered. "I don't think I could bear it if it weren't for Joanna."

And Margaret nodded, knowing at last that Kate would be all right, that after the first terrible pain had dulled, she would begin to live for herself again as well as for her child. Briskly she got to her feet. "And now I'm going to make us some tea," she said. "Then I'll phone and have Justin send the car for us." She had started toward the kitchen. "I'm taking you and Joanna home with us for a few days."

Kate's voice stopped her halfway across the room. "No, Margaret. I want to stay here." She quickly stood. "Oh, I'm terribly grateful, but—well, I must stay here. I have to learn right from this moment how to face it alone. And . . . it's home, you see." She looked around.

"Oh, my dear," Margaret said, starting back to her, then stopping. "Of course. I understand perfectly. I think I would feel the very same way." She went on to the kitchen.

Kate watched her as she disappeared through the small foyer, then turned back to the window. For a moment she didn't move, then she leaned forward slowly and placed her hand against one of the casement panes, as though reaching beyond to touch someone, and her lips soundlessly formed the name Philip.

Jeanne watched as Liz carefully lay Julie down in the white bassinette, then gently loosened the pale pink bonnet and matching bunting.

"I'll wait until she wakes up," Liz whispered, "then take these things off her."

Jeanne stood behind Liz, her hands half raised in a gesture of helplessness, her face tightly masking a look of deep anguish. She watched as Liz untied the satin ribbons and tucked the bunting away from the sleeping baby's face, then pulled off her own hat and coat and tossed them onto the bed.

"Oh, Jeanne, just look at her," Liz exclaimed, still whispering. "Isn't she beautiful?"

"Beautiful," Jeanne echoed, forcing her voice to sound

normal, but Liz heard something and slowly turned around. "She's gorgeous, Liz," Jeanne enthused, but she caught her lower lip between her teeth.

"What is it, Jeanne?" Liz asked, taking hold of Jeanne's hands.

"Come in the other room." Jeanne led Liz out of the bedroom and into the wide living room overlooking Riverside Park. Snow had topped the evergreens with caps of white, and on the slope falling steeply toward the river a group of children in bright snowsuits and stocking hats threw themselves down on sleds and raced to the bottom of the hill.

"It's Bill," Liz said, standing in the doorway, hands to her mouth, her blue eyes wide with fear. "You've heard something."

Jeanne had stopped in the middle of the room and turned to her, her face white beneath the piled mass of reddish hair. She nodded, trying to speak, but the words wouldn't come for a moment. Slowly she walked back to Liz and took hold of her shoulders.

"The telegram was for you, Liz, but—" Her hands tightened on Liz's shoulders as Liz began to shake her head back and forth. "I decided to open it. I thought it was best if I—"

"He's dead, isn't he, Jeanne?" Liz whispered, her face turning a ghastly white, her blue eyes darting wildly from Jeanne's eyes to her mouth and back again. "Isn't he, Jeanne?"

"Oh, God, Liz!" Jeanne grasped her wrists and led her to the couch as Liz's legs began to buckle. She felt tears streaming down her own face, and as Liz rocked back and forth on the edge of the couch, Jeanne knelt down in front of her and put her arms around her. For several moments they simply held each other, Liz now deathly still and quiet. Finally Jeanne pulled back and looked at her.

"Where's the telegram, Jeanne?" she asked in a strange voice.

Jeanne pulled it from her jacket pocket and handed it to her, then watched as Liz unfolded it and slowly read the printed words, her lips moving silently. She read and reread it, then folded it again, carefully creasing it. She had become utterly still, her face a mask of stunned composure. She rose and walked out of the room, simply shaking her head as Jeanne tried to grasp her hand.

Chapter 6

JENNY STOOD AT the entrance of the sprawling old newsroom, peering through the Sunday gloom. As she had expected, he was there. Beyond the sea of desks and clutter she saw Henry Fremont, all alone and hunched over his desk, at work in the small circle of light from the gooseneck lamp, pencil moving swiftly across the copy.

Halfway across the room she stopped and he looked up, hearing her footsteps. He scrambled to his feet, almost knocking his swivel chair over. "Jenny!" he called out, hands stretched toward her.

As she slowly walked toward him he bumped into a wastebasket while hurrying around the desk to meet her. "You've had the baby!" he exclaimed, then grabbed her and held her in a close hug. "Christ, honey, we've tried to call you time and again, but you never answer your phone, and Alison had it all figured out. You must have been home a couple of months now. Here, sit down, sit down." She sat at the desk opposite him, slowly pulling her gloves off. "What is it? A girl or a boy?"

"Boy," she said.

"What's his name?" He was trying, a smile pasted on his face.

"Christopher."

"Must be a great looking kid, with such swell looking parents."

"He looks like a baby."

"Hey, come on," he said, starting to jump to his feet. "Down to the Blue Ribbon. I'll buy you a drink in celebration."

But she didn't move. Just stared at him, and slowly he sat down. "What is it, kid?" he asked.

She looked away, off toward the big grimy windows. "Alan's dead."

He didn't move, just kept watching her for a long moment, then started to get up and come around to her, his arms open. "God in heaven, honey, what can I do for—"

"No!" She jumped up and backed away. "I don't want your sympathy, Henry. All I want is my job back."

He just shook his head, angry with himself, angry with the world. "The rules haven't changed, honey," he finally said in a low voice.

She watched him for a long moment, then turned and walked swiftly toward the stairway.

"Jenny!" he called out.

She stopped and turned. "Don't tell me you're sorry, Henry. Just run a little fudge box down in the corner of page one, telling all of Jenny MacKenzie's good friends the latest news about her. Will you do that for me? I made a couple of good friends in the hospital. They were in the same room with me and"—she laughed mirthlessly—"the same boat, too, you might say. Their husbands were at Pearl Harbor too. I wonder how they made out. I promised to keep in touch with them. But I'm not in the mood right now. Just let them know they won't be hearing from me for a while. If ever. And that goes for you too."

He heard her footsteps echo on the marble steps of the stairway and finally disappear.

Henry Fremont phoned Mother Frances, explained his visit from Jenny, and asked her to give him the phone numbers of the two young women who had been in the same hospital room with Jenny. When he reached his apartment that evening, he stood with his back to the crackling fire in the fireplace, then finally said to Alison, who sat in a wing chair mending, "Jenny came to see me today. Alan's dead."

"Oh, dear God," Alison gasped, one hand to her lips.

"She mentioned two other young women who shared her room in the hospital. Husbands at Pearl Harbor too. I called them to tell them about Jenny." His head sank sadly on his chest. "Same story. Dead. All three husbands dead."

Alison had pulled a hanky from her sweater pocket and was softly weeping.

"Jenny asked for her job back again. I had to tell her, of course, that nothing's changed." They were quiet for a moment, only the sound of the fire breaking the silence. "She had a little boy," he said. "Named him Christopher. She

31

didn't want him, you know, and it sounds as though she still doesn't."

"Poor, poor little baby," Alison murmured sadly. After several more moments of silence she sighed and stood up, putting her mending away in the basket. "I'll fix you something to eat." At the kitchen doorway she turned. "I'll go down and see Jenny tomorrow."

"Well, don't be surprised if she tells you to get the hell out," he said, walking over to the radio and switching it on to the news.

Chapter 7

"COME BACK TO work just as soon as you want and feel you're ready," Justin Wheeler had urged.

And Kate, being Kate, pulled strength from her reserve and set about putting her life back in order. Carolyn Harrison, the English nurse from the hospital, had phoned and said that she was tired of living in a boardinghouse and wondered if Kate might need someone to care for Joanna during the daytime hours. "My shift is from four to midnight," she had said. "If you can find someone to take over from three thirty until you get home, it would work out fine."

And it did. It left Kate alone in the evening hours, feeding Joanna and putting her to bed; left her alone with her grief, disposing of his clothes, putting away his books and mementoes, weeping her silent and private tears, and carefully reconstructing the shattered pieces of her life.

"I'll be back on February second, Justin," she had told him.

"You sound fine, Kate," he had said, sounding relieved. "Just fine. How are your other two friends taking it?"

"Badly, I'm afraid, but for different reasons. Jenny won't even answer her telephone. And Liz refuses to accept it at all, keeps saying he might have been on shore leave that weekend and that the records are mixed up. In fact, I'm on my way to see her right now."

Jeanne Starrett pulled the green Nash coupe to the curb and turned the ignition off. They had just returned from Larchmont, where they had attended a memorial service for Bill at Dr. Oldingham's church, leaving Julie with one of Jeanne's neighbors on her floor. Bill's parents had come from Florida, where they had moved in the autumn, and Jeanne had just driven them to Pennsylvania Station, where they were catching a train back to Palm Beach.

33

"I'm going for a walk," Liz said in a wooden voice, and without looking back, she crossed the drive, pulling her coat collar higher around her neck against the bitterly cold wind. Jeanne stood beside the car, watching her for a moment, feeling utterly helpless and frustrated in the face of the dry-eyed and silent grief that Liz was suffering. Since early in the week, when she had been informed that the missing-in-action status had been changed to killed-in-action, Liz seemed like someone walking in her sleep.

Even from a distance her hopeless acceptance was apparent as she walked down the path that sloped toward the river. In her dark coat and hat she was a figure of infinite sorrow against the wintry sky, like the bare branches above her, stark and lonely in the gray waning light of late afternoon. Hurrying across the street, Jeanne followed her at a distance, stopped and waited for a moment as Liz sat down on a green bench, then slowly walked on down the slope toward her and leaned against the end of the bench, where she stood gazing across at the Jersey shore.

"You know, somewhere along the line you have to stop this dying, Liz, and start to live again," she finally said, her own sorrow for her brother's death lost somewhere among the tangled threads of Liz's grief and her parents' bereavement. "Your life has to go on, because somewhere in that life of yours there's a baby that has to be cared for." She sat down beside Liz and took one of her hands. "Even if nothing seems to matter to you right now, honey, you have so much to live for. You have Julie, and you have to care about what happens to her. And finally, it *is* going to matter someday, because you're young and pretty and sometime there will be someone else in your life who will—"

Liz stood up and started to walk away, but Jeanne quickly grasped her arm. "No! You're going to *listen* to me. You're too young to bury yourself in the same grave with Bill, and he'd hate it if he knew."

Neither of them saw a tall, slender young woman in a dark fur coat step out of a taxi on the street above. Seeing them on the slope below her, the woman stood and watched as Liz struggled, trying to get away from Jeanne, tears streaming down her face.

"He was too full of life to want to see you turn into a living corpse," Jeanne half shouted as she stoutly held on to the distraught Liz's arm, her gray eyes flashing, her red-gold hair like a bright streamer in the gray afternoon. "Damnit, Liz, he

34

loved you. Not only because you're sweet and pretty and warm, but because he thought you had guts and good sense."

Kate started down the slope toward them.

"He knew what the odds were for himself, so he wouldn't have married you if he'd thought you were going to fall apart," Jeanne cried out as Liz broke loose and started down the hill, half stumbling. "Damnit, Liz, he trusted you!" The running figure stopped.

"Liz!" Kate called out. Liz slowly turned and looked up and saw Kate at the top of the path. Liz started toward her, hands outstretched in an open, helpless kind of gesture. When she was just a few feet away, she stopped, her lovely face torn with grief.

"What are we going to do, Kate?"

Kate slowly closed the gap between them and took hold of Liz's hands. "We're going to go on, Liz," she said, so softly that Jeanne, just a few feet away, had to strain forward to hear.

"We're going to always remember them, and . . . miss them terribly—" Her voice broke. "But we're going to be all right, because that's exactly what they would expect of us."

Jeanne backed off a little into the growing shadows. She saw tears slip down Kate's face and the movement of Liz's shoulders as she sobbed silently, then watched as Kate put her arms around Liz.

"There are going to be times when we're going to wonder how we can bear it, and there are going to be times when the loneliness will make us want to give up. But we knew it, Liz." Kate held her away a little and looked into her face. "We knew when we married them that there was always this possibility, always the chance this could happen. Isn't that true?"

For a long moment Liz stood stiffly with her eyes closed, her face wet with tears. Then she slowly shook her head up and down. "Yes," she whispered. "Yes, we knew. Bill said . . . the war was coming to us. He didn't know where. But it was coming."

Kate pulled her close again, and for several long moments the only sounds were the distant clanging of a bell on a barge gliding up the river and the flow of traffic on the drive above.

Jeanne turned and walked up the hill. When she reached the top, she stopped and looked back. They were still standing there, holding on to each other, two dark shadows in the deep twilight.

Chapter 8

As THE HARSH weeks of winter slipped into the soft months of spring, the initial sense of shock and outrage at Germany and Japan changed to unabashed patriotism. Even the most extreme of the isolationists did a complete about-face, and Winston Churchill's V-for-victory hand signal was seen everywhere. People cheerfully grumbled at the shortages of butter and meat, of coffee and silk stockings, but lined up to buy war bonds and stamps and flew the American flag every day of the week instead of just Memorial Day and the Fourth of July. Housewives started rolling bandages for the Red Cross, and their daughters went to work in defense plants.

About a week before Kate returned to Wheeler, Byfield, and Mason, Liz phoned to tell her that she was taking Julie and moving back to Larchmont, where they would live in the Rectory with her parents. "Tomorrow morning," she said sadly.

"Then come with me today," Kate urged. "I'm going down to the Village to try and see Jenny." It would help Liz as much as Jenny.

"If she won't answer the phone, Kate, she probably won't come to the door either."

"We'll get in somehow," Kate said firmly.

At the Minetta Lane address they couldn't find Jenny's name on the lower hallway mailboxes, so Kate rang the superintendent's bell.

"Yeah?" he said as he shuffled into the narrow hallway from a door at the rear, pushing his stained brown cap back on his head.

"We're looking for Mrs. MacKenzie," Kate said as he stared at them appraisingly in their pretty spring coats and close-fitting hats.

"She moved," he finally said. When Kate started to ask him a question, he turned back to the door. "And don't

36

bother askin' me where, 'cuz she didn't leave no forwardin' address."

"None?"

"None," he said and disappeared behind the door.

Kate took Liz's arm and they went to a drugstore on the corner, where Kate phoned Henry Fremont. But he knew less than they and, discouraged, they boarded an uptown bus on Fifth Avenue.

"Two new accounts to start you off," Justin said, handing her two manila folders. "Both with high budgets." The first was a big Detroit automobile manufacturer that had taken on war contracts. "Their last civilian car rolled off the production line two months ago," he explained, his silver head tipped toward her. "They're building tanks now, four hundred a month to start."

"But why this massive ad campaign?" Kate was puzzled.

"Good will," he said, swiveling his chair to look out at the Manhattan skyline. "Morale factor, keeping the product's name in front of the public until the war ends and they go back to making autos again. Your job will mainly be involved with a big hour-long variety show on the air with Hollywood, Broadway, and radio stars. Eddie Cantor is heading the first show.

"Your second account is the war bonds campaign. We're giving the government a free assist on this, doing our bit too. I'll be in Washington most of the time as a dollar-a-year man, and you'll be my account executive here. The goal this year is seven to ten billion in the sale of bonds."

"Dollars?" she asked, and when he nodded, she gasped, "Good God!"

She felt a ripple of excitement up her spine as she rose to leave. Between Joanna and her job, life was finding meaning again.

"Just one other thing, Kate," Justin said, and she turned at the door. "A friend of mine who publishes the *Sun-Post* in Boston wants a series written on Rosie the Riveter, but he wants it written by a woman, and unfortunately he has no women on the staff, except—"

"On the society pages," Kate echoed, smiling.

"I know, I know," he said, putting his hands up apologetically. "Wasn't that young friend of yours from the hospital a newspaper reporter?"

"Yes," Kate said quickly. "Jenny MacKenzie."

"Think she'd be interested? It would give her about two or three months' work, all expenses paid, even someone to take care of the baby while she's out doing her interviews. An airplane factory in Connecticut is the spot."

"I don't know if I can find her," Kate said and explained about Jenny's disappearance.

"Simple," Justin said with a smile. "Widow's pension. I've got a friend in Washington who owes me a few favors. He'll find her."

Jenny stood in the hallway, carefully closing Christopher's door and swaying slightly, her wrinkled robe hanging open at the top where buttons were missing. Then, after steadying herself on the doorjamb, she walked back to the tiny kitchen, poured herself another drink, and carried the glass into the living room.

She looked around as though seeing it for the first time. It could be pretty, she thought, like her other living room on Minetta Lane; the antiques she had so lovingly selected, the good prints and chintz-covered couch and chairs, and all the books still packed in boxes. Who cares? she thought, kicking at the rolled-up oriental rug, staring at the drapeless windows and ashtrays overflowing with cigarette butts and ashes.

At the sudden sound of the door buzzer she didn't move. Even when it rang several more times with insistence. Then, remembering that she had asked the superintendent's wife, Mollie, to pick up some Scotch and an evening newspaper for her, she wandered to the door, muttering, "All right, all right, I'm coming," and flung it open.

"Well, Jenny, you certainly make it hard for anyone to find you."

For a few seconds she looked bewildered, then reached out and tried to slam the door shut, but Fred Baldwin quickly put his foot in the way and pushed the door open again.

"You have a nerve!" She was suddenly shaking with an uncontrollable rage. Instinctively pulling her robe about her neck as his gaze slid down over her body, she stepped back. But he pushed into the small foyer and shut the door, then stood there looking into the living room and in one glance absorbed all the information he needed to know. One silk stocking hung over the back of a chair, and half-filled coffee cups and crumpled newspapers littered the tables. A skirt was tossed on a chair.

Beneath veiled lids she watched him as he slowly walked

around the room. She had never liked Alan's brother-in-law and wondered why Mary, who seemed nice enough and was rather pretty, had married him. Of medium height, but stocky and slightly paunchy from too much beer, he had features that had coarsened with years and weight. And he had a way of looking at women with an insolent, suggestive gaze, where he half dropped his lids, apparently believing that this made him appear sexy and attractive. "God," she had once laughed to Alan, "he must think he's another Clark Gable."

"First you wouldn't answer your phone, then it was disconnected, so we decided I'd better come down to New York and see what's what."

"How did you find me?" She spoke between clenched teeth, despising the way his gaze seemed to rake up and down her body.

"Not too difficult," he said, walking into the small kitchen and making himself a drink, all the time talking over his shoulder as she stood glued to one spot as though afraid to move. "A little bribe with your old superintendent to tell me the name of the moving company who moved your furniture over here, then a nice schmaltzy story to them about how you're grief-stricken and about to have a breakdown." Coming back into the living room, he shook a finger at her. "You shouldn't worry Mary and her mother like this. They've been concerned about you and Christopher—"

"Christopher is fine," she said, the words clipped.

"—and whether you're taking proper care of him. After all, the one time Alan's mother managed to talk to you, you were pretty drunk, you know, and—"

Jenny had moved to the door and opened it. "Get out of here," she said, venom fairly dripping from the words. But Fred quickly stepped to her side, forced the door shut, and took hold of her wrist. He led her back into the living room, where he eased her down onto the couch.

"So I had to come to New York on business," he said, seeing her wince as he tightened the grip on her wrist, but never losing the smile on his face or the dulcet-soft tones in his voice. As he stood over her, first putting his own glass and then hers down on the coffee table, she felt fear for the first time. "And I thought, why not drop in and see my pretty little sister-in-law?"

He sat quickly on the couch beside her and ran his fingers up her arm. As she pulled away he grasped the back of her neck and tried to kiss her, but she twisted her head aside.

39

"After all," he said, struggling with her, "she hasn't had any loving for a long, long time now, and sexy little broads like her need a lot of—"

"You pig!" she screamed, lunging out of his arms, but with one powerful move he pulled her down again, this time suddenly pushing her onto her back, where with a single tearing motion he ripped her robe and gown upward from the hem to the top, then held her flat with his fingers cupped over her neck. One of her hands was twisted beneath her, but with the other she raked her fingers down his face, and in the split second that followed knew she had made a grave mistake. Cursing her, his breath exploding in short little excited gasps, he fell with his full weight on her. His breath was hot on her neck, and then she felt his flesh against her, heaving and pressing, and nausea rose in her throat in waves. With her free hand she tore at his face again, her nails gouging the same cheek from under his eye down to his chin.

"Bitch!" he snarled, and she felt a smashing blow to the side of her head from his fist, then a shattering pain as the same fist crashed into her face. She tried to scream, but he had pushed her head sideways with his arm into a small corner pillow and held it there with the butt of his head while her free hand clawed at the air. She felt as though she were strangling, tasted blood from a split in her lip, and gasped desperately for air as her face was driven into the pillow. Trying to move, she flailed helplessly, then suddenly heard a guttural, rasping sound tear from her own throat as he thrust her legs apart with the sheer power of his body and drove into her with a force that ripped a high-pitched scream from her deep down inside.

She lost all track of time and reality. For what seemed like forever, in a tormenting nightmare, he pounded into her, his breath erupting in groaning gasps. The pain seemed remote, as though happening to someone else. And then, at last, it was over, and all of her senses slowly returned—light and sound and odors and the revolting feeling of his flesh against hers.

As she felt the crushing weight lift from her body, she kept her face buried in the pillow. Slowly she rolled to her side and pulled her knees up, burying her face even deeper, waiting and wondering what would happen next as her heart pounded in her throat. For crawling minutes she heard the rustling of clothing, then soft footsteps across the carpet, the door opening and quietly closing, and finally nothing. Just the

40

ticking of the clock on the desk. A stillness like death, and far off, sounds of traffic, sounds from a world beyond that had nothing to do with her.

She huddled there for perhaps an hour, not moving. Then there was a small cry from the bedroom—Christopher waking. Dragging herself to her feet, she pulled the ripped robe around her and crept to the kitchen to warm his bottle.

Chapter 9

KATE LEFT WORK a little early and flagged a taxi on Fifth Avenue heading south. She checked the slip of paper Justin had given her and told the driver Jenny's address. It was on Waverly Place, not too far from where Jenny had lived before.

The building was another brownstone, and as Kate climbed the front steps she looked up, wondering which windows were Jenny's. In the gloom of the vestibule she read "MacKenzie" on one of the mailboxes. Apartment 4A. She climbed the stairway to the fourth floor, found the door and knocked, waited, then knocked again, but there was no answer.

"Jenny?" she called out softly, leaning close to the door. "It's Kate. Please open the door. I have something important to tell you." She waited a moment, then knocked again. "It's terribly important, Jenny." She heard a small noise, then the door slowly opened.

Waiting a moment to let her eyes adjust to the dim light in the shade-drawn living room, Kate watched as Jenny moved away.

"How did you find me?" Jenny asked, slurring the words.

Kate ignored the question as she watched the disheveled figure in the rumpled seersucker bathrobe and worn slippers. She saw how Jenny's fingers trembled as she picked up a cigarette from a pack on a table and lit it. Slowly Kate walked across the room to her, took hold of her shoulders, and turned her around. It was then that she saw the bruise beneath one eye and another on the side of her neck and gasped.

"Good Lord, Jenny! What happened?"

"I fell," Jenny said bluntly.

"That's not from a fall," Kate said, her green eyes flashing.

Jenny walked to the window and pushed back the blind at one side. She looked down into the street for several moments, then turned and started to say something flippant. But as she saw Kate's face, she suddenly sat down in a chair and hugged her knees while rocking back and forth. Tears began to slide down her face. "He—he came yesterday—"

"Oh, God, Jenny, what happened?" Kate hurried across the room and knelt down in front of her.

In a controlled outpouring of words, Jenny began to talk, the monotone gradually giving way to hysteria.

"I didn't want to see or talk to anyone. But ever since Christopher was born, Alan's mother and sister, Mary, have been phoning me from Massachusetts. I'd just hang up, and when they wrote, I threw the letters away. All they care about is having Alan's child, and twice Mary's husband, Fred, got on the phone and insisted I come live in Craddock Corners. I finally moved so they would stop bothering me. But yesterday Fred found me."

As her shoulders started to tremble the words spilled out in wracking sobs. Kate put her arms around her and held her.

"He came here and rang the bell and I thought it was the super's wife. But he pushed his way in when I opened the door . . ."

When she finished the story, she sat perfectly still for several moments while Kate simply held her. Finally she stirred.

"I feel so dirty, Kate. I stood under the shower, just stood there letting the water run over me, for an hour, maybe longer, scrubbing and scrubbing. But it wouldn't wash away."

"We should take you to a doctor," Kate said softly.

"No!" Jenny half shouted, pulling away.

"But that kind of thing happening, so violently, just months after the baby was born. And . . . you might be pregnant."

"Then I'll have to get an abortion." The words were muffled, frightened, as Jenny buried her face in her hands. "This time I'll *have* to." She suddenly looked up. "Oh, God, Kate, I feel like hundreds of broken little pieces . . . scattered all over, like . . . like a jigsaw puzzle—"

"Lean back, Jenny," Kate said gently. "Let me get a compress and put it on those bruises." Jenny put her head back and closed her eyes. For a few moments she was still as Kate brought a wet towel and put it against her cheek and neck. But then she sat forward, pushed the towel away, and began to twist her hands.

"I can't," she muttered. "I can't. I need a drink." She got to her feet and started toward the kitchen.

"Don't, Jenny," Kate said sadly. "That won't solve anything."

Jenny paused, glancing at her for a moment over her shoulder, then went on to the kitchen and after several minutes walked back into the room with a tall glass of Scotch. She leaned on the back of a chair and was silent until the glass was half empty.

"I feel so much hatred," she said in a low voice. "For everything."

"You can't, Jenny. Christopher's only a baby. He needs love."

"I don't have any to give."

"That can't be true." Kate threw the towel down.

Jenny looked deep into her glass, then slowly looked up again at Kate. "Golden girl," she said softly, an edge of sadness to her voice. "There's just no way I can even *try* to make you understand. You have your job again. It's as simple as that. Everything's just the way you want it, the best it can be without Philip. But me? I can't even mourn for Alan. That shocks you, doesn't it?" She finished her drink.

As Kate sadly shook her head Jenny went on, "Oh, God, yes! I'm sorry he was killed. He really loved life. But I can't mourn for him, Kate, because I didn't love him. And I didn't want his child; I didn't want to go to Hawaii." Her voice was breaking. "I only wanted what I had. My job!" In sudden anger she threw the glass at the wall, where it shattered and fell to the floor in fragments. Kate gazed at it, then looked up at Jenny.

"But now you have Christopher," she pleaded softly.

"I feed him, bathe him, keep him on a schedule, pay Gina, the janitor's niece, to walk him in his carriage once a day." Her mouth was set, her hands clenched in a kind of rage. "More than that? No!"

"Oh Jenny, Jenny," Kate said, taking her wrists. "Don't be so afraid to love him."

"Love?" Jenny pulled away scornfully. "What's that, Kate?"

Kate turned away and slowly picked up her purse and gloves. "Something you'll discover someday," she said quietly. "Maybe when you stop working so hard to find someone named . . . Jenny." She walked toward the door without waiting for a reaction, then, as though suddenly remembering something, she stopped with her hand on the doorknob.

"Oh, by the way, Jenny, I have what may be good news for you. A newspaper publisher whom Justin Wheeler knows wants a woman reporter to write a series on women working in an airplane factory in Connecticut. Rosie the Riveter."

Jenny's eyes flickered in confusion. "A—a series?"

"Justin suggested you. Gave him all your credentials and told me to ask you to send him some of your clippings. That is, if you're interested. And if you are, and this man likes your work, you'd go up to Connecticut for several months to work on it. You'd get a flat fee, all your expenses, even someone to take care of Christopher."

Disbelief flooded Jenny's eyes. "Oh, God, Kate! Is it true?"

"It's true." Kate was laughing. "*If* he likes your clippings."

"I can't believe it." Jenny ran to Kate and threw her arms around her. "Oh, Kate. A series. I can't believe it." She hurried over to her desk, opened a drawer, and pulled out a portfolio filled with newspaper clippings. "I'll send him the one on the abortion series, and the soup kitchens—"

"Here's the man's name and address," Kate said, putting a slip of paper down on the foyer table.

Jenny quickly turned and looked at Kate, her pale, drawn face suddenly filled with excitement, then breaking into a wide smile. "You really are a golden girl," she said, looking at her directly for the first time, admiring the smart beige suit, the cool chiseled beauty of her face beneath the wide-brimmed hat. "You're so damned wonderful, and I'm such a bitch." Tears came to her eyes.

Kate laughed gently, her hand on the doorknob. "You're Jenny," she said. "Don't ever be any other way."

The door closed softly as she left.

As Jenny stepped from the train in Bridgeport, balancing Christopher on one hip and dragging a heavy suitcase in the other hand, she stopped for a moment and looked around. It still seemed like a dream. Finally she walked through the busy station and headed for the taxi stand, mentally pinching herself. It was true. Out on the street she blinked for a moment in the sunlight, then held up her hand as a yellow cab pulled to the head of the taxi stand.

She gave the cab driver the address of Mrs. Blaney's

boardinghouse, then settled back, absently shifting the baby on her lap.

Christopher sat there quiet as a mouse. His solemn little eyes were round with wonder as he watched the automobiles and buildings and people on the crowded sidewalks slide past the window of the taxi. Never in his short six months of life had he seen so much. A quiet baby who rarely cried, he gazed at the bewildering world beyond the taxicab with wide eyes and parted mouth.

"Pretty baby you got there, missus," the driver called out over his shoulder, shifting gears as he raced around a corner.

Eagerly leaning forward a little, Jenny asked, "Do we pass the aircraft factory on the way?" They were on the outskirts of the city.

"Just up the road," he said. And as Jenny anxiously watched from the window Christopher turned and gently touched a button on her dress.

Jenny followed the young woman along the wide aisle of the noisy, cavernous building with its overhead girders stretching the length of one whole block. Towering to her left and right were long rows of shining planes, like giant silver bugs crouching in wait, but without propellers and with their spreading wings folded upward.

"Corsairs," Virginia Cochran shouted over her shoulder to be heard above the shattering roar of machinery. "Fold-up wings for aircraft carriers."

Beyond one row of almost completed Corsairs, Jenny saw women dressed like Virginia in coveralls, close-fitting caps or wrapped scarves, and goggles, working with welding machines and acetylene torches on wide slabs of armor.

At a bisecting aisle Jenny followed Virginia through another maze of planes, these halfway through completion, with workers clambering over each fuselage in what seemed like chaos and confusion but was actually an efficiently operating production line. At another juncture they came to a wall and a door, where Virginia led her into a long room with a row of small windows looking out upon the impressive and bustling scene. Pushing up her goggles, Virginia shut the door, cutting the deafening noise to a distant hum. They sat at a long table facing each other.

"I'm dumbfounded," Jenny said, her eyes filled with excitement. "I had no idea so many women worked in these plants."

"About fifty-fifty here," Virginia said, lighting a cigarette and offering Jenny one, somehow managing to seem dainty and feminine in her gestures in spite of the oily coveralls and the smudges on her face. "Most of the men are over forty, and family men, of course." She blew out a pensive stream of smoke. "But that didn't stop my Joe." She thought about it, her blue eyes squinting.

Jenny looked up for a moment from her notebook, where she was scribbling notes. "What do you mean? Is Joe your husband?"

"We have three kids, ten, eight, and four. But Joe's brother was at Corregidor when it surrendered to the Japs in May." She looked off at the vast indoor field of planes and machinery and scurrying workers. "He stood it until two months ago, then joined the Seabees. Construction battalions that go into the combat areas. My sister-in-law takes care of all the kids while I work here and bring in extra money to supplement the government allotment, which isn't near enough to live on."

"They—know you have children here?" Jenny asked, surprised.

"Sure," Virginia said, then laughed. "Honey, when they need you, when the male manpower is shrinking to the point where they're delighted to see you walk through the door of that hiring office, you know they're desperate and will take anything. Even women. But remember you heard it here: When this war is over, the men up at the top will throw us women out faster than we can run."

Jenny pounded her anger out on the little portable typewriter that night, pausing only to light endless cigarettes in the golden pool of light over her makeshift desk. Smiling grimly into the darkness beyond the boardinghouse room window, she slowly flexed her fingers, bent and unbent her arms. She had been hammering at the keys for hours, leaving Christopher downstairs in Mrs. Blaney's quarters, where he spent most of his time anyway. Poor little kid, she thought fleetingly in a remote corner of her mind, you sure picked the wrong mother. Then she looked back at what she had written.

When they need you, when the manpower is shrinking to the point where they're glad to see you walk in the door of the hiring office, Virginia Cochran had said. Well, Henry Fremont didn't need her. Not yet. There were still enough *old* newspapermen around so that he didn't have to dip into the

47

ranks of young mothers. Now and probably never. Her fingers began to pound again.

Liz had moved back to the Rectory after receiving the War Department telegram. As she watched from the church office window one morning, she saw the postman climb the steps of the Rectory veranda. That meant that in approximately half an hour her mother would have lunch ready. If she hurried, this would give her twenty minutes to spend with Julie, who would just be waking from her morning nap.

She ran across the church lawn, took the steps two at a time, scooped the mail from the mailbox, found one for herself, and dropped the other letters on the foyer table. Then she ran up the stairs, a slight figure of golden light in the rays from the landing window.

She tiptoed across the shade-drawn room and for a long moment looked down at the sleeping face of her child. As the fingers on one tiny fist curled and uncurled twice in some infancy dream Julie was having, Liz caught her lower lip between her teeth, feeling a rush of love and amazement at creation. Damp golden curls lay against the baby's petal-soft cheek, and the tiny mouth moved, as though in whispers. Then she settled into a light sleep once more.

Finally Liz turned and sat down at her dressing table. She read the letter from Jenny, savoring every word, laughing softly at a bit of humor, sobering again at the descriptions of the factory production lines, the enormity of the war effort, the exhilaration, the hubbub in her life, and the vivid way she described it.

She looked at the postmark on the envelope. It was only Bridgeport, Connecticut. But it seemed like somewhere thousands of miles away, a place filled with wartime excitement, where people were doing important things. And in spite of the fact that Julie filled most of her life, she ached with wanting to feel a part of it.

The Rectory and church office were the perimeters of her world except for the rare Saturdays when she took Julie into the city where the doctors still checked her over. She often stayed on for the weekend with Jeanne, cherishing those hours. They had gone to museums and once to a concert, hiring a young girl in Jeanne's apartment building to take care of Julie. Then, twice in recent weeks, they had gone to the theater, where Liz had seen her first stage plays. She had walked out of the theaters as though in a trance.

"What are you going to do about the rest of your life?" Jeanne had suddenly asked one night as the taxi sped up Broadway. Liz looked toward her in the summer darkness, feeling an irony in the question. Jeanne's own life was in chaos. She was involved with a high-level broadcasting executive whose wife was doomed to an iron lung for the remainder of her life, and saw him go off each weekend to his Long Island estate. Liz had at first been shocked when Bill told her about his sister's affair. But as time passed she began to understand. Jeanne's life with Glenn Griffen began on Monday nights and ended on Friday mornings. Whatever private hell she suffered, she kept it well hidden from Liz, behind those wise gray eyes and tightly smiling mouth.

"You have to start thinking about it, Liz," Jeanne said, pulling off her gloves and lighting a cigarette, the glow from the match etching the strong but pretty features in a flash of light. "You can't go on forever typing tithing envelopes to parishioners and keeping the church books."

Liz saw it stretching before her, leading to a dull nowhere. Even in the dim-out, the street outside the taxicab windows pulsed with life and noise and excitement. Crowds filled the sidewalks. Moviegoers poured from the theaters. Taxis and cars jammed the streets.

"We need a part-time typist at my office," Jeanne said. Jeanne was administrative assistant to Claudine Marais, the Parisian designer who had escaped from France just before the Germans marched into Paris. "It could be a beginning, and as you said earlier, your work at the church only takes three days each week. Why not come into the city and work with us the other two days?"

"Oh, Jeanne, my father would never approve of anything like that," Liz had said as she hungrily watched the theater crowds from the moving taxi windows.

"Did it ever occur to you," Jeanne answered with patience, "that you can decide for yourself what you're going to do with your life?"

"You don't understand, Jeanne—"

"That your father has nothing to say about it, that you work for him three days each week for your room and board and never see a penny of it? Damnit, Liz, what you do with the other two days is your business. And you've said your mother *loves* taking care of Julie. So tell him, Liz! Just tell him what you're going to do."

Liz recalled the firmness in Jeanne's voice. Looking up at

her reflection in the dressing table mirror, she saw a new expression in her eyes, a different set to her mouth. She had walked into her father's office at the church the Monday morning following that conversation in the taxicab and told him about the job in New York two days each week. He had dismissed it at first with cold logic and finality, saying she could find a part-time job nearby. But with a new stubbornness she had persisted, and he had looked up from the sermon he was working on with surprise, eyes behind the steel-rimmed glasses revealing a brief glimpse of alarm. "What kind of defiance is this?" he had asked.

Trembling as she answered, she had said, "It's not defiance, Father. But—I'm twenty-three and I've been married and I—I want to make some kind of life for Julie and myself."

He had stared at her, then looked off out the window, and she knew he was thinking of her brother, Frank, of what he had seen as defiance in him, but what was only Frank's determination to make a life away from the Rectory. She and Frank had been so close, close in age, but close in spirit too.

"Please, Father," she had begged him that Monday morning, still nervous but holding on to her courage. "I want to do it with your approval, but—"

"But if you have to without my approval, you'll go ahead with this foolishness, is that it?" She heard the cold thread of anger in his voice, and in that moment she knew she could lose all the ground she had gained, and set her chin stubbornly.

"If I have to," she said in a whisper.

He looked out the window, his face flushed, his eyes distant. "Do as you wish," he said through tight lips and picked up the sermon, his way of dismissing her.

She trembled a little, remembering. He had been such a strong force in her life, but as she looked in the mirror she could see the determination. She reached into the dressing table drawer under a pile of hankies, took out a flat box of letters, and pulled out the one on the very bottom. Worn and creased from many readings, it still had greenish stain marks on the envelope from where he'd hidden it in their secret chink in the peach tree five years before.

"Don't let him turn your life into the drab and dreary mess he made of Mama's life," Frank had written that night he ran away. "I remember when she was still pretty. As for me, I was never able to do what Father wanted and approved of. I never could. That's why I'm leaving."

Looking up into the mirror, she smiled. Frank would have been proud of her that morning in her father's study. She smiled through a soft blur of tears. *Both* Bill and Frank. If they only had known. Kate and Jenny too. She pulled a piece of stationery from a box in the top drawer, sat in deep thought for a moment, then began to write.

"Dear Jenny . . ."

"But what a beautiful young woman," Claudine Marais exclaimed the first morning Jeanne took Liz in for introductions. The small, dark-haired woman circled Liz, looking her up and down as though she were a prize sculpture. "Somehow I have a feeling her talents will be wasted behind a typewriter."

Jeanne winked at Liz behind Mme. Marais' back as the designer kept circling, and later Jeanne said, "One of these days, and probably sooner than you think, she'll have you modeling in the showroom."

Jeanne was right. Within a month Liz was a showroom model. Her blonde beauty was perfect for the softly molded, clinging gowns that Marais had built her reputation on in her salon on the Rue du Faubourg Saint-Honoré before the war. And even though wartime regulations had placed great restrictions on the fashion industry because of growing shortages in materials, her creations were still exquisite and in great demand. And Liz soon became her favorite model.

"I thought we were going to Colucci's for lunch," Liz said as Jeanne hurried her through the revolving doors of the RCA building one September day and then maneuvered her through the lobby crowds.

"I have an errand here first," Jeanne said vaguely. After running a little to keep up with her, and wondering why Jeanne was acting so strangely, Liz suddenly grasped her arm and stopped her.

"I won't go another step until you tell me what you're up to," Liz demanded, out of breath. Jeanne led her off to the side.

"Liz, it's time you faced facts. But as long as you haven't, I've been facing them for you. It's obvious you love working in the city. And for a long time I've noticed how fascinated you are whenever we go to a movie or the theater. The minute that movie starts or the actors walk on the stage, you're completely lost. It's as though you're on the screen or stage with them. I was telling Glenn about it, and he said he'd arrange for you to have an audition on one of the soaps, like *Guiding Light* or *Stella Dallas*."

Liz's mouth dropped open and her eyes went wide with astonishment.

"I don't know why," Jeanne hurried on, "but something tells me you're one of those naturally gifted actresses. Your voice, your laugh, everything about you. Now, all you have to do is read a page or two of the script they hand you, and—"

"This is insane!" Liz gasped.

"What do you want to be, a file clerk, or even just a showroom model the rest of your life?" Jeanne's eyes snapped as she raised her voice. "Or just Julie's mother, maybe? Is that enough?"

"Yes, that's enough!" Liz snapped back, her eyes filling with angry, hurt tears. "It was enough with Bill and—"

"But Bill isn't here, Liz," Jeanne said in a hard low voice, grasping her arm. "And he isn't going to be. This is something you're going to have to do all by yourself, make a new life for you and Julie."

"No!" Liz cried out softly, trying to pull free, but Jeanne hung on.

"You said it yourself when you took the job with Claudine," Jeanne said.

"That was different," Liz said, sounding confused. "It's—well, just two days—" She was looking off at the people who passed.

"And leading nowhere." She took hold of Liz's wrists and forced her to face her. "You have to make a commitment to something, find a place for yourself. Liz—" She shook her arms. "Bill isn't coming back. You've got to make a future for yourself and Julie, and this could be a wonderful one. *He's not coming back, Liz*." Seeing the stricken look on Liz's face, she softened. "Oh, honey, I'm sorry. I'm not trying to hurt you, but only make you see that you have to do something with your life."

As Liz nodded rapidly, unable to speak and forcing back the tears, Jeanne looked away, wondering why she was always the one who had to comfort others. First her parents, and then Liz when word had arrived about Bill. Never me, she thought, never me. "I don't know what we would do without you, Jeanne," her mother had wept on the phone from Florida when word had come about Bill. "Our Rock of Gibraltar," her father had told someone at the memorial service.

She and Bill had been close as brother and sister, close enough that it mattered deeply to him what she thought about Liz when he said he was going to marry her, close enough that he was saddened by the hopeless situation she was embroiled in with Glenn Griffen. "I loved Bill too," she wanted to cry out, but instead held Liz's hand tightly and led her on through the crowded lobby.

"What you do with it after the audition, well, that's entirely up to you," she said as she pulled Liz through the bronze doors of an NBC elevator just as they were closing.

"All right," Liz said finally in a small voice. "I'll try."

Much to Liz's astonishment, she was given a tiny role. At first she had been terrified, but as she stood at the microphone and began to read the script they had given her, she forgot who and where she was and her nervousness disappeared. Jeanne had told them her name was Elizabeth Lowndes. "My middle name," she said, "and just in case your father should pick up a fan magazine someday." She winked.

Liz's father accepted her explanation that she would have to put in extra time occasionally at Claudine Marais', just as he had accepted her working in the city in the first place: with a cold shrug and dismissal. "I'll do the church books and typing when I get home at night on those days," she said eagerly, and he had merely nodded and left the room. But Ellen had smiled, almost as though she knew the truth. "Oh, Mama," Liz said softly, kissing her cheek. "Thank you for understanding."

Liz would appear three or four times over a period of several weeks, Axel Berglund, the director, explained, and the serial was scheduled to start in early October.

On the day she was to first appear on the show, she arrived at the studio, feeling somewhat ill at ease. She knew no one, but the others seemed to know one another. Soon Berglund introduced her around, went into the control booth, and quiet settled on the studio.

Two of the other actors began to read their lines, sheets of paper from their scripts floating noiselessly to the carpeting to eliminate any paper-rustling sounds as they finished with each one.

Suddenly it was time, and tingling with nervous excitement, she stepped to the microphone, sharing it with the actor who played Shannon's father. He smiled warmly at her, and she began to relax. In a miraculously firm voice the first line came out without a quaver. As the rehearsal went on, her tension flowed away. Suddenly she was no longer Liz but the young schoolteacher, struggling with the problems of children growing up in the slums of New York. And all too soon her scene came to an end.

"Nice job, Elizabeth."

Liz looked up. Axel Berglund was speaking to her over the intercom. "Just watch that pause before your final line. Make it a little quicker. It would be perfect for the stage, but this is radio."

Liz smiled at him gratefully. It was then that she noticed a young man sitting next to him, broodingly handsome with dark eyes and hair and fine, sensitive features. She quickly glanced back down at her script. She had felt someone watching her, and as their eyes locked for a moment, she remembered Jeanne mentioning a young man who was the writer of the show. Dan Coleman was his name. But when the on-the-air light flashed red, she promptly forgot him and watched Bart Gregory, the announcer, nod toward the control booth that he and the cast were ready.

As the director signaled thirty seconds to air-time and then started the countdown, Liz felt a delicious wave of excitement. Suddenly Axel's arm swept in a wide arc downward, and his hand shot out, pointing at the organist. They were on the air.

The next fifteen minutes flew past in a vivid montage of sight and sound, the velvety voice of the announcer and the rippling notes of the theme song leveling out under the sound effects, then the interweaving of voices, the punctuating organ music and melodious tones of Bart Gregory as he launched into the soap commercial, and the final minutes of drama as the episode wound to an end.

Dan Coleman watched her as she leaned close to the microphone, her silvery voice and clear pronunciation taking the lines he had written and so effortlessly making them her own. He strained forward, listening, then looked at Axel. "She sounds like a natural," he said quietly. Axel nodded as he watched through the glass.

Dan tried to define it to himself. New York was full of beautiful actresses, even ones with exquisite features and large intense blue eyes. Her eyes were almost *too* large for the delicately molded face and pale sweep of ash-blonde hair that fell over her shoulders.

"Something so real about her off-mike too," Axel said as

the organ crashed into the last notes of the theme song. There was a note of irony in his voice as he added, "An unusual quality in these halls of network broadcasting." He rose from his chair. "Come along, Dan. I'll introduce you."

But Dan had slid down into a slouch in his chair and was scribbling some notes. The situation in San Francisco with Connie had taught him to avoid pretty girls with innocent blue eyes, particularly girls who were working on a show he was writing.

Actually Dan Coleman despised the show. But at least it was writing, working at what he loved to do. Writing. Better than selling insurance to support himself while he finished his play, he'd been telling himself for weeks as he pounded out episodes on his typewriter.

"Not today," he muttered without looking up at the big silver-haired man waiting by the control room door. "I'm behind two episodes on this damned piece of junk." Suddenly unfolding his lanky frame from the chair, he shot Axel a rare grin to soften the insult.

"Sorry I'm holding up your Pulitzer prize, my boy," Axel said, laughing fondly. "But come along and say hello anyway."

Liz was standing in the wide corridor excitedly hugging a young woman, tall and stunning in a handsomely tailored gray suit. Axel and Dan pushed toward them through the crowds streaming to the elevators.

"Kate, my dear, how are you?" Axel exclaimed, taking hold of her hands and kissing her cheek. He turned to Liz. "If you don't mind my barging in, why don't I take you both to lunch?"

"I didn't know you knew each other," Liz said, surprised.

"Axel was the director of the show on my first big account two years ago," Kate said, smiling. "Now I'm hoping to get him for another one."

"You can tell me about it at lunch," he said, then turned to Dan. "I want you both to meet Dan Coleman. Elizabeth Lowndes and Kate Gray, Dan. Dan is the writer on *Shannon O'Shea.*" His eyes twinkled mischievously. "Although Dan would probably rather I didn't mention it. He considers writing soaps a mark of utter degradation and shame."

"Really, Mr. Coleman?" Kate said coolly. "Anything that pays someone such a handsome fee surely deserves some credit."

"You don't like writers, Miss Gray?"

55

"Oh, did I say something about writers?" she said, green eyes flashing.

"Touché," Dan said with a mocking bow and the hint of a smile that never reached his eyes. "Sorry. I have to run."

Tipping his hat, he moved off toward the elevators while Liz watched. As the bronze doors slid open he disappeared from view.

"Weren't you a little rough on him, Kate?" Axel laughed while helping Liz into her coat.

"Such obvious conceit deserves reward," Kate smiled as they set off along the corridor.

"He's very talented," Liz said quickly. "*Shannon* seems to be a much better show than most of the other daytime serials."

"Writing talent's a dime a dozen in this town," Kate responded.

"Not his kind," Axel said sharply, but still smiling.

Kate looked at him as they reached the elevators. "Oh? He's *that* one in a thousand?"

"Maybe even a million. He's good. Damned good. And he's writing a play. I predict that when it's finished, produced, and opens on Broadway, it will be a hit."

"It's as certain as that? To be produced, I mean?" Kate seemed surprised.

Axel pushed the elevator button. "Hackley Crawford is very interested. He's taken an option on it."

"How wonderful," Liz said. "But then, I'm not surprised."

Doubt still seemed to plague Kate. "Mr. Coleman seems to be young enough for the draft, Axel. What's his excuse?"

Axel didn't answer until they were sitting at a table overlooking the sunken plaza and Prometheus Fountain and had ordered their lunch.

"Dan went to England in 1938. He had a friend who lent him a flat in Bloomsbury, and he went there to write plays, supporting himself by occasionally going out and barnstorming the English and Scottish countryside fairs as a stunt flyer. Then when Britain's entry into the war came that September of '39, he tried to get into the Royal Air Force. But the red tape meant months of delay, and in the meantime something happened. He doesn't talk about it, but I gather he was in love with a young Englishwoman, and she was killed. So he took off for China. It took him weeks, going to Spain first, then hitching by whatever means he could—broken-down airplanes, tankers—and when he got there, he joined General

56

Chennault, first helping him to train fighter pilots for the Chinese government, then becoming part of the Flying Tigers that the general formed in early forty-one."

He turned to Liz. "That's where he wrote the radio script about the British soldier wounded at Dunkirk, while he was flying in Burma against the Japanese. A friend coming back to the States from the China–Burma–India Theater brought the script to me and I did it on *Starlight Theater.*"

"Isn't that the one that won the Lidster Cabot Award?" Kate asked.

"That's the one," Axel said. "But awards don't pay the rent. Dan was wounded in Burma. A diving Zero got him, so he was sent back to the States and recuperated on the West Coast. By the time he got here, he needed a job, looked me up, and I put him on the *Shannon* script. The writer on that show had gotten drafted before I could even get it on the air."

Kate nodded as the waiter placed a cup of asparagus soup in front of her. "I guess I owe Mr. Coleman an apology," she said slowly, looking long and pointedly at Liz.

But Liz was far away in her thoughts, wondering at the depths of sadness in Dan Coleman's eyes, the measure of mistrust and hurt in his aloof manner.

Chapter 10

SEVERAL TIMES IN the next few weeks Dan and Liz walked along the corridor together as they were leaving the studio. They chatted briefly as they waited for the elevator and rode down to the lobby floor, then separated just outside the revolving doors at Rockefeller Plaza, Liz going one way, hurrying toward Grand Central Station in the autumn sunlight to catch a train to Larchmont, and Dan heading for his apartment in the East Fifties.

Each time, as he watched the slim figure cross Fifth Avenue and disappear in the crowds, he felt an odd kind of emptiness steal over him. He was puzzled by it. In their brief meetings they had said little, talking only about the weather or having some inconsequential bit of conversation about the show or a cast member. But each time she lifted those clear, blue eyes to his and smiled, he was startled at his reaction. He found it deeply disturbing and vowed each time, as he walked toward his apartment and typewriter, to avoid her. She was interfering with his work. Frequently, while sitting at his desk working on a script, he found himself staring into space. He was thinking about her, the way she tipped her head when she listened to him, her thickly lashed eyes, steady and such a deep blue. Her slim figure and graceful walk, her silvery clear voice. But . . . it was more than that.

There was something that reminded him of Vivian—her way of looking at someone, a directness as she listened and then spoke. And a tone in her voice. Filled with silken half-notes.

But then . . . not really like Vivian at all.

Vivian had been a music hall singer, with just the slightest trace of her cockney heritage left in her speech. She and Dan had met at a friend's flat in Soho, and Dan was immediately attracted to her. She made his pursuit of her difficult at first, but as he stubbornly persisted the dark-haired, vivacious

Vivian laughingly capitulated. "We might just as well get on with it," she said, finally accepting his dinner invitation. "You'll give me no peace until we do. You're frightfully persistent, you know."

The rather languorous affair became charged with the feverish pitch of war when the blitz of London began that September. Each hour they were together became the most important hour of their lives as they watched the devastation of London through the incessant bombings from the Luftwaffe. And when it seemed imminent that the Royal Air Force would form a squadron of flyers made up solely of American pilots and that Dan might be one of them, she agreed to marry him. All that was left was for her to set the day for their marriage that autumn of 1940. It would be October fifteenth.

Long after the fifteenth of October had come and gone, Dan walked the streets of London day and night, oblivious to the scream of sirens, the acrid smell of smoke and cordite, the feathery contrails of fighter bombers high in the sky, the shriek of falling bombs, the dreadful beauty by night as London burned with thousands of fires. Nothing mattered as he walked on and on. There were times when he imagined he saw or heard her, a dark-haired girl disappearing around a corner; a voice just behind him in a bus.

At last he could stand it no more and left, traveling first to Spain by way of clipper to Lisbon, on his way to China and General Chennault, taking her memory with him like an open wound that it seemed would never heal. Even the briefly diverting but ultimately unpleasant affair with Connie in San Francisco had left him with nothing, emptier than before. Only his writing mattered. And at times that deserted him, too, and his sorrow enfolded him like soft black wings. Until the day he first saw Liz through the studio window.

Liz stopped and turned halfway across the main floor lobby when she heard someone call her name one late November day. With his soft brown felt hat slouched over his eyes and his trench coat collar turned high, Dan Coleman was striding toward her. Taking her arm, he led her through the weaving crowds of people to the revolving door.

"I want to talk to you for a few minutes," he said, "if you have the time. It's business."

He was pushing her ahead of him through the door. Out in the gray biting cold, she let him lead her across Fifth Avenue and along the shadow of St. Patrick's Cathedral toward

Madison Avenue, where he took her into a small coffee shop. Neither of them spoke until they were seated at a small table by the window.

"It's about the show," he said after ordering their coffee. "Your part runs out next week."

"I know," she said, disappointment clouding her face as she gazed out at the traffic. Quickly looking back at him, she smiled. "But I loved it while it lasted. And I've already started going to other auditions." She kept looking at him as she pushed back her coat.

He smiled briefly, and she was glad. For just a moment his eyes had lighted up, the sadness momentarily gone. "That's what I want to talk to you about. I'm writing another radio serial, a new one, my own from scratch, one that will have some relevancy to what's going on today about the war. It involves a refugee family, escaped to this country from Occupied Europe. But only the women. The men have stayed on to fight with the free forces. The leading character is a young woman in her early twenties. Her name is Anna. I've discussed this with Ax. He's going to direct it, and he agrees with me about you." Each sentence had been short and clipped, and he gazed off at the waitress who approached them with their coffee. "I want you to play that role."

"Me?" She seemed stunned.

A slow smile spread across his face. "You *are* new at this business, aren't you? Is that small part in *Shannon* really the first one you ever had?"

"I'm afraid so," she said in a small voice.

"Well, how about it?"

She stared at him for a moment, disbelieving. "Are you serious?"

"Absolutely," he said, the smile gone, the brooding look in his eyes again.

"I . . . I don't know what to say." She was bewildered. "I mean, I want to, but—"

"Then say yes." He laughed. "Your eyes are saying it."

"I'd be crazy not to, wouldn't I?" she said breathlessly. "And Jeanne would—" She nodded excitedly. "Yes. Of course, yes."

"It goes on the air this winter," he said, stopping to sip his coffee. "You'll need an accent. Very slight. Just to suggest the Czechoslovakian background. They'll hire a voice teacher for that. I've already told them to put that in your contract."

"Contract?" she said, voice faltering.

"You'll get two fifty a week, whether you're written into each script or not."

"Dollars?" she gasped. "Two-hundred-and-fifty dollars?"

"Dollars." But he said it absently. He was staring at her.

"Mr. Coleman, I . . ." She moved uncomfortably, trying to look away.

"I—I'm sorry," he said. "I didn't mean to stare. But . . . you remind me a little of someone I used to know." He looked out at the traffic, laughing ironically. "That's an old line, isn't it?"

"I look like her?" Liz asked, not knowing what else to say.

"No, but . . ." He gazed at her again, intently. "There's something about you, the way you talk . . . move your head."

Liz waited a moment, then said in a soft voice, "Who was she?"

"A girl in London." He looked at the traffic again. "We were going to be married. I'd gone to Kirton Lindsey to see an RAF friend of mine, to ask him to be our best man at the wedding, and I'd taken the train. But train service into all five rail terminals in London had been brought to a standstill, and I couldn't get back until the next morning."

Liz shivered inside at the terrible dark expression that crept across his face, the haunted look in his eyes.

"There had been three daylight raids, and then they kept it up all night by moonlight. I looked for her for two days. And then I found out what had happened. If she had been with me—if I had stayed in London that day, it wouldn't have happened. Someone told me a kid ran up out of the shelter. This woman had nine kids. And Vivian ran after him . . ." He spread his hands helplessly.

"I'm so sorry," Liz said in a whisper.

"If I hadn't gone to Kirton—"

"You don't know that for sure," she said.

"I know that," he said tonelessly. "She would have been with me."

At that moment Liz wanted to reach out and touch his hand, hold it, let him know he wasn't alone.

"It seemed important that I tell you this," he said, looking at her with a sudden directness. "Axel told me about your husband. Until then, I'd felt . . . well, as though I was the only one in the world who knew what it was like to lose

61

someone you loved. But knowing about you, suddenly I realized there are others, so many others, and that life *does* go on, for the one who is left."

She smiled and nodded, then waited out the long silence.

"It's strange," he said, shaking his head a little as though to clear it. "I might never have met you. When I got that first check for the *Starlight Theater* show, I bought a train ticket east from San Francisco, but for Washington. I'd heard about a guy by the name of Wild Bill Donovan, close friend of Roosevelt's. He'd just formed the new Office of Strategic Services, and I wanted to try and get in on the ground floor. So I went to see him, told him I wanted to join the OSS. But the minute they saw my service record with the Tigers, they sent me packing. No bad legs in the OSS," he said wryly. "They sent me over to the OWI, Office of War Information. Robert Sherwood, the playwright, had just been made one of the deputies, and they were looking for writers. But it wasn't what I wanted." He suddenly sounded bitter. "Every branch of the service had turned me down, and all I could get was a desk job in Washington. So I took the next train and came here."

They rose to leave, and as they walked out to the street Liz found herself wishing they could sit on for hours, just talking. As they said good-bye he held her hand for a moment. And when she turned south toward Grand Central Station, she felt her heart beating hard and knew as she hurried along that he was standing in the middle of the sidewalk watching her.

Kate stood just behind Margot Wilson's shoulder, peering at a brilliant red sea of flame serving as the background on the poster board for the huge black swastika. Glittering above it and ready to slash the swastika in half was an Allied bayonet, and the lettering read, "Slavery or Victory. Buy War Bonds Now!"

"You really have the gory touch," Kate said, smiling.

"Well, that's what you asked for, boss." Margot grinned over her shoulder as she looked up from the drawing board, her short red hair curling around her face, a daub of paint on her chin. "Wait until you see the one I sketched out last night—bestial, leering creatures, just like you asked for."

"I know. That's the directive, to make the Nazis and the Japanese look as terrifying as possible."

"I'm sorry to interrupt." Lloyd Mason's secretary was at

the door. "Mr. Mason would like to see you, Kate." She turned and Kate followed.

Kate walked past the bank of elevators into the executive corridor and entered Lloyd Mason's large corner office.

"Well, Kate," Lloyd said, waving her to a chair.

Kate glanced briefly at the good looking young man casually slouched in the leather chair to the right of Lloyd's desk, then sat on the opposite side, crossing her legs as his eyes slid appreciatively from her head to her toes. He appeared to be tall, his gray tweeds draped in casual elegance across his broad shoulders. He had perfectly groomed dark blonde hair, and he was smiling at her, the smile flashing from a deeply tanned face. A rotogravure face, she thought, belonging with sleek picture spreads on the America's Cup trials at Newport or the winner's circle at Belmont. After politely returning his smile, she looked at Mason, the one partner she made a point of avoiding.

"This is Adam Barnfield," Mason said, nodding toward the young man. "Adam is Justin Wheeler's nephew."

Kate glanced at the young man again. If he was Justin's nephew, then . . .

"Kate is on the war bonds project you'll be working with, Adam." Kate's heart sank. Adam Barnfield was appearing somewhat later than the usual crop of rich young sons, nephews, cousins, and sons of friends who arrived at the agency in the autumn to take their first jobs after graduation from college and a summer at Watch Hill or Newport.

"He was graduated from Princeton last June, and actually he'll be a tremendous help to us on the project. Adam has been working since last winter on the war bonds committee at college."

Kate nodded, tried to smile appreciatively.

"Justin called from Washington and asked me if I'd show Adam around. He'll be here with us only for a few months while taking a special course at New York University, then he goes up to Connecticut to work with his father."

"Where in Connecticut?" Kate asked Adam, only to be polite.

"Brookton," Adam said with that easy smile. "Small-town kid."

Kate vaguely remembered hearing that Justin had a brother-in-law named Jonathan Barnfield, owner of the sprawling Barnfield Mills in lower Connecticut and married to Justin's sister Amanda. Small-town kid indeed.

"What's the name of that course, Adam?" Mason asked.

"Well, *efficiency expert* is the big word in management these days," Adam said, then grinned. "The boy wonders with the slide rules, you know. I had other plans, but—"

Why not Officers Candidate School, where so many June graduates of top colleges were just completing their ninety-day stretch, Kate wondered. Young men like Adam Barnfield didn't usually wait until the draft board caught up with them. It was as though he had read her mind.

"—I'll have to postpone OCS for a while. My father asked me to hold off, because the Barnfield Mills are in the process of changing over to wartime production, manufacturing Army and Navy blankets instead of carpeting for the duration. I've been down in Washington with my father these past few weeks, observing contract negotiations with the War Production Board. It's a good place to start training for a job in the mills, watching government and business getting together. And the course I'm taking while working here with you will add to that expertise, hopefully."

His smile became serious as he leaned forward. "Father managed to convince me that I'll be doing as much for the war effort working in an essential industry as I would as a line officer or flyer."

As Mason rose from behind his desk Kate and Adam stood up. "So meanwhile," Adam said charmingly, spreading his hands, "I'm afraid you're going to have to put up with me. For a few months anyway."

"We'll be happy to have the help." Kate moved toward the door.

"Thanks, Kate," Mason said with a nod of dismissal. "I'm taking Adam to lunch, but he'll stop by your office later."

"Damned good looking," Adam said offhandedly after she left.

"Bright too," Mason said as they started along the corridor. They could see her up ahead. "Sad story, though. Her husband was killed at Pearl Harbor. The baby was born the same day."

Adam's eyes suddenly followed her.

"But that's just between us," Mason said in a tone of confidence as they reached the elevators and he pushed the button. "Justin promised Kate we'd keep it quiet. It's Justin's idea, letting women work here after they've had children."

As Kate's slender green-clad figure disappeared around a

bend, Adam watched her, then slowly followed Lloyd Mason's gray flannel back into the elevator.

By the time Kate reached her office, she had almost forgotten Adam Barnfield, certainly dismissing him as a charming but frivolous type. "Too rich for my blood," she muttered, lighting a cigarette, then opened a package on her desk. It was a set of the series Jenny had written on Rosie the Riveter, with a note from Justin's secretary saying that the Boston publisher had sent it to Justin. For the next hour she sat with her door closed and read it. Kate realized as she finished it that it was some of the best newspaper writing she had ever read. Jenny must be back in New York and hadn't called her. Kate picked up the phone and called her number, letting it ring and ring until she knew Jenny wasn't going to answer. Up to her old tricks again, she thought, just as her own phone rang.

"Kate?" Liz sounded in a hurry. "I've been trying to reach you. Can I see you? I need to talk."

"How about meeting me at Jenny's? I think she's been back for two or three weeks. I don't like the fact that we haven't heard from her."

"That's right," Liz said. "The last letter I got from her was postmarked about a month ago."

"I have to go down to Madison Square Garden to discuss the program for the bond rally two weeks from tonight, but I could get down to the Village after that. Why don't you meet me at Jenny's at four? Then we can talk in the taxi on the way back."

"That's a wonderful idea. I'll just phone my mother and tell her I'll be a little late for dinner, and I'll meet you in front of Jenny's building at four."

Chapter 11

LIZ TIPTOED INTO the bedroom where Christopher was sleeping while Kate stood in the middle of the living room looking around. She could hear Jenny in the small kitchen beyond, the refrigerator door opening and closing, and a muttered "Damn!" as a cupboard door slammed. She looked around at the clutter—books and magazines scattered on the floor and tables, empty cups and two glasses with the remains of drinks in them. Clothes were draped over furniture, and unopened mail, clippings, and newspapers were piled in corners and on chairs. But beneath the confusion and clutter, Kate could see a love for pretty things, for harmony and comfort. Good taste was obvious in the blending of dark rich woods, brass and copper pieces, and a wonderful old tapestry hanging on the wall opposite the books and fireplace. She didn't expect Jenny to be a fastidious housekeeper. But there was a sense of organization about her, a harmonious arrangement of thoughts and ideas. It was hard to believe she could live in this clutter and mess.

When Jenny first opened the door, Kate wasn't surprised, but Liz had been startled by Jenny's appearance. Kate turned to the high wall of bookshelves, and let her eyes wander over the titles—Wharton, James, Proust, Fitzgerald, Hemingway.

"Quite a library," she said as Jenny, still in a robe and slippers, shuffled through the door carrying a tray with two cups of coffee, a highball, and a tall nursing bottle filled with milk.

"Take whatever you want from it," she said, putting the tray down on the cocktail table with a thud.

Liz was walking in from the bedroom, carrying a sleepy Christopher, the top of his head peeking from the blanket she had wrapped about him. She picked up the nursing bottle, sat in a chair, and began to feed him. "I hope you don't mind,

66

Jenny, but he was smiling at me and I couldn't resist him," Liz said.

"It's okay," Jenny answered in a weary tone as she curled up on the couch and sipped at her highball. "I usually let him hold it or just prop it on a pillow in the crib."

Kate and Liz exchanged quick glances, then looked back at Jenny, who seemed unaware of their concern. Her hair was uncombed and tangled, and she was pale. Her drawn face was devoid of makeup, her eyes were darkly circled, and her cheeks were hollow from loss of weight.

"We tried to phone," Kate finally said. She sipped her coffee. "I read the series, Jenny. It's fine stuff. You're a very talented writer and reporter."

Jenny simply shrugged and took a drink from her glass. "You'll have to forgive me if I seem ungrateful, but I should never have taken the assignment."

"Oh?" Kate asked. "Why not?"

"Because I thought it would lead to a permanent job. I thought this Lumley guy would think I was so great that he'd have them hire me. When I finished the series and sent it to him, I wrote and asked him for a job as a reporter." She laughed bitterly. *"No women,* he had his managing editor write back to me. Not on cityside. And there weren't any openings"—she said it sneeringly—"in the Society Department." She rose and walked over to the window, where she stood looking down into the street. "Right back where I started."

"Well," Kate said softly, "I guess you're going to have to accept it, Jenny, and turn to something else. We've all had to make changes in our lives."

Jenny turned and looked at her. "Don't preach, Kate," she said rudely. "Next thing you'll be telling me I drink too much. And you'll be right." She waved her glass. "But so what?" She finished her drink, then swished the ice cubes around in the glass. "Usually I take it straight. But in deference to you, I made it with ice cubes."

"Jenny," Liz said softly, "we didn't come here to pry. We came because we care about you. We missed you while you were gone, and were glad to hear you're back."

"That's more than I can say," Jenny said bluntly.

"Well, we'll keep right on trying," Kate said, her tone offhand, casual, and Jenny stared at her. "After all, we promised to keep in touch, and that's what Liz and I intend to do." She walked over to stand in front of Jenny and said, "Too much happened to us when we were in that hospital, to forget each other."

Jenny dropped her eyes. "You'd better give up on me. I'm a rotten friend, Kate. If you keep this up, you'll find out."

"Oh, don't worry." Kate's voice was softly pleasant. "We'll keep it up. We don't give up easily, especially with someone like you, Jenny. Because we happen to think that underneath all that apathy and feeling sorry for yourself—" Jenny's head snapped up, but Kate bore on relentlessly. "—a decent human being still lurks there somewhere."

With that, she walked over to Liz, took the baby from her, and crossing to Jenny, placed the curly headed Christopher in her arms. Then, beckoning to Liz, she walked to the door, pulling on her coat as she went. Liz hesitated, then quickly ran to Jenny, gave her a soft hug, and gently bent to kiss the baby on the cheek.

"You have my phone number, Jenny," Kate said from the door. "Liz's too. But if we don't hear from you, well, we'll start phoning you and coming here again."

Opening the door as Liz joined her, Kate smiled and said, "You might as well face it. We'll never give up."

For a long moment Jenny stood at the window, hands stiff at her sides, watching down in the street. Finally she walked into the kitchen, poured herself another drink, and drank it down quickly. For several minutes she gazed blankly at the kitchen wall, then leaned against the doorjamb and pounded her fist on the wall. Finally she put her forehead against it and began to cry long wracking sobs.

"Damn, damn, damn," she cried as she beat both fists against the wall, then slumped to the floor, sobbing.

"It's just no good," Kate said as they hurried along the street. "I called this Harry Fremont last week, when I knew she'd be coming back soon, but the rules are rigid. They hire very few women as reporters in the newspaper business as it is, and at the *World-Dispatch*, none. Jenny was the only one, and only because she hounded him, he said." She smiled grimly. "He told me that the publisher almost fired him when he hired Jenny."

"Then what's the answer, Kate?" Liz said, half running to keep up with her as they hurried through the winter twilight. As they stopped at a corner, Kate pointed across the street to a tea shop. Inside, they loosened their coats and ordered tea, while she shook her head.

"I don't know what the answer is. Newspaper jobs are finished for her, I'm afraid. They just won't hire a woman with a child, so that's that. All we can do is be around in case she needs us." She looked up, smiling suddenly, as the waitress put their tea down. "You said you had something you wanted to talk about?"

Liz told her the whole story, about Dan Coleman's new daytime serial, how he wanted her to play the leading role, and also about a script for the new *Sixth Row Center* anthology show on Friday nights.

"He's written a script for that and wants me to play in it," Liz said in bewilderment. "What am I going to do?"

Kate laughed. "What a lovely dilemma." She sipped her tea while looking around at the small tea shop filled with women chatting softly. "You're going to take it, of course. All of it. The time has come when you have to take one big step forward. It's an opportunity you don't dare pass up, Liz. Why, do you have any idea at all how many thousands of people are pounding the streets looking for the chance you've had handed to you? New York is full of actresses looking for jobs."

"I know," Liz said, "and I'm terribly grateful for everything that's been happening to me. It's just that it's beginning to—"

"Liz, I think you've reached a point where you're going to have to make a very big decision." Kate leaned toward her. "It looks as though you're going to have an important career as a radio actress, and maybe something even *more* important someday. Maybe you'll go beyond radio. I just don't think you can afford to ignore it. The time has probably come where you'd better take a small apartment here in the city and—"

"What on earth are you talking about?" Liz said, shocked.

"Wait until I'm through," Kate cut her off. "And for the time being, until you see your way clear to bringing Julie into the city to live, too, I think you should leave her with your mother if you can. You could be there on weekends, Liz, and from what you tell me, I think your mother would be more than willing." Laughing at the astonishment on Liz's face, she pushed her teacup closer. "Here, drink some of this. It will warm you up."

But with an unexpected show of irritation, Liz pushed the

cup and saucer away and leaned toward Kate. "You don't understand. It seems so simple to you, Kate. Many people's lives just aren't as uncomplicated as yours." She suddenly looked miserable, her lovely eyes troubled, her mouth drawn tight. "I hate what I've been doing, telling lies, pretending things that aren't true—"

"Well, then," Kate said slowly, wisely, "do you want to back down and undo all that you've done, go back to Larchmont and spend most of your days doing clerical work for your father?" When Liz shook her head, Kate rushed on. "And it seems to me there's something more to the situation with this Dan Coleman than just a writer-actress relationship." At the look of surprise, then confusion, on Liz's face, she laughed softly and put her hand over Liz's. "It's all right to feel again, you know."

"Oh, Kate," Liz cried, her voice heavy with doubt. "I keep thinking—"

"Just plain common sense tells me it's normal and natural. It's all right to want to be loved again, to love a man. Think of it this way. If you were the one who had . . . died, would you want Bill to never be in love again, never to marry?"

"Of course not," Liz cried, and then she smiled a small smile and nodded. She picked up a lump of sugar and thoughtfully stirred it into her tea. "I've thought about it and felt I was being disloyal even to think about it . . . to want to have those feelings again." They looked at each other and smiled. "I hope you find someone, Kate."

Kate suddenly seemed far away. "I think I hope so, too, Liz."

Jenny got to her feet and shuffled across the living room to the windows, closed the blackout curtains, then switched on another lamp. As she stood for a moment, letting her eyes adjust to the brighter light, glaring black newspaper headlines leaped up at her from the top of the coffee table. U.S. FORCES LAND IN FRENCH NORTH AFRICA, she read. REPORTERS KEEP LANDING A SECRET.

Reporters, she thought bitterly. Angry tears filled her eyes as she pushed the newspaper to the floor. Panic filled her. Suddenly she knew she had to get out, away from the apartment, if only for a few hours. She picked up the phone and dialed a number, rapping her fingers against it nervously while it rang.

"Gina?" she said into the phone. "I have to go out for a while. Can you come up and take care of Christopher?"

An hour later she walked into a small bar on Macdougal Street. It was almost full, but she managed to find a bar stool where the lights were dimmest. She ordered a drink and drank it slowly. As the anxiety began to ebb she slipped off her coat, put a dime into the jukebox near the door, and pushed the buttons for a couple of records, Ellington's "Mood Indigo" and a Tommy Dorsey number. Sliding back on the stool where she was nearly hidden in the shadows, she signaled to the bartender for another drink. She closed her eyes and began to sway a little to the music.

"Would you like to dance?" She looked around, startled, into the eyes of a young man in an army uniform. "The name is Tom Winter." He had the insignia of a private first class, and his face was sprinkled with freckles. The blue eyes beneath the neatly combed reddish hair were smiling as he leaned against the bar next to her.

"Thank you, but—I don't think so." She turned away.

"Aw, please," he begged. "I haven't danced with a girl since I left home last April. In fact, this is the first time I've been in New York."

Jenny smiled in spite of herself. His bright blue eyes were pleading with her, and he had a wistful smile on his lips. She slipped down from the stool into his waiting arms, and in the small space by the jukebox they swayed to the music of Glenn Miller.

"You know something?" he said, looking down at her. "You're the prettiest girl I ever danced with."

She glanced up at him and laughed. "Some line, Tom Winter!"

The blue eyes rounded and grew serious. "Heck, that's no line. Do you ever look in the mirror? I think you're beautiful."

She started to laugh again but smiled instead. "Thank you," she said softly. "And I think you're the nicest person I've met in a long time." She added with a touch of bitterness, "For a man."

"Wow," he said softly, pulling away from her a little and looking down into her eyes. "Somebody must have given you a rough time."

Suddenly leading him back toward the bar, she said, "Let's have another drink and sit and talk about you."

71

He told her all about himself, about the small town in southern Ohio where he lived in a big white house with a veranda that was covered with roses, about his two younger brothers and his parents, about the drugstore that his father owned and where he'd always worked on Saturdays and after school, making deliveries, about the high school football team he played on and his two years at the University of Ohio before he enlisted. She could tell, by the way he told her of *home* with a soft yearning in his voice, that he would be going overseas soon. He had finished basic training and was stationed at a camp in New Jersey, taking advanced instruction in weapons.

They sat for hours, drinking Cuba Libres and talking like old friends who hadn't seen each other for years. Hungrily she listened as he told her about growing up in the big old white house, about fishing and rafting on the Ohio River, Christmas and the huge tree in the living room bay window, the fragrance of turkey roasting and the sound of church bells, the snow forts and tree houses he and his brothers built, his first car, a six-year-old coupe with a rumble seat that he'd bought with his own money.

"Hey," he said as they walked out of the bar and stood for a moment on the silent, dark street, "you haven't tol' me an'thing about you." He slurred his words and stood in front of her, swaying slightly, a foolish little half grin on his face. As she started to walk he caught up with her and held her arm through his.

"There's nothing to tell," she said softly after a moment, pushing on along the empty, dark street. "I grew up, I got a job, I got married—" As he pulled her to a stop, she looked up at him. "My husband was killed overseas." Her face was a blur in the darkness.

Slowly he pulled her to him and held her. "I—I'm sorry," he said, his voice soft, comforting. They stood there for a long time, not moving or speaking, then she pushed away and, taking his hand, pulled him along the sidewalk with her.

"Come home with me, Tom Winter," she said, the words barely audible as she led him into Waverly Place. Smiling happily, he hooked his arm through hers again and, turning his head, glanced down at her. But in the darkness he couldn't see her face, the look of loneliness or the haunted expression in her eyes as they neared the brownstone in the middle of the block, and he began to sing softly, mumbling the words.

*"A cigarette that bears a lipstick's traces,
An airline ticket to romantic—"*

"Shhhh," Jenny hissed. "You'll wake up the whole street."

"—these foolish things remind me of you."

Chapter 12

DURING THE NEXT week Kate only saw Adam Barnfield once or twice, and only as they passed each other in the corridor. Then one morning he came into her office to ask for a briefing on the war bonds campaign. She showed him charts, brought him up-to-date on the project, and outlined the entertainment schedule. "We channel it through radio, movie theaters, vaudeville shows, and on stages," she explained. "It's been well tested already, and the public loves these big star-filled rallies."

They had lunch almost every day from then on, rarely discussing anything but the war bonds campaign.

"Freddie March was at a dinner party my parents had last week," he told her, "and he said he'd be glad to help out. Then I'm sure we can get Tallulah Bankhead and Crosby, of course, Carmen Miranda, probably Ann Sheridan, Dietrich, and Hayworth. Don't worry, we'll get more than we can possibly book."

What happened between them was gradual. And yet to Kate it seemed sudden. She found herself thinking about him more and more, and when he accidentally touched her or clasped her hand in a moment of friendly banter, she felt a shivery tingle run up her spine.

"It frightens me," she said miserably to Liz one day at lunch. "Maybe it's all just—just physical. I don't want only that."

Liz was astonished. "You? That could never happen to you, Kate. Or to any man who ever fell in love with you."

"I didn't say he was in love with me," she said in surprise.

"Well, of course he is," Liz said, laughing. "How could he help but be?"

"Dear Liz," Kate said softly, putting her hand over Liz's on the table, then laughing delightedly. "What would I do without you?"

For the next several weeks Adam persisted, asking her to dinner, the theater, dancing, a ride in the country, anything, anywhere. But she was firm in her refusals, bewildered by her feelings, and plagued, still, by a sense of betrayal to Philip. At the same time her practical side argued that this was ridiculous. She was allowed to feel again.

One day in the office she finally faced him, carefully keeping the desk between them.

"Adam, we must understand something. I—I haven't been out with any man since my husband was killed a year ago."

"I can understand that," he said softly. "But it *is* a year now, Kate. And from what Justin's told me about him, he would want you to live as normal a life as possible—"

"That isn't all." She paused for a moment, then drew a deep breath. "Very few people here at the agency know this. And I'm only telling you so you'll understand." She turned to the window and looked out across the Manhattan skyline, the bright winter sun turning the building tops to gold. "I have a child, Adam—"

Adam had been prepared for this moment but had not been certain that he would appear properly startled. In the fleeting second or two before Kate turned back to look at him, he remembered Lloyd Mason's words: *Her husband was killed at Pearl Harbor. The baby was born the same day. But that's just between us. Justin promised Kate we'd keep it quiet.* For only the briefest moment he thought of telling her he knew, that he'd been told in the deepest of confidence. For that briefest moment he wanted to tell her. Wanted to be completely honest with her. But the moment passed.

"It's a little girl. She's a year old." Kate saw the startled expression on his face, then watched as it slowly changed to a wide, warm smile. To her surprise she felt relief flooding through her.

"Kate," he said softly, taking her hands in his as he came around the desk to her. "How wonderful. Really wonderful. Justin has told me how close you and your husband were—"

Seeing the sudden tears in her eyes, he put his arms around her and held her to him.

"I'm sorry, Katy. I didn't mean to upset you." He took his handkerchief and slipped it into her hand.

She tried to laugh and casually pulled away from him. "Sorry, Adam. I've never done that before."

"Well, maybe it's about time," he said softly. He walked to the door of her office, then turned and smiled.

"Dinner tonight?"

Laughing and shaking her head, she crossed to him and gave him the handkerchief. "All right. Dinner tonight."

As the weeks flew by they had dinner several times, then it was the theater, and then dinner and dancing, and finally he begged her to come to Brookton for a weekend. One night, as he parked his car in front of her apartment building and they sat for a moment in contented silence, smoking, watching the shadowy passage of cars in the dim-out, he leaned over and kissed her. It was a whisper of a kiss, gone almost before it started, and yet it affected her deeply.

"Please come to Brookton this weekend?" he asked softly. "I've talked so much about you, and they're all anxious to meet you."

For a long moment she was silent. "All right, Adam," she said, then quickly stepped out of the car and disappeared into the darkness.

He was waiting on the Brookton station platform in the pale January sunshine, and grabbed her bag as the train puffed out of the station. He took her hand and ran with her to his car, a long blue Packard convertible, parked on the other side of the small Victorian station house. Silent but smiling, she listened to his steady stream of conversation as they swept through the small town and he pointed out the places of interest. He was particularly handsome this day, she thought, his profile sharp above the beige turtleneck sweater and brown suede jacket.

Glancing out the window again, she noticed that the streets were becoming narrow and were lined with three-story wooden tenements and small brown cottages.

"Up there," he said, pointing, "the Barnfield Mills."

Ahead stretched a solid wall of red brick buildings, dark and grim and four stories high, as far as the eye could see along one side of the cramped cobblestone street. Each building had mansard rooftops and narrow windows like fortress slits. Tall chimneys belched black smoke into the winter sky. A pall of soot seemed to hang over everything, just as the deafening roar of machinery from inside set the rhythm of the long narrow road. Opposite the mill buildings nestled a long row of tiny houses, attached and identical, hugging the edge of the narrow dirt path next to the road. Children in dark coarse clothing played in the snow-patched dirt while several women in dark baggy coats swept the stoops or scrubbed away at the grime on the small windows.

"These houses are owned by the mills," Adam explained as they drove along. Kate looked away. One of the women was leaning on her broom and staring at the car. "The rent is extremely low, and there's a long waiting list to move into them."

Kate nodded, trying to understand. She had never seen settlements like this one before. As they turned a corner she caught a glimpse of outhouses in the tiny yards and looked away again. It was all so bleak and crowded; the endless stretch of mill buildings, tall and grim and dominating the small town of Brookton, strangely disturbed her. They spoke silently of a power and wealth and influence that Kate had only read about: the great textile empires of New England, almost always owned by one family who had amassed its fortune when the industrial force of America had exploded into the twentieth century.

As they drove into the countryside Kate breathed easier. They passed snowy fields and ice-covered brooks, and then Adam said, "We're almost there." As the car slowed she looked up at the elaborate black iron gate that soared high across the wide driveway, then glanced beyond at the Tudor-style gatehouse that rambled along one side of the driveway just inside the gate. An elderly man hobbled out of the gardener's cottage opposite it and opened the gate. Adam waved, then drove on along the winding road through a thick forest of birch and pine.

"My sister lives in the gatehouse," he said.

"Your sister?"

"Marianne. You'll meet her and her husband, Reed, at dinner. They have two children, Brenda and Jamie. Reed works for Father in the mills. He has a fancy title." Adam was looking down at her, an amused expression in his eyes. "For the life of me, I couldn't tell you what he does, but he's paid very handsomely for it, I assure you."

The car slowed almost to a stop, then continued on around a long circular driveway. Far across a snow-covered parklike lawn filled with great old elm and oak trees was the house. Like a jewel placed down on the setting of a formal French garden, it was brooding and beautiful, its Tudor-style stone facade crowned with steep roofs and gables, patterned areas of brickwork and tall mullioned windows, gothic arches, and a profusion of fantastically formed chimneys. The imposing size of the mansion was softened by hundreds of rectangular and bay windows, all glittering in the afternoon sun.

"Finisterre," he said in a soft tone.

"How beautiful," Kate breathed.

He pulled the car up behind a Cadillac sport phaeton and led her into the great center hall, a circular area with a polished flagstone floor, a fire leaping in the huge stone fireplace, and a carved staircase climbing to a gallery, all paneled and inlaid with heavy scroll designs. A houseman took her bag and led her up the broad curving staircase, along a wide, deeply carpeted corridor to her room.

As the houseman left, Kate looked around, feeling almost out of breath. From the long french windows she could see stables and tennis courts and rolling hills that were probably a golf course stretching around the end of a long lake that was covered with a blue sheath of ice in the winter sunshine. In the other direction was a covered swimming pool with white-columned porticoes at each end and cabanas along one side. Her room, large and all in a soft dove gray, was filled with flowers, satin boudoir chairs, dainty Dresden figurines, and crystal lamps. There was a satin bellpull in the corner, silver-backed brushes on the dressing table, a mirrored wall, and a small balcony outside one set of the french doors.

For a moment she wanted to run, wanted to find a deserted staircase and flee from this massive place. She wanted to run back to her apartment with its chintz-filled living room, Joanna sleeping in the next room, and the distant sounds of the city far below. Instead she turned to open her suitcase when there was a soft knock on the door. A thin dark-haired girl in a black uniform and frilly white apron and cap came a few steps into the room.

"I'm Carla, miss, the upstairs maid. You're expected in the solarium for lunch. I'll unpack your suitcase, miss, while you're gone."

Back in her apartment Sunday night, Kate tried to assemble her thoughts as she prepared for bed. The weekend had flown by in confusion, but pleasant confusion. She was an expert horsewoman from her growing years in California, and had joined Adam and Marianne for a ride on the estate's snow-cleared bridle paths. That evening, at cocktails in the book-lined library, with firelight leaping up the walls, she had met other family members who hadn't been present at lunch. Kate felt she had to talk to someone about the weekend,

78

and picked up the phone to call Jenny's number. She wasn't surprised when there was no answer and looked at the clock, but realized it was too late to call Liz at the Rectory. Finally she turned to her small desk, pulled out some stationery, and wrote:

Dear Jenny,

I tried to call you tonight, but again, as always recently, no answer. If this letter doesn't come back, I'll know you're still there, but apparently trying to still find your way through what seems empty and futile to you. You'll find your way out of it, I'm sure. I only wish you'd let Liz and me help. We're here, you know, when you're ready or if you need us. Please don't ever forget that, Jenny dear. Now to bring you up-to-date on me.

I've told you a little bit about Adam Barnfield, and I guess I'm ready to admit I find him most attractive, and that I'm more than just idly interested in him. Trying to understand my own feelings, remembering how deeply I loved Philip, makes it all very confusing. I went to Finisterre, the Barnfield estate up in Connecticut, this past weekend and met Adam's family, all except a cousin who is off in the Air Corps.

I liked Adam's mother so much, but suspect from her appearance that she's terribly ill. She's sweet and withdrawn, pretty with just touches of gray in her hair. His father? I don't know yet. A handsome man, with piercing blue eyes, a voice like an actor, towering over everyone, except Adam who is as tall as he. Jonathan, Adam's father, is charming, but there's something, a certain quality that men of great power and influence often have. I don't quite know what it is yet, but it's fascinating and a little frightening.

Adam's sister, Marianne Shaw, is beautiful in a thoroughbred, glamorous kind of way. She's slender and blonde, amusing, and terribly bored, I think. Oddly enough, I liked her. I gathered from conversation that she spent most of her time before the war broke out in places like Saint Moritz or Deauville or Paris. Her husband, Reed, is quite handsome—that is if you find the Adolph Menjou type handsome, small dark mustache, elegant manners, a bit foppish.

And there was Sarah Wheeler, whom I liked most of all. Tiny and positive, about eighty-six, she came from

*her place, Windward Hills, about four miles away in her
chauffeur-driven Pierce Arrow. To meet me, she said.
She's the grande dame of the family, Adam's grandmother on his mother's side. It was an interesting weekend, as
you can imagine . . .*

Looking up from the letter, she remembered one strange
note. As they were leaving, Marianne had pulled her aside
and said, "I wouldn't get mixed up with this bunch if I were
you, Kate. Oh, we're swell for parties, wonderful for cocktail
and weekend houseparties, even rather good at hosting for
Father when some twitty senator comes for dinner. But,
darling, over the long haul, well—"
Kate hadn't known what to say, when Marianne suddenly
laughed. "Just joking, of course." And she warmly hugged
Kate good-bye.
Remembering the incident left Kate with a sense of uneasi-
ness. She picked up her pen again, but the mood of Finisterre
was gone.

*Please call, Jenny. Liz and I have lunch once or twice
each week, and we miss you terribly. If I don't hear from
you soon, I'll be knocking on your door again one of
these days. Unless you call me first. Please do. Love,
and . . . let's keep in touch.*

                                                    Kate

Just as she finished addressing the envelope, the phone
began to ring. She reached out slowly and picked it up.
"Kate?" Adam said at the other end of the phone, and
Kate caught her breath sharply. Until this moment she hadn't
let herself think about those last moments in the car earlier in
the evening when he pulled up in front of her apartment
house. He had slowly pulled her into his arms and kissed her,
a long lingering kiss that left her trembling. Then he had
kissed her again, and she had clung to him. "There's no going
back now," he had whispered. Suddenly she had opened the
door on her side and climbed out, calling back as she grabbed
her overnight case, "Don't get out, Adam. And thank you for
a lovely weekend." Before he could move or say anything,
she had run into the lobby.
"Kate?" he repeated. "Damnit, I can't sleep."
"Please—" She tried to keep the tremble out of her voice.

"I'll come right to the point. It's the only way to handle something with you. I want to marry you, Kate."

She drew in her breath sharply. "Adam, please . . ."

"No, darling." His voice was soothing, reassuring, strong. "I don't want you to say anything. I just want you to think about it. Think about it tonight. I'll be gone tomorrow and Tuesday in Boston, then Tuesday night we'll have dinner, and you can—tell me then. Good night, darling, and I love you." He hung up before she could say another word.

Chapter 13

JENNY READ THE letter twice, then tossed it onto the coffee table and stared at her drink. She shook it a little, but the ice cubes had melted, so she put the glass down on top of the letter. Kate's letters. Damn her letters, she thought.

She walked unsteadily to the window, pulled the curtain aside, and looked out. The night beyond was a blank, as though all life had been erased. But there *was* life out there, she told herself. Sounds, music, low lights, someone to talk to who wouldn't ask questions or even care what her name was.

She called Gina first, then showered and quickly dressed. As soon as Gina arrived to watch Christopher, she left, walking carefully, holding the stairway bannister so she wouldn't fall, feeling lightheaded and unreal, her mouth dry and stiff.

In the bar she sat in her usual darkened corner, near the jukebox. After her first drink she began to feel better, put a dime into the jukebox, and pushed the button for Bunny Berigan's "Can't Get Started." The bar was crowded and noisy, but she felt anonymous in her slouchy hat and dark suit. She lit a cigarette, then glanced down the bar, finding the usual cast of characters lined up, soldiers and sailors, a couple of Marines, a few men in civilian clothes, four or five women, and the gray-haired bartender. She smiled. All bartenders were gray-haired these days.

Yes, the cast was all in place, the curtain had risen, and the play had begun. She knew all the moves, the lines, everyone's role. In a few moments one of the soldiers or sailors would slide down off his bar stool, and with a wink or a nudge at his buddy, he'd swagger around the end of the bar and stand or slide up onto the stool next to her. For a few minutes he wouldn't say anything. Then after a while he'd look around as though surprised to see her sitting there and ask if he could buy her a drink. But she never let them buy her drinks. She always bought her own.

For the first ten or fifteen minutes he'd talk about inconsequential things—the weather, the record that was playing, or maybe the war, the North African offensive, Roosevelt and Churchill's meeting at Casablanca. Finally he'd talk about his hometown and his friend at the end of the block who got killed at Guadalcanal.

This one looked like Tom Winter. As he slid up on the stool she saw the Army uniform, the reddish hair and stocky build. But Tom had been wearing the Screaming Eagle armpatch of the 101st Airborne Division, and his olive-drab trousers had been neatly tucked into shining paratrooper boots. Tom had been the first, and she had taken him home with her. She had taken a few others, but she didn't even try to remember them. She had just danced in the tiny space by the jukebox with most of them. She remembered Tom because he'd been the first.

"What does the T stand for?" she asked the soldier sitting next to her, touching the armpatch, a black T against blue.

"Why, Texas, ma'am. What else would a big T stand for?" he said, grinning and speaking with the broad accent of his native state.

Later, she couldn't remember the exact time that it happened, but she and T for Texas walked through the bitterly cold streets of Greenwich Village and turned onto Waverly Place, laughing softly as they teetered along the curbing as though on a tightrope. T for Texas had a bright shiny flask in his pocket, which they kept drinking from.

When she tried to stop him in the vestibule, explaining that she had to send Gina home before he came upstairs, he pushed into the hallway with her, laughing and loudly shushing her. But they both stopped at the bottom of the stairs. Gina was sitting halfway up the staircase, a frightened expression on her narrow little face.

"There're some people up there in your apartment," she said, pointing upward. "They sent me out, down here."

Jenny tore up the stairs, the soldier following, not understanding, only aware that Jenny was getting away from him. Drunkenly he caught her at the top with a "Not so fast, gorgeous!" then grabbed her and whirled her around in his arms just as the door to Jenny's apartment was flung open.

With her eyes riveted on the apartment door, Jenny pulled herself from the soldier's hold.

"Just what I might have expected," Fred Baldwin said sneeringly.

"What the hell!" the soldier muttered to Jenny. "Y'all told me you lived alone." And with a livid look at Fred Baldwin, he turned and pounded down the stairs while Jenny and Fred watched each other. They heard the outer door slam four flights below, and only then did Jenny move, circling warily toward the door as a chilling fear stole through her.

"What are *you* doing here?" she asked as she edged past him, half in fear, half in revulsion. But he didn't answer, merely stepped aside to let her pass, his mouth formed in a contemptuous smile. She stopped at the door. In her living room beyond the small foyer she saw Mary Baldwin, her sister-in-law, and a stranger, a middle-aged man in a shiny brown overcoat and rimless glasses.

"Who is that man?" she demanded, her voice trembling. It was then she saw one of Christopher's blankets dangling from Mary's hand. Hearing a small sound, she knew Fred had moved closer behind her. In a blinding flash she realized what was happening.

"No!" she shouted, lunging toward the bedroom. But Fred grabbed her arm and pulled her back, his touch sickening her.

"Fred—" Mary timidly started to protest.

"Get Christopher, Mary," Fred snapped as he struggled with Jenny, who thrashed about wildly trying to free herself. As Mary disappeared into the bedroom, Jenny felt Fred's hands close tighter on her arms until she felt pain, but she kept on struggling. This was the man who had raped her, and now he was taking her child.

"You can't do this!" she shrieked. "There are laws—"

"There are laws that protect innocent children, too, Jenny," he said as he pushed her down onto a chair and held her there. "You'd better listen to what Mr. Hagen has to say. He's a private detective we hired and he's been following you for weeks."

Jenny froze. With a rush of exploding awareness, the full horror of it sank in. They were really going to take Christopher away. They had no children of their own, never could have any, and wanted Christopher. So they had hired a detective to watch her.

She made a move, but Fred held on. Terror filled her throat. She heard words coming from her mouth as she fought to stand up, unintelligible words. In a split moment she knew what she had been hiding from herself all along, that she loved Christopher and wanted him, wanted to care for him, raise him, see him as a little boy and then growing as tall and taller than she. "Oh, God," she cried. "No!" It came out in a long wail from the depths of her new anguish as Mary came from the bedroom carrying Christopher. She struggled to get to him as he twisted about in Mary's arms, trying to see Jenny, his eyes wide and bewildered, one little hand outstretched toward her, the other clutching a small brown teddy bear. Mary half ran across the living room, eyes turned away, as Fred wrenched Jenny back in the chair.

"I love you, baby," Jenny cried out, lunging forward as Christopher sobbed something that sounded to Jenny like "Mama." "I always loved you, Christopher. I just didn't know!"

But Mary and Christopher were gone, and Mr. Hagen had shut the door and was leaning against it. Still straining against Fred's hands, she saw Mr. Hagen take a notebook from his pocket.

"Okay," Fred said to the other man. "Read her a few of those names, dates, and places."

In a droning voice Mr. Hagen began to read, "—wearing the slash marks of a sergeant and an armpatch of the Americal Division, about six feet two, weight approximately one hundred sixty-five pounds, brown hair and a —"

"Stop it," she moaned. "That doesn't mean anything."

"I have pictures, Mrs. MacKenzie," the detective said in a dull nasal voice, "and signed statements from witnesses, people who live here, who saw specific men go into your apartment at night and come out in the morning. Other witnesses followed—"

"Stop it!" she shrieked, her hands over her ears. Fred was holding some papers in front of her.

"You'd better sign these, Jenny."

"I won't sign anything," she said, suddenly lunging toward the door, but Fred caught her and pulled her back to the chair.

"I think you will sign them," he panted. "We have more evidence than we'll ever need to go into court and prove that you're an unfit mother. So I think you'd better just sign these papers, waiving your rights and giving Christopher into our care until the adoption is finalized."

Adoption? She froze, clutching the arms of the chair.

"If you want to fight it, you'll need lawyers," Fred said, standing in front of her as Mr. Hagen picked up his hat and walked back to stand in front of the door again. "And lawyers cost a lot of money. But you'd lose, Jenny. Any lawyer would tell you that. So why waste the money?"

She knew he was right. They had all of the evidence and information they needed. When she'd worked at the *World-Dispatch*, she'd seen stories like this. UNFIT MOTHER LOSES CHILD AFTER LENGTHY COURT BATTLE. She had seen the headlines, perhaps even written the story. She couldn't remember, couldn't think of anything; everything was a jumble in her head.

"You'd lose the minute that evidence is produced in court," Fred said, prodding her with one hand while he pushed the papers in front of her with the other.

"I'll never sign anything, Fred Baldwin," she said through her teeth. "And somehow, some way, I'll get him away from you."

For several minutes Fred stared down at her, then with an angry shrug he walked to the door. "Never, Jenny. I'll start legal proceedings tomorrow."

Long after they had left, Jenny sat in the chair, staring at nothing. Then she got a blanket and huddled on the couch until it was light, when she got up and showered and dressed, and after several cups of strong black coffee caught a bus for uptown.

"I'm sorry, Mrs. MacKenzie," the third lawyer said, repeating what the first two lawyers had already told her. "I wouldn't be doing my job if I didn't tell you the truth. You wouldn't stand a chance in court. Even with all the extenuating circumstances, your husband's death at Pearl Harbor, the loss of your job—it just wouldn't matter. The child is all they think about in these cases." He looked away in embarrassment. "These men, you see, who came to your apartment—"

She dragged up the three flights of stairs, unlocked the door of her apartment, and went in. For several long minutes she stood in the middle of the living room, listening for sounds that were no longer there. Then she went into the kitchen, reached for the bottle of Scotch, and poured a tumblerful.

By mid-winter of 1943, Liz had signed contracts for *Across into Twilight*, Dan Coleman's new daytime serial. The show was to start on the air the following week, but Liz found herself pushed to a hurried decision. The same week she had been offered a small role on *Ellery Queen,* a popular night-time show, but had reluctantly turned it down.

"You can't do things like that, Liz," Jeanne scolded her as they sat in the Algonquin over lunch. "You simply can't refuse parts on radio and expect to keep working in the business. So that means you've got to move into town, because you're going to be getting more and more offers for nighttime shows."

"Well, Kate *did* tell me about a sublet available in the building right across from hers," Liz said tentatively as she picked at the chicken salad on her plate. "The tenant will leave the furniture for whoever takes the lease off her hands."

"There you are then," Jeanne said, stirring her coffee.

"It's just not that simple. You and Kate think—"

"You *have* to make the break from your father if you ever expect to make anything of your career. And with this other offer to do Hack Crawford's *Sixth Row Center,* you've got to make a decision now, not tomorrow or next week or next month, but now."

"It's terrifying," Liz said. "Like stepping off a cliff."

"Lots of things in life are." Jeanne was casually lighting a cigarette. "But maybe you're not that keen on a career in radio?"

"You know I am," Liz said, leaning forward, her voice sharply intense.

"Then make a decision." Jeanne dropped the match in the ashtray.

Liz toyed with the food on her plate for a moment, a deep frown on her lovely face. Then she looked up. "I'll tell my father tonight." But she was still frowning. "I'll hate only seeing Julie on weekends."

"It won't be any time at all before you'll be able to have her with you all the time," Jeanne said, comforting her. "You're already the most talked about new actress in radio, according to Glenn. Before you know it you'll be getting bigger and bigger roles and you'll be able to hire someone to take care of Julie."

Her father, again surprisingly, said little. It was as though he knew it would do no good to oppose her and so reacted in only the most passive sense, saying little and leaving the dining room as quickly as he could. Her mother was quietly thrilled, and Liz dreaded the day when she would take Julie away from her. The wrench, she knew, would be dreadful.

The furniture in the new apartment was simple but adequate. With new drapes and slipcovers, Liz knew she could make it attractive. And the new show, *Across into Twilight*, had gotten off to a good start.

Liz was walking out of the studio after the first program when she saw Dan Coleman coming toward her, smiling and shrugging into his coat.

"Lunch?" he simply said and took her to a saloon in the West Forties. They talked only about the show and yet Liz had never known an hour to fly past so rapidly. The following day he asked her to lunch again, this time in a smoke-filled, dimly lit brownstone half-basement that had been a speakeasy just ten years before. This time he asked her questions about herself and told amusing stories about when he was a youngster growing up on Chicago's west side.

"When I'm with him, it seems so right," she told Kate one evening as they hung her new living room drapes. "I mean, we have so much to talk about, and it feels so easy, even exciting, to be with him. It's fascinating to listen to the stories he tells about England during the blitz and when he was in China and Burma. But then when I leave him, or when I'm in Larchmont on the weekends, I feel as though it's wrong, Kate. It's only been a little over a year since Bill—"

"I know," Kate said, shaking her head wisely as she put hooks into a drapery. "But I'll tell *you,* Liz, just as I have to keep telling myself, that it's all in the past." She was quiet for a moment. "We can't bring them back. And we're here . . . with so many years ahead of us."

From the top of the small stepladder where she was sitting, Liz looked down at her, her eyes filling with excitement. "I *knew* it. You and Adam."

Kate nodded, her green eyes dreamy.

Liz jumped down from the ladder and threw her arms around Kate. "How exciting. When?"

"Next month. And I want you and Jenny to be there. At Finisterre." She was quiet for a moment. "I won't pretend, Liz. It's going to be a wonderful kind of life, especially for Joanna, growing up in such a beautiful place, and with a family." She smiled. "No more remodeling last year's suit or stinting on the bedroom rug to buy Joanna's playpen, no more quick lunches at Walgreen's counter."

"You are in love with him, aren't you, Kate?" Liz asked softly.

"Oh, Liz, he's such fun. And he's exciting, marvelous to be

with. I didn't think it could ever happen to me again."
Suddenly she was all business. "Hand me that drape, and I'll
put the hooks in it."

By late winter *Across into Twilight* had sponsors waiting in
line. It was rumored to be the top contender for the Peabody
Award. Liz was in rehearsal for Dan's hour-long drama to be
broadcast on *Sixth Row Center* and had also been signed to
play several roles on other evening shows, including the
prestigious *Cavalcade of America.*

"You're what is known in the trade as a hot property," Dan
teased her as they sat in Cherio's at dinner one evening. Then
his darkly handsome face grew serious. "I *am* in love with
you, you know."

She nodded slowly and put her hand in his.

They walked through the dark streets to her small East Side
apartment, hands clasped tightly. Her heart beat fast as they
went into her foyer. Then, standing in the dark of her
bedroom, he kissed her. With gentleness he undressed her,
and as he did, for only a brief moment she thought, no, I
mustn't. But they were side by side on the bed and he was
holding her close. "I'd never do anything to hurt you, Liz,"
he whispered. "If you tell me to leave, I will."

But she pulled his head down to hers, and then his hands
were touching her, one exploring her breasts, the other
sliding beneath her and holding her to him. He kissed her a
long and lingering kiss while his hands softly searched,
making her flesh glow. Then he entered her and she felt the
sweep of his passion and became lost in it, writhed in it, their
bodies entwined in a miracle of motion that drove them on to
a pitch until it all burst inside, and she heard her voice cry
aloud, but it was like a cry from someone else.

They held each other closely, as though to let go would be
to lose each other. And then he caressed her again, but with a
gentleness that brought tears to her eyes, and as he kissed her
he tasted her tears.

"I adore you," he said.

"I love you," she whispered. "You've made me whole
again."

After a while, a long, long while, she rose in the darkness,
walked over to the windows, closed the curtains, and, returning to the side of the bed, flicked on a lamp, which cast a soft
glow on the room. He lay on the bed watching her, and as she

leaned down to kiss him he said, "I never knew I could love anyone again like this."

"We're both starting over, Dan," she said, a thread of sadness in her voice. "But it's right for us. I *know* that, darling."

For a long, long time he held her in his arms, then rose to dress. She pulled on a silk robe and watched him, propped against a pushed-up pillow on the bed. Suddenly he turned to her and said almost angrily, "I don't want it this way, Liz. I want it to be right."

Looking up, she smiled and touched his arm. "It *will* be, Dan." But he had quickly turned away to pull on his jacket.

She walked to the door with him. He looked down and held her for a moment and told her he was going to the West Coast the following day to talk to the producers of *Suspense* about doing several scripts for them. "Then I have some business to take care of in San Francisco. But I'll be back in a week."

"I don't want you to go," she whispered.

"I'll call you every night."

Liz noticed the strain on Jeanne's face as she walked toward her across the restaurant. A stringed trio was playing near the trickling fountain in a bower of ferns.

"Sorry I'm late," Liz said, catching her breath as she slid into a chair opposite Jeanne and loosened her blue coat. "But Ax wanted to tell us about the rebroadcast to the coast."

"It's all right," Jeanne said, tense. "I hope you don't mind, but I ordered for us. I only have half an hour more." As Liz busied herself pushing her coat onto the back of her chair and pulling off her gloves, Jeanne watched her closely, then suddenly leaned forward. "I didn't know you were dating Dan Coleman." Her voice was accusing.

Liz gazed at her, puzzled, then slowly unfolded her napkin and placed it in her lap. "Well, I didn't see any reason to talk about it. Not—not until now, actually." She smiled brightly. "I mean until it began to be serious."

"Then it is serious?" Her voice had risen sharply. Looking around, she lowered it and leaned closer. "Don't you realize what you're doing? What a terrible mistake you're making?"

Liz was bewildered. "I don't know what you're talking about."

"God! I can see it in your face." Jeanne lit a cigarette. Her voice was bitter. "You've been sleeping with him. Good God,

Liz, it's not really my business, but—damn it!" She puffed furiously.

Liz's hand instinctively went to her cheek, flushed now with embarrassment. "Jeanne . . . ?"

"I don't want you to go through what I've been going through," Jeanne said, leaning even closer, her voice low with desperation.

"What—what do you mean?" Liz asked, alarmed. "I don't understand." As it began to register, her face went white.

"Oh God," Jeanne said grimly, "why do I have to be the one to tell you?" Her eyes were steady but sad. "Dan Coleman is married."

Liz didn't say anything. She slowly looked around the crowded restaurant as though wondering why she was there. "Who is she?"

"Her name is Connie." Jeanne watched her carefully. "Oh, he doesn't live with her. In fact, she's out on the West Coast."

"West . . . Coast?" Slowly her eyes turned back to Jeanne.

"That's where he met her. Of course, there's talk the child isn't even his, but—"

"Child?" Liz was trembling.

"It's a little boy, Liz." Jeanne's voice was gentle as she reached across the table and held Liz's hand. "While she was pregnant, he believed her when she said it was his. It was born about five months after Dan married her. She said it was premature, but it weighed around six pounds. Hardly a preemie at that weight. Dan was still in China when *that* child was conceived. She probably didn't even know *who* it belonged to. Connie was apparently a party-loving gal, who worked nights as a volunteer at a USO club in San Francisco."

"But . . . but, why would Dan get involved with someone like her?"

"Well, he was alone, and just back from the CBI. He was lonely and was getting treatment at a hospital there for his wounds. He wanted in the worst way to get into this war in one of our military branches but they wouldn't take him, and as second best was trying to write for radio. That was when he met her."

Liz was white. Her eyes were stricken, and when she spoke it was barely more than a whisper. "I want to leave," she said, rising, then shook her head. "No, don't come with me. I have to be by myself."

* * *

She let the phone ring four or five times, then with dread moved toward it and picked it up.

"Liz? Liz, are you there?"

"Yes," she said, but it was only a whisper.

"I can't hear you, darling. This connection—"

"Yes, Dan."

"There, that's better."

"Dan . . . I heard something yesterday—"

"Hey, is something wrong? Honey, before this connection goes bad again, I want to let you know I'm catching a train up to San Francisco. I'll leave from there and be home by Sunday."

"Dan, you've got to listen!"

"Is something wrong?" He sounded alarmed.

"Yes. I—I heard about Connie."

There was a long silence, then she heard him sigh, and her throat began to ache with the held-back tears.

"I didn't want you to hear it this way," he finally said. "I was coming back to tell you. And you've got to believe this. She was getting a divorce. When I met you, the papers were all set, and all she had to do was go to Reno and set up residence. Then something happened. She didn't go. And that's why I'm making this trip, to find out what happened." There was a pause. "You've got to believe me, darling. And I can't lose you now. You mean everything to me."

"I . . . I can't talk anymore, Dan." She felt the tears coming.

"Just as soon as she gets this divorce, honey, we'll be married."

Liz hung up the phone, then put her head down and sobbed.

In long loping strides, with his trench coat collar turned high and his hat pulled low against the wind, he walked along Powell Street, smiling grimly to himself. "I don't like to meet a man in a bar," Connie had said on the phone when he suggested the Oak Room Bar of the St. Francis, where he was staying. "I'll be at the Sir Francis Drake, on the mezzanine. They serve afternoon tea there." Connie? Tea?

At the entrance to the mezzanine he saw her before she caught sight of him. She had once seemed pretty to him, but now she was too heavily made up. A smooth reddish pageboy fell from beneath a smart hat, and a silver fox scarf was draped over one shoulder.

"Sit down, Dan," she said after realizing that he had no intention of kissing her. He threw his hat and coat on a chair between them and sat opposite her. "The same old Dan," she laughed. "Keeping his hat and coat close for the quick exit."

"How *are* you, Connie?"

"Not too well." The lower lip pouted a little. "The doctor thinks I may have hypoglycemia."

"Thinks?"

"Well, he's testing. I'm nervous, exhausted all the time." She looked extremely well rested. Dan had been about to comment on it. "I had to give up that part-time job I had."

"What was it? Receptionist?"

"Well, then I heard about this wonderful opportunity of working just afternoons in a photography studio, making appointments, assisting him in the studio, answering the phone, sending out bills. Bobby is old enough now that I can put him in one of these new nursery centers. Oh, you forgot his birthday, you know—" She was fitting a cigarette into a long shiny gold holder. "But I was absolutely exhausted, trying to keep a job and taking care of Bobby and the apartment, and it was all just too much. Which of course means I'll have to have more money from you, Dan. I can't possibly get along on what you send me." She paused while she ordered tea and Dan told the waitress he didn't want anything.

"How much more?"

"Well, with my rent and gas for my little car and the utilities and Bobby's nursery school and clothes and—"

"If you're not working, why does he have to be in nursery school?"

She was lighting her cigarette. "Well, several afternoons each week I take singing lessons."

"Singing lessons?"

"A band leader who came into the photography studio one day told me I had a wonderful musical quality in my voice, and said I should be a singer, study voice."

Dan simply stared at her. When he met her, she had been taking ballet lessons, because a soldier she met at the USO told her she was the most graceful person he had ever danced with.

"My vocal coach thinks I have operatic possibilities."

He looked at his watch. His train was leaving at six and he hadn't packed yet. "About the divorce, Connie? Could we talk?"

"Oh, I threw that last letter from your lawyer right into the wastebasket, Dan. And I've decided a divorce is out of the question."

"But we have nothing between us. You live here, I live there. And the child isn't even mine, so—"

"Legally he's yours, Dan. And at the moment I have no reason to want a divorce." She waited until the waitress put her tea and finger sandwiches down. "Oh, by the way, I hear you're doing extremely well in radio."

So that was it. It was always money.

"That big soap opera? *Across into Twilight*? And all those other shows? My goodness, Dan, you must be living very well there in New York, while back here, poor little Bobby and me, we're—"

He had stood up, placed a bill on the table, and was picking up his hat and coat. "I have a train to catch. As for more money, I guess you'd better talk to your lawyer." Angrily he pushed his hat on his head and strode from the restaurant.

Hack Crawford's knock on the door was steady and insistent, enough to finally bring Dan to the foyer where he turned the lock, let Hack in, then walked away into his den.

"Well, you're certainly a sorry sight," Hack said from the door of the den as he gazed at Dan's back, hunched forward in the rumpled sweater, hands shoved in his pockets, hair uncombed, sporting a three-day beard. "How long have you been back from the coast?"

For several moments Dan didn't answer. "I got back Sunday."

"And?" Hack's ruddy but handsome face settled into patient lines."

"And nothing." He was slouching against the desk.

"Nothing what?"

"Nothing anything." Dan looked at him wearily. "Connie won't give me a divorce. And when I called Liz to tell her when I'd be back, she hung up on me. Someone had told her about Connie." He went over to the big window and leaned against the sill, lighting one cigarette from the end of another one.

"Well, that doesn't particularly surprise me," Hack said, unbuttoning his camel's-hair coat and putting his hat down on

Dan's typewriter as he sat behind his desk. "You should have told her about Connie right from the start, and not just hope the divorce would go through before she found out. I must admit I was pretty surprised myself when you told me. You just never seemed married."

"Maybe because I didn't consider myself really married." He laughed emptily. "I didn't want to marry Connie right from the start. But it seemed like the *gentlemanly* thing to do. For some reason I never was able to kiss and run. Okay"—he heaved his shoulders and arms helplessly—"I'd been sleeping with her. And when she told me she was pregnant and that the baby was mine, I—well, I believed her. Until it was born. Then I knew."

He walked to the small bar in the corner, poured them each a short Scotch and handed one to Hack, then went back to the window.

"She'll give you a divorce," Hack said slowly.

"Huh?" Dan said. "Why do you say that?"

"Because, from what you've told me about Connie, she won't be able to live without a man for very long. She may even have someone now."

Dan studied his face. "You're obviously suggesting something."

"People like Connie pick on the good guys, because they're easy to take. Why do you think she picked on you in the first place?" He sipped his drink while Dan scowled. "Good guys play the game by the right rules. She knows that. The trick is to play the game by her rules. She'll never expect it from *you*."

"Have her watched, you mean?"

Hack nodded. "You'll get your divorce."

Dan shook his head. "I'm no good at that game."

Hack finished his drink, stood up, and walked to the door. "Good guys usually come in last, you know, Dan."

"You don't really believe that?"

"My boy, I do." With a small wave he left.

"Liz," Kate's voice was strong through the phone. "I thought you should know. I've asked Dan to come to the wedding."

"Oh, Kate, no." Liz cried out. "Then I—"

"Ax told me yesterday that Dan has his lawyer working on some new financial settlement that will be acceptable to that bitch." She sounded almost angry. "He's doing everything he can to try to make things work out. You owe him at least that much. And frankly, Liz, when I pick up a morning newspaper and read that ten thousand innocent people can be killed in just one night from the bombs dropped by two or three hundred planes, well, I just don't think it's terribly important, if you're in love, whether you're married or not."

There was a long silence, then in a small voice Liz spoke. "I'll be there, Kate."

Chapter 14

LIZ SAT AT the dressing table in a pale blue silk nightgown, slowly brushing her hair, while Jenny, in pajamas, sat cross-legged on one of the twin beds, creaming her face. Kate had just come through a connecting door from the next room, her yellow silk robe flowing behind her.

"Tell me, Kate, how in the hell do you raid an icebox in a house like this?"

Kate laughed. "I wouldn't even know where to find it. Adam is going to have to give me a map until I know where everything is. But seriously, if you're hungry, I'll ring for Carla. She'll get you something."

"Crackers and milk, like in the hospital?" Jenny teased, and Kate looked at her, noticing how thin she was, how pale, how much bravado there was in her voice.

"Beluga caviar and champagne would be more like it," Liz said as Jenny and Kate looked at her in surprise.

"Well, listen to her!" Jenny said. "I heard there was a new man in your life? What does he do, bring you orchids and pearls?"

Kate looked sharply around at Liz, who quickly lowered her eyes and brushed at her hair harder and harder.

"Who is he, anyway?" Jenny asked, wiping the cream from her face.

"He's the writer on her show. And he writes many other radio shows," Kate said, sitting on the flowered chaise and lighting a cigarette, carefully watching Liz from the corner of her eye. "He's also writing a play."

"Couldn't you have picked a banker or a lawyer?" Jenny said. "Playwrights are usually broke and all wound up in themselves."

"Oh, but Dan isn't," Liz said suddenly and defensively. "Of course, he's very involved in his work, but—"

97

"But he's bright and talented, and he's had a wonderfully interesting life, flying with the Tigers in China and Burma; then he was in London all during the blitzkrieg," Kate said.

"What's wrong with him?" Jenny asked, wary of Kate's tone.

Kate and Liz looked at each other, then Kate said, "He's married."

Jenny stared at Liz for a moment. "Married, huh?" She turned to Kate. "Well, my friend, it looks as though you're the only one coming out of all of this with a piece of cake." Her laugh was bitter.

Kate looked at Jenny. "You started to say something earlier about Christopher, when I asked you how he was."

Jenny slowly put the cap back on her cold cream jar and dropped it in her overnight case. "Christopher's gone."

For a long moment no one moved or said anything.

"Gone?" Kate asked, leaning forward. "Gone where?"

"They came and took him away." Her voice had sunk almost to a whisper. "Fred Baldwin, Alan's brother-in-law. And Mary. Alan's sister. They came to my apartment one night and took him away."

"But this is insane," Kate said after a moment, jumping to her feet and crossing to Jenny. "Somebody can't just walk into your house and take your child like that." She grasped Jenny's arm and tried to turn her toward her. "Somebody can't just walk in the door and . . ." Her voice trailed off and she let go of Jenny's arm. "All right. Apparently they could. At least, that's what the look on your face seems to be saying." Kate sat down on the end of the bed. "Aren't you going to tell us what happened?"

"Let's just say I found some playmates." Jenny's voice was flat, low, almost toneless. "And I brought a few of those playmates home. Oh, not many—"

Liz, slowly understanding the implication of the word *playmates*, said, "Oh, Jenny."

"But some." Her voice hardened as she tried to sound as though she didn't care. "The trouble is, my timing was bad. I brought somebody home one night and there was Fred, with Mary and a detective. They had the papers all ready for me to sign, papers releasing Christopher to them. T for Texas, of course, took off down the stairs like a jack rabbit."

"T for Texas?" Liz asked, bewildered.

"Well, I didn't know his name," Jenny said, wanting in her

own hurt to hurt someone else, even Liz. Kate watched her, knowing it was best to let her get it out in her own way. "They were all soldiers and sailors. After all, I was doing my bit for the war effort." She laughed. "No civilians. You don't have to worry about that."

"Stop it, Jenny," Kate said gently. "We're your friends, remember?" Jenny jumped up from the bed and walked to one of the windows, where she stood looking out as Kate went on. "I gather this detective had been following you for some time, and on this night they threatened you with the information. Is that right? Did you sign something so they could get custody of Christopher?"

"I didn't sign anything, and I never will," Jenny said grimly without turning around. "I've lost one round. In Family Court. But that's only the beginning. It's going to take a long time, and at least by fighting them, they'll never be able to adopt him." She suddenly turned, her eyes filled with tears. "But I'll never give up."

"All right," Kate said, crossing to her and putting her arms around her. "The next step is to put your life back together again. It won't be easy. But if you do, someday you'll have Christopher back with you again. I'm sure of that, Jenny."

Jenny leaned against her, and Kate heard a long sigh escape. She led Jenny over to the twin bed and pulled back the silk coverlet and sheet and blanket. "Start by trying to get some sleep, Jenny," Kate said. And Jenny slipped wearily down into the bed. Turning face down, she cradled her head on her arms.

The ceremony was brief. It was held in the solarium in the midst of all the carefully tended flowers and tropical foliage, turning March into summer. Liz, watching Kate and Adam standing in front of the Brookton justice of the peace, felt Dan's hand gently squeeze hers, and she gazed up at him. She felt whole again as he looked down at her. Just before the ceremony the guests had gathered in the small dining room for coffee. She and Dan found a corner.

"It's only a matter of money, and how much," he had said to her quickly. "That's all that's holding the divorce up."

"But I don't want you to—"

"It's not important," he argued quietly, holding her hands tightly in his. "The money doesn't matter, and apparently the sky's the limit when it comes to what I can make in radio."

"But you wanted more time to work on your play," Liz protested just as Jenny walked toward them, carrying her coffee.

"The play can wait. The divorce and you can't."

"Introduce me, Liz," Jenny said. "I want to be able to say I met him *when.*" Liz's heart went out to her, knowing how much pain was behind the smile.

Dan looked down into a face made smaller by the hugeness of her eyes, an arrestingly pretty face, the eyes boldly beautiful, brown with flecks of gold, and a wild tousle of dark hair about her face. She was small and as slender as a young boy, and yet there was something sensual about her figure, even in the tailored gray suit.

"This is Jenny, Dan." Liz was clasping Jenny's hand warmly.

"Jenny," he said suddenly, his face breaking into a smile. "I've been wanting to meet you."

"She's worth her weight in gold and silver and diamonds and rubies, but then I suppose you know that," Jenny said, smiling. Then, with utter candor, she said, "Whatever you do, don't hurt her."

"Oh, Jenny," Liz said with a small laugh. But Dan simply nodded.

"I promise," he said.

"All right, everyone," Jonathan Barnfield called out from the doorway, a wide smile on his face. "It's time to go to the solarium."

To Kate the Palm Beach house was the perfect honeymoon spot. More casual than Finisterre, with glass walls opening onto gardens and the sea, it had an unobtrusive couple as cook and houseman, a palm-lined sweep of beach, and terraced pools and gardens leading down from the Italianate house on a rise facing the ocean.

They sunned and swam and sailed, dined at the Everglades Club, danced at the Breakers and the Colony, shopped for Joanna on Worth Avenue, and walked late at night along the beach, dark and mysterious in the coastal blackout and perfumed with exotic flowers that drifted down from the gardens.

Kate was almost surprised at the intensity of her happiness. Adam was far more than just fun to be with. The careless kind of wit, charm, and arrogance deepened to something more interesting. They talked for hours on end and she discovered that he loved good books, theater, ballet, even opera. The slight physical resemblance she had seen between Adam and Philip ended there. Where Philip had been quiet and serious, Adam was outgoing, enthusiastic; where Philip had been circumspect, Adam was daring; where Philip's lovemaking had been gentle and tender, Adam aroused her to a pitch she had never known existed.

On their last night they took a final swim at midnight. Then he led her up from the beach through the open glass wall of their bedroom. A trail of moonlight shimmered out across the sea.

He kissed her, gently at first, then with a mounting surge of passion that swept her on and on while his hands moved swiftly over her body. She could hear her breath tearing from her throat in uneven little jabs. And as his body crushed down on hers she rose to him, finding it like music, powerful, stirring music, that swept her into a center current, where she rose and fell with the orchestration of his hands and mouth and words of love. And when he finally slept, she remembered the wildness and unleashed passion and softly smiled, then closed her eyes, her body curved to his.

As soon as Kate and Adam returned to Finisterre, preparations were under way for Amanda's fifty-first birthday. While in Palm Beach, Adam had told Kate that his mother was dying of cancer, and when she put her arms around him and held him as she saw the stiff set of his jaw, he had whispered, "Thank God I found you." For weeks Amanda had been almost completely bed-bound, but for the birthday celebration she was brought down to the long dining table in her wheelchair, wearing gray satin and her famous emeralds.

With the entire family present Jonathan beamed from the head of the table, his ebony cigarette holder tilted rakishly as he sipped his liqueur. "These living arrangements, of course, are only temporary," he said, patting Kate's hand where she sat at his left. "Amanda is afraid you're going to start disliking us, all living under one roof."

Kate smiled across at Amanda, who sat for this evening at Jonathan's right, then said with a teasing smile, "Well, we're not exactly cramped for space. I told Liz and Jenny I could go for a week here just looking for Adam."

As they all burst out laughing Amanda said in her frail voice, "But a bride wants her own home."

"And she'll have it," Jonathan said gently, "just as soon as this war ends and building materials and manpower are available once more. Directly across the lake. A four-acre section."

"Didn't I tell you he'd want to get rid of me, Kate?" Adam bantered.

And as the voices rose and fell Kate followed Amanda's eyes as they traveled slowly around the table, seeing that Amanda knew it would be the last time she saw Marianne glittering and beautiful in her white jersey gown, Reed yawning from time to time in boredom, Sarah Wheeler carefully watching her daughter for signs of pain and exhaustion, Brenda and Jamie squirming in their chairs, an excited Joanna in Carolyn Harrison's lap, eyes wide at the large cake and fluttering candles, and Justin and Margaret Wheeler, up from the city for the party.

"Oh, I understand," Jonathan was saying as Kate returned her attention to the conversation between him and Justin, "anti-fascist political parties quite true, these members of the French Underground in General de Gaulle's Conseil National, but basically coming from the communist party, isn't that correct?"

"Both communists and non-communists, Jonathan," Justin said.

"Strange bedfellows for the haughty Mr. de Gaulle, don't you think?"

"But necessary ones, Jonathan," Kate said. "The Russians are encouraging the French communists to support de Gaulle's leadership of the Free French, and because he *is* haughty and difficult he'll undoubtedly go to great lengths to escape complete dependence on us and the British, and swell the Free French ranks at the same time."

"Enough," Adam teasingly groaned.

"Quite a girl you've got here," Jonathan said to him, "and a well informed one, too, I might add."

"Oh, aren't women supposed to be well informed?" she asked quickly, but tempered her question with a smile.

"It makes interesting dinner conversation," he said, his eyes laughing.

"For those who care," Reed yawned as he lifted his demitasse.

When the nurse took Amanda off in her wheelchair to the small elevator, Marianne and Kate followed more leisurely, pausing on the broad staircase to look up at the stern portraits of John Adam Barnfield, who had come from England in 1858

102

and opened a small carpet store in Brookton, and Adam Wolcott Barnfield, who had started the mills.

By the time they reached Amanda's bedroom, she was almost asleep, her face almost transparent in the low light, her eyes closed in exhaustion. As Kate and Marianne stood beside the bed she opened her eyes and smiled.

"You must be very relieved, Kate," she said, speaking with great effort.

Kate glanced at Marianne, who simply shrugged.

"Relieved? About what, Amanda?"

"Adam." Amanda nodded slowly, her eyes half closed. "So relieved."

"About what, Mother?" Marianne bent down close.

"Jonathan told me just before dinner." Amanda's voice kept fading with the effort. "The draft board . . . his new classification." She was almost asleep. "So . . . relieved."

Kate and Marianne looked at each other, puzzled, then walked from the room.

"Adam said nothing to me," Kate said as they walked to the staircase.

"Probably didn't get a chance," Marianne said as they hurried down the stairs, Marianne heading toward the playroom to gather up Jamie and Brenda, Kate going to the library.

"You have to understand, Adam, the National Labor Relations Act was passed a little over seven years ago," Jonathan was saying as she entered and sat in the wing chair opposite him. "And of course this opened an entirely new production aspect to worry about. It meant that unionism was not only increasing, but beginning to gain national support." He looked at Kate. "Forgive me, my dear," he said as Adam came from the bar with brandy glasses for both of them. "But Adam was asking about the NLRA problems at the mills."

"No, please, I'm interested," she said, taking the glass from Adam. "It's just that Amanda said something just now about a reclassification for Adam by the draft board."

Jonathan and Adam glanced at each other for the briefest instant, then Adam walked back to the bar to make himself a drink.

Jonathan looked down into his glass. "Kate, Adam has just been reclassified three-A, which as you undoubtedly know translates into a man with a wife and a child."

There was a long pause as Kate began to understand.

"Three-A?" She was groping. "But that's not possible."

"As a married man with a child, he classifies three-A."

"But—" She looked at Adam but he had his back to her. "The regulations are very clear on that. Adam and I were not married before Pearl Harbor was bombed, and Joanna is not his child, so—" Something in Jonathan's face made her pause. She stared at him, then slowly rose, putting her glass down. "You're going to have to explain this."

"All right," Jonathan said. "You're a sensible young woman, so you'll understand." His jaw had hardened and she saw steel in his eyes. "But I'll preface it by saying that under no circumstances is Adam going into military service. I lost a younger brother in the First World War. Never again. And this is where you and I will surely agree, Kate. You lost your first husband. You know what—"

"Wait a minute, Jonathan!" Kate kept glancing from one man to the other. "Philip's death has nothing to do with this. You're right, no woman wants her husband to go to war, but it's no longer a matter of choice. And it *is* a matter of conscience."

"The local draft board has reclassified Adam on the basis that he is a married man with a child, sixteen months old, and conceived long before we went into this war." As she started forward he put his hand up. "Everything is in proper order, I assure you."

"Our marriage license had to be changed," she said wildly.

"Quite right," Jonathan said, watching her closely.

It was a long moment before Kate fully comprehended his meaning and what he had done. She looked at Adam but he still had his back turned. "Somehow you've managed to have the records doctored so that our wedding date is different." She remembered the justice of the peace who had come to the house one weekend with the marriage license papers for them to sign. He was also the town clerk in Brookton and the man who had married them.

Still watching her closely, Jonathan marveled at her, a slim, almost regal figure in the black velvet dinner gown, her wide green eyes beautiful in their anger, her skin like alabaster, her dark gold hair gleaming in the light from the fire.

"Joanna?" she asked slowly. "How did you manage that bit of forgery?" She felt a nauseated, growing panic.

He paused, then sat down. "Joanna was born in the Adam Wolcott Barnfield Memorial Hospital in Brookton."

Kate was stunned. As the room filled with a long, tense

104

silence she didn't move. "So it was all nothing but one huge, terrible lie, Adam?" she said, fighting the tears and hysteria.

He flung around, his face white. As he started toward her she backed away. "My God, Kate, no! I love you. I've loved you right from the start. That has nothing to do with this."

"That has nothing to do with this!" she said with a terrible mockery. "That has *everything* to do with this." She backed to the library door and leaned against it, her hands behind her. "All the lies. All the months and months of lies."

"No, Kate." Adam came halfway across the room. "Please. My God, Kate, please believe me." He started toward her again, arms outstretched.

"Don't come near me," she cried out, holding her hands up. "I'll have to go to them, of course, and tell them the truth."

"You'll not tell anyone anything," Jonathan said, the words cutting like a knife as he took several steps toward her and stopped. "You will only say, if anyone should ever ask, that you and Adam were married while he was still in Princeton, but you were married here in Brookton, quietly, so that it would have no effect on his standing at school, and that you continued to work in New York until you returned here to have the baby at Barnfield Memorial Hospital."

Kate shook her head slowly. "You have it all figured out."

"And, of course, should you be so foolish as to try and say anything to anyone in authority, it would be a simple matter to include you as a party to the action that was taken, and to suggest that you were under the impression you were going to receive an extremely large amount of money for your role in the whole situation, but that when you realized this wasn't true, you tried to turn the burden of guilt elsewhere."

The nausea rose to Kate's throat. She felt frozen in time and space. She wanted to take Joanna tonight and run. But where? She knew she was trapped. Jonathan's kind of power was awesome. In the end he would simply win through sheer power and money and influence. Better just to leave in a day or two, go to California probably . . . try to forget.

As she slowly turned, Jonathan's voice stopped her. "May I suggest you don't make any preemptive or rash move. Running off somewhere in the night, Kate, will gain you nothing. Joanna is now . . . *legally* Adam's child. If you try to leave, we'll find you. Make no mistake about that. By staying . . . there's much to be gained."

There was simply no way out. She knew that. "I can almost forgive what you've done, Jonathan, because Adam is your son, and you don't want to lose him. But I'll never forgive Adam."

Adam's hands were clutching the back of a chair. "Don't, Kate! Please listen to me. You mean more to me than—"

"I couldn't believe anything you told me," she said, her words like a whiplash. Then she turned to Jonathan. "Tell me, Jonathan, what date were Adam and I married? I'm sure he wouldn't know. He doesn't seem able to make any decision in this house." From the corner of her eye she saw Adam go to the bar and pour a drink.

"February tenth, 1941," Jonathan said, his voice cold.

Kate nodded, thought about it for a moment, then walked out the door, softly closing it behind her. She somehow reached the center hall and started up the staircase, then grasped the bannister and leaned on it, half collapsing and crying softly, "Oh, God, what's happening? What's happening to all of us?"

Dan raised his head and listened. The buzzer at the front door, just barely audible down the long hallway from the apartment's foyer, was ringing insistently. He looked at the clock on the bedside table—ten after ten—then down at Liz, softly sleeping, her pale golden hair spread across the pillow, the slight flush of sleep just visible in the low light from the bedside lamp.

He slid carefully out of the bed and pulled on his robe, then stole across the bedroom and pulled the door quietly closed behind him. He went along the half darkened hallway to the foyer and paused for a moment, waiting for the buzzer to ring again, wondering who it was. He ran his hands quickly through his hair and shook his head a little as though to shake out the sleep. Well, almost time to take Liz home anyway, he thought, wishing for the thousandth time that he could keep her with him all night long, remembering how she felt in his arms as she slipped off to sleep, then holding her close until he, too, slept.

The buzzer suddenly ringing again sharply interrupted his reverie and he pulled open the door. A stranger, an older man in a brown hat and raincoat, stood there.

"Mr. Dan Coleman?" When Dan nodded, the man pulled a long envelope from his pocket and shoved it into Dan's hands, then turned and ran down the narrow stairway of the brownstone and disappeared. Dan looked at the envelope for a moment, then pulled out the folded papers from inside and let his gaze slide down the closely printed lines. His eyes stopped at one phrase. "On charges of adultery." As his glance leaped downward he saw the name Elizabeth Lowndes and the word *Corespondent*. Staring at it for a moment, he muttered, "Christ!" and put one hand over his eyes, then looked along the corridor toward the bedroom. He'd have to tell her. "Christ," he said again.

"I'm going to Washington," Dan said on the phone. "The Office of War Information called me. They want me to work on a special project for about a month. I'll do the soap scripts from there and send them to New York." He remembered how calm she had been the night before.

"A month?" Liz said, trying to hide the shock. It was all happening too suddenly, the papers naming her as corespondent—and now Dan leaving.

"Might even stretch into six weeks," he said, his voice noncommittal. Then there was a long silence, and when he spoke again, she could hear the strain. "It's probably best this way, honey, until we know Connie will actually go through with the divorce, and I really have it. I've offered her a better settlement if she'll just drop the adultery charges. Had my lawyers get on it this morning."

"Dan—" she said, trying to interrupt, her voice breaking.

"Honey, it's just no good." She could hear the anguish now. "You're not this kind of person, getting named as corespondent, sneaking around hallways and stairways, trying not to let my neighbors see you. Good God, honey, I know better than anyone how miserable you've been, how cheap it's made you feel. It's best that I keep away from you for a while, and this gave me the opportunity."

"When are you leaving?" Her voice sounded dead.

"Tomorrow from Penn Station, on the Congressional Limited."

"I want to come there and see you off. Please," she whispered.

Liz let the crowds swirl around her. She watched past the quickly moving faces, and saw Dan coming back, scanning the newspaper he had just bought. The noise was deafening. Over it a voice bawled through loudspeakers, calling out a stream of stops between New York and Chicago. As he walked up to her he folded the newspaper and shoved it in his pocket, then took hold of her arms.

"I'm going to get on the train, honey." He looked down at her, thinking that she had never looked so beautiful, but never had her eyes been so sad. Suddenly he crushed her to him and held her. "God, how I'm going to miss you."

Before she could say anything, he had let her go, reached down, and picked up his suitcases, and without looking back he pushed through the crowds at the train gate and disappeared. She tried to peer over heads to catch a glimpse of him, but he was gone.

She walked across the rotunda, not heeding the tears that slid down her face. In less than two hours she would be on the air, playing the role of a young refugee girl from war-torn Europe. More than twenty million people would be listening to her. But at the moment it didn't matter.

Nothing mattered as she walked out into the May sunshine and climbed into a taxi. "Radio City, please," she said and sat back against the seat.

Now is the time, she thought, to make the final break from her family and bring Julie into the city to live with her. I have to do something right, she thought, and this was right for now.

Chapter 15

JENNY STOOD ON the station platform for several minutes after the train pulled out. Then she tugged the brim of her hat low over her eyes and walked to the window of the station house, where she saw a man in suspenders and a station master's hat. When she rapped on the window, he slid it open, eyes suspicious, and said, "Yes?"

"Is there a public phone booth around here?"

"Inside," he said, pointing to the door along the side. She walked around the old building, feeling his eyes on her as she entered and went into the phone booth, where she looked up a number and placed a call.

"Is Mr. Baldwin there?" she asked into the phone, raising her voice in an effort to disguise it.

"Yes, ma'am," a man's voice said. "But he's with a customer. Who shall I say is calling?"

"Just tell him Mrs. Perkins called, and that my husband and I'll come by late this afternoon to look at tractors." She remembered that Fred had switched to selling farm equipment when the auto industry came to a standstill.

She left the booth and walked rapidly toward the center of the small town, realizing that it was even smaller than she remembered from her one visit with Alan. It was shady and sleepy in the warm spring afternoon; huge leafy old elms formed a canopy over the streets, and green lawns stretched back to big white houses with deep verandas and awninged windows.

When she reached Main Street, she saw a taxi just pulling up to the curb of the taxi stand and ran across to catch it. She jumped into the rear seat, and gave the driver the address of Alan's mother's house.

"Going to visit Miz MacKenzie or Miz Baldwin?" the driver asked, looking at her in his rear-view mirror.

109

"Well—both of them," she said with a bright smile.

"Miz MacKenzie just got back yesterday from visitin' her sister over in Dedham."

"Yes—yes, that's right, I remember she wrote me that she was going there. Her sister—Henrietta." Dredging her memory, Jenny grasped the name.

"That's right," he nodded. "Henrietta Brown."

Jenny vaguely remembered the house as she walked up the front steps, hands trembling, heart pounding. The house gleamed with new white paint and the green shutters were closed against the afternoon sun. She lifted the brass knocker and tapped it several times.

Doris MacKenzie was wiping her hands on her apron when she opened the door, but before she could recover from her surprise Jenny pushed into the hallway and closed the door behind her.

"Jenny!"

"Mrs. MacKenzie, I have to talk to you."

"Wait," Doris MacKenzie said, trying to grasp her arm as Jenny pushed past her into the living room. "Here now, Jenny, just you wait a moment! Fred said you aren't supposed to come here. You have no right just to burst in here as though—"

"Any more than they did?" Jenny asked as she quickly hurried over to a door that led to the dining room. She could see a playpen in the back sitting room in a flood of sunlight, but it was empty. A fragrance of cinnamon and apples cooking filled the house.

"Where is he?" Jenny demanded, pushing her way back into the center of the room just as Mary appeared in the hallway door.

"He's taking his nap," Mary answered, quickly barring Jenny from the stairway beyond, her thin face frightened but resolute. Jenny looked back at Doris. There was a smudge of flour on her cheek. She looked like everybody's grandmother, gray hair wound high in a bun, but there was steel in her eyes.

"For God's sake, Mrs. MacKenzie, I'm his mother."

"From what Fred told me, I don't think you were behaving like one. All those men!"

"You don't understand," Jenny cried, trying to push past Mary again. But Doris grasped her arm and whirled her around. "When you brought those men home, Jenny, you gave up your child."

"Mother . . . ?" Mary said faintly.

Jenny, hearing the doubt in Mary's voice, turned and faced her, hands outstretched, tears streaming down her face.

"Mary, you understand, don't you?" But she heard the door open, then saw Fred's angry face, right behind Mary.

"What the hell are you doing here?" he shouted.

Suddenly bursting past Mary, Jenny hurtled up the stairs and almost reached the top when she felt him grab her ankle and drag her back down. She clung to the bannister and, lunging her leg downward, caught him off guard and heard him stumble backward with a series of shouted oaths. She ran to the top of the stairs and saw the corner of a crib in the bedroom in front of her, and a beautiful wide-eyed child staring at her as he held on to the sides of the crib.

"Christopher!" she cried out, running into the room and falling to her knees beside him just as Fred grasped her arms and dragged her from the room. She was crying his name over and over, as she saw Mary hurry past them on the staircase and quickly close the bedroom door just as Christopher, eyes round with bewilderment, put his hand out as though to reach toward her.

It was almost dark when they got to the railroad station. Fred took her around the darkened station house to the platform, where they stood in the growing twilight. Jenny could hear a train whistle down the track, high and mournful, like an echo from her soul. The tears were gone; she felt wooden, numb.

She could see the headlight on the train's engine, pounding toward them along the track.

"Just thought you'd like to know, Jenny," Fred said. "I'd given the station master a snapshot of you. Figured you'd try something like this."

She didn't look at him, but just kept watching the train as it pulled into the station. When it stopped, she walked across the darkened platform, climbed the steps, and opened the heavy coach door.

Kate settled back in the cab after telling the driver to take her east to Sutton Square and Riverview Terrace, where Sarah Wheeler had her townhouse in a tiny, cobblestoned cul-de-sac.

"How good to see you, Mrs. Barnfield." Elsie Ford clasped Kate's hands and drew her into the foyer. For more than thirty years the tall, smiling, gray-haired woman had been

111

Sarah Wheeler's housekeeper and companion. "She's been looking forward to your visit all day."

Sarah was waiting for her in the small sitting room with its comfortable chintz-covered furniture and cheerily burning fireplace.

But she wasn't alone. Standing by the fireplace with one elbow on the mantel was a young man with broad shoulders neatly encased in a tan military shirt open at the neck. His short light hair was neatly combed and still damp from the shower. This must be Del, she thought, liking him at once. His face was open and friendly, with strength about the mouth, laughing blue eyes, a sharp, decisive jaw, and a slightly crooked nose, broken in college boxing, she later learned. He was wearing pinks, the dress trousers for Army officers, and his dogtag and chain glinted in the light from the fire.

"Gran said I had to meet you," he said, grinning and turning to glance at Sarah, who sat by the fire knitting, her short gray hair curling around her heart-shaped face. He shook Kate's hand. "She's sold on you."

"I am indeed." Sarah smiled, kissing Kate's cheek as the younger woman bent down. "She's a favorite already."

"Making it mutual," Kate said, sitting on the small loveseat near the windows that looked out on a rear walled garden.

"Del is home on leave." Sarah's eyes rested on him with a mixture of affection and worry. "Just thirty days."

"What she really means," Del said, smiling at Kate, "is that I'm on that long delay-enroute before shipping for points unknown."

"Will you be up in the country at all?" Kate asked politely.

"Can't wait to get there. That's really home, you know." He looked at Sarah fondly. "Gran actually raised me, most of the time there. I'll be up as soon as I get a few business matters settled in town."

"Del, dear, I hate to rush you," Sarah said, looking at her small wristwatch. "Your two thirty appointment—"

"I'm on my way." He bent down to kiss her, then shook hands with Kate and said, "See you up in the country."

Elsie Ford brought in a tea tray, and as Sarah's hands moved deftly about the silver tea service, she told Kate about Del's fascination with airplanes and his eagerness to enlist in the Army Air Corps. "He was eight when Lindbergh flew solo to Paris, and he's worshipped him ever since. Del came to live with me eight years ago when he was just sixteen."

112

Kate remembered that would have been when the *Morro Castle* sank, when his parents were lost, on their way home from a Havana vacation. Sarah handed Kate her tea.

"He just came in from Texas last night, from a base near Byron, an instrument school. He's a fighter pilot." They were silent for a moment, then Sarah looked at her. "I'm worried about you, Kate. You look pale, and you've lost some weight." She held out the silver sugar bowl, but Kate shook her head and kept stirring her tea. "It's Adam, isn't it?"

Kate looked up from her tea in surprise.

"My dear, my dear," Sarah said, sighing, "there are things I've known about Adam over the years that I'd wished Jonathan and Amanda had kept from me. Sometimes I think he knew I wanted him to be more like Del, and resented it, resented Del. Adam is my grandson, too, and I love him. But I've always wished he could be like Del, level-headed, sensible." She smiled sadly. "Adam was always the handsome devil who tried to win with his wit and charm. And my daughter was never a match for him. Jonathan and Amanda spoiled both of their children, let them have their way in everything. Marianne will survive it. There's something underneath that will come through and hold her together." She sighed. "But Adam? I don't know. There's still that wildness in him, that lack of responsibility." She looked at Kate. "And now you." She paused. "Do you want to talk about it?"

·· Slowly Kate unburdened herself while Sarah nodded from time to time, the faded blue eyes revealing no surprise or shock.

"Jonathan will stop at nothing to protect Adam," she said. "Or perhaps *shield* is a better word. When he was expelled from prep school for cheating, Jonathan enrolled him in a school that needed a new gymnasium, and of course donated the money for it. There were other incidents. Del probably knows more than I."

Kate left Sarah that afternoon feeling comforted. As they stood at the door Sarah said, "It's outrageous what they've done to you, and yet, oddly enough, I know that Adam really loves you."

Tears came to Kate's eyes as she looked out into the flooding sunshine. "I loved him so," she said, so low that Sarah could hardly hear her. "I still love him, I think. But I hate him for what he's done to me. And for the shame I feel for him."

"I know, my dear," Sarah said, nodding. "I know."

113

Kate took a taxi to Saks Fifth Avenue to pick up a bedjacket and some nightgowns for Amanda. From there she walked across Forty-fourth Street to Grand Central Station to catch her train to Brookton. As she came down from the balcony on the Vanderbilt Avenue side and plunged into the moving mass of people, their voices echoing upward in a muffled roar, she stopped halfway across the rotunda. A long line of men and women inched patiently toward a gate leading to one of the trains, the Chicago-bound all-coach Pacemaker. Beyond Chicago were other trains, she thought, waiting to rush passengers toward the West Coast. In a matter of hours she and Joanna could be on their way on one of these trains and halfway across the state before anyone at Finisterre missed them.

She pushed on. Jonathan would search for her until she was found, block any attempts for a divorce, fight her every inch of the way. Loosening the gray jacket of her suit in the pressing heat, she circled around a large group of people saying good-bye to a sailor, when suddenly she saw a familiar face.

"Jenny!" she called out, not certain it was Jenny. She'd only caught a glimpse of the face as it disappeared in the crowd. "Jenny!" she shouted again, running after her, pushing past the crowds around her, recognizing the hurried walk, the way she ducked as she darted past people. Catching up to her, Kate grasped her arm and turned her around. "Jen, didn't you hear me?"

"God!" Jenny said rudely, trying to jerk her arm free. "Of all people!"

"Well, exactly what does *that* mean?" Kate demanded, anger flaring as she dropped Jenny's arm. She started to walk away.

"Wait a minute, Kate," Jenny called out, and as Kate turned around a few feet away Jenny said, "I'm sorry. Please." She sounded distraught.

Kate took a long look at Jenny's face, then slowly came closer. "What is it, Jen? What's happened?" When Jenny didn't answer but simply stared off at the crowds, Kate said, "Are you coming or going?"

"I just came back from Craddock Corners." Jenny's eyes seemed blind as she watched a soldier hoist a small child onto his shoulder. "Fred Baldwin escorted me to the train. But when I got to Boston where I had to change trains, I just . . . just wandered around the station all night. I . . . I

114

didn't know what to do. Finally I got on a train for here. There was nowhere else to go."

"What were you doing in Craddock Corners?"

"I thought I could just pick Christopher up and walk out of that house," Jenny said hopelessly. "I—I don't know what I thought I was going to do. I just went there. I had to do something about Christopher. Oh God, Kate, I had to do something about something!"

"Let's go someplace where we can talk," Kate said, hooking Jenny's arm through hers.

They took a taxi down to Jenny's apartment. While Jenny showered and changed her clothes, Kate called Sarah Wheeler and asked if she could spend the night at her house, then phoned Carolyn Harrison in Brookton and explained where she could be reached if she was needed, and that she would catch a train for Brookton in the morning.

They went to Mother Bertolotti's restaurant on West Fourth Street, where they both merely picked at their food.

"You don't look so hot yourself," Jenny said as she crumbled bread between her fingers. She was on her third glass of wine, but Kate knew better than to comment. "I'd say something about your own life is wrong as hell."

Kate took her time lighting a cigarette. "I found out something quite by accident," she said, sipping her cappuccino. "If Adam's mother hadn't unwittingly told me, I probably would have gone on forever not knowing."

As Kate told her the story Jenny sipped her wine and lit one cigarette from another. Sensible, careful, cautious Kate, she thought, the only one of the three of them she had been certain would never make a mistake about men.

"Bastards," she muttered. "But, Katy, you've really got them. You could spill everything."

Kate slowly shook her head. "I'd never win. In the end we'd all lose. Jonathan said he'd swear I'd been a party to the fraud all along, thinking I was going to get a huge financial settlement out of it." She watched the couple at the table next to them laughingly trying to eat spaghetti. "I can't do anything that will hurt Joanna. And they need us until the war ends. If I tried to leave, Jonathan would force me to come back."

Jenny nodded slowly. "Doesn't leave you much choice, does it?" She shook her head in disbelief. "But from what I saw at the wedding, I'd say Adam is crazy in love with you."

"What kind of love is that?"

"I guess I'm not the person to answer questions about love," Jenny said, draining her glass and signaling to the waiter for another. "I never had time, or maybe it was room, for love in my life. I was in too much of a hurry to try to get other things."

"But Alan—?"

Jenny shook her head slowly. "Alan was wonderful. He gave me something I needed at the moment. But I wasn't in love with him, Kate." She blinked back tears. "I didn't want marriage or a husband or kids like nice normal ladies do. But then . . . when Christopher was gone, I found out too late that I . . . really loved him, really wanted him with me." They were quiet for several moments. Jenny took a long drink of her wine, then said, "Oh, did I tell you I got a job? Three days a week. I demonstrate cosmetics at Macy's."

"Well, that's *something*, Jen. Good for you."

"The money I make from it goes to the lawyers." She fidgeted with her spoon, then spun the glass around and around. "I've gone to court three times now, trying to get Christopher back." She was trying to toss it off, but her lips trembled, and her eyes filled with tears. "Oh God, Kate, I want him back so badly. But it won't work. They have everything stacked against me."

For several minutes she held a handkerchief over her eyes, then slowly finished the wine in her glass.

"I go out every once in a while at night and walk by the river. I think a lot while I'm walking there, in a different way from when I'm anywhere else. I think I become a part of something, something that's very big and mysterious. When I walk by the river, it just keeps flowing past me, ignoring me, ignoring everything. I think about the war there. And I think about all that death. But the river doesn't give a damn, just keeps flowing along. If I stepped into it, for a minute there'd be a ripple, in one tiny little place. But then the ripple would be gone. If I stepped into it, it wouldn't matter." For a moment they stared at each other, as the soft laughter and voices in the restaurant rose and fell around them.

"You couldn't do that, Jenny." They were quiet for another moment.

"Kate," Jenny said hesitantly. "If I get one more shot at it, this court thing about Christopher, would you appear as a character witness for me?"

"You bet I will," Kate said, her green eyes flashing, and

116

Jenny, her eyes filling, reached over the table and clasped her hand.

When Kate rang the bell at Sarah Wheeler's front door later that night, it wasn't Elsie Ford who answered, but Del, a book in his hand.

"Just reading," he said, holding up a copy of Ernest Hemingway's latest novel, *For Whom the Bell Tolls*. "How about a nightcap?" He took her hat and coat and put them in the guest closet.

"Thanks, Del, but I think I'll go on up to bed." She smiled.

He walked back in the direction of the library. She could see firelight flickering in a reflection on the door. He turned and smiled, an open, engaging smile. "Just a touch of sherry?"

Kate hesitated by the staircase. "Well, just for a *touch of* sherry." She smiled again as she walked toward him, and he saw the sadness. They didn't speak for several moments as he busied himself at the bar while she sat down in a chair by the fire. From the corner of his eye he studied her, her dark gold hair falling softly to her shoulders, gleaming in the firelight, her lovely long green eyes suddenly glancing up, her flawless skin and molded cheekbones. He'd always dreamed of someone like this, of it hitting him like this. Christ!

After he handed her the glass of sherry, they talked of inconsequential things. Then Del leaned forward.

"I hope you don't mind," he said slowly. "But Gran told me something of what has happened. Only because she knew I was wondering why Adam hasn't been drafted."

For a moment Kate was angry. But the blue eyes gazing at her were filled with understanding, and she silently forgave him. "I'd rather not talk about it, Del," she said almost apologetically, then added, "It's happened. There's nothing I can do about it. Not until the war is over."

Del nodded. "It's just that I know Adam pretty well, probably better than most. We were together a lot when we were little. So—" He spoke carefully. "I'm around, if you ever want to talk."

"Thank you," she said, putting her glass down and rising. "I think I'll go upstairs now."

"If you're going up to the country tomorrow morning, I'd be happy to drive you. Gran is going up later."

Kate smiled from the door. "Thank you, Del. I'd like that."

They met again two days later on horseback. Their horses came almost head to head on the narrow bridle path at the far side of the lake in a fine, drizzling rain. Del turned in the direction she was headed, and they cantered together in single file until Del broke down into a trot and she pulled up alongside of him.

"I was hoping I'd run into you," he said, smiling. "I hate to ride alone. Gran says you ride just about every day."

"Usually at six a.m.," she said, then laughed as she saw the expression of horror on his face. "Before I go off to Red Cross or into New York to the agency. Do you always ride here?"

"No. In fact I never did until the past few years. But Uncle Jonathan lets me keep two of my horses here. Gran always had stables, even after Grandfather died." He laughed. "Would you believe she was still riding until about eight years ago? She's eighty now. When I went into the Air Corps, she decided to close the stables."

"Eight years ago!" Kate pulled the reins up and stared at Del. "Still riding at seventy-two?"

"She was a great horsewoman," he said, pushing aside some low-hanging branches. "Showed horses for years, traveled everywhere to shows, even took them to Europe a few times for events there. And Grandfather was a fine polo player. In fact, Windward Hills was a farm for brood mares for a number of years. Grandfather got into racing, and as a matter of fact, on the day he died one of his two-year-olds came in second in the Futurity at Belmont Park."

Kate laughed. "All that history! And I'm just learning to ride English saddle."

"That's right. Gran said you're from the West. Where?"

"San Francisco. Summers at Carmel. My father kept horses at the beach house and we rode all summer."

They chatted amiably for the next half hour, then he reined in and turned to her at a fork in the path. "If we go right, it will take us to a small country road, and about a half mile down that road there's a wonderful little old inn with a great fireplace and tremendous food. We could have lunch and dry out." He smiled.

She watched him for a moment, caution returning.

"But if we go that way," he said, pointing to the path on

the left, "we'll be back at the stables in twenty minutes at a slow walk."

She heard the rain dripping mournfully on the leaves overhead. A crow cawed deep in the forest behind them.

"Lunch," she said, suddenly smiling. "I need a cheery fire to brighten my spirits. And besides, I'm hungry."

It was early and the inn was almost empty. The smiling owner threw her arms around Del in an excited greeting, then sat them at a table in front of the crackling fire. Del ordered two dry martinis, and lunch was a rich lentil soup and a moist, flaky fish, served with a subtle lemon sauce.

"My meat rations are low," Mrs. Desmond explained. She was buxom and in constant movement, even when talking, but her face was worn and tired looking and she wore her graying hair like a little girl would, in a Dutch bob. "Wrestling with these food stamps is a pain in the neck. That's why we have nothing but fish and eggs on today's menu."

"No need to apologize," Del said, fondly patting her arm. "This food is great." She threw him a kiss as she hurried to the door to greet customers. "She used to give me cookies and milk when I'd come by as a kid. Ken, her son, was my friend. He was killed last autumn when we landed troops at Guadalcanal."

They were quiet for several moments, lounging back comfortably in the old captain's chairs, boots stretched toward the fire, sipping their coffee. Del smiled with amusement as he noted Arlette Desmond constantly looking over her shoulder at them.

"She thinks we're a twosome," he said. "But then, she thinks I should be married, raising a family. I can just see what's going through her mind, fantasizing me right into a romantic situation."

Kate looked at him, then away, and started pulling on her jacket.

"And why not?" he teased. "We're a very handsome couple."

They had lunch at the little inn twice that week, and met again at a small dinner party Sarah Wheeler gave at Windward Hills, her lovely big old colonial mansion overlooking the Connecticut countryside. The fourth time was unexpected. Kate stopped at Marianne's for a cocktail late one afternoon and found her and Del in the sunroom. She had just come from the military hospital in Bridgeport, where she

119

had driven an ambulance all day long for the Red Cross, and was still wearing her uniform.

"It was one of the *better* runs," she said with a bitter smile. "Two soldiers, both under twenty. I picked them up right off the troop transport, one with a leg gone and blind, the other a paraplegic."

Del put his hands over his eyes for a moment while Marianne murmured, "Oh God! Why, why, why?"

Suddenly Kate wanted to go home, crawl into a warm bath, and weep. She still felt battered and confused, and Del's presence disturbed her in some oddly dependent way. She wanted to put her head on his shoulder and weep, weep for Adam, for herself, weep for all the mangled bodies, the haunted eyes, the silent whys that rode in the back of her ambulance.

"I have to go," she said, suddenly rising and putting her drink down, afraid she would start to cry before even reaching the car.

"Wait a minute, Katy pal," Marianne said, running after her while giving Del a strange look over her shoulder. At the door Marianne grasped her hand. "I'm a friend, remember? And I know what happened. I feel sorry for Adam, because *first*, he really does love you." As Kate violently shook her head, Marianne went on, "Oh, he may not have planned it that way, but he *did* fall in love with you. I know, because he told me. And I believe him. And now, Katy, he has to live with it, with what he's done to you. It's bad enough, Katy, that he has to live with what *caused* him to do this to you."

Kate opened the door stiffly. "Please, Marianne—"

"I told them both, my father *and* Adam, I could never forgive them."

Kate turned to her quickly, the mask gone, her face troubled. "Don't let this affect your relationship with them, Marianne."

"Kate," she said softly, taking Kate's hands in hers. "I'm vain and spoiled, and sometimes I can be a real bitch. I often drink too much, I curse and swear and get a lot of speeding tickets that somebody always fixes for me. But, damnit, I have a few principles. Not many, I admit, but a few. And besides, I like you one hell of a lot!" She quickly put her arms around Kate and hugged her, then slowly pulled away, her hands still on Kate's arms. "Listen to me for a few minutes, because it's important. Del told me before you got here today that he's never met anyone like you before." Kate tried to

120

pull away, but Marianne held on to her fiercely, shaking her a little. "And you're trying to run, because you feel something, you're afraid of something, something you recognize in him and that you feel in yourself. Adam wrecked your marriage before it even had a chance. Oh, there's no doubt in my mind that he would have fallen in love with you anyway, and the moment he met you, and he knows that too, but he knows it too late, found out too late. He used you and Joanna even before he discovered that he really loved you—"

"Don't—" Kate tried to break away, but Marianne held on.

"Well, it's too late for all that," Marianne said. "But it's not too late for whatever it is that I saw between you and Del, the look in your eyes when you first saw him this afternoon."

"You're imagining—"

"I'm imagining nothing. I saw it, Katy." They stared at each other for a moment, then Kate looked away, and slowly they walked down the path to her car. When they reached the end of the path, they stood in the growing twilight, watching the shadows of the deep forest spread across the grass and newly turned flowerbeds.

"Del is one of the finest men I've ever known," Marianne said softly. "He's always known exactly who he is and where he's going. Even as a kid, when his parents were lost in the sinking of the *Morro Castle,* he picked himself up and pushed right on."

She broke off a branch of early forsythia from a nearby bush and, leaning back against the fender of Kate's car, carefully examined the petals.

"Father offered him a position at the mills, and Uncle Justin wanted him to go into the agency with him, but Del knew exactly what he wanted to do when he got out of college. He got a job with an engineering firm in New York, and got it on his own, with no help from anyone, and at a time when jobs weren't easy to get, at the tail end of the Depression a few years back. He always wanted to build things. Ever since he was a kid. That and flying were his passions. Until—he met you."

Kate looked around at her, startled, then away.

"I've never seen him like this," Marianne said softly. "Not about anything or anyone."

Kate kept her head turned and started to get into her car. Then she stopped. "This is crazy," she said, and Marianne heard the anguish in her voice. "I'm married to Adam. I—"

121

"If Del hadn't known about Adam right from the moment he met you, and what Adam did to you, he still would have fallen in love with you, but no one would ever have even guessed."

"Oh, dear God!" Kate cried out softly, her hands clasped and beating gently against the side window of the car. "If only Del and I had met first, if only—oh, Marianne," she said, turning quickly to her, "all the *if onlys* in life. When I found out about Adam and why he had married me, I asked myself over and over why I had married *him,* if I could stop loving him so easily. If only I had loved him more, I told myself. If only I had never found out, I thought. And then, in the deep of one night, I realized I had *wanted* to love him. But wanting isn't enough."

Marianne nodded sadly. "How dreadful that so many of us find out too late."

Kate studied Marianne's face. But then, she had known that Marianne's marriage had been wrong almost from the start. She leaned down and opened the car door.

"Del's leaving, you know, in less than three weeks," Marianne said.

Kate paused, then slowly nodded and, without another word, climbed into the car and drove toward Finisterre.

Kate turned from the dressing table where she was brushing her hair, hearing a knock on her door. "Come in," she said.

Adam entered, wearing a maroon dressing gown crested in white with his initials. He had a silver cocktail shaker in one hand and two crystal glasses in the other. She stared at him in disbelief.

"We haven't had a nightcap for weeks, Katy," he said as he crossed to the matching settees in the window bay, a forced joviality in his voice. "Thought you might like one." He put the glasses on the table and started to pour.

"I don't care for any," she said, stiffening warily.

His hand stopped in midair. Slowly putting the shaker down, he looked at her, his smile fading. "How could your feelings for me change so fast?"

She shook her head slowly, sadly. "You really don't understand, do you, Adam?"

"Love doesn't just stop. I haven't stopped loving you. What you said you felt for me—"

"You destroyed what I felt for you." She couldn't even

weep. She felt dead inside. "I wanted to love you, but you killed it."

"Kate, please listen to me!" He moved toward her.

"Don't, Adam. There's nothing more to say. Just go and leave me alone." He had almost reached her. "Please, Adam—"

But he was beside her, had pulled her to her feet and was kissing her. For a moment she was limp in his arms. Fleeting memories of the first magic confused her. But then she stiffened and tried to push him away. His hold tightened, and he was pushing the pale blue satin robe from her shoulders. She felt his hand on her breast and trembled violently. He had excited her once. Now she only felt rage.

"Take your hands off me," she said in a low voice.

"You're my wife," he said, his voice urgent in her ear.

"Not anymore!" She pushed out of his arms and stumbled backward, clutching her robe about her, her voice low and desperate. "Keep away from me, Adam. I'm not your wife anymore. Legally, yes, but those are simply words on a piece of paper; official, yes, but nothing but a fraud."

All gone. It was all gone, whatever feeling she'd had for him, and something wept inside of her at the loss. He had swept away her terrible loneliness, brought laughter into her life, given it meaning again, meaning for her as a young and vibrantly alive woman. She had thought it was love, wanted to love him, and was certain it would grow. And at the time it had been enough, a full, exciting life, a husband that other woman envied, a husband who had seemed to adore her, who lavished her with gifts and attention, who seemed to honestly love Joanna, whose eyes lighted up each time he saw her. Oh God, she thought, I believed it would be everything I wanted.

"Just words, Adam. Nothing more." She heard the venom in her voice.

"You've never let me explain, never let me tell you—"

"What about, Adam?" she asked cruelly. "How can you explain *cowardice?*"

His face went white, and raising clenched fists, he stepped toward her. She ran to a corner of the room and put her hand on the satin bellpull.

"If you take a step closer, I'll have to call for someone. I don't think you'd want that. I think you'd rather we keep up our little pretense for the servants, even for Jonathan."

For a long moment he watched her, his jaw clenched

123

tightly, then silently he turned and left, closing the door behind him. In a moment she heard the door to his bedroom on the opposite side of the suite close. Quickly she ran back to her door and, fumbling, turned the key, then leaned against it, trembling, tears running down her face, and slumped to the floor.

For the next few days Kate and Del didn't arrange their meetings. They met at the stables, on the bridle path, again at Marianne's, always by accident, and yet each knew the other had made a conscious effort. On the fourth day Del was waiting for her in the hospital parking lot as she came back from her ambulance run, and they went in his car to a small place outside of Bridgeport for cocktails. At the end of the week, as they quietly rode their horses back toward the stable, they stopped as though by signal and he took her hand in his.

"I've loved you from the moment I met you," he said softly, and her hand tightened in his. "When I saw you at Gran's that afternoon, I said to myself, 'Someday she has to belong to me.'"

She tried to pull her hand away and looked off into the forest.

"All right, Kate." He spoke slowly, deliberately. "If we're going to stop it, it has to be now."

She climbed down to the ground and walking over to the side of the bridle path, sat on a slab of stone as he watched her. She bent her head and with a small stick drew endless circles in the dust below. He dismounted slowly and walked over to her just as she looked up at him. She shook her head.

"No, Del." Her voice was soft. "I don't want to stop it. But . . . I don't know how I feel. Not completely. I'm so confused. I only know I want to be with you. Something happens when I'm with you, and if that's enough—"

"That's enough, Kate," he said and pulled her to her feet. He touched her cheek softly, lovingly. "Do you have any idea how lovely you are?" And then he kissed her, and she felt her body grow warm—a warmth she had never thought she would feel again, and she kissed him back, a long, deep kiss that left her breathless.

She pulled a little away from him and looked up, whispering, "I need you. Desperately."

* * *

124

The following afternoon he met her near the Red Cross headquarters, where she had spent the morning rolling bandages and working on the records for the blood bank.

"We'll leave your car here," he said as she climbed into his low-slung sports car, "and pick it up later."

They stopped for lunch at a small restaurant on the edge of a lake, then drove toward Long Island Sound, turning off the main highway onto a country road that led to a lovely small cove. They passed boarded-up houses on the road circling the cove and pulled into the driveway of a white Victorian house hugging the shoreline.

As he turned off the motor she put her head back on the seat and closed her eyes, breathing the fragrance of pine and sea and the May sun on new grass. She opened her eyes and looked at Del, who was staring at the house.

"It was our summer place when I was a kid. Gran kept it for me after they died. I come here every once in a while when I'm home. But . . . I've never brought anyone else here in all these years. You're the only one, Kate."

Taking her hand, he led her to the back veranda with its lacy gingerbread trim and unlocked the door. She followed him through the shadowy house, which echoed with their quiet footsteps as they climbed the stairs. In a large bay-windowed room the light was a soft green until he threw open the shutters and let in the sunshine. They stood at the window for a moment, his arm about her, watching the soft whitecaps as they danced on the water. Somehow it was all so right, the deep silence of the house, the way he held her, drawing her closer, their lips touching, softly searching at first, then the deep and passionate need of each other rising as they closed everything else away.

He slowly undressed her at the side of the big double bed, softly kissing her small, creamy breasts and swelling nipples. With languid fingers she unbuttoned his shirt as she lay back on the bed and he hovered over her. He cradled her in his arms, and as his mouth covered hers his hands touched her in a series of sensations that made her twist beneath him in pleasure. Her body came alive under his, moving with him in uncontrollable response when he pressed deeply within her, and then they clung in close embrace, flesh joined in rapture as the fiery glow spread and spread. At last he slid down beside her and stroked her face, her hair, brushed her fragrant skin with his lips, murmured her name over and over. "I'll always love you," he said.

She turned her head and saw his uniform jacket over the back of a chair, the silver first lieutenant's bars gleaming against the dark olive-green of the tunic, and she moved in his arms.

"We only have two weeks," she whispered.

She had thought it would be difficult facing Jonathan and Adam each night at dinner, with Del always hidden away in her thoughts. But everyone was playing a game as they faced one another at the long table, faces handsome in the flickering light of the tall candelabra, all secrets safe within the large charade where each of them was playing a role. Jonathan, of course, thought Kate had recovered more quickly from the initial shock following the scene that night in the library than even he had hoped, and saw relations among them as cordial, even pleasant and improving as time went on.

But behind Adam's smile and charming banter, the bitterness dug deeper and deeper. The more unattainable she became, the greater his desire for her grew. In his wildest fantasy he could almost imagine himself joining the Air Corps and sitting down to dinner one night, then casually announcing it and seeing her eyes widen with surprise, her lovely mouth smile in admiration. But he would suddenly break out in a cold sweat, and his throat would close with the old familiar feeling of unknown terrors, the kind that plagued him in nightmares.

And so as the nightly ritual of dinner became a predictable and graceful part of their day, with coffee and cordials in the library afterward, Kate quite unwittingly began to absorb an impressive amount of information about the Barnfield holdings, particularly the mills. For as Jonathan talked and she listened, Adam spent most of the time wandering from the bar to the radio and even at times to the playroom where he played a lonely game of billiards or put stacks of his big-band records on the record player.

And then as Jonathan climbed the stairs to sit for a while with Amanda, and Kate went to peek at the sleeping Joanna and then on to her own room to read and then to bed, she would hear the faint roar of Adam's sports roadster as it tore along the driveway and down through the forest to the main road.

"Jonathan notices, I'm certain, but he never says anything," Kate told Del. "He knows, but he pretends he doesn't. Carolyn Harrison told me that twice a bar owner in Brookton called Nelson and that he had to waken Martin so they could drive into town and bring back Adam and his car. Sometimes I—" She looked from the car window and bit her lip.

"Sometimes you what?" Del asked sharply, his hand on hers.

"Sometimes I feel so destructive," she whispered, looking down.

Del slowed the car. "Whatever you do," he said in a hard voice, "don't start blaming yourself for his mistakes and stupidity. If he wants to drink himself to death, there's not a damned thing you can do about it."

"I know, darling, I know," she said, clutching at his hand. Del's bags were in the trunk of Kate's car. He was catching a train at Westport at four o'clock. His train for the south would leave Penn Station at six. They were driving to the house at the shore for their last few hours together. She didn't know when she would see him again. "Please, let's not talk about it anymore."

For a while they walked along the water's edge, tossing pebbles into the small waves that lapped at the beach. Then they turned back to the house and climbed the stairs to the big old-fashioned room that looked out onto the cove. The sky was overcast; the ominous clouds of a squall hung low in the southeast while whitecaps skipped over the water, and pines along the shore bent in the gusty wind.

They wanted the clock to stop, the hours to last and last, and for long moments, as they lay on the bed, their fingers traced each other's faces, as though to memorize each feature. In that moment Kate knew she could never feel this way with another man. Philip had been her first love. There had been an innocence, a kind of purity and gentle seeking that a first love often holds. With Adam there had been a dazzling kind of excitement that had filled her loneliness and made her believe it was love. But this—she caught her breath and held it. This was as deep and old as the world.

"What is it, Kate?" Del whispered.

"Just . . . that I'm so full of love for you," she said. "And I'm afraid."

"I suppose everyone at this moment says 'I'll come back.'" He was caressing her, hands gentle but growing more demanding. "But with you here, waiting, I *know* I will."

127

As they made love she forgot for a while, forgot that he was leaving. His touch was sure and knowing, intoxicating, leading her seductively toward complete possession. She felt the ripple of muscles on his back and cried out with joy as he took her, flesh blended into flesh, their bodies consumed with a fire that neither had ever known before.

Slowly it ebbed away, but they held each other close, eyes turned from the clock. Finally he reached to the bedside table and picked up a key. He put it in her hand, closing her fingers over it. "It's the key to this house. Keep it for us, Katy. And come here whenever you want. I want to say good-bye to you here. This is where I want to remember you." He looked at his watch. "I've ordered a taxi to pick me up." He stood above her, hard and golden-fleshed in the light.

They dressed silently. As she stood at the mirror to comb her hair she saw him pulling on his uniform jacket, slowly buttoning it and buckling the belt. Reflections, she thought. It all seemed so unreal, the way it had that morning Philip had left and she had watched him in the mirror. Something cold clutched at her heart. But he came up behind her, his arms encircling her, and she turned and held on to him hard.

They didn't speak. Then he bent and kissed her, a long kiss.

As he pulled on his hat, tossed his trench coat over his shoulder, and picked up his bags, she turned and watched him through the mirror again, the gold buttons of his uniform flashing.

And then he was gone. She listened, not moving. First she heard a door close, far off, then the distant sound of the taxi as it stopped at the back. When it pulled away, and the sound of the motor grew farther and farther away, there was finally a nothingness. Just the lapping of the waves and the shadow of a sea gull as it wheeled against the gray sky.

Chapter 16

THEY STOOD AT the bottom of the courthouse steps, oblivious to the lunchtime crowds swarming through Foley Square, three slim young women in pretty springtime linen dresses and shading hats, two of them clutching the hands of the small dark-haired one between them.

"Thank you for coming," Jenny said in a low voice husky with unshed tears. "But I'm sorry you wasted your time."

"Don't say that, Jenny," Liz said, turning to face her. "We'll be here every time you bring it into court again."

"No more," Jenny said wearily. "I can't go on with it anymore. It's hopeless. And it's tearing me apart."

"Nothing is hopeless," Kate said firmly. "We'll try it again."

"No," Jenny said, shaking her head. "Maybe when he's older . . . or if things change, if the men who sit up on those benches begin to see things differently, or if something . . . something . . ." She was crying dry, heaving sobs, softly, like a child, and there in the June sunlight Liz put her arms around her and held her until the sobbing finally stopped.

"Come home with me and stay for a while, a few days, Jenny, until you feel better," Liz said.

Jenny shook her head back and forth almost violently, then forced a wan smile to her lips. She walked toward the curb, Liz and Kate following her, looking for a taxi. "No, I want to go home." Quickly clasping Liz's hands and then Kate's, she said, "Please, I know I sound ungrateful, but I—well, I just have to be alone right now."

As a taxi spun up to the curb she quickly kissed them both on the cheek and stepped into the cab.

Kate and Liz watched as the taxi roared away and disappeared around the corner. Then Kate turned to Liz, a gleam in her eye.

"How would you like to pay a call on Mr. Henry Fremont at the *World-Dispatch* office?" It took a moment for Liz to grasp the meaning.

"I'd love to," Liz said, looking for another taxi.

"Come on," Kate said, starting off at a clip. "We can walk."

Jenny tried to ignore the sound of the door buzzer and the insistent tapping on the door. She stood near the kitchen, holding her rumpled robe together, as though the person could see through the door.

"Come on, Jenny, let me in," a voice said, softly urgent, right at the crack of the door. "It's Henry Fremont."

Henry . . . she pushed her hair back from her eyes. She hadn't called him. Or had she? She couldn't remember.

"I just want to talk to you for a couple of minutes, Jenny." She started away from the door.

"Damnit, Jenny, don't make me go all the way down these four flights to get the superintendent. These stairs are killers."

She hesitated.

"If I have to get the super, I will. I'll tell him you're sick. Probably passed out from all that booze." His voice was fading.

She turned the knob and he walked in.

For a moment they just watched each other, then he took off his hat, slowly walked into the living room, looked around, and turned to watch her again. She stayed by the door, back against the wall.

"You look like hell." She shrugged, but he saw her lower lip tremble. "Christ, you're skinny." Sitting on the edge of the couch, hat in hand, he watched her. She didn't move, kept shifting her eyes.

"Okay," he said softly, placing his hat down beside him. "A couple of your friends came to see me this afternoon."

Jenny stiffened with anger. Kate and Liz.

"You don't like that? Well, tough. You just want everybody to go away and leave you alone. But what you really need is someone to give you hell, yank you back up on your feet, and tell you to get the devil out there and start fighting again. All right, that was bad, losing the baby, but—"

She turned her head away, pressing her cheek against the wall.

"If you're ever going to get him back you're going to have

to stop feeling sorry for yourself and start battling." He looked around. "This place looks like a pigsty."

"Go to hell, Henry Fremont," she sobbed.

"I don't know, Jenny." He shook his head back and forth. "For somebody as scrappy and tough as you, I don't understand what's happened. You've really been hitting the bottle, haven't you?" He stood up and walked over to the window, then pulled the blind back an inch or two and peered down into the street. "No good. Not high enough. You'd probably just break a couple of legs and your thick head, but that's all—"

"Damn you, Henry!" she shouted, hitting her fists against her sides. "Get out of here and leave me alone."

"You want a job?" he asked matter-of-factly, not even turning around but still looking down into the street.

She stared at him. She wasn't certain she had heard what he said, that he had even spoken. He turned around, casually twirling his hat in his hands.

"Well?" He was looking at her with raised eyebrows.

He was both elated and ashamed. The first because at last he could give her a job again, a job she deserved, a job she should never have lost. She was a fine reporter, a gifted writer, and those were the only things that should count, he thought with a return of the usual anger and frustration. And ashamed—well, because he perhaps could have fought harder to help her keep her job. He would probably have been fired and had to walk out right beside her. But at least he would have taken a stand against the publisher.

"You're certain, Fremont, that the child is gone?" the steely-eyed publisher had said, leaning over the gleaming desk toward Henry.

"Certain." Henry clenched his jaw, holding back the anger, not even concerned about the lie that followed. "She just couldn't take care of it by herself, with her husband killed at Hickam. She felt—well, she felt the kid needed a normal home. So her brother-in-law—"

"Well, if you're certain, Fremont, and can assure me the child won't be brought back. I don't want to set any new precedent here that's liable to get us into trouble."

Henry looked at her, the tiny, thin frame and pale face, the deep shadows under the huge brown eyes, and his heart wept.

"What . . . what did you say?" she asked in a harsh whisper.

"A job. I said, do you want a job?"

131

She pushed away from the wall and slowly walked toward him. She started trembling and held on to the back of a chair for support.

"What kind of . . . a job?"

"Reporter. What did you think? Publisher? Board chairman?"

"Oh, my God!" She sat down, stunned. "Oh, my God!"

He pulled a chair over from the desk, put it in front of her, and sat in it, facing her. He took hold of her hands. "Okay, kiddo?" She shook her head, unable to speak. "But if you cross me up and goof on this, so help me, I'll blackball you out of this business clear to Timbuktu where you can report on mosquitoes for the local *Mali Gazette*." She was crying. He pulled a large handkerchief from his pocket and awkwardly dabbed at her face. But she pushed his hand away, stood up, and walked across the room, her back to him.

"I talked to a man I know over on the *Times,* and he said he thought he could get me on the metro desk."

"Baloney!" Henry snorted.

"What do you mean, baloney?" She started to shout, facing him.

"Even if it were true, the *Times* isn't your kind of newspaper."

"How do you know what's my kind of newspaper?"

"I know you like I know my foot, the one with the bunion on it. You like the kind of beat you had, the nuts and bolts of the business, the meat and potatoes. All the *Times*'d give you is obits, if you were lucky. They'd probably put you on the society page, where you could write up the weddings for all those society broads."

"Shut up, you!" she shouted.

"Shut up yourself," he said, half laughing. "You want a job or not?"

She watched him, still angry, but with traces of tears on her cheeks. "Can I have my old beat back?" she finally asked, hesitant.

"Nope," he said cheerfully, and she slumped into a chair. "Because I have something else in mind for you, Jenny. A very specific job, like nothing you've ever done before."

"What is it?" She was suspicious, on edge.

"War correspondent. England first."

She stared at him. For several moments she couldn't comprehend what he had said, then asked in a stunned voice, "What?"

"England." He smiled. "What's wrong, sweetie? Did you pickle your brains with all that booze you've been putting away?"

"England," she repeated numbly.

"Look, if you're not interested, I have plenty of guys—"

"Yes! Oh God, yes."

"—who'd jump at it." He acted as though he hadn't heard her. "But newspapers and wire services are beginning to send women across. Especially to the European Theater."

"I said yes, Henry!" she shouted. She suddenly grabbed his hands and pulled him to his feet. She was laughing, on the edge of hysteria. "I can't believe it! War correspondent! I can't believe it."

"You have to be ready in ten days," he said. "Stop at the office tomorrow, early. Mabel Sedgewick in the employment office will take care of your departure details. You'll travel with a group of correspondents, probably on a troop ship."

"Oh, my God!" She was hopping up and down in one spot.

"It won't be easy, Jenny," he said, pushing her down onto a chair. "The ships are crowded and hot, there's not much air below, and half the guys get seasick as hell. The food's terrible, and there's always the danger of attack. The goddamn U-boats are still roving in packs. And even though you travel in a convoy, there's always a chance."

She seemed oblivious.

"Did you hear what I said? About possible attacks?"

"I heard," she said, trancelike. "I'm not afraid."

"You know, you really do look like hell."

"I'll eat, Henry, stuff myself, put on weight like crazy, ice cream and mashed potatoes, take vitamins, get my hair cut, drink milk by the gallons. You'll see."

"Well, with all that eating don't forget to go and see Mabel in the morning. She'll tell you all about uniforms, shots, papers and—oh, you may have to shoot down to Washington to the State Department to get your passport, so you'll have it on time." He walked to the door, putting his hat on. "Don't make me sorry, Jenny."

"You'll never be sorry. Oh, Henry, I never even dreamed of anything like this." She ran to him and flung her arms around him.

"Hey, it's okay," he said, patting her awkwardly. "And—well, you'll do one helluva job." He walked quickly out the door.

* * *

133

A high school marching band in red and white uniforms and high white-plumed hats strutted up Fifth Avenue toward Central Park where the war bonds rally was being held, the sun flashing on the brassy trumpets and trombones, the Sousa march blaring loudly up into the canyons of buildings. Jenny swung along beside it on the sidewalk, keeping step and looking back over her shoulder at the bands and the red, white, and blue floats as far down the avenue as she could see. She pushed through the crowds jammed along the sidewalk edge, singing and shouting and laughing with them, feeling pretty in her new beige dress, liking the way it slid over her hips, liking the way men turned and smiled at her.

She dodged into the next street and started to run. She was ten minutes late. Entering Henri's on Fifty-second Street, she squinted in the sudden half-darkness, then followed the maitre d' through the crowded restaurant, waving as she saw Kate and Liz in a corner, Kate cool and stunning in a lime-green linen suit, Liz more beautiful than ever in lilac silk. Grinning, she slid into a chair.

"Sorry I'm late, but I got stuck with the parade."

"You're forgiven," Kate said, smiling. "Now, what's this *incredible* news you said you have?"

"Let's order first, then we can talk," Jenny said as she opened her menu, a secret little smile playing about her lips. "And I'll do the ordering. I'm taking a crash course in French at Berlitz."

"French?" Liz said, raising a curious eyebrow. "Why?"

But Jenny was looking at the waiter, who suddenly smiled widely as she enunciated each word with exaggerated care. *"Qu'est-ce que vous recommandez, monsieur?"*

"Of course, mademoiselle. Perhaps—"

"No, no," she said, laughing, then struggled. *"Nous voudrions un dejeuner à la française."* She threw her hands out helplessly. "I give up. What I was trying to say—"

"I understood perfectly," he said with a gallant bow. "And I will select it for you, a typically French meal."

They watched her expectantly as the waiter left. "Well?" Kate demanded. "You're killing us with suspense."

"Henry Fremont, as both of you well know"—she mockingly leered at them—"came to see me. And I have a job." She held her breath. "I'm going to England as a war correspondent."

They sat in stunned silence.

"Where in England?" Kate asked.

"I can't tell you that much. I'll be with the Eighth Air Force somewhere in England, that's all I can say, at one of their bases, reporting on the Flying Fortresses and their crews, or maybe the P-47's. But the important thing"—she clasped her hands excitedly—"is that I'll be there for when it all starts."

"Starts?" Liz was puzzled.

"The invasion," she said. "Everyone knows it's just a matter of time. And, of course, with the landings a success in French Morocco and Algeria this past winter, we proved that a full-scale amphibious assault can be done. With strong air and sea support it can work."

"Then that accounts for the French lessons," Kate said as she flicked open her gold lighter to light her cigarette. "But good heavens, with that accent you're liable to end up in Les Halles eating onion soup when you really want to just go to the Louvre."

They all laughed.

"Won't it be terribly dangerous?" Liz asked worriedly. "And for a woman to—"

"When you're a reporter, it doesn't make a damn bit of difference if you're a man or a woman." Jenny leaned toward Liz and tapped a finger on the table to emphasize her point. "Women have been proving this ever since the war first started. Rhea Clyman was in Germany back in the mid-thirties. Helen Kirkpatrick from *The Daily News* in Chicago was reporting on the Battle of Britain three years ago. So was Mary Welsh for *Time*. Martha Gellhorn and Sigrid Schultz are there, Shelley Mydans was a reporter for *Life* and was trapped in Manila when the Japanese invaded. Analee Jacoby kept right on filing dispatches after her husband was killed."

"Listen to her!" Kate said in mock horror, then smiled and shook her head admiringly. "We knew you'd bounce back."

Jenny looked at them both for a long moment. "Not without a lot of help." She smiled, then said softly, "I guess that really *is* what friends are for." She took a cigarette from Kate and lit it, then blew the smoke out. "Trouble is, I've got a lot of catching up to do."

"Who's counting?" Kate said, laughing as she lit her own cigarette.

"I am," Jenny said quietly. "I haven't really cared a damn about what was happening to you two." She quickly put her

135

hand out and clasped Liz's. "I was down in Washington getting my passport, and I bumped into Dan Coleman at the Wardman Park, where I was staying."

"Yes, I know," Liz said with a quiet smile. "He calls several times a week. He said, 'Your friend Jenny doesn't pull any punches.'" Liz laughed in spite of herself. "Jenny, you're incorrigible."

Kate leaned forward. "What's *this* all about?"

"Well, he asked me to dinner." She laughed. "I'll bet he was sorry about that later. But after finally admitting he'd taken this Washington assignment with the OWI to put a few hundred miles between Liz and himself, to protect her from gossip, from being hurt any more than she already is—his words, not mine—well, I told him I thought he was pretty dumb. All that heroic baloney."

Kate glanced quickly at Liz, who was gazing intently at Jenny, more curious than disturbed.

"But he's mad about you, and somehow he'll get that bitch to go through with the divorce. Meanwhile"—she leaned forward—"don't take a chance on losing him, Liz."

"But Jenny," Liz said softly, putting her hand on hers, "Dan is the one who went to Washington. I made my choices long ago and I haven't regretted them for a minute." She looked at Kate and then back at Jenny again. "I think the three of us learned something in that hospital room in one awful moment that most other people still don't know about, that with the war everything can just suddenly disappear for you. So you'd better hold on to what you have as hard as you can."

Jenny was nodding sadly. "I remember something you said, Kate, that right from the first day of the war, something new was created. War widows. Thousands and thousands of women with no husbands. Suddenly we were oddities, didn't fit into any neat little category. Well"—she laughed bitterly—"there's a nice little social problem for the American people to sweep under the rug." They were silent for several moments as the waiter put their first course down, then Jenny looked at Kate. "And you, my friend. Are you all right, Katy?"

"We're civil, all very civil, even rather pleasant to one another," she said, attempting a normal smile as she put her cigarette out. "Joanna makes everything bearable." She wouldn't tell them about Del. She couldn't talk about him yet. It was all too new and painful. "And Jonathan seems ready to believe everything is under control."

"Men like Jonathan Barnfield always think they win," Jenny said.

They said good-bye outside the restaurant, hugging each other, crying and laughing at the same time. Then Kate and Liz watched as Jenny ran off across Fifth Avenue and jumped on a bus heading downtown just as it roared away from the curb.

In the deep hours of the night in early June 1943, Amanda Wheeler Barnfield died. For two days cars drove slowly along the driveway beneath the leafy oaks and elms, relatives and friends and people from the town of Brookton paying their respects.

On the day before the funeral Kate went to the children's center that Amanda had opened in Brookton for the mothers of small children, mothers who worked in the mills and had no one at home to care for their children during the day.

"I'm Kate Barnfield," she said, putting her hand out to the slender dark-haired woman with sea-blue eyes who ran the place for Amanda. "You're Edwinna McCauley, aren't you?"

"I've seen you around town," Edwinna said cautiously, nodding.

Kate looked around her, smiling at a group of four-year-olds who were quarreling over a ball, then gazed beyond to youngsters seated at low tables, coloring in books, molding objects with clay, and cutting figures out of colored construction paper with stubby little blunt scissors. In one corner two little girls were standing at a dollhouse, rearranging the furniture.

"It's wonderful," she said, looking back at Edwinna and smiling.

"Would you like to look around?" Edwinna asked, her eyes still wary.

"Very much," Kate said, following her as she pulled off her gloves. After touring the center's three spacious rooms where she chatted with some of the children, helped one little boy tie his shoe, and tasted a cookie that three little girls had helped to bake, Kate followed Edwinna into the small office, where they sat facing each other.

"Amanda has left funds in her will to keep the center going." Kate saw the relief on Edwinna's handsome face. "I wanted you to know as soon as possible."

"Thank you." It was almost a whisper, and Kate thought she saw tears in Edwinna's eyes. "I'm going to miss her very much," the young woman said in a low voice. Then suddenly she looked up at Kate and smiled. "Somehow I had the feeling, each time I saw you, that you'd be like Amanda Barnfield."

"That's the nicest compliment I've ever had," Kate said softly, tears coming to her own eyes. She looked at the pretty blue curtains on the narrow window and the colorful rag rug on the floor and somehow knew Edwinna had made them. "Would you let me come here one day a week and help?" she asked.

Edwinna nodded. "Amanda came, you know, until she became too ill to leave the house. We'd like to have you, Mrs. Barnfield."

"It's Kate," she said, rising. She left Edwinna sitting on the floor, reading a story and surrounded by the children.

"Fine young people, Edwinna and her brother, Mike McCauley," Amanda had told her shortly before her death.

Several weeks after Amanda's funeral Kate called for the car to be brought around. She avoided the chauffeur-driven limousines as much as possible, preferring to drive herself, but she was taking six of the center children to the hospital's out-clinic for eye examinations and needed the larger car. Then, after dropping the youngsters back at the center, she went on to Dr. Berwin's office on the other side of town.

"Adam will certainly be pleased," the doctor said after she had dressed again following the examination. "Mr. Barnfield, too, and wishing for a *grandson* this time, I'm sure."

She had been almost certain for weeks, only needing Dr. Berwin's confirmation. And he had given it, smiling, his gray head nodding.

As the car headed toward the countryside Kate sat as far back in the corner of the rear seat as she could, aware that the long black gleaming Rolls Royce was a familiar sight on the town's streets. Jonathan and Adam were driven to the mills in it each morning. It had undoubtedly become a symbol to the townspeople. She carefully peered out at the narrow Brookton streets and ugly houses. All she heard was the purring of the powerful motor and the tires on the road below. She wished Del could know. But they had agreed there could be no letters. Nothing until the war was over, when perhaps everything could change for them. Surely then it would change, she thought, closing her eyes tightly, seeing his face, his crooked smile and sparkling eyes.

"I'd like to go straight home, Nelson," she said into the speaking tube, hoping her voice sounded calm, seeing him nod through the glass between them. She needed some time alone before dinner, time to absorb what Dr. Berwin had confirmed for her. Only Adam would know the truth, and then he would know only that it was someone else's child. Del's child, she whispered silently, closing her eyes again, feeling a shiver run up her spine. Del's child.

Following dinner, as Jonathan rose to walk to the butler's pantry to give Martin an order for the cook, Kate spoke in an undertone to Adam.

"Please come upstairs for a moment, Adam. I'd like to talk to you." At the suggestive smile on his face, she spoke again, almost angrily. "The solarium, anywhere, it doesn't matter. But I have something I have to tell you."

Adam followed her up the broad staircase. She felt cold and brittle, but her bitterness over what they had done to her hadn't cooled. As she closed the door to the sitting room of their suite, he lounged against the end of the settee and lit a cigarette, then watched her through the haze of smoke, desirable and lovely in the green chiffon dinner gown, the small diamond clips in her ears, her dark gold hair falling in gleaming waves to her shoulders.

"I won't go into all kinds of unnecessary preliminaries, Adam," she said, "but I warn you my news won't be pleasant for you." She sat down in a chair, cool, detached, her eyes a stranger's.

Adam tore his eyes away from her, a cold premonition stealing over him. Where had the Kate he had known gone, the lovely vibrant creature he had married, made long and passionate love to, the woman he had held in his arms, danced with to the Dorsey records, linked hands with as they drove through the countryside? God, what had happened? he wondered; everything had crumbled around him. "All right," he said, a lazy, insolent little smile at the corner of his mouth.

She drew a deep breath. "I'm pregnant, Adam."

For several moments there wasn't a sound in the room as he simply looked at her, the smile frozen on his face. Then he slowly walked across the room, all trace of insolence gone, and in a brief second as he passed her she saw the hurt, the pain in his eyes, his mouth, and wished somehow that everything could have been different.

"Wait, Adam. I haven't finished." He didn't turn but stopped. "No matter what you do or say, it's not going to change anything. I'm pregnant, and in about seven months the baby will be born."

He continued to the door, then stopped with his hand on the knob.

"You can rush down to the library and tell Jonathan. But it won't matter, Adam." He slowly looked around at her. "Tell him the truth, if you want to. I really don't care."

Adam stood at the half-opened door for several moments. She couldn't see his face. But when he spoke, his voice was dry and harsh.

"I don't suppose you'd care to tell me who it is?"

"Not any more than you cared not to tell me why you married me."

A long and painful silence grew between them, then he flung the door wide. "You may have the pleasure of breaking our news to my father," he said with a smile that was more a grimace than anything else.

"No, Adam," she said quietly. "You'll have to do that."

"He'll be delighted, you know," he said, suddenly turning. "After all, a Barnfield grandchild, one bearing the name Barnfield, but the *real thing,* one whose records will be absolutely unquestionable." There was a softly menacing thread in his voice, and Kate felt a chill run up her spine.

"Here's a grandchild he'll *never* give up."

Chapter 17

JENNY WAS ON her second cup of coffee and reading the morning newspapers when the terse phone call came. A large wardrobe suitcase stood packed and locked in the living room, and a smaller one was open in the bedroom for last-minute items.

Boxes packed with books were sealed and neatly stacked on one side of the living room, ready for the movers who, at a phone call from Mabel Sedgewick, would pick up the furniture and cartons and put them into storage until Jenny returned.

"You're to be at Service Command Headquarters by four o'clock this afternoon, Jenny," Mabel said.

"I'm leaving then?"

"That's all I was told to tell you. And remember, you're to tell or notify no one."

"Of course," Jenny said. She was learning that censorship regulations were even stiffer than she'd heard. Troop movements, with Nazi U-boats still prowling the eastern coastline, were being kept in the utmost secrecy, Henry had told her. Well, she was prepared, she thought, sitting in silence for a moment and watching the clock.

By three o'clock she was ready, lugged her suitcases down the four flights, and waited for her cab at the curb, feeling a little self-conscious in one of her two new correspondent uniforms. At Command Headquarters, after her papers were approved, she found herself waiting in a holding room with benches on three sides. She was joined by three other reporters, all men, then finally a young woman, and they welcomed the sandwiches and coffee brought to them by a harassed looking army private. When she queried him as to why they had to wait so long, he mumbled some reply and hurried out.

Close to midnight a burly sergeant opened the door and

beckoned all of them to follow him. He explained that their luggage had gone on ahead as he led them through a maze of corridors and down some steps that ended in a large garage filled with dark green military vehicles and some nondescript trucks and cars.

They were told to climb into an unmarked gray van, where they sat on hard benches along the side and looked at one another, then away, in silence as the truck drove out of the garage.

For perhaps ten minutes they swayed on the benches as the van tore through the nighttime streets of New York. After a short time they knew they were near one of the two rivers. A ship's whistle called out hauntingly into the blacked-out night, and the wheels of the van passed over the rumbling, hollow-sounding boards of a pier. They glanced at each other expectantly, as they climbed out of the van onto a dock where a gray Navy ship hovered alongside. In the dim light, as they walked toward the ship, in a small straggling group behind the sergeant, Jenny could just make out the lettering against the hull. USS *Thurston*.

For the next eleven days, she realized they would be in a cabin just large enough for two, but with bunks stacked three deep for Jenny, another woman correspondent named Joyce Collier, two WACs, and two pretty Red Cross workers. She grinned at what was ahead for them.

Too excited for sleep, they hurriedly introduced themselves, stowed their belongings as best they could in the cramped quarters, and went on deck just before dawn as the hook was raised and the ship stood out to sea. She was wearing her trench coat in the chilly air, and leaned against the rail, her collar turned up, as the ship glided silently down the Hudson River and into the harbor. Jenny peered ahead, and suddenly tensed. In the first streaks of pale dawn she saw it, looming out of the harbor and darkened now for the wartime regulations, but the outlines, so familiar to all Americans, clearly visible. Something tightened in her throat as she watched, and for the first time she knew what the symbolism of this towering Statue of Liberty really meant as the lady stood in silent watch over the harbor that they were leaving.

"Funny," murmured Joyce Collier, standing next to her, her voice catching a little, "I must have seen that lovely old girl half a dozen times before, but she never looked as beautiful as she does now." Jenny simply nodded, too moved to speak.

She and Joyce stayed at the rail as the *Thurston* slipped out of the harbor, heading for the open sea and toward the center of the huge convoy that they could already see forming as they plied the choppy gray waters. Finally, as the sun broke on the horizon, they went below to sleep.

The first few days were difficult, with a succession of storms tossing the ship in great heaving rolls, leaving all but Jenny and Iris, one of the Red Cross women, hopelessly seasick.

But on the fifth day they were all recovered enough to go on deck and study the vessels nearest to them and up ahead. Some of them were escort ships, but many were troop ships whose decks were crowded with men. Jenny and Joyce leaned on the rail and watched.

"Our news editor was telling me just before I left that the *Queen Mary* and *Queen Elizabeth* are both being used as troop ships," Joyce said, "but they're so fast—they make the crossing in less than five days—that they can't travel in convoys. Nothing can keep up with them, and they carry about fifteen thousand troops."

"I know," Jenny said, turning to the red-haired young woman, whose bright blue eyes peered with curiosity at the nearest troop ship. "The German radio keeps reporting the *Queen Mary* as sunk, but she always turns up again without a mark on her."

Joyce slowly turned and looked at her. "I know why *I'm* here. What excuse do you have?" She was smiling.

Jenny looked at her while holding on to her cap as the wind blew her brown curls into a frenzy. For a moment she felt resentment, disliking the intrusion into her closely guarded privacy. But all she could see in the lightly freckled face and level-gazing eyes were friendliness and a smiling humor.

"Okay. You first. Why *are* you here?" Jenny said.

Joyce looked off at the sea and up ahead as the bow of the ship plunged into the heaving water, unleashing geysers of white foam that hurled upward to spew over the prow and stream deck-high along the sides of the hull.

"I was dumb enough to think I could have my job and my marriage too. But my husband, Howard, had very different ideas." She spoke lightly, seeming almost amused. "Especially after he was classified four-F by the draft board. For a punctured eardrum. The goldbrick's dream. So he decided he wanted me to creep into my well-padded housewife-corner and meekly sit back and over the next six years produce three children, two boys and one girl." She grinned. "The girl should be the youngest, according to Howard's plan for the well-structured family."

"Did Howard propose how he was going to work that little miracle?"

"No, but he *did* say that if the first three children were all boys, we would stop there; but if the first three should happen, by some terrible misfortune, to be girls, we'd just have to try, try again. I walked out while he was still in the planning stages."

Jenny watched her with far more than curiosity.

"First of all, I loved my job. Second, my parents and even my two sisters kept telling me where my place was in the scheme of things. And when an aunt started telling relatives and friends that apparently I couldn't have any children, I knew the time had come to pack my bags and leave." She looked at Jenny as she pushed a wisp of stray red-blonde hair under her cap. "What none of them knew was that a most enlightened young doctor I went to delivered me from bondage with a female contraceptive. He fitted me for a diaphragm, and that did it. In my ignorance I had been unaware that for several years there's been this gadget for women. Hallelujah! As a result I'm here, on my way to the most exciting place in the world instead of stuck in Engle-wood, New Jersey, with a three-bedroom house and a baby."

Jenny looked away. She had first learned about the dia-phragm after Christopher was born, when she had gone to the doctor for a final checkup. He had given her a prescription for one then, and she had merely said, "Too late." The doctor had looked up at her coldly, and as she left his office she had squeezed back tears of bitter disappointment.

"Suddenly I was in control of my own body," Joyce was saying with almost an exhilarated shout. "I had a choice. And I chose this. At the risk of being tied at the stake and sent up in flames, I told Howard, and then I told my parents and sisters. They acted like I was demented. My sisters already had houses in the suburbs and two kids each, a family station wagon and their Tuesday luncheons and bridge at the Woman's Club with the Junior Section. Needless to say, Howard is getting a divorce. I think he'll marry Midge Armbruster. Midge loves children."

144

Joyce and Jenny looked at each other and burst out laughing.

The ship dropped anchor at Liverpool in a heavily overcast dawn. For most of the day they waited impatiently while debarkation was held up. A small epidemic of scarlet fever had broken out aboard ship, but finally in late afternoon the troops and other personnel poured onto the docks and walked to a nearby waiting train. The five reporters, Jenny and Joyce and the three men they had first met back in New York at Command Headquarters, climbed into the first empty compartment they could find and settled behind the blue-painted windows—painted over for the blackout. By this time a strong camaraderie had developed among the group, and whatever prejudices had been formed by the men against women as correspondents, both before and during the Atlantic crossing, the barriers were gone.

Cigarette and cigar smoke soon filled the small compartment. Jumping to his feet, Hobey Loman, a brisk little man of about forty from the *Chicago Daily Express*, lowered a window as the other four shivered down into their coats.

"This is supposed to be June," Joyce grumbled.

"August in England can be a lot colder than this," said Tom Dunne, a bear of a man with a gray-streaked crew cut who always seemed to have a cigar clenched between his teeth. He burrowed deeper into his trench coat and scowled through the window at the weather.

"Well, take your choice," said Hobey cheerfully. "Enjoy the cool breezes and mellow fragrances of the Dock of a Thousand Smells, the Liverpudlian nickname for their *scenic* waterfront—or die choking to death at the mercy of Tom's cigar."

Wesley Campbell, the young Pulitzer prize-winning reporter from the weekly news magazine *Report*, smiled shyly at the camaraderie, then turned to the book he always kept in his pocket.

Finally at eleven p.m. the train began to glide silently through the outskirts of the city and into the dark countryside, heading for London's Paddington Station. Two hours on their way Hobey opened the window a crack and peered out. "Black as pitch out there," he said.

"What'd you expect?" Tom Dunne growled. "Klieg lights to show the Luftwaffe where to drop their load? And shut

145

that blasted window, will you? This isn't the upper deck of the Fifth Avenue bus."

At midnight Jenny opened a ditty bag one of the *Thurston* sailors had given her and produced sandwiches and a steaming thermos of fragrant coffee while Joyce dug into her knapsack and came up with a nested set of celluloid drinking cups.

"Well, you girls are good for *something,*" Tom said with a grin, biting into his sandwich.

"Of course we are," Jenny said too sweetly. "After all, we're women, biologically and emotionally fulfilled, suited to all the little duties around the house."

"If I'd thought that," he said with a glint in his eye, "I'd have pinched you the first day out, sweetie."

"If you had, sweetie," she said with a smile, "I'd have punched you right in the mouth."

"I believe you would," he said admiringly. "Well, all I ask is don't climb in my foxhole once the invasion starts."

The invasion. The landing on the coast of France.

Jenny and Joyce found that the invasion was the talk of London, when it would start and where the troops would land. The Pas de Calais was everyone's guess.

They found rooms in a small hotel in Montague Street just off Russell Square near the British Museum and trooped to their beds with a weary good night to one another. The following morning Jenny and Joyce had a hurried breakfast and then parted at Bloomsbury Way, Joyce heading for the Russell Square underground station, and Jenny, armed with a map, setting off on foot for the small *World-Dispatch* office just off Fleet Street.

Jenny was cheered by the pace and evident good spirits of Londoners on their way to work, and her eyes were caught by the massive barrage balloons floating like sausages above the rooftops, and the piles of sandbags lining the building walls. On such a peacefully beautiful morning they seemed incongruous.

But turning a corner, she came to a sudden stop and gasped. The scene first stunned and then horrified her, in spite of the fact that she had been more than well prepared for it. More than half a block of smoking rubble and mountains of bricks and stones that had once been buildings stretched in front of her; a bus with shattered windows stood upended against one of the few remaining buildings that were standing.

Criss-crossing the street were coils of rubber hose like miles of writhing snakes, and working above them were hundreds of rescue workers and firemen in tin helmets, bending over the piles of still-smoking debris with shovels and pickaxes. Jenny watched a woman in a torn and soiled housedress, her face grimy with the smear of smoke and tears as she wandered among the rubble, dazed and hollow-eyed and always looking down. Every now and then she reached beneath her and tried to move a heavy piece of timber or large block of stone.

At a hand on her arm, Jenny looked around. A tall policeman said, "I'm sorry, miss, you'll have to move on." Nodding dumbly, she turned and hurried down a side street just as the woman stumbled toward two rescue workers who were emerging from a half-destroyed building with a body on a stretcher.

Shaken, she consulted her map and walked on. "Look for Ludgate Circus," Henry Fremont had told her, "near Reuter's." Looking across the street, she saw a gray stone building with the small gold and black Reuter's sign on it and knew she was close. The *World-Dispatch* office was on a small side street where numerous foreign newspapers had their branches, and it seethed with activity. In the second floor office Jenny found Joe Bernstein, long the head of the newspaper's London bureau and main headquarters.

He was grizzled and slightly stooped from too many years of looming above most people, and had keen hazel eyes that crinkled deeply at the corners when he smiled.

"Anyone that Henry Fremont sends over is okay with me," he said in his softly southern-accented voice, pointing her to a chair that looked down on the narrow street. "He wrote me that you're the best damned reporter in the city of New York."

"Wouldn't you know I'd have to come all the way to London before hearing that," Jenny said, laughing. "And thanks for not adding 'for a woman.'"

"Well, when you meet my wife, Robbie," he drawled, lounging back in his swivel chair opposite her, "you'll know why I'd never say a thing like that, let alone think it. She's English, works for Consolidated Press and does every bit as good a job as a man, if not better."

He showed her around the three-room headquarters, introducing her to Molly Winship, his secretary, a thin, dark-haired Englishwoman with exquisite skin and thick glasses, and Paul Blakely, a sixtyish American reporter who had been in London so long he spoke with a British accent and wore a long drooping white mustache.

"I want you to get your bearings for a bit," Joe said, pouring her a cup of coffee from a battered pot perking over a one-burner electric plate. "Then we'll shoot you off to one of the newer American bomber stations not far from London. We'll want the routine stuff—statistics, figures, strike reports, loss averages, all camouflaged enough, of course, so that it'll get by the censors; reports on bomber runs, bomb tonnage if you can get it, numbers of planes. But what we really want from you is the human interest tale, the slice-of-life story that the readers eat up back home."

Jenny's excitement grew. She could hardly believe that she was actually in London, where everything was happening, at the edge of the war and in a city sometimes right in its midst, its streets overflowing with military personnel from dozens of countries, reeling with the feverish gaiety of wartime.

". . . and the story here right this minute and for the reader back in the States is the story of the B-17," Joe was saying, pausing for the effect. "The Flying Fortress, and the men who are flying them out of the Eighth Air Force bases here—just about the toughest, scrappiest bunch of young guys who ever flew an airplane. They came here as raw, unseasoned, undertrained kids and have proven the Fort to be the greatest bombing machine of the war. We have a concept of unescorted daylight precision bombing, and that's what the Flying Fortress is proving. It's the answer, you know."

"But with heavy losses, Joe," Jenny said, holding out her empty cup for him to refill. "At least that's what I've been reading. With fighter escort not having that capability of distance once they pass the Channel, the Forts are sitting pigeons for the Germans."

"Aha, she's been doing her homework," said Paul Blakely, looking up from his typewriter.

"They're cutting their losses with tremendous fire power, those big roaring fifty-caliber guns, and something new and pretty hush-hush that has to do with synchronizing sighting and holding a steady course, and of course the fact that this plane can fly at greater heights than other bombers and can take unbelievable amounts of punishment. Why, I saw one that made an emergency landing at Biggin Hill, and it landed safely with its whole waist and belly torn out by flak."

"Every teenage boy just graduating from high school in the United States wants to fly a Flying Fortress," Jenny said, her eyes shining.

"Well, we're going to need them," Joe said soberly, standing up behind his desk and handing Jenny a metal helmet and a gas mask. "Come on, I'll introduce you around at the embassy. Then we're meeting Robbie for lunch. Oh, they call these their battle bowlers here," he said with a laugh, pointing at the helmet. "But they make sense."

For the next two weeks Jenny covered SHAEF, the Supreme Headquarters of the Allied Expeditionary Force, writing summaries for the "War News Roundup" column and turning out numerous daily rewrites on communiques phoned in by other correspondents. In her spare time she and Joyce, sometimes with Tom Dunne or Hobey Loman, went sightseeing, finding many of the tourist attractions closed for the duration, but enough of the historical landmarks available for history buffs.

She was most fascinated by the original city of London, "first called Lyndin by the Celts," she wrote in a by-lined news story, "then Londinium by the Roman conquerers." Covering a square mile area only, from Fleet Street to the Old Tower of London, it was an area she haunted, feeling the history, trying to reach into its past, to the time when it was first defended by the Romans and Emperor Hadrian, then invaded by the Saxons and regained by King Alfred from the Danish invaders until it was finally taken by William of Normandy in 1066.

She fell in love with the Bernsteins' London, too, the locals, or pubs, and particularly those in the Fleet Street area. Especially El Vino, jammed to the doors with newspapermen, most of them in correspondents' uniforms. Jenny and Joyce were politely snubbed when they first walked in.

"They don't particularly like women in here," Joe explained.

"Too bad," Jenny said, pushing through to the bar and ordering a ginger ale. "With ice!" she shouted over the din, and when the proprietor looked up with something between surprise and disgust, she grinned and saluted him with a V-for-victory sign. "Have to keep these bloody Americans sober, y'know." And he laughed.

"What are you?" Tom Dunne muttered. "Some kind of alcoholic?"

"Well, let's just say I'm not trying to find out anymore," she said, her eyes smiling beneath the smartly tipped overseas cap as she lifted her glass.

The pubs became their meeting places at the end of the day, with Joe and Robbie Bernstein often joining them. A vivacious brunette, Robbie—"Short for Roberta," she explained—welcomed the two young women with open arms. They all usually gathered at Rules or the Prospect of Whitby by Wapping Wall, or sometimes the Grenadier on Wilton Row behind Hyde Park, but the place Jenny loved best was the Lamb and Flag on Rose Street, where the theater people went. It was where she often picked up local color and fascinating tales for her feature pieces.

Pushing through a small laughing crowd gathered around one end of the bar one evening, Jenny listened and took notes as a tall young American flyer, his arm looped casually around the shoulders of a showy-looking blonde, regaled the group with humorous but what Jenny suspected were tall tales about the flyers at his base. He glanced at her, then away.

"This one is about one of yours," he said to the crowd, "and it was just told to me by an RAF friend of mine stationed at Coltishall. It was during the blitz, and this character walks in the door of a pub here in London, a Spitfire pilot in all his gear. He had been shot down and baled out over the city one noontime and simply walked in the door and cheerfully asked the landlord, 'Would you be a good fellow and ring up a cabbie for me?'" The crowd roared while Jenny, from the corner of her eye, carefully studied him. He was tall and rakish looking, with dark hair, a thin, well-groomed mustache, and startlingly blue eyes that suddenly gazed at her with a lazy insolence. He wore the Air Corps uniform as though it had been designed exclusively for him, and was handsome in a way that Jenny didn't trust, with roving eyes and a sardonic smile.

"In a matter of minutes he was in a taxi and on his way back to his aerodrome, where in an hour or two he would be back up in a Spitfire or Hurricane that same afternoon." The crowd laughed again and clapped as he continued to gaze at her. "Apparently our lady reporter from the United States doesn't swallow that one," he said, and laughter pealed from the actressy blonde's mouth while Jenny scowled and started to back out of the crowd. "But then I guess she didn't see many Messerschmitts over New York or Cleveland or wherever she came from in the States." And the blonde laughed again as Jenny walked back to her friends.

"You look like you just saw the person who killed Santa Claus," Joe Bernstein said.

"Come to think of it, he probably did," Jenny said angrily, her face still a deep red. "What an insufferable, cocky, conceited, baloney-shoveling artist that was! If all our Air Corps men over here are like him, then God help us with the English and what they probably think of us as a nation of pea-brained, overbearing nitwits."

"Wow," Joyce said, laughing, as Robbie and Joe looked over at the loudly laughing group of American airmen and young women. "It's a good thing you don't carry a gun."

"I may go out and buy one," Jenny said.

"Well, if it's any consolation, Jenny, most of the Air Corps men here are pretty decent chaps," Robbie said, "and the Londoners are quite fond of them. Oh, they may be a bit taken with themselves, rather jaunty types, but under the circumstances they can be forgiven a great deal. They're really quite splendid fellows, you know."

"This one," Jenny said, emphasizing each word grimly, "is the most arrogant, insulting boor I have ever seen."

"Well, forget him," Joe said, laughing, "and let's move on to someplace else for that late dinner."

But Jenny couldn't forget him and worried that when she was finally assigned to one of the Air Corps bases, she might find she had an aversion to these cocky, sure-of-themselves types that the Air Corps seemed to draw for training back in the States. She only hoped that Robbie Bernstein was right, that most of them were at least *bearable,* and was thinking it when she walked into the office the following morning. Joe looked up from a pile of cables on his desk and said, "Well, this is it, Jenny. Your assignment." He handed her a sheaf of papers.

She stared at him for a long moment, almost as though afraid to move on to the next step. The two weeks in London had been an exciting and wonderful experience, and she was almost reluctant to enter the second phase of her work as a correspondent.

She reached out and took the papers from him.

"Before I even look at the assignment, Joe," she said, her voice husky, trembling a little, "I want you to know how much I've loved it here, how I appreciate the way you've made it so easy for me."

Joe laughed softly, reached across the desk, and ruffled her hair beneath the small cap.

"I almost don't want to leave here," she said, lowering her head to hide the rush of tears. Then she laughed shakily. "Just—well, thanks for everything."

"Hell," he said, smiling, "you'll come for weekends. We'll see you often. Meanwhile, you leave tomorrow. Take a train from King's Cross Station. Your ticket's there. You go to a B-17 base, with the air station right at the edge of a tiny hamlet called Chipping Epworth. A Mrs. Barrington rents rooms, and she's expecting you. It's not too far from Cambridge, and the area's crawling with air stations, a lot of Fortress groups. You'll be fairly close to the big air stations, Alconbury and Mildenhall. Lot going on up there."

She felt a surge of excitement and looked up and smiled, eyes dancing, just as Paul Blakely came into the office.

"Well, she's off, Paul," Joe said, relieved at Jenny's smile. "Headed for Chipping Epworth."

Paul made a face. "Wait until you see it, Jenny. You can throw a spitball from one end to the other and catch it before it lands."

"Well, it's my own beat, so it doesn't matter," she said with a grin, her enthusiasm growing. She turned quickly to Joe. "It's beginning to sound better and better. But I'll still miss all this." She looked around a bit wistfully at the battered furniture and grimy windows. "I've really loved it. But this is what I've been waiting for. And any reporter that's worth his or her paycheck wants her own territory."

Joe handed her a sealed envelope. "Your censorship instructions."

"How about a pair of boxing gloves and some brass knuckles to keep the flyboys at their distance?" Paul asked with a scowl.

"Don't worry, Mr. Blakely," Jenny said with a gleam in her eye. "In the neighborhood where I grew up in New York, a girl learned to take care of herself."

Jenny paused in front of the building on her way out. The old gray city pulled at her in a strangely indefinite and out-of-time way. For the rest of the day she walked about, revisiting places that had touched her in some impalpable way: the red brick house on Gough Square where Dr. Johnson had lived, the bookstores on Charing Cross Road where she stopped to browse and buy books to take with her, and finally Westminster Abbey. She sat for a while in the dim hush of the nave, feeling its vast space and centuries of history swallow her. Behind its ancient walls lay buried kings and queens. She paused at the Tomb of the Unknown Soldier from the First World War, sensing the continuity and quiet stoicism of the people of this island empire, then stood in Poet's Corner, where voices seemed to whisper to her.

Finally heading toward the hotel, she went into a small tea room in Bloomsbury, where she wrote two V-mail letters, one to Kate and one to Liz, explaining that she was leaving London but to continue writing to her at the London *World-Dispatch* office, where Joe Bernstein would forward their letters to her. A shriveled little white-haired lady with twinkly blue eyes, who owned the tea room, read her tea leaves and told her she saw a tall, dark-haired man coming into her life, and he would be wearing a uniform.

Jenny smiled as she crossed Russell Square toward Montague Street. *All* of the young men at the air station would be in uniform, and surely half of them would have dark hair.

By the time she reached Chipping Epworth, it was late evening. She completed the final seven miles of the journey by taxi from the nearest railroad station and was enchanted by the centuries-old charm of the hamlet. It was once apparently a market town; the main road widened at the center into a triangular cobblestone area. This was closely bordered with an old coaching inn called the Swan, a postal station, two pubs, some small shops, and off to one end a narrow walking bridge across a stream.

Beyond the stream a deep green area led to the towering Norman church, its features dating back to the twelfth century. Twisting off from the village center were tiny winding cobblestone lanes with cozy thatch and plaster houses and patches of neat gardens, brilliantly green in the still-light summer evening.

Mrs. Barrington's cottage at the edge of the hamlet sat close beside a duck pond at the end of the small stream that wound through the village. It looked exactly as Jenny had imagined, with timbered eaves and a garden of riotously colored flowers all across the front. Mrs. Barrington completed the picture. She was tiny and cheery, and her bright blue eyes welcomed Jenny. She immediately sat Jenny down at a small table in a bay window overlooking the garden with a cup of tea and dozens of curious questions. She explained that she was a widow with a son in Field Marshal Montgomery's Eighth Army in Sicily and that her daughter was in the Women's Royal Naval Service, affectionately called Wrens, where she operated a motorboat that ferried men and supplies to ships anchored in home ports.

"You'll sleep in Pamela's room," she said, bustling Jenny and her luggage to a small room up under the eaves with a high four-poster bed covered with a patchwork quilt and deep down-filled pillows.

"Pam's bicycle will do you nicely," she said just before Jenny closed her door, ready to wearily sink into the big, comfortable looking bed. "You'll need something to get you about, you know. The bomber station is almost two miles off, and the one cabbie in town just never seems to be about when one needs it. There *is* an Army bus, of course, and it stops at the Swan on its way to and from the railway station and the aerodrome. But I think you'll find the bicycle a handy bit of transportation."

The road between Mrs. Barrington's cottage and the bomber base became as familiar to Jenny in a matter of days as the streets of Greenwich Village had. The following day, when she presented her credentials to the information officer, Lieutenant Wayne Parker, she was admitted to the base and given a tour. She was somewhat unprepared for the totally professional way she was treated by Lieutenant Parker and the other administrative officers she met. Past experience in her job as a reporter had made her accustomed to good-natured but sometimes sarcastic gibes and amused stares from men, and when Jenny thanked him, he said, "Well, Joe Bernstein said you're good at your job and that you'll strictly adhere to the rules of censorship, and that's all we care about. It doesn't make the slightest difference to us here whether you're a man or a woman, just so long as you play ball with us."

She was also totally unprepared for the enthusiasm she drew from the ground and flying crews when they first spotted her. She broke into a run, laughing and waving as she headed for the administration building, holding on to her small overseas cap while a wild chorus of shouts and whistles went up from a group of young men piling off the big lumbering dark green bus.

When she arrived on the third morning it was a different story. Rising at three a.m., she tiptoed down the creaking staircase only to find Mrs. Barrington in a warm flannel robe waiting for her with a cheery smile and steaming cup of tea and bun. "You didn't think I'd let you pedal off with nothing warm in your stomach, did you?"

With a shrouded flashlight Jenny set off on the bicycle in the dark, grateful for the first streaks of dawn that crept up the horizon. She arrived at the bomber station just in time to watch the start of the day's mission as a group of men crossed in front of her. They looked almost surreal in the bulging layers of electrically heated flying suits that plugged into outlets on the plane. The suits were topped with brown coveralls, fleece-lined boots, and Mae Wests, the orange rubber life preservers that would inflate in an instant, and finally their parachutes, held on by thick canvas straps between the legs and over the shoulders. Some were pulling on helmets with throat speakers and attached earphones, while others carried them in their hands.

They hurried toward a truck, a few shouldering their fifty-caliber guns, turning and smiling at her as they walked past and climbed onto the truck. She watched as they were driven down alongside a runway where she saw faint silhouettes looming out of the half darkness—the great Flying Fortress bombers, like a scattered flock of giant birds.

It was chilly in the misty gray dawn and Jenny shivered, pulling her trench coat collar closer, eyes straining through the mist to watch the flyers cluster around their planes.

"They've been up since two thirty a.m.," Lieutenant Parker said moments later when he escorted her up to the control tower deck, steaming mugs of coffee in their hands. They watched the huge planes dotting the runways on the field spread down before them. "First a briefing, then breakfast in the mess hall and getting all that gear on."

Jenny watched the plane closest to them. A jeep with several officers had spun onto the field and pulled alongside the Fort. Before climbing aboard, the officers distributed packets to the other men. "What are they giving them?" she asked.

"Money from the countries they'll fly over, in case they go down, and some concentrated food. Maps too."

Peering hard through her binoculars, she read the name on the plane nearest to them. *Spirit of Times Square.* The men were clambering aboard; then the captain, turning to say something to the ground crew chief, happened to glance up toward the control tower deck, and in that moment she thought he somehow looked familiar. Putting the field glasses

155

to her eyes again, she stared at him and, after a long moment, slowly lowered the binoculars. It was the Air Corps officer she had seen that night at the Lamb and Flag, the one who had been so insulting.

She watched him as he disappeared up into the Fortress, then several minutes later saw him salute the ground crew from the high cockpit window above and behind the ship's nose. Suddenly there was a burst of sound and then a deafening roar as the engines began to turn over and catch, sending a sweep of wind across the deck. She clapped her small hat on tighter and held it there.

"This is a small station," Lieutenant Parker shouted down into her ear. "Just twenty-four Forts. They'll rendezvous with squadrons from other fields. You'll see when they take off." He pointed north. "They'll head in that direction, then come past again on their way toward the Channel."

"Can you tell me where they're headed?" She stood on tiptoe to shout in his ear. He simply shook his head, gray eyes serious behind horn-rimmed glasses.

She watched as the *Spirit of Times Square* slowly turned, the huge silvery wings and fuselage flashing in the early morning light when it glided along the runway, picking up speed, then lifting with another flash of silver into the sky. Something caught in her throat and ached there, and she quickly brushed at her eyes. One by one the other planes followed, climbing skyward and sailing northward in a long line, the deep-throated thunderous roar of the motors drifting farther and farther away and finally disappearing.

"Watch now," Parker said, pointing. "Keep your eyes in that direction. Pretty soon they'll come back." She glanced at him quickly before looking north, saw the expression on his face, and began to understand the love that the men on this base had for the Flying Fortress.

She first heard the faint roar, and then high in the sky and in tight formation they flew overhead, followed almost seconds later by another formation, and then a third and fourth. For long minutes hundreds of planes passed high above them, then disappeared. They were heading for the Channel and some target in Germany, she guessed.

The base suddenly seemed almost deserted and lonely. Men from the ground crews wandered about in their coveralls and fatigue caps, obviously nervous, eyes to the ground.

"It'll take hours before we know anything," Parker said as they left the deck and went to the mess hall for a second cup of coffee. Another correspondent, Zeke Raymond from Bakersfield, California, had joined them, his freckled face smiling and eager.

"We can bike back and forth together from town," Zeke said with a grin, holding her hand long after shaking it, refusing to let go.

"Well, that depends," Jenny said sweetly as she extricated her hand. "If you're nervous about riding on the road alone in the dark these early mornings, Mr. Raymond, perhaps we can arrange it."

"Ouch!" he said, grinning even wider. "You really bite."

"But if you had something else in mind, I have a friend in London who would be perfect for you. She says she's not as choosy as I am."

"Hey, you really know how to land a punch, don't you?"

"And you don't lose any time, do you?" she said, laughing, as she looked at him over the rim of her cup, knowing they'd become friends.

Jenny was working on a story about how the men lived on the base, so Parker took her on a tour of the Nissen huts and Zeke trailed along. The walls behind and above the double-decker bunks were literally plastered with sexy pictures of Lana Turner, Betty Grable, Rita Hayworth, and Marlene Dietrich in tight bathing suits or low-cut evening gowns.

"Oh my God," Jenny said, "how boring."

"Beautiful," Zeke murmured. "These guys have excellent taste."

"Yeah, you'd like Joyce," Jenny said, nodding her head as she followed Lieutenant Parker out the door. "She's about five foot four, weighs about one hundred and ten pounds, and does a wicked jitterbug, and she's looking, pal, she's looking."

"Well," he sighed, pushing a lock of sandy hair back from his forehead, "if I can't have you, bring on your friend Joyce."

Jenny had planned to return to Chipping Epworth before noon to wash out some lingerie, mend stockings and write letters to Liz and Kate. But for some reason that kept eluding her, she lingered, lunching with Lieutenant Parker and Zeke in the mess hall, then distractedly tried to write a story on the pinups in the enlisted men's quarters as she sat at a typewriter in the press cubbyhole. But she kept walking to the window and looking off into the skies in the direction of the English Channel.

In the late afternoon she first sensed the stir of excitement outside, then as she rushed to the door she heard the high and distant drone of motors. As they swooped down onto the field, she ran to the wire fencing and, with her binoculars trained on the end of the field, watched each plane that landed and taxied in until she saw the name—*Spirit of Times Square*. She waited for a moment as it glided gracefully down the runway, then quickly walked away and around the control tower building, climbed on her bicycle, and swiftly pedaled off the base, heading toward Chipping Epworth.

Jenny spent much of her time at the base in the next few days and began to learn everything she could about the Flying Fortress, both technically and emotionally. For she had discovered it was the kind of plane that men talked about in reverent tones, as though it lived and breathed and imparted a wisdom of the skies that only it and the men who flew it understood.

She hung around the ground crews, at first finding them difficult to talk to when the planes were still out. They seemed to resent any intrusion into those strangely somber hours when life and death hung in the balance out there across the sky. But after the planes had returned, they greeted her with lusty yells and shrill whistles, and not only answered her questions but taught her how to shoot craps and play gin rummy, discussed their wives, their girls, and even the Dear John letters some of them had received.

She interviewed eight or nine of the men who came from the New York area, and each morning in the press cubbyhole she pounded out their stories on her typewriter. A series on the flying crews, she thought, would come later. And this, she told herself, was why in that first two weeks she avoided the early morning mission takeoffs and late afternoons when the planes returned to the base.

"Too early in the morning for you, Jenny?" Zeke teased her as they sat one evening at the big round table in the Dove, the larger of the two pubs in the village. The center table was always filled with a changing stream of young officers from the Fortress crews, brash in their handsomely cut uniforms, many with decorations and their silver pilot's wings, and all with the fifty-mission-crush hat, the officer's service cap with the wire stiffening removed so that it could be worn with earphones while flying.

"I'm busy with the series on the enlisted men," Jenny said, scowling at him, then looking around the pleasant room, light from the big stone fireplace flickering on the timbered ceiling. Her gaze trailed along the line of men laughing and talking at the long bar, then settled on the group tossing darts at the pictures of Hitler and his henchmen over in one corner.

"Well, it's a good idea for a while anyway," Zeke said, suddenly turning serious as he twirled his glass on the table. "You should be here for a time before you let yourself in for the daily death watch. Get used to it all—"

Jenny looked around at him sharply. "Death watch?"

"The casualty figures, the torn-up planes *when* they make it back, the guys they pile into the ambulances, the missing arms and legs, even faces, day after day until it begins to get to you." He suddenly tried to smile and took a drink. "But as they say, baby, this is war. It ain't patty-cake time. And speaking of patty-cake, here comes Bud Corwin headed our way and with his eye on you. He's stretching it if he's nineteen, but then he claims he prefers older women."

Jenny laughed. *"Who* and *what* is he? Quick, Zeke."

"Bombardier. On the *Spirit of Times Square,* I think."

Jenny stiffened a little.

"Zeke, my friend," the brightly smiling young man said as he ceremoniously pulled over a chair from another table and squeezed it in next to Jenny. "It's time to share the wealth. Introduce me."

Zeke introduced him without enthusiasm, then, picking up his empty glass, he stood up and pulled back Jenny's chair. "Let's move to the bar, Jenny. This guy is a number-one moocher."

But Bud Corwin followed right along behind them, smiling cheerfully. "Like I said," he called out loudly as he walked along in their path, "I'm a firm believer in sharing the wealth. And, my friends"—he winked at smiling airmen as he passed, gesturing ahead toward Jenny's trim figure—"*that* is wealth, if I've ever seen it."

About two miles from the Dove, on the other side of the village, Doug Gilbert skidded the jeep over to the edge of the dark road and pulled to a stop just as Jenny and Zeke were squeezing into a small space at the bar of the pub.

Doug had been heading for Cambridge but suddenly changed his mind after glancing at the illuminated dial on his watch. He was flying in the morning and had to hit the sack early. The Dove would have to do.

He sped back through the tiny village, slid the jeep into a

159

spot in front of the pub, and gracefully leaped over the side and headed for the door.

Once inside, he paused for a moment as his eyes adjusted to the light. He lit a cigarette, letting the smoke curl lazily upward. The room, as usual, was filled with men from the station and a few locals. Since the Americans had moved into the area, most of the village people went to the Bull and Bear down the road, leaving the Dove clear territory for the men from the base.

He let his eyes rove slowly as he propped himself with a lean kind of grace against the doorjamb, the firelight and low-hanging lamps lightly shadowing his face. It was a rather narrow face, skin drawn over high cheekbones, a thin well-groomed mustache lifting slightly at one corner with the rather sardonic smile. His eyes roamed the room with a lazy amusement, then stopped.

He had seen her somewhere before.

While searching his memory, he walked slowly toward Bud Corwin, who was standing next to her and waving his hands as he told her some story. Her head was slightly thrown back and she was laughing at something Zeke Raymond had just said to Bud. He saw the long lovely line of her neck, her lips parted in laughter. And then he saw the insignia on her uniform, and something glimmered in his memory.

A news-hen, he thought with a scowl. Yes, that was it. She had been furiously scribbling notes in a notebook one night at the—where was it? He pushed his memory further. That was it. The Lamb and Flag, in London. She had suddenly looked up at him as he stood with his friends, telling a story, complete disbelief on her face, her expression as much as telling him he was a liar and a fool. He stopped halfway across to the bar, studying her, the brown hair a cloud about the small triangular-shaped face, a face more expressive and animated than beautiful, the tiny figure exquisite in the well-cut uniform, long slim legs and hands that moved gracefully as she talked. There was something about her, a vibrant, intense quality, just in the way she stood or moved.

Suddenly feeling his gaze, she turned and looked at him. For a moment their eyes locked, then she turned to Zeke and threw back her head in laughter again. Continuing on to the bar, Doug pushed in next to Bud and ordered a drink, answering a number of greetings with a casual wave of his hand.

"Doug! For crissake, Doug," Bud shouted, slapping him on the back. "I thought you went to Cambridge."

"Changed my mind," Doug said, looking past him to Jenny, who was looking at him with a steady and intense gaze of recognition and dislike. "That two thirty a.m. call rolls around fast."

"Well, look who's here," Zeke said, laughing. "Doug Gilbert in the Dove. To what do we owe this honor?" He turned to Jenny. "Doug is one of the roaming types—Cambridge, Northampton, Bedford, Letchworth, Saint Alban's. You name it, he's been there. Knows them all—Gwen, Lily, Wilma, Meg, Jill—"

"Jenny, this is Doug Gilbert, my boss on the *Spirit of Times Square*," Bud said proudly. "Jenny MacKenzie."

"We've met," Doug said with a smile. "But under far more formal circumstances. London, wasn't it, Miss MacKenzie? When I was trying to spend a quiet evening with some friends in the Lamb and Flag?"

"Quiet?" Jenny said with a bright smile. "Oh, I thought it was a leftover act from one of the music halls." His eyes never left her, the most startlingly blue eyes she had ever seen, and she felt a tight little butterfly knot at the top of her stomach, fluttering. She had never seen such bold eyes, such a deeply brilliant blue, seeming to peer into her very soul. Suddenly she turned to Zeke, took hold of his arm, and said, "Hey, how about that movie you promised to take me to at the base? With Akim Tamiroff."

"The what?" Zeke stared at her, then recovered with a slow smile and said, "Oh, sure. *Five Graves to Cairo* with Franchot Tone." He looked at his watch. "It starts in about twenty minutes. We can just make it." Grasping her arm, he rushed her across the room and out the door, calling back over his shoulder, "Take care of my bill, Bud. I'll settle with you tomorrow."

Every night for the next week Jenny saw Doug Gilbert at the Dove. Sometimes he sat at the big round table in the center, where she was usually sitting; other times he stood at the far end of the bar, always surrounded by members of his crew and other young officers, obviously a popular man on the base. He sat with his hat pushed on the back of his head, a cigarette hanging from the corner of his mouth, an amused smile that traveled from his lips to his eyes as he listened to the others—until he looked at her, when the laughter disappeared. At first, when their eyes met, there was a mutual dislike that flickered before they each turned away. But as time went on, it slowly changed. Some kind of recognition flared each time their eyes locked, if only for a brief moment —intense, probing, stirring emotions and needs in her that she had thought were safely buried, even lost.

Once, when she unexpectedly turned and their eyes held, she caught a glimpse of raw sensual desire and became frightened.

She began to stay away from the Dove and carefully avoided Major Gilbert at the base. Staying in the press cubbyhole until late in the evening, then bicycling back to Mrs. Barrington's where she would eat a late supper and fall into bed in utter exhaustion, she would still find herself staring up through the darkness at the ceiling, sleepless and wondering what was happening to her, remembering his eyes, his hands, the fingers long and graceful and strong, lighting a cigarette, cupping the flame . . . touching her . . . always touching her. . . .

From the deck of the tower Jenny glanced back at the field once more as the last Fortress glided in and touched down. She had come up for a breath of air and to stretch her legs after long hours at the typewriter and stayed to watch the squadron return. Greatly relieved that all were accounted for, she headed down the narrow stairway at the side of the building, then stopped about three steps from the bottom. Looking up at her was Doug Gilbert, leaning against the railing, hands deep in his pockets.

"You've been among the missing," he said with a lazy smile. "So I decided to check."

She looked at him for a moment, seeing only amusement, even friendliness in his eyes. Carefully making sure not to brush against him as she passed him at the bottom of the steps, she went on down and quickly crossed to where she had parked her bicycle.

"Well, I *do* have a job, you know, and it's been one of those weeks. Busy. I've worked every night."

"By choice?" he asked, smiling while he walked alongside her. "Or by design?"

She ignored the remark and started to climb on her bicycle, which was parked near the entrance to the building, but he had taken hold of it and was walking it toward a jeep nearby.

She half ran next to him, protesting, "If you don't mind, Major Gilbert, I—"

"I'll drive you into town, if that's where you're going. After all, we're in England and it's time for tea, and I know the perfect place for it." He had lifted her bike into the rear of the jeep, then, without any warning, turned and picked her up and put her down into the front seat.

"You have one hell of a nerve!" she said furiously, starting to get out, but he had jumped into the driver's side and quickly turned the motor on. He slammed the jeep into gear and they peeled off.

"Too late," he smiled down at her as the jeep roared along the access road and off the air station onto the main road going toward Chipping Epworth.

Arms folded, looking straight ahead and with eyes blazing, she said, "Fine. I'm in a hurry anyway."

"I know," Doug grinned. "Zeke told me you're going up to London, where you're introducing him to a friend of yours, but you're taking the six o'clock train."

"Zeke has a big mouth. I may not introduce him to Joyce after all."

"Fortunately for me he has a big mouth."

For several moments neither of them spoke, then he looked down at her again. "Let's not kid ourselves," he said softly. "Something happened the second time we saw each other. And it's been happening ever since."

She kept her eyes straight ahead, not trusting herself to look at him. When he reached over and gently turned her head to look at him, she closed her eyes. She felt the jeep slow down, heard the motor begin to idle, and knew they were standing still. Slowly opening her eyes, she saw they had pulled to the side of the road in the heavy forest between the air station and Chipping Epworth. Slowly he leaned down and kissed her, a gentle but long kiss that made her ache with longing. She felt something slip away, like a second skin that had safely held her close within herself. Now she was unprotected, stripped of her defenses.

As he drove on she didn't move, keeping her eyes straight ahead again, watching the road but seeing nothing. Something was crumbling deep inside. She was bewildered, suddenly unsure of herself. The kiss had been tender, soft, questioning, but with a promise of something else, something dangerously threatening, prying gently at her senses, forcing them to reel upward to the surface, making her feel. She

163

didn't want to feel. Feeling meant pain. It meant destruction. It ate away at you until there was nothing left. She shivered in the sunshine, then slowly turned her head to look at him, unable to stop herself.

"Please let me off at the edge of the village, Major," she said, surprised at the calm in her voice.

"Tea first," he said, smiling down at her. As he brought the jeep screeching to a stop in front of the Swan, he turned off the ignition and looked at her. "Ready?"

"Well, tea," she said hesitantly, quickly climbing from the jeep and walking around it. "Then I have a train to catch."

Chapter 18

BEFORE HACKLEY CRAWFORD left his hotel for Union Station in Los Angeles, he made two phone calls. The first one was to the Wardman Park Hotel in Washington.

"Just checking," he said when Dan Coleman picked up the phone at the other end. "I see you haven't gone home yet." There was a long silence, then Dan finally spoke.

"Another couple of weeks, Hack," he said, then added unconvincingly, "I have to finish up some work here."

"That's a lot of bullshit, Dan, and you know it."

"Look, Hack, I'm working on the play and—"

"Liz thought you were coming back five weeks ago. What the hell are you trying to do to her?" There was no answer. "I'll tell you what you *are* doing to her. You're killing her, that's what. And as for the play, you'll never get that finished until you've straightened your life out with Liz."

"A girl like Liz doesn't deserve the only kind of arrangement I can give her," Dan started to shout.

"Oh, now we're going to play God Almighty, are we?"

"I'll go back to New York when I can offer her the kind of life she should have."

"You know something, Dan, you're just too goddamn good to be true. Your halo is even beginning to show."

"Get off my back, will you?"

"Not until you get on that train and get yourself to New York."

"When Connie tells me the divorce is finally going through, then I'll leave here and go back."

"Well, I have some news for you, buddy boy. I had somebody do a little investigating while I've been out here on business in L.A., and I found out your Connie hasn't even *started* divorce proceedings. Sure, she had a lawyer send you a letter charging you with adultery, but that's just a lot of legal mumbo-jumbo. But she's sitting in Reno having a ball, just seeing how far she can go, sweating every nickel out of you she can get in a settlement promise, and you want to know something? She'll do it just as long as you let her."

There was another long silence. "I don't know what to do, Hack." He sounded lower than he ever had, and Hack's heart went out to him. "Connie's holding all the cards."

Don't be so sure of that, Hack said silently. "Look, Dan—" His voice had become gentle. "I'll talk to you when I get back to New York. In a few days."

As soon as he hung up he asked the hotel operator to get him another long-distance number.

"This is Hackley Crawford," he said.

"Oh, I'm glad you called, Mr. Crawford," the male voice on the other end of the phone said. "I finally located her."

"And?"

"It's like you figured."

"All right. I'll be on the eight forty train out of Los Angeles tonight. Meet me, and we'll take care of it."

"Okay. Meet me in the train station by the baggage window. Just give the baggage master your name, then I'll know who you are."

"Right, I'll see you then."

Hack Crawford and Charley Kane stood in front of room 412 and looked at each other. With a gesture from Hack, Kane carefully, quietly inserted a key in the lock, turned it without making a sound, then; with a nod of his head to Hack, swung the door wide. They both rushed in, Kane immediately pressing the light switch near the door and flooding the room with light.

As Hack stood in the doorway surveying the scene, Kane whipped a camera from his pocket and snapped one picture and then another and still another as the couple in the bed turned and looked at them in shock.

"What are you doing?" Connie shrieked, pulling the sheet high to her neck to cover her nakedness as the man, dark-haired and young, slid off the bed and rolled under it, dragging half of the sheet with him.

Hack almost laughed, but instead answered her with a ridiculing kind of half bow. "I'm paying you a visit for your husband, Mrs. Coleman." He walked to the bed, took a card from his pocket, and placed it on the bedside table. "And here is the name of Dan's attorney in New York. I suggest you

166

give it to your attorney, and perhaps they can come to some kind of immediate terms."

With another half bow, he turned and walked from the room, her mascara-streaked face burned into his memory for all time as she glared up at him from the rumpled bedcovers.

The conductor had opened the train gate for the arriving Twentieth Century Limited, and with a tip of his hat, while holding others back, he let Evelyn Crawford through to the track area with Proctor, the Crawford chauffeur, following.

"There he is," Evelyn said, catching sight of Hack as he hurried toward them along the red carpeting beside the long train, its drawing room windows glowing softly in the dimly lit train shed. "Darling," she called out as Proctor rushed forward to take the bags from the smiling redcap. Throwing herself into Hack's arms, she said, "You look wonderfully rested for all those thousands of miles." She nuzzled his cheek and murmured, "Mmmmm, lovely."

"Just give me a train to ride on and I sleep like a top," he smiled, holding her away from him for a moment to drink in the sparkling eyes and figure of his wife. Then he held her close for a moment. "God, how I've missed you." Shaking hands with the chauffeur as they walked on, he said, "How are you, Proctor? And how's Tommy doing these days?"

"Fine, sir," Proctor said, tipping his hat and smiling and leading the way to the Vanderbilt side of the rotunda as they pushed through the early morning commuting crowd. "Still teaching weapons down at Camp Maxey, thank God, sir, and not overseas."

Settled in the long black limousine, Hack leaned forward for a moment and, with a sidelong, mysterious smile at Evelyn, spoke to the chauffeur as the car pulled out into the thick traffic. "Drop Mrs. Crawford and me at the Pierre, Proctor. We're having breakfast with some friends on the roof garden. Then after you've taken my bags home, come back for Mrs. Crawford at around eleven, at my office. We'll take a cab over there when we're through here."

"What's that all about?" Evelyn asked.

"You'll see, you'll see," Hack said, patting her hand, then holding it tight and smiling down at her as Proctor headed north along Madison Avenue.

"Well, aren't we the mysterious one, though," she laughed, looking out at the traffic, and then settled back in the seat, content that he was home and here holding her hand. There was no point in pushing him, insisting on an answer. In his own good time Hack would let her know what the mysterious mission was all about.

As they crossed the roof garden to their table, following the maitre d', Evelyn saw Dan Coleman rise from his chair, and she hurried in his direction.

"Dan!" She hugged him and kissed his cheek, then hugged him again. "You big beautiful dope! You've come back!" Hack and Dan shook hands and affectionately slapped each other on the back. "When did you get back to New York?" she asked as she sat down at the table.

"Last night," Dan said, looking at Hack for signals as the two men sat on either side of Evelyn. "I'll go back to Washington later this afternoon."

"Well—we'll talk about that later," Hack said, suddenly getting to his feet. Evelyn and Dan, following his eyes, saw Liz coming across the restaurant. Dan's eyes widened and he leaped from his chair while Evelyn, beginning to unravel Hack's mystery, watched her.

Liz stopped for a moment when she saw Dan, the composed expression on her face quickly turning to consternation. Then, getting control, she slowly moved toward them again. She had paled but was still lovely in a white summer suit and white cartwheel straw hat accentuated with a navy blue silk blouse and purse. After greeting Evelyn and Hack with a small hug, she slowly turned to Dan, and he saw the raw hurt in her eyes. He took her hands and simply held them.

As Hack sat down and discreetly turned to Evelyn in conversation, Dan ran one hand distractedly through his hair, then blurted, "I'm ten different kinds of coward, staying away like I have. I was coming back several weeks ago—even told Jenny I was—but I just couldn't face you with nothing resolved, little or no hope of anything *being* resolved."

"Dan, it doesn't matter," she said, her lovely blue eyes filling with tears, her voice low and hurried. "I don't care how we—"

"No," he said, his voice matching hers. "Somehow I'll get the divorce. I don't know how, but—" He took her arms and turned her directly to him. "She has all the cards. There isn't a law in my favor, not a state I can go to, as long as she has the cards in her hands. But my lawyers haven't given up. They—"

"Will you two please sit down," Hack said. "I have something I want to show you."

As they sat Hack pulled a long white envelope from his inner pocket and handed it to Dan, then turned to the hovering waiter and said, "Just bring us all orange juice, scrambled eggs, and bacon, please."

Dan slowly pulled the folded piece of paper from the envelope, opened it, and began to read silently while Liz watched, her eyes expectant.

"Why don't you read it out loud?" Hack said softly, nodding at Evelyn, who was watching them with curiosity.

Dan started to read: "'Dear Dan: I have decided that waiting any longer to start divorce proceedings is unfair to both of us. I have therefore instructed my attorney to get everything moving again, and as I am already in Reno, the divorce should be final in about six weeks. I have also decided to only ask for child support from you and no alimony—'" Dan looked up at Hack, puzzled. "'After thinking about everything, it just didn't seem like the right thing to do.'"

Dan looked up at Liz, who was watching him, a tremulous smile on her face. "I knew it, darling. I knew *something* would happen."

With spilling, excited laughter Evelyn turned to her. "You'll be married at our house. As soon as the divorce goes through."

Dan rose and pulled Liz to her feet, then said to Hack and Evelyn, "Do you think you could each eat two orders of eggs and bacon?"

Hack laughed. "Delighted."

They had taken a few steps away, Liz's hand firmly in Dan's, when he turned and called out to Hack, "Lunch tomorrow?" When Hack nodded, he said, "Then you can tell me how you got hold of this letter."

"And don't forget, now you don't have any excuse about finishing the play, Dan," Hack said. At a wave from Dan's hand he added, "And I want it soon."

"Four months," Dan said, looking back and smiling. "I promise you."

And all the way across the restaurant, as the couple headed toward the elevator, Hack and Evelyn could see the broad smile on Dan's face.

"It's all right, Kate," Liz said into the phone, eyes dreamy, remembering the evening, the hours of soft conversation as they sat over a long candlelit dinner at the Sky Garden of the St. Moritz, then walking back to Dan's apartment through the summer darkness, and the hours of lovemaking while music played softly from the record player in his living room. "It's all right. He'll have the divorce in six weeks, and then we'll be married."

"Liz darling, how wonderful!" Kate said from the other end of the line. "I'm just finishing a letter to Jenny, and I'll tell her the good news. She keeps writing and asking me how you are."

Kate slowly hung up the phone and looked down at the half-finished letter on her desk, the box of Jenny's letters beside it. She had been rereading them, one in particular, over and over, that Jenny had written while she was still in London, before going to the Air Corps base she had been assigned to cover.

. . . and Joe Bernstein had sent me out to Bushy Park. That's where the U.S. Army Air Forces headquarters and SHAEF are and I was just getting my feet wet on the job. I caught the tail end of some conversation from a group of Air Force men who were just being processed through, and realized several of them were from the New York area, so I asked them if I could talk to them. One of them, it turned out, was Adam's cousin. A Captain Delevan Wheeler, and miracle of miracles, he said he was a good friend of yours, Kate. So we had lunch and talked of nothing but you. Ships that pass in the night, but a touch of home. Much as I love it here, and love my assignment, it's wonderful when you can talk to someone from home. And home, somehow to me, is you and Liz. Write soon and often.

Love,
Jenny

Kate smoothed the letter out with her fingers, slowly, lovingly, as though to bring Del and Jenny, two people she loved, closer. Pulling the half-finished letter she had been writing toward her, she picked up her pen.

Something you will be happy to know is that Dan Coleman is finally going to be given a divorce by that dreadful woman he's married to, and he and Liz will be married as soon as the decree is final. Her career is exploding with all kinds of recognition and offers, so all

*will soon be well with her. How far we have all traveled
since that day we met in the hospital. Before closing, I
should tell you . . .*

She hesitated. She had told no one outside of the family.

. . . I'm going to have a baby, in January . . .

Jenny pedaled fast, her eyes straight ahead, peering into
the waning evening light and trying to pretend she didn't hear
the half-idling motor of the jeep as he tried to keep the speed
down to match that of her bicycle. The lumbering old Army
bus passed them, going in the opposite direction, headed for
the base, young men hanging from the windows and whistling
and hooting, but she ignored them and pedaled on.

Just as she reached a tiny thatch-roofed white cottage that
always signaled to her that she was at the edge of Chipping
Epworth, he suddenly swerved the jeep out in front of her.
She slid to a stop and waited, one foot on the ground as she
balanced the bike. She watched him with a set, cold expression on her face, saw him climb out of the jeep and walk
around to her, then very gently pry her hands from the
handlebars.

"Please, Major Gilbert." She spoke in a stilted voice. "I
told you at lunch that day that I'm just not interested in some
casual little wartime romance. Ever since I arrived here, I
haven't—"

"Shhh," he said, his voice as gentle as his hands as he took
her arm with one and the bicycle with the other and walked
them both to the jeep. "I know all about it. You've turned
down every date offer you've had since you got here, and you
have no intention of starting anything with anyone here on
the base." First he put the bike in the rear of the jeep, then
inched her into it, and as she sat in rigid silence staring
straight ahead down the road, he walked around, leaped over
the side and behind the wheel, and sent the jeep roaring
toward the crossroads, where he made a sharp left turn.

"We'll go to a pub I know about over in Duxford where
nobody knows us and we won't be interrupted."

But as they passed through a tiny village much like Chipping Epworth, he saw a small but attractive inn by the name
of the Bell nestling at the edge of the road. He stopped the
jeep and took her inside, feeling her resistance as he took her
arm and led her along the path. But he felt more than saw

something else, a quick glance from her in the half darkness, and tightened his hand on her arm.

As they sat at a small table in a darkened tap room, he ordered drinks, then sat back and looked at her over the flame of a lighter as he lit two cigarettes, first one, then the other, and handed one to her.

"You can't force me into something that I don't want to get involved in, Major Gilbert," she blurted out stiffly, avoiding his eyes.

"Doug is the name," he said softly. "And I don't think I have to force you." She was even pretty when she was angry.

"Such conceit," she tried to jeer.

"Not conceit," he said. "It's just something that one recognizes. You meet a hundred, a thousand people, you say hello, how are you, a few you keep as friends, a few more as acquaintances, and most you never even see again. But then one day you meet one. And that's it."

She looked away, then down at her hand holding the glass. If she let go of it, she knew her hand would tremble. She felt the tiny knot inside, fluttering right at the top of her stomach, and something tingled down the length of her spine.

"That's crazy," she said, expecting it to sound amused, with a note of mockery, but it came out a whisper.

"No," he said. "That's the way it is."

Finally she found the courage to look up at him, and for a long moment they looked deeply into each other's eyes. Again she was startled by the deep and probing blue of his eyes and how they seemed to see past everything, into her very thoughts. There was a magnetism about them that almost frightened her, as though she would never be able to look away again, as though she were doomed to live in his eyes forever if she didn't look at someone or something else.

Forcing her head to turn, she gazed about the room, at the dark beams overhead and the tiny panes of narrow mullioned windows at the front, the shuffling old waiter who was putting drinks down on a nearby table.

"You don't understand," she said, as though he had spoken. "And you don't know anything about me."

"I know your husband was lost at Pearl Harbor. And I know you love your work, almost to the point of being neurotic about it." He was smiling as he leaned toward her, and he touched her fingers, which clutched the glass, tracing the edges and sending shivers along her arms. "But then, I love my work too. I'd rather fly than eat or sleep."

172

"No, you don't understand," she said, sounding confused, and suddenly she pushed her chair back and dashed toward the door. He slapped some money down on the table and followed her out into the night.

For several moments they just sat in the jeep, silent, the dark and quiet all around them. She heard crickets and smelled a sweet fragrance on the soft wind, then felt his hand touch her hair and lightly ruffle the curls.

"You don't understand," she said again, and it sounded like a muffled cry. "I don't want to feel again. Feeling hurts. God, how it hurts!"

"Oh, baby," he said softly, pulling her against him, and she quietly wept as he stroked her hair and kissed her tears. Finally pulling away from him, she slowly slid over into the far corner of the jeep. She felt as though she had died and was now coming to life again, and the pain was unbearable.

"Please," she pleaded, "please take me home. I can't—"

He reached over and tipped up her chin and kissed her on the mouth. For a moment she leaned against him, then she sat rigid and straight and looked directly ahead and said it again. "Please."

"Slow and easy," he said, turning on the ignition and looking down at her with a smile that was a promise. "I won't push, much as I want to. We'll go at your pace, whenever, however, wherever."

And for the first time, she smiled a tight little smile as the jeep skidded into the road and headed toward Chipping Epworth.

Each night they met at the Swan, avoiding the pub where the Fortress crews and correspondents hung out. She told him about everything except Christopher. That would come later, if there was to be a later, she thought, and found herself silently praying there would be.

Since she had met him, she had begun to feel the implacable sense of mortality that men face when they suddenly begin to taste the acrid smoke of war and see friends die.

But still, she held him at a distance, unable to take the final step that she knew would carry her past the place of no return. This was no idle flirtation or casual romance. She felt it deep inside. It was painful yet wondrously new and exciting, opening old wounds but filling her with new life. And when he told her about himself, she listened eagerly.

"There wasn't anything very unusual about my life," Doug

173

smiled one evening as he slowly twisted his glass on the small table between them. "I was just a typical, middle-class American kid, I guess, like most of the guys in my outfit. I have two older sisters, both married and with kids, and a younger brother, a father who's a small-town lawyer, and a mother who practically runs one of the local women's clubs singlehanded, and a Model-A Ford from my Rutgers days that's probably rusting in the backyard back in Plainfield, New Jersey, where I grew up. I gave it to my brother when I left college, but he's with the Marines now in the Pacific . . ." His voice dropped and he looked into his glass as though there might be an answer there. "I worry about him. A lot."

Jenny slowly reached out and touched his hand. Quickly looking up, he took her hand in his. But in moments she drew hers away.

That night at the door of Mrs. Barrington's cottage she turned to say good night, but he pulled her into his arms, and before she could move into the doorway, he was holding her close and kissing her. With a breathless little cry she tried to back away, but he held her tight.

"No," he said as she pushed against his chest. "This is something we have to face, baby. We can't keep walking around it, treating it like it doesn't exist."

"No, Doug," she said as she struggled. "Please—please—" She felt the panic rise in her throat. "Everyone, everything I've ever had, I've lost! You—it could happen with you too."

"It could happen with anyone," he said, sounding almost angry. "Especially now. Especially in this war. Everybody's vulnerable, everybody can have it happen without any warning. You're not any different from—"

"No!" she cried, tears sliding down her cheeks, trying to twist out of his arms, but he held her as though in a vise, forced her face up to his, and kissed her hard, and then as her body slowly melted into his he kissed her again with aching tenderness.

"I have a full weekend pass," he whispered into her hair. "Tomorrow night we'll go to London." He kissed her again with an exquisitely slow and searching passion until she was breathless, reeling, clinging to him, not able to get enough of him now. Slowly he pulled away. "Tomorrow night, darling," he said and strode away into the night.

He saw her through the gray dawn, standing high on the deck when his jeep spun past the control tower and down the runway, and he waved. She put her field glasses to her eyes and watched him, then waved wildly as he stepped from the jeep next to the plane. She wanted to roll back the days and nights, relive the time they had lost, while watching him swing up into the plane and out of sight. Moments later the plane's engines exploded into a deafening roar; the *Spirit of Times Square* taxied into position, then flew along the runway and lifted into the sky. She watched until it was a speck in a line of moving specks that finally disappeared over the horizon.

Too excited to sleep the night before, Jenny felt exhausted but elated, tense in the face of the waiting hours ahead but tingling with excitement, remembering his arms, the way he kissed her and touched her breasts, the promise of the two whole days and nights in London. She tried to work in the press cubbyhole, but couldn't concentrate and wandered aimlessly about the somber base. At one point the loudspeakers announced that a film would be shown that night with John Garfield, entitled *Air Force*. She heard a group of men suddenly hoot with laughter and realized that this had been the first sign of life since her arrival that morning, and without a doubt since the Fortresses had taken off. She glanced at her wristwatch and gazed up at the sky once more, then headed for Wayne Parker's office. She would force herself to pound out the story about the tail gunner who painted landscapes in his free time. Perhaps that would help to pass the time, take her mind off the mission he was flying.

"Fighters at six o'clock!" the voice barked in Doug's earphone. Then the tail gunner shouted again, his voice rising to a yell, "The bastards are climbing! Jesus, it looks like the whole goddamn Luftwaffe's coming at us!"

Doug began to curse under his breath. The intercom was crackling with half a dozen voices, everyone shouting at once. "Christ, shut up!" he yelled over and over until finally he could hear only his own voice telling everyone to sit tight. "Give it to me, Jake," he said through the intercom to the tail gunner.

"So far, nothing," he said. "They're just sniffing."

"Keep an eagle eye." The important thing, he kept thinking over and over, was not to break formation. As always, he felt nothing, and sometimes it worried him—no fear, no foreboding, just the incredible tension and the damned little flick in his right eyelid, constant, continuous, flicking and flicking.

"Jesus, Major, there's at least seventy or eighty of them and they're climbing fast." Suddenly he let loose with a long curving yell, like the shrill call of a football crowd in the stands when the cheerleader raises his arms in a long swooping motion. "Here they come!"

Behind him there was a loud explosion, and the ship lurched then rocked, and he heard a scream. He wanted to break formation, but he knew it would be fatal, knew the Focke-Wulfs would swarm over the Fort like jackals leaping on a wounded animal. He held it tight as a steady stream of curse words spilled from his copilot's mouth, almost like a prayer, in a strange and hurried chant.

There was another explosion, then a series of them, and the ship rocked again, battered from both sides as voices yelled and cursed through the intercom. He felt another kind of vibration as their own guns opened up, roaring, spitting tracers into the fighters that whipped past them like unseeing bats, sheering close with that ungodly scream that sent chills down the spine.

The ship shuddered, careening from side to side as the fighters shrieked past. From the corner of his eye he saw a Fort drop from formation and knew it was as good as dead as three Messerschmitts dove with it.

He felt a sudden rush of air and knew the ship had suffered a mortal wound, then braced himself as a long drawn-out tremor shook and jarred the Fort, and in that moment he wondered how it could take all of the punishment it was taking and still remain aloft. If they could just hang on another few minutes, he kept thinking. They were nearing the rendezvous point with their own fighter escort, just another few minutes . . . coming home . . . coming home . . . the phrase kept echoing and re-echoing, and suddenly he knew they had to make it. They had to. Had to.

In that instant he buckled slightly as something hit him with a force that shocked him, even within the greater sense of shock that had possessed him for the past five or six minutes as the plane reeled and staggered through the air. He knew he had been wounded and grabbed at his shoulder. Icy wind was whipping through the cockpit, and it was then he heard the copilot babbling incoherently. As he clutched his own shoulder he glanced at Alec Poynster and saw blood pouring down his face. Suddenly there was another shuddering jolt as a broadside of cannon fire shattered through the side of the

176

Fort, and Doug yelled hoarsely into the throat mike, "Give it to them! Give 'em everything you've got!"

Then miraculously the fighters peeled away one by one, then in twos and threes, and again miraculously Jake, the tail gunner, screamed through the intercom, "I see ours, Major! I see our guys coming. Those big ugly sons-of-bitches Thunderbolts, Major, the prettiest goddamn sight I ever saw."

He sounded as though he was laughing and crying all at once as he kept on shouting into the intercom. Doug shook his head as though to clear it and almost smiled, his lips tight, his teeth clenched in pain. They were going home. Going home! And goddamn it, if he had anything to say about it, they were going to make it, make it all the way to England.

Lighting cigarette after cigarette, one off the other, Jenny kept right on working at the typewriter until about noon, then went up to the deck. Little clusters of men had already started to form, with one cluster near the flagpole, the men leaning or sitting on the concrete base or kneeling on the ground nearby on one knee. All faces kept turning toward the direction where the planes would first appear. There was little conversation. One man, with an olive-drab knit beanie shoved to the back of his head and his hands in his coverall pockets, paced slowly in a circle, kicking at the earth with one toe as he walked. At last she really knew. Oh, how she knew!

"Some of them live the whole thing right along with the ship crews," she had written in a dispatch two days before. "They know, minute by minute, step by step, what their ship and crew is going through, and then the imagination begins to go to work. The ones who have been here the longest have gotten so they almost know where their ship is going to hit the heaviest flak, or what kind of fighter attack they'll get and about where. It's uncanny sometimes, especially when you hear the debriefing reports later on and remember what some ground crew member had said. They seem to have developed a seventh sense about their ships and men."

At a stiffening of movement on the edge of the field and near the flagpole base below her, she looked first at a group of crewmen and then off in the direction where they were watching, hands shading their eyes, bodies tensed. An unearthly kind of silence had descended over the airfield, then piercing through the stillness was a faint drone, gradually growing louder and louder. Straining forward, eyes squinted against the sunlight, Jenny saw something far, far off, the very first dot on the horizon, the lead plane in the formation, a V within a larger V, as the entire group came in sight and flew closer and closer.

No one moved as they watched. She was only vaguely conscious of Wayne Parker and Zeke Raymond climbing the stairs and coming to stand beside her as she began to count. Everyone was counting the small specks that grew larger and larger and began to take shape.

Jenny felt more than heard the gasp that went up, and her hands gripped the railing. One plane, far in the lead of the others but beneath them, was obviously in trouble and coming straight in. Suddenly small rockets spurted from the side of the fuselage, and Lieutenant Parker turned and raced off down the steps. Hearing the scream of a siren, then leaning over the railing to watch as an ambulance hurtled from behind the tower building and out onto the landing field, she realized the rockets had signaled that there were wounded men aboard. Her mouth felt dry and her shaking hands gripped the railing. She had seen crippled planes come in before, but today . . . today it was different. God, how it was different.

As the rest of the formation roared past overhead, the crippled plane lurched in low, just barely clearing the treetops in the distance, its landing gear sliding down stiffly. She was only vaguely aware of the sudden activity below, trucks racing toward the point where it was estimated the plane would stop, men hanging on the sides and shouting, and Zeke, beside her, muttering over and over, "Goddamn, goddamn, goddamn!"

"Can you see the name?" she shouted up at Zeke, but he didn't hear her. She shrieked, "What's the name on the plane?" He still didn't hear her.

As it careened once and then righted and bounced along the runway, the huge Fort appeared at first to be many pieces of grotesquely shattered and burned wreckage loosely held together. As it sheared past, she saw the pilot high up behind the smashed nose, his window glass gone and the skin on the fuselage torn away to reveal the metal ribs. It was only later that she remembered having prayed over and over that it wasn't the *Spirit of Times Square*. As it skidded to a stop she saw that two of the engines were dead and that huge obscene holes gaped along the fuselage, the wings, and the belly; only the tail seemed intact.

Even as the brakes still squealed, men from the ground crew were clambering over and around it, spraying it with hoses as crew members leaped from the hatch, pumping fire extinguishers. Flames spurted from an engine, then exploded in huge dense clouds of black smoke while the rescue squad pulled two men out and ran with them on stretchers to the ambulance.

In a matter of moments, it seemed, the fire was out and the ground crew had returned to their regular posts as the trucks hurried off the field. The rest of the formation had circled and was peeling in one by one to land, one after the other, each roaring past, billows of dust swirling upward and the screaming pitch of sound tearing at her on the sudden gusts of wind.

"Two are missing," Zeke shouted. Then, as the whine of engines sank to a low roar, he said, "And from what I can tell, on that first wreck that came in three or four of the crew must have either parachuted or been blown right out the sides."

Jenny, still straining her eyes at the crippled plane, felt her legs threaten to go out from under her. "What's the name of the plane?" she begged, clutching his arm. For a moment Zeke stared at her, then lifted his field glasses and looked through them. "The *Spirit of Times Square,*" he said, slowly lowering the glasses. "And all I can say is that Gilbert's one helluva pilot." But she was racing down the steps. Zeke hurried across the deck, stopped at the steps, and looked down at her as she ran toward the ambulance. She was halfway across the tarmac when she saw two of the men from the *Spirit*'s crew being helped into the ambulance behind the two stretchers. She then saw a medic close the doors and the ambulance speed away toward the main road. As she stood and watched it, Zeke ran up beside her, out of breath.

"What the hell's going on?"

"Where's the ambulance going, Zeke?" she cried out. Her face was white and taut with fear as she grasped his arm.

He saw the tears sliding down her cheeks. "Come on," he said, grabbing her hand. "I'll commandeer a jeep or something. The hospital's about ten miles from here." They ran back toward the administration building.

Located at the edge of a larger airfield, the field hospital was a series of big Nissen huts, where the wounded were treated on a short-term basis, or given initial aid, then processed through to larger hospitals. Jenny and Zeke pushed their way through the confusion at the main Process Center, where airmen and soldiers stood in long snaking lines, and managed to find a corpsman who told them where to go.

Zeke had to walk with long loping steps to keep up with her as they hurried from one aid station or processing point to another. Jenny darted in and out of several huts to ask questions. The roadway areas were filled with the grinding noise of jeeps and command cars and ambulances, and at one interval planes swooped in to land on the nearby airfield with a thunderous roar. It was an orderly kind of pandemonium, Zeke realized, with ambulances shrieking in and out of the area, and men swarming like bees on the aid stations.

Searching for Doug Gilbert and other crew members of the *Spirit of Times Square* proved almost entirely in vain until they returned to the main hut, where they finally found a clerk behind a desk who told them that Major Gilbert had been taken to an Army hospital just a few miles northwest of London, near High Wycombe.

"It's okay," Zeke said as they piled into the jeep again. "Wayne told me to keep it until tonight if I had to."

It was almost evening by the time they found him. Zeke stopped at the head of the long corridor lined with rows of beds that were separated and surrounded by white screens. "I'll wait for you here," he half whispered, and she nodded, grateful for his discretion.

She turned and walked toward the far end, closing her ears, or trying to, to the low moaning sound that came from one of the beds and rose in pain above the murmur of voices and the soft padding noise of nurses' footsteps as they hurried about.

She stepped through a narrow gap between two screens and stopped, looking down at him. His eyes were closed and his breathing was even. Above the sheet she saw the bandaging over his shoulder. For several moments she stood perfectly still, holding her breath, her eyes wide with fear, then without a sound she moved closer and leaned a little over him. Slowly he opened his eyes, and for a moment they simply looked at each other. Then he reached up and pulled her down to him, and with a small sob she knelt beside him. "I love you," she kept whispering, "I love you . . . love you."

Jenny was just coming out of the administration building when he first saw her. It was late evening, and she had started to swing up onto her bicycle when she stopped and looked at the jeep that had just pulled into the area behind the building. He climbed from the jeep and walked toward her. She watched him as he came closer, her heart pounding. She hadn't seen him since the day he had left the hospital near High Wycombe. He had been taken to Scotland to a recuperation center. But now he was back.

She couldn't move as he came closer and closer. She had waited for this moment and tried to say his name, but it had come without any warning, and she could only watch him, aching to feel his arms around her, longing for the hardness of his body against her. When he reached her, he grasped her and held her close. They stood in the darkness, unmoving and silent, then he kissed her, a kiss that said she was his. Still holding her with one arm and rolling her bike with the other, he led her to the jeep.

"We'll stop and pick up some things for you," he said softly as he started the motor and swerved out of the air station. "You can tell Mrs. Barrington you're going to London for the weekend."

They went to a small inn in Cambridge, where Doug had phoned earlier for accommodations. She tried to eat as they sat over a late supper in the small dining room, but she was too excited. He closed the door of their room and leaned against it, watching her as she walked about the room, running her hands lovingly over the antique chairs and bureau and high canopied bed. She was wearing slim white pumps and a pretty summer dress instead of her uniform.

"I've never seen you like this before," he said, walking toward her and softly ruffling her hair. He lifted the dress away from her and she slipped out of the pumps. In moments she stood before him, naked and lovely, then lay back on the bed as he stripped off his clothing and lay down beside her. Just one light burned dimly in a far corner of the room, turning their skin to a satiny gold.

An August rain tapped softly on the rooftops and against the half-opened window, as gentle and rhythmic as his hands slipping in voluptuous torment over her breasts and along all the curving contours of her body.

He kissed her again and again, her mouth and eyelids, down her throat, and teasingly over her small, firm breasts. Her response was instant in the seeking softness of her mouth, the exquisite pleasure of her hands touching him in light little darting motions. With a groan he moved above her and pressed deeply within; then, as her legs tightly circled him, he pressed harder and harder, pulling her to the peak of their passion, until they fell back and held on to each other, their breath coming in short jabbing gasps. Finally they lay still and close and slept for a while, never moving in each other's arms. When they awakened, they made love again. And when he slept once more, she watched him, her fingers tracing his mouth and trailing down with gentleness to the vivid red scar just below his shoulder.

Finally she too slept, just as the rain started again, and she curved in closely to him as he murmured her name, a smile on his lips.

The following morning he rented a boat at the Magdalene Bridge and they rowed on the River Cam, then wandered through the open air market and on into the King's College Chapel as sunlight flowed through the centuries-old stained glass windows like a celestial revelation.

They finally climbed into the jeep and drove back to Chipping Epworth, circling up through Alconbury where Doug had first been stationed.

"The 482nd Bombardment Group," he said as they drove along Great North Road and stopped in at the Crown for a leisurely drink, oblivious of the crowd, the shouts and laughter, aware only of each other. "I was going to stop and introduce you to some of my old buddies but decided to keep you all to myself."

They were together every moment they could find. Doug took a room at the Swan, and on the nights when he wouldn't be flying the following morning, they slipped through a side door up to the room and stayed until just before dawn, when he would take her back to Mrs. Barrington's.

"I have to tell you about Christopher," she suddenly said into the darkness as they lay against hunched-up pillows on the bed, his arms about her, the tips of their cigarettes glowing.

"Christopher?" he said, momentarily puzzled.

"My little boy," she said, and he heard the pain.

"Baby," he whispered, holding her closer, "you don't have to tell me anything."

There was silence for several moments. "Yes," she said slowly, "I have to tell you. Because, you see . . ." She paused, trying to find the words. "He was taken away from me." She waited again. "I went a little crazy after Alan was killed. I'd lost my job, and that was all I wanted, my job. I hadn't wanted to be married, to have a child. And then suddenly one day I heard that Alan had been killed at Pearl Harbor. All at once nothing mattered. I didn't care about anything. I began to drink too much, hung around this one bar in Greenwich Village. It was a place where a lot of servicemen came, and . . ." She was half crying.

"Baby, baby," he said, stroking her hair, kissing away the tears that slid down her face. "Don't, baby."

"I have to, Doug, I have to. My brother-in-law . . . he came to my apartment and waited for me one night. He'd had detectives following me and—"

"It's all right, Jenny. Don't talk about it anymore. I think I understand what happened. The brother-in-law took your little boy, is that right?"

He slowly put their cigarettes out as she nodded. "If you want to talk about Christopher, Jenny, then I want to listen." He pulled her down onto her back and hovered over her. "But if it's too painful, then just keep remembering, I understand."

"It hurts too much to talk about him," she whispered, pulling him down close to her, her arms about his neck. "It's just that I wanted you to know."

Jenny rarely went to the airfield in the early morning hours of dawn anymore. It was all too close, too frightening to watch Doug's plane taxi down the runway and lift off into the sky. But she always awakened, sat up in her bed, and listened, hearing the great roar of motors as the planes climbed overhead.

But there was something different about this morning as she woke. She turned on her little bedside lamp and looked at her watch. Two a.m. She dressed quickly and stole down the stairs and out of the little cottage, climbed on her bicycle, and pedaled away through the darkness.

She felt more than saw the activity on the field as she parked her bicycle. Moments later, standing on the deck of the control tower building, she turned up her trench coat collar against the fine rain and held on to the railing. The full wing was revving up, trucks and small vehicles tore along the edges of the field delivering crews to their planes, just shadowy shapes and figures in the half light of the misty dawn. She heard the distinctive coughing sound, then the roar of the engines as they caught. As she peered through the soft drizzle, she wondered why this morning seemed different from others. For one thing there was no delay, in spite of the weather.

She looked hard at one of the Fortresses as it wheeled past

to circle and take its place on the runway. She lifted her small field glasses and watched for several moments, at first seeing nothing but the silhouette of the plane and a dark shape in the high window of the cockpit. Then there was a flash of something white, and she caught a glimpse of his hand waving and then his face as his smile flashed. She pulled a handkerchief from her pocket and waved it wildly just as Zeke joined her on the deck.

The plane was moving into the middle of the field, a distant blur in the mist and drizzle, then in moments the great silver bird fled down the airstrip and gracefully lifted off with a flash of wings in the gray morning light above the field, soared above the distant line of trees, and disappeared into the horizon. She watched through a blur of tears as other Fortresses followed, some simply shadowy shapes, still camouflaged with the dark green and earth-colored zigzags of earlier years.

"Something's different today!" she shouted to Zeke above the roar.

"The censorship lid's down tighter than a drum. We can't leave the base until they're back," he shouted back as the planes rose into the air and grew smaller and smaller. "But I hear talk they're on their way to Regensburg, the Messerschmitt factory there, and Schweinfurt. That's where fifty percent of Germany's ball bearings are made."

Regensburg. Her head whipped around.

"That will be the deepest they've gone into Germany, right?" When he nodded, seeing her fear, she asked, "How far can the fighter escort go?"

"Not far enough." He was shaking his head. "They'll get plenty of penetration and withdrawal support, our P-47's and the RAF Spits, but they're sure to hit opposition at the Dutch border, or near Antwerp. And Regensburg's halfway across Bavaria, about fifty-five miles below Nuremburg."

Jenny watched the sky where she had last seen the planes. Then, shoving her hands deep into her coat pockets, she walked down the stairs, went over to the flagpole, and hunched against it, her arms clasped around her knees.

For three days, pedaling back and forth to the base, she waited. Confusion had clouded all communiques. The first announcement of a disastrous loss of aircraft and men had been finally amended when it was learned that many of the three hundred and seventy-six B-17's that flew out from

various bases in England that drizzling morning had continued on to bases in North Africa because of the great distance
to Regensburg.

But as she stood at the window of the day room looking out
across the empty field, she heard Zeke's voice behind her as
he talked to one of the other correspondents. "Sixty Forts,"
she heard him say. "Known losses."

She walked out of the building, climbed on her bicycle, and
pedaled her way toward Chipping Epworth.

Chapter 19

MARIANNE LOOKED AROUND the table, her eyes finally resting on Kate in the soft candlelight. She was puzzled. Kate and Adam's marriage had seemed finished only a matter of months ago, cold but civil boundaries had been drawn by Kate, and Adam spent evening after evening in most of the bars between Brookton and Bridgeport. But now it looked as though everything was all right again. Well, *almost* all right, she thought. There was something there that she couldn't quite put her finger on.

"Well, bring Joanna and come to lunch with me here one day this week," Sarah was saying to Kate from her place at the head of the table. "I miss that precious child when I don't see her."

"I'd love to, Sarah." Kate smiled, her face serene.

"I hate to break this up," Adam said, taking Kate's arm and drawing her to her feet.

"You're right," Reed said, stifling a yawn and looking at his watch. "The last showing of *Watch on the Rhine* starts at nine."

"Well, drive carefully," Jonathan said. "That's a heavy rain out there. Another of our bad summer storms."

"I'll drive," Reed reassured him with an ironic smile toward Adam. "We'll get there in one piece if I do."

As their voices faded in the distance Sarah and Jonathan sat quietly for a moment, Sarah with a guarded but puzzled expression. Jonathan put a cigarette into his holder and carefully lit it. "Nice to see them looking so happy, isn't it?" he said.

Sarah glanced at him sharply, then down again as she poured their coffee from the silver coffee service.

"I suppose you've guessed?" Jonathan said with a slow smile.

"Guessed?"

"The good news. Kate's pregnant. They're going to have a child."

Sarah stared at him, but he was gazing upward at a series of smoke rings that looped lazily toward the ceiling.

"You seem surprised." He took a sip of coffee.

"Surprised?" She recovered quickly. "Well, to tell the truth, Jonathan, I had thought Adam and—that Adam and Kate were having some difficulties."

"Nonsense." Jonathan laughed, waving his cigarette holder. "Early growing pains in their marriage. That's all in the past now, however. And needless to say, they're thrilled about her pregnancy. Well, you saw them just now."

She *had* seen them. It was something of a reversal of what she had seen two months before and of the way Kate had talked the past spring. Well, she thought with some misgivings, Kate had apparently made her peace with the situation. Perhaps the love she'd had for Adam was strong enough to overcome her anger—no, her rage—over what they had done to her.

"Excuse me, Mr. Barnfield." Morgan, in his white coat, stood at the door of the dining room. "Nelson is here with the car, sir."

Sarah said good night to Jonathan, then as she heard the car drive off, she walked up the curving staircase to the sitting room off her bedroom and sat down at her desk. She sat there for a long time, staring at the monogrammed vellum stationery before her on the desk top, then slowly picked up her fountain pen and began to write.

My Dearest Del,

Although we never spoke about it in all the time you were here at home before leaving for overseas, somehow it always hung there between us, unsaid but understood, your feeling for Kate. That's why this is such a painful letter to write. I can't let you go on any longer hoping for something that can never be, something that your letters have only hinted about.

Kate and Adam seem to have overcome whatever unhappiness came into their marriage several months ago. They were here for dinner tonight with Jonathan and Marianne and Reed, and it seems that everything is all right between them. Kate is pregnant, Del. Jonathan is thrilled at the thought of having a grandchild whose name will truly be Barnfield. Adam, naturally, is beside himself with happiness. I won't dwell on this, my dear. But I knew you had to know.

She went on for several pages, telling him news of other things and people, then sorrowfully addressed and sealed the envelope. Though Del had spoken only once of his feelings for Kate, she knew what a deep effect her letter would have on him.

As Kate started up the broad staircase she called good night to Adam and Jonathan, who stood near the door to the library. Hesitating for only a moment as Jonathan called up an invitation to a nightcap, she smiled over the bannister and said, "Thank you, Jonathan, but I have to leave for my ambulance run at six in the morning."

Kate crossed the sitting room to her bedroom and went in and closed the door.

Her thoughts all through dinner at Sarah's and even later during the movie had been filled with Del. His photograph in a silver frame had been on a table with other photographs in the library. She was startled when she'd first seen it. He was wearing his uniform and was smiling into the camera. She had almost forgotten how his eyes laughed with his smile, how much strength there was in his mouth.

She walked slowly over to her dressing table and began to undress, absently throwing her dress and slip over a chair and peeling off her stockings. Then she sat down at the dressing table and with long slow strokes began to brush her dark gold hair.

She remembered back to their last hours in the house at the shore, the long and languorous lovemaking that became more intense as the hours passed and the moment of parting grew near. She thought of how he had touched her, how he had leaned over her as the clock ticked the minutes away, cupping her face with his hands and kissing her.

Kate crawled into bed liking the feel of the sheets against her nakedness, stretching longingly as she turned off the bedside lamp and stared up into the darkness as the night closed over her.

Del, she thought, where are you, Del? Wherever he was, it was far, far away. Jenny had seen him in England, but then what? Where had he gone from there? She turned face down, felt her breath in warm, feathery little spurts against the skin of her shoulder, closed her eyes tightly against the pale glow of moonlight that patched the carpet beneath the french windows. She tried to remember how it had felt, Del's hands on her flesh, his mouth on hers . . . but he was so far away, in a place she knew nothing about . . . and his child would be a . . . Barnfield. It would always be a Barnfield, she thought in lucid moments that came and then drifted away as sleep stole through her, weighting her eyelids, pushing consciousness farther and farther away.

Murmuring, she rolled to her side, then felt his warmth first and murmured again. As his hands slipped down her body, she drowsily moved closer, opening herself to the skillful caresses, hands that knew her, knew her so well, all the places to touch, mouth kissing her, tongue probing, gently at first then with a demanding ardor, and she, Kate, responding, wanting more, curving to him, moving in a rhythmic motion until they were like one person, their bodies drinking desperately of each other.

At what moment she knew it was Adam, she wasn't sure. She had come fully awake as he entered her, but she was engulfed in a wave of passion as sensation and desire flowed back into her like a rushing stream. For one brief, fleeting second she thought . . . no . . . no. But his mouth closed over hers again, and she felt his life leap within her; there was a roaring in her ears and her head reeled. Slowly reason returned, and she pushed away from him, but he held her tight in his arms.

"Kate," he whispered. "God, Kate, how I've missed you—"

"No, Adam," she cried out softly, pushing farther away from him and swinging her legs to the floor. She caught her breath, forcing back the panic, and in one quick, softly rustling move, ran across the darkened room to her dressing room and bath and locked the door behind her. She slipped down to the floor, hands pressed to her mouth in shock.

"Kate?" he called through the door.

"No, Adam—please—please just go away. I—I'm sorry. But it's something that shouldn't have happened."

There was a long, long silence. Straining her ear against the door frame, she listened. When she finally heard the door on the far side of her room open and close, she put her head down on her arms and wept.

Chapter 20

"WAIT HERE," ADAM said curtly as Kate stood in the wide entrance hall, smoothing on her long white kid gloves. "I'll be back in a few minutes with the car." As he buttoned his black chesterfield, he started toward the door, his handsome face sullen.

"Phone the garage, Adam," Jonathan said as he paused near the staircase. "Nelson can bring it around. It's sleeting out there."

"I need the air," Adam said, closing the door behind him.

For a moment neither of them spoke, then Jonathan walked over to her, took the sable coat from her arm, and helped her into it. "What's happening, Kate?" Jonathan asked, sounding bewildered. "For a while there, through the summer, everything seemed to be all right again with you two after that first—first misunderstanding."

Kate winced inside. Jonathan honestly believed she had forgiven them. "As right as it will ever be, Jonathan," she said with a weariness of spirit.

"I don't understand." He was watching her as she walked over to the long refectory table against the wall, where she picked up the small beaded evening purse and took out a lipstick and small mirror and retouched her mouth. He didn't think he had ever seen her looking so beautiful, the long green velvet gown so ingeniously designed that one would have to look intently to see that she was pregnant. She was wearing the diamond necklace and earrings he had given her for her birthday, and he remembered how she had protested when she opened the gift. Slowly she turned and looked at him. Her lovely face was filled with sadness.

"Please don't try, Jonathan," she said softly.

At that moment the door burst open, and Marianne, glittering in bright silver lamé and a long white fox cape, rushed in.

"Just wanted to make sure you didn't change your mind and decide to stay home, Kate." She crossed to her father and kissed his cheek.

"I'd never do that, Marianne," Kate said warmly as Marianne linked her arm through Kate's and drew her toward the door. "After all the work you've done on this dinner dance?"

Jonathan slowly followed them. "Kate tells me you even have a kissing booth set up where you're going to sell war bonds and stamps," he said, appalled. "With daughters of members selling kisses."

"Don't look so distressed, Father," Marianne said, laughing, as they turned at the door. "*All* the country clubs are doing it when they hold these war bond parties. It's wonderful. Every old fool who ever thought about cheating on his wife gets a quick little thrill this way, and legitimately, and all it costs him is eighteen dollars and seventy-five cents. Then he goes home and dreams."

Jonathan's eyes rolled toward the ceiling as he spread his hands helplessly. "You have such a delicate way of putting things, Marianne." But he smiled and waved them off as they went out the door to where Reed was waiting in his car under the porte-cochere.

"Adam's gone for his car, Marianne," Jonathan called out as he waved, then closed the heavy oak door.

All laughter gone, Marianne turned to Kate while Reed watched them with curiosity from inside the car. "Adam roared past just as we drove up and called out that we should bring you with us, that he has an errand to run." She peered closely at Kate in the dim light. "Things're still pretty bad, eh?" When Kate nodded, she asked, "Still drinking a lot?" Reed was racing the motor in annoyance.

"At times it's dreadful, Marianne," Kate confessed as they walked slowly toward the car's open door. "Thank God Jonathan isn't aware of how bad everything really is. He'd be sick at heart."

"More women?" Marianne spaced the two words carefully.

"I had two anonymous phone calls this week alone," Kate said sadly. They paused several feet from the car. Kate laughed, a sad, empty little laugh. "It's funny, almost. Because it . . . bothers me. I hadn't thought anything like that would, but then I remember that I loved Adam once. Very much. And there are times when he's . . . trying very hard to be sweet"—she was finding it difficult to speak—"that

191

I almost—" She shook her head, as though to rid herself of the thought and, taking Marianne's arm, walked on to the car. "We should hurry, Marianne."

"Well, it's about time," Reed complained as they climbed into the car and shut the doors. "I'm wasting gas stamps, sitting here."

The evening was half over before Kate spotted Adam, his blond head and elegant figure towering above the crowd in his dinner clothes. She was sitting at their table at the edge of the dance floor between Reed and Dean Cliborn, leaning across Dean to say something to his wife, Amy, when she saw him. Dean and Amy were old friends of Marianne and Adam, and both of them followed her eyes nervously, seeing him at the exact same moment that she did.

"I'd like to punch him," Marianne said between clenched teeth while reaching across the table and clasping Kate's hand.

"Really, Marianne," Reed said in his bored tone. "The things you say about your devoted brother."

"Please, Reed," Marianne said acidly. "Don't play any of your vicious little games tonight." But Reed was watching Kate in obvious amusement as he casually lit a cigarette, the match flaring to catch a glint of mockery and pleasure in his eyes. Kate glanced at him distractedly. He was actually enjoying this, she thought, welcoming these confrontations. Anything to anger or annoy Marianne, anything to add tension and unpleasantness to their marriage. She wondered if Marianne had ever really loved him, or if it had been one of those marriages where two young, attractive people from socially prominent families did what was expected of them.

"Well, *here's* my lovely wife." She looked up to see Adam with an almost empty highball glass in his hand. A stray lock of blond hair on his forehead and the dilation of his pupils revealed how much he had had to drink. "How about it, lovely wife? Shall we dance?" He took her hand and tugged at it.

"Please, Adam," she said in a low voice, pulling her hand away. He sat suddenly in the chair beside her and raised his glass in a mocking toast. "To our marriage," he said loudly, then drained the liquor in it. "As full and rewarding as this glass."

His thin face anxious, Dean took hold of Adam's arm and

tried to pull him from the chair. It was evident to everyone now that Adam was very drunk. "Come along, old chum," Dean said, peering through horn-rimmed glasses. "Let's step outside for some air."

But Adam flung Dean away from him and suddenly leaped to his feet. He sidestepped Dean and grabbed a pretty young waitress with long dark hair who was just passing them. As her tray clattered onto the table, Adam swung her out onto the dance floor. Movement in that part of the crowded, candlelit dining room seemed to stop while all heads turned toward them as the music throbbed on. Kate stared at the huge lighted Christmas tree opposite the bandstand, then shut her eyes tight. Adam and the girl were whirling wildly when she opened her eyes and, as though mesmerized, she watched them. She suddenly felt Marianne's hands on her shoulders as the girl's laughter rang out.

In that stricken moment she saw Amy's pretty little face staring in shock, Reed's half-amused, half-surprised smile, and Dean suddenly moving forward as he said, "I'll get him."

"No." Kate grasped his wrist. Hearing the low agony in her voice, he turned and looked down at her. "Please don't do anything," she begged.

As they watched, Adam pulled the laughing girl from the dance floor and in moments they disappeared through the crowd of dancing couples toward the direction of the central lounge.

For a moment a few people glanced at Kate, then started dancing again, and the room around her fell back into its normal pattern. She waited one long agonizing moment, then stood up.

"He's just had a little too much to drink, Kate," Dean said lamely. "If you want me to, I'll find him and take him home."

Kate merely shook her head, smiling her gratitude. She turned to Reed and Marianne and said quietly, "Please tell Adam that I'm taking the car, and I'll send Nelson back for him." As Marianne made a move with her, Kate stopped her. "No, your place is here, Marianne. And I want to go alone."

They watched her hurry away.

Kate walked away from the long sweeping curve of the clubhouse toward where the Packard was parked in a row of shining cars. As she reached the car and opened her small beaded handbag, she remembered that she hadn't brought

193

her set of car keys; she had dropped them back on the dressing table because of the bulge they caused in her tiny purse.

She started back toward the clubhouse to phone for Nelson. But as she thought of the brightly glittering chandeliers in the lobby, the crowds of friends and acquaintances and strangers, and even the possibility of seeing Adam and the girl again, she recoiled at the idea of returning. She turned slowly and climbed into the rear seat of the Packard, where she wouldn't be seen by anyone coming to their cars.

It was several moments before she realized how hard she was trembling. But after a time the trembling stopped, and she felt a wave of despair, and utter futility as she silently admitted how hopeless and empty her marriage had become. As she pulled the fur robe over her knees, she huddled down into her coat, trying not to remember what had happened. But in minute and horrifying detail the pictures filed through her mind: the girl's laughing face, the way they whirled crazily across the dance floor, crashing into other dancers, Adam's face wild with laughter. And then . . . suddenly leaving.

She knew where he had been leading the girl. Everyone else knows, too, she thought, her face flushing in the darkness. He would take her down to the men's locker room. And though it was strictly against the rules of the club, no one would try to stop him or do anything about it, because he was Jonathan Barnfield's son.

He kept liquor in his locker and would ply the little waitress with drinks. Oh, she knew the scenario. He had boasted about it to her one night when he had returned late with lipstick on his face and collar and found her in the library still reading. She had fled to her room, not wanting to hear the details, but had heard enough before she could get past him and out the door. He had half followed her, shouting, "Well, what do you expect me to do? *You* won't sleep with me! Not since that one night when—"

She shuddered, then looked off toward the clubhouse. It would probably be another hour or so before Adam would come to the car . . . through with the little waitress. She shuddered again and drew down even farther into her warm coat. When he came to the car, she would be outside of it waiting for him, would take the keys from him, and drive them home. But if he insisted on driving, she would have to go back to the club and find Marianne or call Nelson.

Fifteen minutes . . . perhaps half an hour passed. She

wasn't sure, she thought, stretching stiffly. She had been dozing, and something, a jolt and then laughter, had wakened her, pulling her from the shrouded folds of sleep. Fighting to the surface, she heard a motor starting, car doors slam shut, and felt a sudden lurching motion before the wheels screeched on the gravel below.

Coming awake with a terrifying clarity, she realized that she was in the rear seat of a car that was roaring onto the main road and skidding from side to side, with Adam behind the wheel and a hysterically laughing girl in the seat beside him. As she clutched at the strap hanging at the edge of the side window, Kate saw the girl pushing a bottle toward Adam. She watched in horror as he held the bottle up, trying to drink from it.

Kate opened her mouth to call out to him, but instead she heard herself scream. The unearthly sound blended with a sudden scream from the girl as the car slid sideways around a curve. Its wheels shrieked across the pavement in a tearing, high-pitched series of screeches that ended with Kate sliding into oblivion just as the car split and exploded with a roar and daylight flash of white light. For a brief second sounds, now far off and muffled, reverberated like rolls of low thunder . . . and then there was nothing, just blackness and silence, and she softly sank down.

Chapter 21

Liz AND DAN were married at the Crawfords' house in Englewood just three days after Christmas. They spent the New Year holidays at the Crawford ski chalet in Vermont, Liz reassured by Evelyn Crawford and Dan that Kate had been unable to attend the ceremony because of her pregnancy and some complications in the final months.

"Don't tell her what has happened, Dan, not until later," a shaken Evelyn counseled after the long-distance phone call from Marianne Shaw. "She'd be devastated."

It was a brief ceremony, with just the Crawfords; their son, Robert, home from Dartmouth for the holidays; Jeanne Starrett, who had arrived with Liz the night before; and Axel and Helen Berglund.

"What kind of a bride *are* you?" Axel teased at the festive champagne luncheon following the ceremony. "Going off to the West Coast just five days after your marriage."

"They wouldn't take no for an answer," Dan said proudly. "DeMille insists he wants her for this particular role. She wasn't going to accept it, but I told her she should. A starring role on the *Lux Radio Theater* is too important."

"That's quite an honor for a relatively unknown radio actress," Hack said, raising his glass of champagne across the centerpiece of orchids. "You'll be right up there with the Dietrichs and Stanwycks and Colberts and Loys." And then he jovially warned her, "Just so long as you don't stay."

"I'll be back before the following weekend," Liz said with a quick smile at Dan.

"She has a reservation on the Superchief for Tuesday," Dan said. "The day after the broadcast. And it took some arm-twisting to get that. With government priorities taking all commercial airline seats for the war's duration, and sometimes months of waiting for train reservations—well, it wasn't easy."

Julie had been taken to her grandparents in Larchmont, with a kind of cold truce effected between Liz and her father. Only the thought of her separation from Julie and Kate's absence from the wedding cast a shadow over the day for Liz. But as she raced to Dan's car in a shower of confetti and rice, her hand in his, Evelyn thought she had never looked more beautiful or more happy. They all stood on the snow-cleared terraced steps, watching and laughing as Dan helped her into the car; then, with a flat manila package in his hand that he had taken from the car, he turned to Hack, who ran down the steps toward him.

"Here it is, Hack," Dan said solemnly, his face suddenly serious, even anxious.

"Your play?" Hack asked. And when Dan nodded, he said, "By God, you did it." Then he gripped Dan's hand and laughed softly. "Don't look so worried. Knowing your work, it has to be tremendous."

And as the car drove down the long circular driveway, Hack looked at the manila envelope in his hand and murmured to Evelyn, "Now if he'd just concentrate on his career and stop going off half cocked on trying to get into the OSS, he'd be all right."

"Darling," Evelyn said softly, putting her hand through his arm and pulling him back into the house, "don't forget how you admired those strong principles and causes. That's why Dan is going to be a fine playwright someday. And if he were any different kind of man, it would be a different kind of talent. Or no talent at all."

"You are so damned smart," he said, ruffling her hair.

"Well, isn't that *really* why you married me?" she said, laughing, as she took his arm and pulled him back into the house.

Liz tiptoed into the shadowy room. At first Kate didn't hear her. She was staring up at the white ceiling from her hospital bed, traction cables looming above her, casts on an arm and leg from the hip all the way down.

"Kate?" Liz said softly, walking across to the bed.

Turning, Kate saw Liz and her eyes filled with tears. "What are *you* doing here?" she asked, putting one hand out. "You're supposed to be on your honeymoon." She grasped Liz's hand tightly. Liz bent over and kissed her on the cheek, then pulled a chair close and sat down, pushing off her fur coat.

"Actually I'm on my way to the coast to do the *Lux Radio Theater* show," she said, her face radiant beneath the small blue cloche. "Dan refused to let me turn it down. It's such a prestige show, you know."

"Oh, Liz, how wonderful!" A smile flooded the thin white face. "And the honeymoon?"

"Five beautiful, unbelievable days in Vermont," Liz said dreamily. "It was absolute perfection. So much so that . . ." Her face clouded. ". . . at times I felt a little guilty, Kate."

"No," Kate said sharply. "You mustn't. Your life with Bill was a different time in your life. It has nothing to do with now. And *you're* different, Liz."

"I know." She was nodding her head slowly. "I feel very different. So much has happened. It's bewildering, in a way." She shook her head. "Why, I make more money in two months than my father makes in a whole year."

"Well, ministers aren't noted for being overpaid," Kate said dryly, half raising herself to light a cigarette.

"And every week it seems there's another offer for programs, actually more than I can take. And Hack has started talking about a play. Imagine!" She seemed stunned simply at the thought. "A Broadway play!"

"I'm not surprised," Kate said admiringly. "You're *so* talented, Liz. You're going to go very far as an actress." She smiled softly and squeezed her friend's hand. "A lot of people are talented, but few are gifted." When Liz laughed with embarrassment, Kate shook her head. "Learn to accept it, Liz. That part of it is very important."

Liz smiled. "But I didn't come here to talk about me. I came to see you. I didn't know anything about this until last night, when Dan told me"—she proceeded carefully—"told me about the accident, and the baby. Is the baby all right?" she asked anxiously.

"He's fine," Kate smiled sadly. "They took him immediately by cesarean section, and he'll be in an incubator for a few weeks." She looked toward the window. "Would you raise the shade, Liz? It's so dark in here." When Liz walked back to the bed and sat down again, Kate pushed the pillow higher behind her head and in the long silence stared at the window. "He's not Adam's child, Liz."

For a moment there was utter quiet, then Liz nodded slowly. "Whatever it was that happened, Kate, I understand."

"If . . . Adam hadn't been killed in the accident, I probably would never have told anyone." She looked quickly at her friend. "Not even you or Jenny, Liz. But with Adam gone, everything is different now." She stubbed her cigarette out in the ashtray beside her and in moments distractedly lit another. "Adam made it very clear, when I told him the baby wasn't his, that it would be a Barnfield and he would never let him go. That meant, of course . . . that whatever Del and I had had together was gone."

"Del? Isn't he—?"

"Yes, Adam's cousin. He's a fighter pilot. Somewhere in the European Theater. Jenny wrote that she met him one day quite by accident at Bushy Park, the Air Force headquarters over there."

"Well, then, perhaps when he comes back—"

Kate nodded slowly. "Perhaps." Her voice was soft, far away. She kept looking out the window as though the answers were there. "War changes everything, changes us. I thought I loved Adam. He was like a part of my youth I'd never known, exciting and so much fun, something I'd never known very much about. And then when I found out why he'd married me, I despised him, even though I knew that in his own very selfish way, he cared for me. But there were times"—she looked at Liz, confused—"times when I wanted him to make love to me, Liz. Can you understand that?"

"Yes," Liz said thoughtfully. "If you loved someone, thought you did, everything just doesn't simply disappear overnight."

"I *did* let him make love to me, Liz," she said, her voice breaking. "Even after Del—even after I was pregnant with Jon—"

Liz leaned over and held Kate for several moments, then took a hanky from her purse and gently wiped the tears from Kate's cheeks.

"And yet . . . I'm in love with Del." She looked around at Liz, and her eyes shone. "He's quiet, in a way that makes you feel warm, safe, and"—her voice softened—"and beautiful. There's something about him, an intensity of feeling, the way he looks at me, as though I'm the only person in a room that's filled with people. We sat and talked for hours, never bored, never tired of listening to each other. And now"—she looked away—"having his child—"

"That's what I want, Kate," Liz said softly. "Another child."

Kate looked at her closely. "And Dan?"

"Well, he wants us to wait. He said we need more time together, time to learn how to be a family. He adores Julie and wants her to grow to feel the same way about him before she has to begin sharing with another child."

"That makes great sense," Kate said. "He's being very wise."

"But I want *his* child," Liz said wistfully.

"Plenty of time, Liz dear," Kate said with a soft smile.

"He also said we need the time to get our careers to a point where another baby would then make sense."

Kate nodded. "Maybe he's right. There's a place one reaches in a career where *nothing* can stop it."

Liz nodded. "Of course. And you're both right. I know it's probably foolish, but I'd be willing to take the chance now." When Kate smiled, Liz reached out and put a hand on hers. "You wanted this baby very much, didn't you?"

"More than anything in my life, I think," Kate said. "We had such a short time together, Liz. And yet it was so full, so completely satisfying in every way. Perhaps that was because we knew we only had those two weeks and only a few hours of each day that we saw each other. We had so much to tell each other. He told me all about his parents, from the time when he was just a little boy, all the wonderful times they had together, and how he cried, night after night in his bed, after their deaths. But his grandmother, Sarah Wheeler, raised him like he was her own child, and he adores her."

She stopped to shift her weight in the bed just a fraction of an inch, her face twisting in pain, while Liz leaned forward to help. "It's all right," Kate said, gasping a little and closing her eyes for a moment until the pain eased. "The doctor said the pain will lessen each day." She paused for a long moment, then looked at Liz. "I named him Jon." She laughed with a touch of bitterness. "I'm stubborn, I guess. Jonathan had named him, told them he was to be Jonathan Adam Barnfield the Third. I crossed it out on the form for the birth certificate and wrote in simply 'Jon.'"

Liz smiled and touched Kate's hand again. "And Del knows nothing? That it's his child?"

"Nothing," Kate said, her lips tightening.

Reluctantly Liz looked at her wristwatch and rose beside the bed. "My train leaves at six." She looked at Kate anxiously. "You're certain you're going to be all right?"

Kate nodded, smiling sadly, then shook her head. "Poor Adam. Born to the wrong father. Born at the wrong time. If he'd been born ten years later, no one would have to have known how frightened he was." She shook her head, her face reliving the horror of that night. "And dying that way. Oh Liz, no one should die that way . . . he and that poor girl . . ." Liz leaned down and held her.

"Thank God you *are* all right, Kate." She pulled back a little. "You're going to be, aren't you?"

"Eventually." Kate smiled. "With the help of a wheelchair for a while, then the doctors say I'll be as good as new. Almost."

For several moments Liz held her close, then kissed her on the cheek. As she walked to the door she said, "Dan is waiting down in the lobby. They'd only let one of us up to see you. But he sends his love."

At the door she stopped, and Kate lifted her one free hand to wave. "I'll listen to the broadcast," she said. "And have a good trip. I'm so terribly proud of you."

Liz threw her a kiss from the door. "I'll come to see you just as soon as I get back from the coast."

Kate listened to Liz's footsteps as they disappeared down the long corridor. Then the sounds of the hospital closed in on her once more; the softly chiming bells, the distant voices calling out in pain, the padded shoes of the nurses as they hurried about, a baby's faraway wail.

Jon, she thought, starting forward a little, then she sank back and smiled sadly. She had seen him only three times. She was not in the maternity section of the hospital, so they had only brought him to her late at night when all visitors were gone. But she had seen that he was healthy and beautiful, a strong baby with a lusty cry and fine long legs. She saw a strong resemblance to Joanna in him, and yet there was something very much of his own in his face. Something . . . of Del, perhaps. If only Del could know, she thought. If only there were some way. . . . No, she'd have to wait until he came back. Then perhaps they could start a whole new life together. And until then she had Joanna, and now Jon.

Another child, Liz had said. Closing her eyes, Kate drowsily wondered if it would ever happen. She and Dan had chosen radio and the theater, with all of its fickleness and uncertain future. Poor Liz, she thought, a nineteenth-century woman in a twentieth-century world.

Liz clung to him as they heard a distant "All aboard!" from the conductor out on the platform. They were standing in her drawing room on the Commodore Vanderbilt, the fragrance of her perfume in the softly lit compartment already making it her domain.

"No more separations after this one, Dan," she was saying. "Please."

Dan held her closer, his lips tightening. "Honey, you can't ask that. Things happen—" They heard the "All aboard" again. He kissed her, a long, hard kiss, then pulled her arms from around his neck. "I have to get off, darling," he said, softly laughing as he untangled himself.

She threw him a kiss as he ran out the door, then pressed her face against the window until she saw him standing on the platform as the train began to move. Smiling and waving, she ached inside, missing him already. What had he meant? "Things happen."

"Good-bye, darling," she cried out, knowing he couldn't hear her but could see her lips moving. As they waved and waved the train moved faster, Dan walking along beside it but losing ground as the train outdistanced him. When she could no longer see him, she sat close to the window long after the train had come out of the tunnel on upper Park Avenue and roared along the tracks above street level.

Dan stood for a moment on the empty platform, watching the small red taillight on the observation platform of the last car as the train disappeared down the tunnel. Then he hurried through the rotunda and collected a small overnight bag he had left in a locker and took a taxi to Pennsylvania Station, where he caught a train to Washington. Though he had accepted the fact that no branch of the military service would take him because of his leg injuries, he stubbornly persisted.

He always hoped there might be a chance with the Office of Strategic Services. He felt somewhat sheepish as he boarded the Congressional Limited, justifying not having told Liz about his trip by reassuring himself that he was protecting her. She was terrified that Colonel Donovan would take him on as an OSS agent. Why upset her? he thought.

As the train sped down through the New Jersey countryside, he remembered some unwelcome advice a top OSS official had given him. "That radio script you wrote on the Commandos at Dieppe probably sold more war bonds than half of the rallies put together. Stick with it."

But Dan refused to give up. A friend of his who had left the Flying Tigers to join the OSS in Burma, helping to lead guerrillas against the Japanese, had stopped over in New York for a few hours the week before Dan and Liz were married. Dan had met him for lunch at Baba Neshan on Twenty-ninth Street.

"I didn't realize how much I'd missed this good Armenian food," Lou Arturian had said, his eyes sparkling as he raised his glass of wine in a toast to friendship. "And good friends," he added warmly. At Dan's persistent, questioning look he finally put his glass down, carefully looked around, and in a low voice said, "All right. If there's one person who'll keep his mouth shut, it's you. I'm going to England, Dan." He took a long sip of his wine and looked around the restaurant with its crowded tables and rich fragrance of Eastern spices and coffee. "I can't tell you much more than that. I wish I could." .

Dan had nodded, then looked away. The excitement in his friend's eyes was almost too much to bear. It told Dan that Lou was going on to some exciting and remarkable experience. He read it in Lou's eyes, heard it in the undertones of his voice, and recognized it for what it *really* was. The love of adventure was strong in both Lou Arturian and Dan Coleman, but it was more than that. It was love of country too. Lou's parents and Dan's father had come to America as immigrants, then planted their roots deeply in its soil. They had taught their children to love their country and then showed them that love and loyalty and devotion by example. Lou had learned it on the Lower East Side of New York, and Dan had learned it in a poor neighborhood on the west side of Chicago. And now Dan wanted desperately to serve his country, and in the way that appealed to him most, as a member of one of its intelligence units behind the lines in Europe.

He knew the terrible risks and knew that life was even more precious now that he had Liz, now that he had discovered how much he really loved her. But the streak of adventure and love of country was strong—strong enough to make him persist even when he knew it was hopeless.

Don Quixote, he thought bitterly with a silent laugh, with a bum leg!

"I wish I could tell you the whole deal," Lou was saying, pulling him back to the dark-paneled restaurant with its bustling waiters and bright, laughing voices.

Dan nodded again. He knew *something* of the OSS operations. Three-man teams would undoubtedly be parachuted into France and Belgium to help equip and organize members of the Resistance groups in preparation for the invasion. This was obviously where Lou was headed.

"I want to get into it, Lou," Dan said, speaking in a low rush.

"Look, fella," Lou said softly. "We always leveled with each other, so I won't stop now. With that leg of yours—"

"It's as good as new! You've seen me walk. I don't even limp."

"Sure, and that's fine. But for the kind of jobs I'm going to be involved in, it wouldn't work, Dan. That leg of yours would never make it. I don't have to tell you what's involved, what you'd have to expect of yourself."

Dan had looked across the restaurant for a long moment, then slowly nodded his head. "I know." There was a sad twist to his smile. "Well, I can dream, can't I? Hell, there must be *some* job they can give me that will get me over there."

The trip beyond Chicago and on to the West Coast was Liz's first. When she wasn't studying her script, she was watching from her compartment window as the snow-covered wheat and corn fields, the rivers and mountains, unfolded before her. All across the midwestern plains she marveled at the flatness of the land and the straight low line where it met the sky, with only a windmill or a silo or a square farmhouse to cut the evenness of the horizon. Then she watched as the foothills rose in gentle swells to meet the soaring mountains, finding an excitement in the unexpected—the sudden rushing of a river or a waterfall as it cascaded down a mountainside or through a valley. And then came the rich warm colors of the canyons and the desert of the deep Southwest, the awesome drama of their silence, the wide bowllike sky that yawned above them in an intense and flawless blue.

But even all of this didn't prepare her for the splashing bright sunshine of southern California, pouring like liquid gold through the valleys and across the hills. A uniformed chauffeur met her train, and while a redcap carried her luggage, the chauffeur led her through the cavernous Union Station. Plunging through the swiftly moving crowds, she followed him along the edge of the long flower-filled patio where on the opposite side an endless column of young soldiers marched toward the train tracks, past long rows of hundreds of poinsettias cutting a brilliant path of blood red down the center.

"Headed for an infantry replacement training camp somewhere in Texas," the chauffeur muttered. "And active combat next."

Shaking the somber mood of that encounter from her thoughts, she watched from the window of the limousine as it sped toward Beverly Hills. It was all so different from New York and the East, she thought, the miles and miles of space and the golden sunshine, the tall, waving palm trees and houses like carelessly scattered bon-bons, all shades, every pastel color imaginable.

Her bungalow at the Beverly Hills Hotel was set down in a garden of poinsettias, jacarandas, palms, and hibiscus. There was a fragrance of gardenia everywhere and soft music in the distance.

She and Dan must come here sometime, she thought, as a waiter wheeled a white-clothed table with her lunch into the bungalow and lifted the silver covers from the dishes. The rooms were filled with sunlight and flowery prints, with casual luxury, and from her windows she could see the sparkling swimming pool. When she had bathed and dressed, she called for the car, feeling the excitement mount. Her first rehearsal was that afternoon. She ran her eyes down the schedule that had been left at the hotel desk along with a copy of the script for her and read that there was another rehearsal scheduled for the following day, Friday, at noon, and a third on Saturday. Sunday she would have to herself, then on Monday there would be two dress rehearsals before the evening performance at the Music Box Theater on Hollywood Boulevard. She knew that Lionel Barrymore was the star of the show and looked forward to their meeting with nervous anticipation.

She arrived at the broadcasting studio feeling that familiar flutter of excitement, only this time more so. This time she knew *no* one. But she needn't have worried. Actress Lurene Tuttle, a regular on the show, introduced her to everyone. As always, her nervousness completely disappeared when the first reading started and she became involved in the role and the script, and at the conclusion Mr. Barrymore led the cast in a round of applause for her performance.

"You have a wonderful quality," the actor said. "Coming from that mysterious wellspring inside we actors all like to think we possess, where the talent takes over and the actress is merely the instrument. I mean that as a compliment, my dear," he chuckled.

"And quite the nicest I've ever had," she said, smiling at him. "Coming from you, Mr. Barrymore."

On Sunday there was no rehearsal scheduled, so she put on a pale blue bathing suit, threw a white beach robe over her shoulders, and went to the pool. After swimming several lengths in a long and graceful breast stroke, she slipped down onto a striped lounge chair, pulled off her cap, and lay back with her eyes closed, only drowsily aware of the shouts of youngsters and the splashing water from swimmers diving into the pool.

"Miss Lowndes?" She opened her eyes and looked up. "My apologies for disturbing you," he said. "But I stopped at the desk, and they called your bungalow, then said you might be here."

"That's perfectly all right," she said, gesturing him to a bright canvas chair near her. He was middle-aged, with close-cropped curly gray hair and a sun-bronzed face, and wore white sneakers, a pair of white trousers, and a pale yellow sports shirt. "You look familiar," she said, then realized she had seen him once or twice at rehearsals. "Oh yes, at the broadcasting studio."

"I'm Jim Ganz," he said, shaking her hand then sitting down. "I took the liberty of ordering us each a nice tall cool lemonade." He smiled. "You look like the lemonade type. And out here that's good." He laughed as a waiter put their drinks down on a small white table between them. "Too many look like the martini type." He paused. "I was telling Mr. Goldwyn about you."

"Samuel Goldwyn?" she asked with a slight gasp.

"Shhh," he laughed. "You're not supposed to be impressed out here. I'm a talent scout with the Goldwyn Studios. The assistant director on the *Lux* show told me about you right after your first reading, so I went over on Friday and heard you, then told Mr. Goldwyn about you. We'd like you to take a screen test."

She stared at him. "A screen test? Are you serious?"

"Perfectly," he said.

"But I'm a radio actress, not even a stage performer, Mr. Ganz—"

"Okay, sure, I understand what you're trying to say"—he grinned—"that you've had no experience in films, not even the stage. Oh, I've done some careful checking on you, Miss Lowndes. But what I noticed was the natural but most unusual quality of your acting. You happen to be very gifted. You have that something that sets you apart, that's very hard to define, a quality that I think is going to make you a very famous actress someday. You've got the gift."

Liz simply looked at him for a long time. Then she laughed a bit shakily. "You *are* serious, aren't you?"

"You bet." He stood up, smiling. "You've got it, Miss Lowndes. I'll stake my job on that." And he walked away, waving.

She'd read about how most screen tests never materialized into anything but shattered dreams. With her it wouldn't matter. She had her career back East. But if . . . something should come of it, she thought as she climbed into the car the following morning, they could move to California. Dan could do his writing from here. That was the wonderful thing about being a writer. He could do it anywhere. And Jim Ganz had said something about Dan writing for films.

"I was just married, Mr. Ganz," she had said. "Ten days ago."

"I know." He had smiled again. "I checked that too. I know all about Dan Coleman. Brilliant writer. Did the Dieppe script, and the one about flying the Hump, over the Himalaya Mountains, to keep an air route between China and India open. Men like your husband usually sign excellent contracts out here."

As she rode along in the rear of the limousine in the bright California sunshine, she felt a sudden chill come over her. Dan would hate living here. He loved New York, the noise and crowds and wild pace. The chill clung, even as she entered the Goldwyn Studios soundstage and sat on the side watching the test director shout at two of the studio grips who had been pushing a heavy dolly with a camera mounted on it. The huge soundstage seemed to be in a state of siege, in constant motion with dozens of people running about until the director shouted through a megaphone and quiet settled over everything.

She did a scene from *A Doll's House,* playing the role of Nora, a role she had secretly loved as a teenager when she read it in school, hiding the copy from her father beneath her mattress. Though her teachers approved of Ibsen, her father did not.

"Wonderful job, Miss Lowndes," Jim Ganz said, walking

toward her with a smile and taking her arm to lead her back to her car. "A bit on the hasty side, but certainly it will give Mr. Goldwyn an idea of what you look like on film. You're extremely photogenic, I'm sure. But it's that particular magnetism that we're always looking for—and rarely find—that projects through the camera, grabbing an audience. I'm betting you have it."

"Well, of course I like to think of myself as an *actress*, Mr. Ganz," Liz said as they walked from the soundstage out into the sunlight, where a crowd of actors and actresses in costumes of the Old West hurried past.

"We already know you're that, Miss Lowndes. It's the other elements we ran the test for."

As he handed her into the limousine she looked back at the costumed extras hurrying along the studio street. "Thank you for everything, Mr. Ganz," she said, smiling as he closed the door.

"I'll talk to you after the performance tonight at the theater," he said as the limousine drove off.

She dressed carefully that evening, in a long clinging black gown with tiny straps over the shoulders and just a single long strand of pearls that Dan had given her as a wedding gift. She slipped a crimson velvet cape over her shoulders, picked up her beaded black bag, and left the bungalow.

Liz had never appeared before an audience before and was nervous when she arrived at the theater. But after encouraging words from Lionel Barrymore and Cecil B. DeMille, the show's producer who also served as its host, she began to calm down. And as the big Louis Silver orchestra swung into the theme song and the announcer stepped to the microphone and said, *"Lux* presents *Hollywood!"* Liz felt all of her nervousness simply flow away and a great surge of excitement take its place.

She looked out into the audience as the spotlights blazed down on her. This was a new and different kind of excitement, a new and thrilling experience—an audience giving something back to her.

The last page of script fluttered to the stage floor as the show came to an end and the *Lux* theme song signaled the end of the broadcast. There was a flurry of voices and movement and then thundering applause. The cast spread in a line across the stage and took their bows, then the curtain swept across the footlights, and the voices of the cast rose in post-performance excitement.

"Splendid, splendid," Mr. DeMille called out as he moved through the crowd, directly over to Lionel Barrymore and Liz. "My dear, you were marvelous," he said, taking her hands in his, then looked to the elderly actor for confirmation. "An extraordinary talent, don't you agree, Lionel?"

"Completely, Cecil. I'll be honored to work with her *anytime.*"

As DeMille moved on, congratulating each member of the cast, the old actor said, "He's right, you know. You're quite remarkable."

"Thank you," she said breathlessly. "It was terribly exciting."

"I understand you've been given a screen test," he said, his eyes peering at her wisely. "Does that mean you may be coming to Hollywood?"

"I . . . I don't know, Mr. Barrymore. It would be very tempting. But I—well, I just don't know." She looked around at the laughing, chattering cast members, then said softly, "I was just recently married, you see. Dan is a very fine writer. He's won several important awards for radio scripts and has completed a play that may be produced on Broadway, so you see . . ." She spread her hands helplessly.

"I see that you love him very much. And does he . . . ?"

"Oh, yes," she said. "If a contract *were* offered to me, he would insist we come here to live. But—I think he would hate it."

"My dear," the elderly actor said, taking her arm and leading her toward the stage door as the cast and their friends began to leave, "an actress who loves her craft as deeply as you do, who gives as much to it as you do, will be happy performing in that role no matter where you are. Hollywood is a difficult place to live and work, and for marriages to survive, in spite of all the success and money and power. Or perhaps it's *because* of it." He patted her arm as they reached the stage door. "When the time comes, and if a contract is offered to you, you'll know exactly what is the right thing to do. I'm sure of that."

On her way to the train station Liz stopped at the Goldwyn Studios. Jim Ganz waited for her at the executive building and led her to Sam Goldwyn's offices.

"You can't tell much from *this* screen test," Goldwyn said, obviously liking what he saw before him. "But you look very good." He then offered her a contract that would more than triple her income.

"I want to discuss it with my husband," she said, glancing at her watch nervously.

"She has a train to catch," Ganz said.

"Her husband?" Goldwyn said, turning to Ganz, ignoring the reference to the train. "Isn't that the one you told me about, the Don Holman who wrote the Dunkirk script for CBS? Any relation to Libby Holman, the singer?"

"No, the name is Dan Coleman," Ganz patiently corrected him. "He wrote the Dieppe script for NBC."

"That's what I said, Dieppe. Well, get him on the phone, Jim, and tell him we're offering him a contract too."

Liz's heart leaped, but she turned quickly to Ganz. "No, please. I want to talk to him about it myself." She moved forward and shook Sam Goldwyn's hand across the big shining desk, appearing cool and beautiful to him in her tailored tweed suit. "Thank you, Mr. Goldwyn. I'll phone Mr. Ganz after I've discussed this with my husband."

All through the next day on the train she agonized over how she would tell Dan and what he would say. Some very important writers had gone to Hollywood to write films. Scott Fitzgerald. William Faulkner. Dan might be thrilled. He could still do some of the more important radio shows and still write his plays. As the western then midwestern landscapes fled past the train windows, she remembered what Jim Ganz had told her on the drive to Union Station. An aging film star was subletting her Santa Monica house right on the beach. She and Dan could rent it until they found a house of their own. And Goldwyn had mentioned optioning the Broadway hit *A Time for Listening*, the perfect role for introducing Elizabeth Lowndes to the American moviegoer. He had also predicted that within a year or eighteen months, she could be as big a star as Crawford or Garson or Hepburn.

Remembering the crowds of autograph seekers outside the Music Box Theater as they left after the performance, she recalled her brief disappointment when the fans pushed around Lionel Barrymore and Kay Francis and Donald Cook, ignoring her as someone with a face they didn't recognize.

"You can be as big a star as Joan Crawford," Jim Ganz had said to her, and she felt a shivery excitement run up her spine.

Before changing trains in the Chicago station, Liz put in a long-distance call to Dan, who had already returned to New York from Washington.

"Darling," she said when she heard his voice. "I'm in Chicago, just getting ready to board the Twentieth Century. I'll be home in the morning. But I have something we must talk about right away—"

"Liz, you were marvelous on the *Lux* show. I went out to Hack and Evelyn's for the evening and we listened there."

"Dan, I—"

"Hack is getting hot on your doing a play and wants to talk about it, maybe for next season or the season after."

"Dan—"

"And I've got tremendous news. I went down to Washington for a couple of days and talked to Elmer Davis at the OWI. To Bob Sherwood too. They have a regular assignment they asked me to do, a radio show called *Medal of Honor,* dramatizing the lives of men who have been given the medal. It'll mean two days in Washington each week, but I knew you would say yes." She put her forehead against the phone booth glass, suddenly weary. "I told them I'd be ready to start next week."

"Of course," she said quietly, closing her eyes for a moment. "Congratulations, darling. It sounds terribly exciting. But—I have to hurry, Dan. I only have minutes to board the train."

She hung up the phone, then leaned against the wall of the booth. *You can be as big a star as Joan Crawford.* One picture could do it, Jim Ganz had told her. *Hack is getting hot on your doing a play.* Wasn't that what she really wanted? A starring role in a Broadway play? But the glitter of Hollywood, the quick riches and fame, had lured her on, and with a place for Dan beside her, writing award-winning films, even films for her.

She pushed out of the phone booth and walked toward the train. Not this year, she thought wearily. Not ever, probably.

Chapter 22

JENNY PEDALED SLOWLY along the road between the air station and Chipping Epworth, seeing her breath in the cold air ahead of her, slapping her gloved hands on the handlebars to try and warm them, the chill damp wind cutting through her with the rawness that only January can bring.

It was almost dark, and no vehicles had passed her either way. The trees on either side of the road stood tall and forbidding, with only the wind high in their topmost branches sighing mournfully.

It was lonely and cold on the deserted road, and she pedaled faster, wanting to get back as soon as possible to Mrs. Barrington's cheerful fireplace and a hot cup of tea. Later she would go to the Dove. Maybe someone would have heard something . . . anything. All through the days of late autumn and early winter, information about the August 17 raid on Regensburg by B-17's kept filtering through. Spitfires and P-47's had escorted the Fortress formations through the enemy fighter belt as far as their fuel would carry them, meeting them on their way back at the rendezvous point, EUPEN, south and east of Antwerp, to escort them back to the English coast.

"*We* went to Schweinfurt," Billy Summerfield, a pilot friend of Doug's, told her one evening following the attack as they sat in the Dove. "Rough! Some Forts never even got a chance to drop their load. We encountered about three hundred enemy aircraft, Focke-Wulfs, Junkers, ME-109's, and dropped our bomb load. The attacks became less vicious then, on the main formation, that is, because then they went after the stragglers." He shook his blond head. "Christ! Those poor bastards!"

Twisting his glass on the bartop, he had paused for a long moment, and when he spoke again his voice seemed forced, his smile too bright. "Hell, Jenny, Doug's probably living it up in some officer's club in Bizerte or Tunis. Or maybe even Naples. We've just taken the air base at Foggia, you know."

But that had been months ago, and his friends rarely spoke of Doug anymore. She pedaled on, pushing harder.

A jeep tore past her, its headlights hooded and horn beeping gaily, leaving the road more lonely and windswept than before as the darkness deepened. She wished Zeke were with her, then was glad he wasn't. She was poor company for anyone these days, either sinking into silence for hours on end or snapping at anyone within earshot.

"Shut up, for God's sake!" she had shouted at Zeke that morning as he rattled on cheerfully about his weekend in London with Joyce, and how they had gone to El Vino where the barkeep had actually asked for Jenny and then on to Rules for potted shrimp and brown bread, and finally to Spaniards Inn for a little old nightcap and back to Joyce's. He ducked as Jenny threw her notebook at him and stamped out of the air station office, where they had been working at their typewriters. "I don't give a damn what you did in London this past weekend!" she yelled as she slammed the door behind her, leaving Zeke scratching his head and wondering what he had said to so annoy her. But twenty minutes later she was back, muttering "I'm sorry" and sitting down behind her typewriter.

She saw the thatched white cottage that was her landmark through the growing gloom, and bore down harder on the pedals, with just half a mile to go.

For long weeks she had tried to pretend to herself that little had changed in her life.

"I guess you have to tell yourself that those were the chances you and Doug were taking," Joyce had said softly in trying to console her friend. It was on a weekend when Jenny had gone to London with Zeke. "And you don't know anything, Jenny. He may be safe someplace, a prisoner-of-war camp or maybe in North Africa somewhere. God knows!"

Jenny left her bicycle in the small shed at the side of the house, walked around to the front, and stood there for a moment, looking up at the sky, hearing the far-off drone of planes. That would be the RAF, heading for the Continent. She looked off in the direction they were heading. All the people over there, waiting, waiting for something to happen, waiting for us to come, she thought. Oh God, something cried inside of her, everyone waiting . . . just waiting.

She turned, her heart heavy, opened the front door and walked in. Only firelight lit the room, casting the corners into deep shadows. Jenny started toward the stairway, unbuttoning her heavy coat as she went. But a tall figure slowly rose from a chair beside the fireplace, and the first thing she saw was the gold insignia gleaming on his jacket.

"Oh, dear God!" she gasped, hand to her mouth.

He walked toward her and she slid into his arms, sobbing. For long moments they stood there as he held her and stroked her hair, then as the sobs subsided he kissed her, the kiss long and deep and searching. All the long months of waiting simply slipped away.

"Don't ask me where I've been," he warned her softly as she started to speak. Nodding, understanding, she wound her arms around his neck, felt her tears against his fatigue jacket. They stood that way for a long time, the old grandfather clock ticking away the seconds and minutes; then, still holding her, he led her out the door and down the path toward the Swan.

"I parked the jeep there," he said quietly, and she paused for a moment to look up at the sky. There were stars there now. She hadn't seen them before, stretching across the top of the universe like thousands of tiny winking jewels. She wanted to reach up and touch them.

She stopped him, looked up into his face in the dim light, and said, "I always thought no one else mattered, that I could take care of myself, never need anyone else in my life, not permanently. But I found out." She shook her head slowly, and he saw a glint of tears on her lashes. "I wouldn't want to go on without you, Doug."

He pulled her to him roughly and held her tight. "Don't!" he said. "Don't ever say that! The way this world is blowing up, none of us can be sure of anything. We just have to take what we can get while it's here, baby."

She looked at him in the darkness, wanting to protest, then slowly she nodded, and he led her on toward the Swan, his arm holding her close against him.

Chapter 23

HE PULLED THE shutter back just slightly, peered down into the Rue Jacob, and watched along the narrow street for a long time. It was late afternoon, the winter sun slanting in long shadows, the Paris shopkeepers beginning to close up their shops. Michel had said perhaps Tuesday. Today was Tuesday. An elderly man wearing a black beret was sauntering toward the small café near the Rue Saint-Benoit, and a small boy with a long loaf of bread beneath his arm was running past him. But no Michel. Well, perhaps Wednesday, Del thought, still watching the street through the narrow slit. Michel had said perhaps Wednesday, if not Tuesday.

The small boy had almost disappeared. In another few years, if the war dragged on, he'd be sent to Germany with a labor battalion, working to repair the bombed-out roads and bridges. Del watched him, his spindly legs running along the curbing, then turning into a doorway. Del remembered when he was that age, reading in study hall, skating and skiing, going on picnics, sailing his boat on the cove, his father patiently showing him how to hoist the spinnaker. Even then, though, he had been in love with airplanes. His huge airy bedroom had been filled with models of planes he and his father had built. Little had he known that he would one day be in a plane that was shot down over Lille, France.

Yes, planes had brought him to this, he thought as he watched a bicycle-drawn taxicab labor along the street, the driver puffing as he pumped the pedals. But it had all been worth it. Even the months of drill back in the States, learning to handle arms and take orders, memorizing the Articles of War as an Air Corps cadet—it all had its moments of excitement. But the real excitement had come with his primary flight training, then on to Randolph Field for advanced training, instruments, formation, night flying; and the most important moment of all, when he first saw and then flew the Thunderbolt.

Everything he'd ever flown before was like a Model-T compared to this powerful, seven-ton, hurtling giant of a fighter plane that screamed through the air like a burst shot out of a cannon. And when he flew his first combat flight in a sweep over the Calais area, he knew when he returned to the base at Manston near Dover that he never wanted to fly anything but this plane.

It had become the sole interest in his life. He had lost Kate, even before he had possessed her. In the few short weeks he had known her, she had come to mean more to him than anyone or anything on earth. But the longer the separation from her, the more hopeless it all had become to him. He could still see her vividly in his mind's eye, her long dark golden hair and chiseled features, her slanting green eyes, wide and opening their secrets to him as they lay in the room above the cove, her graceful long limbs and satin skin.

Softly he pounded his fist against the wall as he continued to peer down into the street.

"There is a train at eight o'clock from the Gare Saint Lazare," Michel had explained to Del and Wayne Brunner, a Liberator pilot who had been passed along the Resistance network like Del to Paris for medical aid for their flak wounds. "You will have tickets for Caen. That is just a few kilometers from the Channel. I will take you that distance, and we will travel as working men, with papers showing we were wounded in 1940. From there, from the Église Saint Etienne, where we will be attending Mass, you will be taken to the coast and hidden until a fishing boat comes for you. You may have to wait there for months. But first, if we are lucky, you will get through."

Del pushed the shutter back, resigning himself to Wednesday. Tonight would be another night, undoubtedly, of helping the woman surgeon, Dr. Rambouillot, with her work, patching up wounded pilots and bombardiers and other assorted British and American airmen who had been shot down over Occupied France. With no anesthetic available, it had been the task of those living in the flat to hold the patient down on the dining table while Dr. Rambouillot proceeded with her job.

As he pulled a carefully hoarded cigarette from his shirt pocket, the folded letter fell out. Creased and worn from many readings, it seemed to sting his hand. It had been mailed to him many months before, and for perhaps the hundredth time he opened it and read it again. His grandmother, knowing he wanted everything straightforward and on the line, had pulled no punches. Kate and Adam had managed to overcome their problems and put their marriage back together again, even seeming almost as close as they had before. And Kate was pregnant.

Shoving the letter back into his pocket, he went to the window again and peered out. Still no Michel. With his luck, he thought, and the way it had been going this past year, Michel would never show up, or if he did show up, they would be caught in the Gare Saint Lazare, or on the train or in the church in Caen.

Slumping down into a chair in the darkened salon, he wondered at his bitterness, at his feeling of hopelessness. What had ever happened to that incredible streak of optimism he'd always had? He lit the precious cigarette and slowly blew a stream of smoke into the gloom. Until Kate he had. . . . He paused, leaned forward, almost as though he had heard her voice, as though she had entered the dark room and was standing in the deep shadows. He could almost smell her fragrance, hear the quick little intake of breath that he always heard when she first saw him. He buried his face in his hands for a moment and shook his head from side to side as though to rid himself of the anguish, then suddenly flung himself to his feet, hands clenched at his sides. Was the thought of her always going to do this to him? he wondered. And what about Meg? Fine, decent, caring Meg.

He began to pace the length and width of the small room like a caged animal. For months he had been grateful for Meg Leighton's friendship. A young Englishwoman who worked as a volunteer with the Red Cross in Dover, near where his squadron was based, she was attractive and vivacious, reminding him just slightly of Kate with her heavy dark gold hair and exquisite skin. He had met her on a chilly morning as she and other cheerful, smiling women passed out mugs of steaming hot coffee and tea when Del and ten or twelve others first arrived at the air station. Mess facilities hadn't been fully completed, and the Red Cross workers had rushed from Dover to help out.

They had seen each other frequently, both at the base and in town. She had told him about Tony, the young man she had grown up with and become engaged to before he went to the Mediterranean to join Montgomery's Eighth Army.

"I'm not certain how serious it actually is," she had told Del with cheerful frankness. "It seemed frightfully romantic at the moment. Everyone was becoming engaged or marrying, and Tony was going off to what we were sure was North Africa. When he comes home, I rather think we'll give it more thought, and I'll return the ring."

When Sarah Wheeler's letter arrived, telling him about Kate and Adam, in despair he had turned to Meg, and a week before his plane was shot down near Lille they had been married in a small church in Dover. Meg had told him how much she loved him. At the time it had seemed enough.

He crossed to the window again and pulled the shutter back a slit. The sun had slipped behind the buildings and the street was deep in shadows. And then Del saw him, striding toward the entrance of the building. It was to be Tuesday after all.

At the sound of footsteps Kate looked up, smiled wanly, and stretched out her one free hand. Sarah was walking toward her slowly, her cane tapping firmly on the polished floor.

"My dear, my dear," she said, "at last they let me come to see you. I've been in bed for days with this wicked back of mine, but finally it's improved, and here I am."

"Sarah, how lovely," Kate said. "I've been looking forward so much to your visit. It's especially nice on such a gray winter day."

Sarah bent and kissed Kate, then sat in the chair beside the bed, lowering herself carefully. "What lovely flowers," she said, looking about. "And so many of them. Goodness, child, you *are* the popular young lady, aren't you? Oh, yes, my dear, flowers certainly do perk one up, don't they?"

Kate watched Sarah carefully. It wasn't like her to chatter on in this way. And there was something about her smile. Stiff. Unnatural.

"And when you leave, my dear, simply tell the head nurse to send them down to the wards. I have Morgan bring flowers each week from my greenhouse all through the winter, then from the gardens in the summer, and he delivers them to the wards with—"

"Sarah," Kate said quietly. "What is it?"

The elderly woman slowly turned and looked at Kate. Then, with a sorrowful expression on her face, she opened her purse and drew out a letter and a yellow envelope that could only be a telegram. Kate started up from the bed, alarmed, then fell back on the pillow. "Oh, God," she cried out softly. "It's Del, isn't it?" Pressing her hand to her lips for a moment, she shook her head back and forth, unable to speak, then said, "You've known, haven't you? All along you've known that Del and I—"

"I guessed," Sarah said sadly. "That first day you met I saw something happen between you." She picked up the telegram and looked at it, then said, "He's missing in action. His plane didn't return from a mission." She reached out and took Kate's hand when she saw tears start sliding down the young woman's face.

"He's all right," Kate said frantically, moving her head from side to side. "Somehow I know he's all right. Oh God, Sarah, we've got to believe he's all right. We have to keep saying that over and over and over—"

"Kate!" Sarah shook her hand a little, then patted it softly with her other hand. Shaking her head sadly, she said, "You must listen to me, my dear, listen until I'm finished."

She took the letter from the envelope and slowly unfolded it as Kate watched, suddenly bewildered.

"The letter was sent in December, just the day before Del's plane disappeared, apparently." She clasped Kate's hand tightly. "He was married, Kate. He'd given up hope that anything between you—back in November Jonathan asked me for his address, said he wanted to send Del some clippings from *The New York Times* about a classmate of Del's from Yale who had just been decorated by the President. I knew he would write him about your pregnancy, and about how happy you and Adam seemed again. But I wanted him to hear it from me. And so I wrote him quickly myself."

Kate covered her eyes with her hand, and Sarah heard a small sob escape. "Oh God, Sarah." For several moments Kate sobbed quietly, then began to talk again, rambling. "I shouldn't say this to you. Adam was your grandson, and in spite of everything, I know how you loved him. And at first when I regained consciousness, I couldn't think of anything but the horror of what had happened, and of how I had once loved Adam, how wonderful everything had once seemed. And then, after a week had passed, I began to think about Del. Oh, I knew it was wrong, I felt so guilty. But Del had come into my life when I needed him most, when I felt humiliated and shamed, and when I'd lost all the love I'd felt for Adam. He made me feel whole again, important to him, he made me feel beautiful and wanted, desirable and exciting.

It took away the shame and humiliation. And then, slowly, I began to realize I loved him, loved Del. And I wanted his child." She quickly reached out and with gentle fingers touched Sarah's face. "Jon is Del's son, Sarah. And I say it without any shame. I had hoped that now—finally—Del would come back to me."

Sarah slowly rose and walked to the window, where she stood with her back to Kate.

"Who is it, Sarah?"

"A young Englishwoman by the name of Meg Leighton." She slowly turned. "I wish I could tell you that she sounds like some trampy nobody who snared him for his money or something of that nature. But she sounds quite lovely."

"Of course," Kate said, nodding sadly.

Sarah walked back to the bed. "He said she looks a bit like you." As Kate put her hand over her eyes again and wept, Sarah sat down in the chair once more and gently patted her arm. "I'll sit here, my dear, until you sleep. Try to take a nap. You need all the strength you can find to get well again and take care of those two beautiful children of yours."

When Jonathan came to see her that evening, she was calm and cool, with a certain sadness in her face, but otherwise in possession of herself, steady, composed. She watched Jonathan as he crossed the room, his footsteps heavy, the lines in his face visibly deepened, his eyes filled with sorrow.

"This conversation won't be easy for either of us, Kate," he said, his voice as heavy as his footsteps. "But there are details you must know, and I want you to listen very carefully." He glanced toward the door and, satisfied that it was firmly closed, went on, slowly pacing alongside the bed, hands behind him. "Adam and the girl were both killed instantly. Afterward"—he paused to gather strength—"I did what I had to do, in order to protect the Barnfield name, which is your name, too, and the name of your children. The girl. She came from Brookton. Her father and brothers work in the mills. They live near there, and that's . . . where her body was found, near their home, victim of a hit-and-run driver in the dark."

Kate turned her head away on the pillow, not wanting to listen. Wanting to scream. Implied threats and bribery again.

"No one suspected Adam. After all, he left the club—with you. Reed saw him leave with you. So did the parking lot attendant. The girl left the country club much later. She became ill and lay down for a while, then the parking lot attendant drove her to the center of Brookton, where he dropped her off and saw her walk off toward her house."

Kate stared at him, her expression under tight control now, the cords on her neck rigid. "I see," she finally whispered. "I'm very tired, Jonathan. I'd like to be alone now."

He reached out and touched her hand for a moment, then slowly left the room. Kate watched the door for a long, long time, then, shivering, she pulled the covers high and clutched them tightly to her neck. She felt so cold. Cold and alone.

Marianne visited her every day in the hospital, and with the exception of two or three more visits from Sarah Wheeler, Marianne became Kate's sole link with the family.

"I don't want to see Jonathan," she told Marianne bluntly.

Marianne took her time pulling a cigarette case from her alligator bag, placing a cigarette in her jade holder, then lighting it. Then, through a swirl of smoke, she looked up at Kate. "It's going to be a long haul for you, even when you get out of the hospital. I'm not telling any tales out of school. The doctors have told you. You're going to be in a wheelchair for a long time until that hip mends. So you have got to reach some kind of compromise with Father." Seeing the closed and faraway look on Kate's face, Marianne reached over and clasped her hand. "Damnit, Kate, you're going to have to call some kind of truce."

She stood over Kate, every blonde hair in place, the gray wool dress clinging to every curve and contour, pearls milky at her throat, and yet Kate heard the distress, saw the crack in the armor.

"I can't," she whispered, shaking her head back and forth. "Not after all he has done. Tell him not to come here again."

She left the hospital in early spring and stayed in her rooms most of the time, taking all of her meals there, wheeling herself to other parts of the house only when she knew Jonathan was away at the mills.

But one day, early in May, she called Carla to her room and said, "Tell Martin I'll come down for dinner this evening, Carla. And please have him tell Mr. Barnfield as well."

She dressed carefully, with Carla's help, selecting a white jersey dinner gown, now that the hip cast had been removed, no jewelry except the simple pearl drop earrings, and her dark gold hair pulled back behind her ears.

She went down in the small elevator and along the wide

gallery to the dining room on crutches, Carla and Carolyn Harrison watching carefully from each side of her, Joanna running ahead of them on sturdy little legs, her blonde hair flying.

"I'm taking Joanna down to the playroom, Mrs. Barnfield," Mrs. Harrison said as Kate paused to watch Joanna tumble, then quickly pick herself up and run on again. "Then later, as soon as I have her ready for bed, I'll bring her to the library to say good night to you and Mr. Barnfield."

Jonathan was waiting for her at the head of the long table, her place set next to him as she had requested. Through the long dinner they spoke politely of matters at the mills. Telling Martin to bring their coffee and liqueurs to the terrace, Jonathan walked slowly beside her as they rose and left the dining room.

"I want to talk to you about the children," she said calmly as, settled in chairs, they watched the sun go down behind the trees beyond the lake. For five or ten minutes they talked of Jon's progress.

"Jon, quite obviously as Adam's son, is completely protected financially, if anything were to happen to me. Joanna, however, would not be." She looked directly at him, pausing for a long moment. "Joanna, at your merest whim, could be totally removed from *everything.*"

For a long moment their eyes held. Then Jonathan rose and went over near the door, where Martin had placed her wheelchair, and rolled it toward her. "Would you come with me to the library, Kate? I have something I want to give you."

Silently, with Jonathan pushing her wheelchair, they went to the library, where Martin had hurried ahead with their drinks. The lamps cast a soft glow across the walls of books and heavy portraits. Jonathan crossed to one of the paneled walls, and pushed aside a large painting. He twirled the knob back and forth on the lock and opened a safe. Kate watched him as he pulled a long white envelope from the safe, walked back across the room, and handed it to her. Kate opened the envelope quickly and began to read the paper. For a moment the words swam in front of her. Then she read it again, slowly this time, to make certain she completely understood its meaning. The paper, with Jonathan's signature, the signatures of two witnesses and the proper notarization, stated that an irrevocable trust fund existed in the name of Joanna

Thompson Barnfield in the amount of two million dollars. It was dated retroactively for January 1, 1944.

Kate finally looked up at him, and with no change of expression, she simply said, "Thank you." She placed the envelope in her lap and started to wheel the chair toward the door, but Jonathan's voice stopped her. She turned to look back at him.

"By the way," he said, "Sarah had some good news today."

Kate felt every nerve in her body tense.

"Word that Del is alive and back in England. He was apparently kept in hiding in France by the Resistance, then after some months smuggled to the coast and taken out at night by British Commandos."

He was lighting a cigarette. Kate watched him for a moment, wondering if he had guessed about her and Del. Satisfied that he hadn't, she carefully let out a long sigh of relief. "How wonderful. Sarah must be terribly excited."

He gestured with his cigarette holder. "This was told her, incidentally, in the strictest of confidence by a man who is a close friend of Justin's from the War Department."

Kate managed to control her feelings until she finally reached her rooms. She sat in the darkness for a long time, letting the bittersweet tangle of emotions drift through her—relief that Del was safe, but sorrow that he was not returning to her.

Kate had been eagerly looking forward to Liz's visit for several days. She had suddenly felt the desperate need to talk to Liz after hearing of Del's safe return to England. When Liz arrived, they went out to the terrace and sat beneath the long green awning, watching Joanna and Julie tumbling about in the spring sunshine on the seesaw out on the lawn. Martin had brought them a pitcher of iced tea and a plate of small finger sandwiches.

For several moments they were quiet, watching the children, Julie with her pale, softly curling hair and huge laughing blue eyes, Joanna, a miniature of Kate with her grave green eyes and dark golden hair tumbling about her shoulders.

"When are you going to have that baby you want, Liz?" Kate asked, rolling her wheelchair closer to the table and pouring tea into the frosty glasses.

Liz kept on watching the little girls, who were shrieking in delight as the seesaw went up and down. She turned then and looked at Kate. "Well, when Hack and Dan talked me into doing Dan's play—" She smiled almost apologetically as she looked away again. "I couldn't refuse."

When she had finally told Dan about the Hollywood offer, several days after her return from the coast, she had made light of it, said the contract they had outlined wasn't worthwhile enough to entice her away from New York and her radio work, let alone the plans for her transition to the Broadway theater.

Unsuspecting, Dan had agreed that she had made the wise decision, and they never discussed it again. Although she thought of it often as plans for her Broadway debut in Dan's play progressed, she had begun to think of it less, and finally convinced herself that, yes, she had made the correct decision. Hollywood . . . another child . . . it seemed that things and people kept slipping away from her. Her father merely tolerated her so that he and her mother could see Julie on Liz's occasional visits. And although her mother yearned for a normal relationship, Liz knew, Dr. Oldingham could never approve of her acting career.

She turned to Kate again and retrieved the threads of their conversation. She had mentioned Dan's play. Absently she began to smooth out the skirt of her pretty flowered dress, her eyes distant and wistful. "And I really couldn't turn it down. It's such a tremendous chance. Perhaps next year, or the year after, depending on how the critics receive the play, of course, and how long it runs."

"But what you really want is a baby, isn't it?" Kate asked quietly.

Liz was silent for a long moment, then with a helpless kind of gesture, she said, "I want so many things, Kate, and all at once. But most of all, I want our marriage bound by something. By a child. I've seen so many show business marriages, the shallowness, the superficiality of them. I want it to have that strong base that a child gives it."

"Isn't your love together what gives it the strong base?" Kate asked carefully. "Liz darling, those show business marriages you talk about have children in them too. But you and Dan are neither shallow nor superficial. And you love each other very much." She looked away, far down to the lake where Carolyn Harrison pushed Jon's carriage along the path by the water's edge. "I wanted Del's child," she said softly. "But only because I wanted something that was part of him. Not because I hoped it would change anything. I knew it couldn't do that. But only because I wanted a child that was his." For a while they contentedly watched their children play. Then in a low voice Kate said, "He's safe. Back in England."

"Oh, Kate!" Liz clasped her hands together excitedly.

"I told you his plane had disappeared, Liz, but what I didn't tell you was . . ." She put her head back against the chair and closed her eyes for a moment. Then she opened them again and looked directly at Liz, her green eyes filled with pain. ". . . that he married someone in England."

"Oh, Kate, I'm sorry," Liz said in a hushed tone.

"He'd received letters saying that Adam and I had managed to work things out, even seemed terribly happy again, that I was pregnant, and that Adam was thrilled, Jonathan beside himself at the thought of a Barnfield grandchild. He never guessed—" Tears brimmed in her eyes. "Why should he guess it was his child? The letters didn't say when the baby would be born. And now, if and when he's told, he'll hear the baby was taken by cesarean section after the accident." Silent for a moment, she twisted a package of matches in her hands, then quickly reached for a cigarette and lit it. "Now that he's married—thank God he doesn't know!" Turning to Liz, she tried to smile. "Poor darling. How I burden you with all my dark thoughts and troubles."

Liz put her hand softly on Kate's. "I'd be hurt if you didn't." She rose slowly, looking at her wristwatch. "I'd better be off. I have a late rehearsal."

At that moment Martin came through the terrace door. "Excuse me, Mrs. Coleman, but Nelson has the car in front. He said if you're going to catch the four ten train, you'll have to leave in ten minutes."

"Thank you, Martin," Kate said, then looked at Liz. "I hate to let you go. We have so much to talk about."

"Once the play has opened, I can come up to see you more often. It was just luck today's rehearsal was postponed until evening."

"Oh, did I tell you that your friends Evelyn and Hackley Crawford stopped by here day before yesterday?" Kate asked as she raised her hand to signal to Carolyn Harrison, who was walking in their direction.

Liz looked down at her in surprise.

"They said they were on their way to see their son up at

college in Hanover, and just wanted to stop and introduce themselves." Kate was smiling secretively. "And guess what? When I told Hack I wished he'd wait one month to open your play, because I'd finally be rid of this wheelchair by that time, he said he was arranging to have two seats removed in the theater so that I could come to the opening night."

"Oh, Kate, how wonderful!"

"Mrs. Harrison and Jonathan and I will be there."

Liz turned to her as she picked up her purse from the chair, her eyes filled with curious concern. "Jonathan?"

Kate paused for a long moment as she looked off across the lawn to the lake. "We have a kind of truce, Liz. And . . . although I can never forgive him, there are some things about him that I admire. And oddly enough I find it fascinating, listening to him talk evenings at dinner about the mills. Actually I'm learning a great deal about the Barnfield Mills, some good and some bad, the labor situation in particular. And I'm thinking seriously of telling Jonathan that as soon as I'm on my feet, I'd like to have a position in the company."

Shaking her head with an admiring little smile, Liz said, "What's he going to say to that?"

Kate laughed. "A great deal, I'm sure. The only women employed there are the spinners and weavers, some in the dye house, and secretaries. It will take a lot of convincing on my part, I'm afraid."

As Liz bent down to kiss her on the cheek, she murmured, "You're amazing, Kate. Knowing you, he'll give you the position."

Kate grasped her hand and held it for a moment. "Well, you're pretty amazing yourself." They smiled at each other, then Liz moved toward the french doors. "Good luck, Liz, and I'll be there opening night. I'll be there for both of us, for both Jenny and me."

On a Monday evening in late May *The Light Under the Door* opened with Elizabeth Lowndes and Peter Rowen Tallner in the starring roles. By the end of the first act Kate knew it was going to be a tremendous hit. Because it was opening late in the season, it already had one strike against it. And with a relatively unknown actress, who had made a name for herself in the suspect world of radio only, starring in a play by a new playwright who happened to be her husband, the critics arrived in a distrustful mood.

It was an extravagantly gowned and jeweled audience for a

226

wartime opening night, mainly because of Hackley Crawford's reputation as a producer and Tallner's following as a major star. But those, like the critics, who arrived in a suspicious frame of mind rose to their feet at the final curtain to shout for the stars and the playwright. Kate clapped until her arms ached and the palms of her hands burned as she watched Liz and Dan come down to the footlights with Hack Crawford between them, Liz and Hack bowing and smiling; Dan, obviously astonished, standing back a little and blinking in the flood of spotlights.

Backstage in Liz's flower-filled dressing room, friends and well-wishers crowded in and out as Hack and the director popped corks on champagne bottles and poured the bubbly liquid into wine glasses while Evelyn greeted guests at the door.

Kate smiled in tired pleasure from her corner near the dressing table where Carolyn Harrison had deposited her wheelchair. She could see Carolyn, tall and spare in her new gray silk dinner gown bought for the occasion, talking with unaccustomed excitement to Clive Malcolm, an English actor who had been wounded early in the war while a pilot in the RAF, according to the program notes.

"He comes from the same town I do, Mrs. Barnfield," Mrs. Harrison called out, her face flushed with pleasure. "Bury Saint Edmunds in East Anglia."

Suddenly Liz hurried through the crowd to Kate, her hands filled with telegrams, her eyes sparkling with excitement. "There's a cable here from Jenny. Read it, Kate."

Kate pulled the cable from the envelope. "Liz dearest: Somehow in my highly intuitive bones I feel this is the beginning of a long and brilliant success in the theater. Don't forget me. We'll celebrate together after the war. Love, Jenny." She read it aloud and looked up, smiling, into the wide blue eyes that were misted with tears. She took Liz's hand and spoke softly. "She's right, Liz. But about both you and Dan. And I know. Because I was here tonight."

Chapter 24

ONE MORNING TOWARD the end of May 1944, Doug and Jenny drove toward the Channel. She had been on special assignment for two months, visiting other military installations, interviewing servicemen in different branches of the service.

Doug was driving to a Spitfire base near the coast to visit an RAF pilot friend and would drop her off at an American fighter base near Ringwood.

"I've arranged for a car and driver to pick you up and drive you to Portsmouth in late afternoon," he said the night before as they walked through the dark from the Swan to Mrs. Barrington's cottage, hands linked, his voice quiet but suddenly tense in the soft spring evening. "He'll take you right to the hotel and I'll meet you there later."

They walked in silence for a moment, then stopped as he turned to give her a cigarette. When she saw his eyes in the light from the cupped match, something cold clutched at her heart. There it was again. She knew every expression now, every lift of his eyebrow or pause in his speech, the distant, closed look that flashed for a brief second in his eyes at a word or newspaper headline or radio announcement. Just as she knew every inch of his flesh, every inflection in his voice, she knew his shift of moods and reactions, all of his desires and passions and needs. But deep within him there was a place she didn't know, a secret place, a place she often contemplated with dread. It would take him away from her again someday, and she knew the time was drawing close. Long after he slept on the nights they were together, she would toss and turn in the darkness, slipping off into a half sleep and then waking. Startled and frightened, she would reach out to softly touch him, make certain he was still there.

Theirs was a stormy love affair. Often, after he returned from a long disappearance, she begged him to tell her what had happened, where he had been, at least to explain why he had gone without warning, pleaded with him to let her know if it was ever going to happen again. At first he had simply held her close and in a quiet, reassuring voice told her he could explain nothing, but one night she persisted and he became angry, shouted that she was unreasonable and childish, and stamped out of their room at the Swan. She waited and waited, but he never returned.

At first she had paced the floor, weeping one moment and smashing something the next. Finally she threw herself across the bed and cried herself to sleep. The following day she looked for him, but he was nowhere to be found. On the third day she waited at the air base, and when the *Spirit of Times Square II* landed, she was waiting for him. When he walked to her and looked down into her face she promised solemnly never to ask him those questions again.

"I promised you that day, Doug," she said softly as they stood in the darkness halfway to Mrs. Barrington's cottage from the Swan, "promised you I'd never ask questions again. But I feel something about this trip to Portsmouth. I'm frightened."

He took her in his arms and held her. Finally they walked on, and when they reached Mrs. Barrington's gate, he kissed her. "I wish—" he started to say, then stopped. "I'll be here at five a.m."

As the darkness swallowed him she felt tears of frustration rush to her eyes. She turned and beat her fists on the gate, then looked back again into the darkness where she had last seen him. She wouldn't be here when he came for her at five a.m. She'd pack a bag and go back to the Swan, where she'd wait for the first early morning bus for the railway station and go to London, stay with Joyce. She'd leave a note on the latch of the gate, telling him to go without her. Finally she turned and slowly walked into the cottage.

And at five a.m. she was waiting for him.

Skirting London, they headed southwest, Jenny at first subdued and quiet, clinging to his arm. But as they traveled farther south, she began to sit forward. They both kept looking from side to side, astonished by what they saw, by the unbelievable transformation that had occurred in southern England since winter. It was like an armed camp. A sea of mechanized equipment covered the countryside. Tent cities, mammoth ammunition dumps, and storage depots were heaped up against each other. The towns and villages were jammed with American G.I.'s, and time and again Doug had to pull the jeep off the road to wait for military convoys to pass, an endless stream of trucks and other vehicles all roaring south. Sudden roadblocks were manned by military police, who demanded to see their identification.

The farther they went the greater were the stockpiles of war equipment. Fields and forests had become leafy carpets and canopies for guns, ammunition, and bumper-to-bumper vehicles. The gentle land seemed to have vanished beneath the grim weight of war. Endless miles of Nissen hut materials, metal netting for airstrips, jeeps, ambulances, halftracks, and tanks filled the moors and valleys.

"Good God!" Jenny said, stunned by the awesome sight, as Doug pulled the jeep up in front of a pub for a midmorning stretch of their legs and something to drink. "It certainly makes you realize the invasion is really going to happen. But how these people who live here stand all of this, I don't know."

"They have to hate it," Doug said with a grim smile as he steered her into the pub and found a narrow space for them at the crowded bar. "They must have a hell of a lot more patience than we Americans would have. Looks like they just grit their teeth and smile or pretend they don't notice."

Later Doug dropped her off at the Thunderbolt base, saying, "I'll get to the hotel as soon as I can tonight."

She climbed out of the jeep and turned to say something, but his eyes told her he had left her. "Tonight," she called out and waved, but he was pulling back onto the road.

As the jeep roared off she watched him, his overseas cap jammed low on his forehead, his intense blue eyes now flinty and hard, already far away and on the road ahead. She watched until the jeep was just a dot on the horizon. He had stopped thinking about her already. Alan had once told her she was like that. "You think like a man," he had said. "Love comes second."

Well, perhaps she had once been like that, she thought as she walked toward the compound of low military buildings at the edge of the airfield. Until she met Doug. Then everything had changed. She grinned a little. Maybe not everything.

"You are the damnedest, most argumentative female," Doug often stormed. "Goddamn, can't you ever agree with anything I say?"

"Well, say something that makes some sense then. And don't try to tell *me* anything about the *Yankees*, my hometown team. It was in 1927 that Babe Ruth hit sixty home runs, not 1928."

"Jesus, what a stubborn dame! It was 1928."

"Prove it!"

"I will!" he had shouted, then the next day had come back, grinning sheepishly. "Well, I was just off by one year." And then he had teased her: "If I ever leave you, woman, it will be because you're so damned stubborn and mulish."

She stopped still in the roadway. If he ever left her. Her heart seemed to fly up into her throat. No, they were too much a part of each other now. And even though he didn't know . . . though she hadn't told him yet. . . . Gently she touched her hand to her still smooth, flat tummy. For over a month she had known she was pregnant, but still she hadn't told him. It had to be at exactly the right moment. Not yet. Not yet. Slowly she walked on. It was all so different from when she had carried Christopher. She wanted this one. Desperately. This was Doug's child, and with Doug her world had turned completely around. She still loved her work, but she would even give that up if he asked her to.

She had a quick lunch with two smiling Signal Corps officers, who then took her to a newly constructed flying control tower at the edge of the field. Within a glass enclosure the two officers worked with loudspeakers, telephones, and remoting apparatus.

Through the afternoon she watched as one of the officers talked a plane in for an emergency landing, a rugged Thunderbolt that skidded in with its engine smoking. The canopy over the cockpit was shattered, and a greasy, boiling plume of smoke rose above it like a knight's pennant fluttering madly in the wind. She scribbled notes while she held her breath, then looked away as a huge crash truck raced toward the crippled plane, the ambulance just behind.

But when she opened her eyes, she saw the pilot jump to the ground and run from the plane, and her heart seemed to stop. Every pilot looked like Doug from a distance. And as her heart raced on with a sickeningly pounding beat, she ran down from the tower.

The driver dropped her off at the hotel in Portsmouth early that evening. At the desk she was told that Major Gilbert had left word he would be delayed, that she was to go ahead and have dinner.

In the late evening she went over her notes, pillows pushed up behind her in the big double bed, wearing the new white silk nightgown and preciously hoarded Shalimar perfume he had given her, her hair brushed into a dark cloud about her face.

When he arrived, he seemed preoccupied. His face was taut and his eyes were veiled. She knew better than to probe, except to ask him if he'd eaten dinner, her hand reaching toward the bedside phone.

"Yes," he answered in a strangely remote voice, turning his back to her and slinging his tunic over the back of the desk chair. Then he pulled a flask from his leather carryall, poured a drink, and slowly sipped at it. He wished he could tell her about this remarkable evening. Oh, how he wished he could tell her.

Dinner had been inch-thick steaks and baked Idaho potatoes, with two generals and a lieutenant colonel, two of them SHAEF tactical and operational officers.

Following dinner he and the two generals and the G-2 man were driven through a woodsy area for about two miles to a large clearing where a long trailer stood. He paused for a moment in the darkness, staring at the bulky outlines of the trailer. Surrounded by a scattering of big tents, it was the Supreme Commander's circus wagon, as he called it.

The deeply sunburned four-star general was standing at a desk in the trailer study looking down at a map—a map of the Channel and France, Doug quickly noted. As they entered the general turned, and Doug saluted smartly. "General Eisenhower, sir," he said.

"At ease, Major Gilbert." The general smiled, but Doug could see the rigid cords on his neck, the strain in his smile, the lines of worry on his tanned face. "I understand you spent several months with the Maquis in France. You were shot down near Reims after the Regensburg raid?"

"Yes, sir, just outside of Reims."

"And the Maquis?"

"We were lucky. My bombardier, Corwin, and I landed near a farmhouse, and after hiding us, the farmer brought a man to us. His name is Armand Moreau. We lay low there for about two weeks, getting clothes, papers, everything but shoes. They couldn't get us shoes, and we had to take a chance with what we wore when we dropped.

"Yes," the general nodded. "I understand the Germans keep their eyes to the ground, always looking for G.I. boots."

"They took us to Paris. Corwin had a piece of flak in his thigh, so they took us to a house where doctors came and performed surgery on the men they brought in. We had to stay there for several weeks until Bud could be moved. Finally they got us to the coast, to Normandy, where we holed up in the cellar of a Resistance member's house in the town of Bayeux. The Rue de Nesmond near the cathedral. But Bud's leg was in bad shape, so the Maquis arranged to get him out. A small landing party of Commandos and Rangers put in near Port en Bessin in small landing craft on an intelligence recon and took him out when they left."

"Moreau came to you then?"

Doug looked at him in surprise. The general's knowledge of details and names seemed astounding. He nodded. "Armand asked me to stay on to take back information. I stayed in the area of Caen and Bayeux and Carentan, twice getting as far over as Gatteville and Cap Levy near Cherbourg and holing up for two full weeks at Grandcamp les Bains, trying to get a reading on Pointe du Hoc. The Maquis say there are several 155-millimeter howitzers on that cliff. But it's completely sealed off. I came back in January, coming out through Spain, and turned in my report two days later."

The general had turned and was gazing down at the map again as the others watched him. Looking up, he said, "We want you to make a drop in there, Major Gilbert, taking vital information in with you. You'll know where to go, whom to contact." He paused for a long moment, and Doug felt everyone in the low-ceilinged room hold his breath. "We have three days, Major, three days to choose from for launching the invasion. June fifth, sixth, or seventh, according to our meteorologists. Normandy is where we will land. And for the landings we need a late-rising moon for our gliders and paratroops, and a low tide right after dawn for our seaborne troops. That's why we have to go on one of those three dates."

Doug merely nodded. It was finally going to happen, and with the realization his heart began to race.

"Colonel Anderson will brief you." The general had nodded toward the G-2 man. "But you're to tell no one anything. You'll go in on May twenty-ninth."

May 29, he thought, looking at the harbor. It was May 26. He felt Jenny creep up against him, and as he slid his arm about her she shivered, and he held her closer. For a long moment they looked out into the deep night, across through the darkness to where they knew the coast of France lay silently waiting.

233

"We're getting close to the invasion, aren't we?" she whispered.

His arm tightened. "You saw the buildup as we drove down this morning. I'd heard about it but had to see it." He still sounded strange, far away and remote. "If . . . something should happen, Jenny . . . I mean, if I should get orders and not be able to warn you—" He closed the curtains, walked to the bedside table, and switched on the low lamp again. As she turned and watched him, he pulled a piece of paper from his wallet and held it out toward her. "I have a close friend in Paris. His name is François Leroux. He spent a year in America, at New York University when I was there. He and his wife, Solange, live on the Rue de Seine. If I know François as well as I think I do, he'll be with some insurgency movement, probably the Resistance. But Solange will be in Paris. She's a cellist of some note. And François is a writer, the kind of people you'll like."

She took the piece of paper from him and glanced at it, then looked up again. "Doug . . . ?"

"Baby, I'm beat," he said, pulling his shirt off, then quickly stripping, his tall muscular body gleaming in the soft light. He downed his drink, and stretched out on the bed, then held out his arms. "Come on," he said softly. "Here, next to me, Jenny."

"It *is* close, isn't it?" she insisted, her eyes wide with foreboding as she sprang onto the bed and hunched forward on her knees.

He nodded, quickly looking away as he reached for her cigarettes on the bedside table. He lit one and dragged on it deeply, then handed it to her. "Just remember what I said," he warned her. "Try to get to Paris. I'll meet you there or leave word with Solange." He took the cigarette from her and slowly put it out in the ashtray. Then, before she could speak, he pulled her down into his arms and buried his face in her hair. Closing her eyes, she gave herself to his touch, his hand cupping her face as he kissed her. With aching softness he caressed her throat and breasts and trailed downward. She heard the sigh from her own lips against his, almost a whimpering moan as his fingers softly probed, and as the minutes winged onward her breath rasped faster and faster, mingling and then racing with his own. "I love you," she said. "I love you so."

"Jenny," he whispered, and she looked up at him. His eyes,

a dark and stirring blue, seemed to be pulling her into bottomless depths, arousing her even more as his hands stroked in a maddening rhythm. "I've never felt this way about anyone before." And before she could speak again, his lips were on hers and she felt his weight, then the exquisite agony as he pressed into her, their flesh and muscle becoming one, her arms and legs coiling hard about him, breath and words incoherently blending, lips still wildly seeking. She clung to him, the passion bursting and flooding her senses, and she repeated his name over and over until it was a drowsy murmur.

Slowly he slipped down to her side, still holding her, his lips in her hair, and in that moment of softly breathing quiet, she whispered once more, "I love you."

Two evenings later she waited at their usual table in the Dove. When two hours had passed, she knew something was wrong. She caught Billy Summerfield's eye for a brief second and tried to call him over, but he had looked away and was pushing through the crowd at the bar. A cold fear gripped her as she hurried across and edged her way up to him. He was trying to avoid her, and when she stood next to him and shouted into his ear, he simply shook his head and muttered something.

"Louder, Billy," she shouted above the noise. "It's bedlam in here." If anyone knew, it would be Billy. He shared a room with Doug in the Bachelor Officer Quarters.

"I don't know where he is, Jen," he yelled down next to her ear. But, looking closely at her for a moment, a peculiar expression came over his face. "Look, he left this morning, or I guess you could call it last night. About one o'clock. He packed all his gear, then just said he was leaving, couldn't tell us any more than that, and went out of the BOQ. A command car was waiting outside to pick him up. And he drove off."

She stared at him. Finally she shook her head a little. She had known something was coming, but suddenly she was stunned. "I don't know what you mean," she said, then, grasping his arm, her fingers digging through the sleeve, she shouted frantically, "What do you mean he just drove off?"

He shrugged, his gray eyes reflecting her pain. Not knowing what to say, he pulled off his cap and ruffled his blond hair. "He's gone, Jen." He looked around nervously. "I'm not supposed to say anything more than that. In fact, I'm not supposed to talk about it at all." Suddenly he gripped her hand and held it hard, then, trying to laugh, he said, "Come on. Let's have a drink."

But she shook her head and pushed her way through the noisy crowd of laughing Air Force men and walked out of the pub and into the fogbound night. She walked and walked, trying to see the sky up through the mist, oblivious to the tears that slid down her face.

Jenny trudged on, hands dug into her trench coat pockets. But she suddenly stopped, feeling the small slip of paper he had given her. She had memorized the address in Paris. All at once, feeling the paper between her fingers gave her comfort, and she turned back and headed for Mrs. Barrington's cottage.

Chapter 25

DOUG SAW THE tracer bullets as he floated down through the dark, the trails of smoke and fire they left behind them marking their flight. He was far enough away to watch almost dispassionately, outside the perimeter set alight by the falling flares from planes in the squadron just ahead of the plane that had dropped him. Hundreds of flares stretched as far as Foucarville and Saint-Martin.

In the glow of the garish blue light he could see that the tracers were spitting viciously from the belfry of a church. He looked down from his harness in the floating parachute. It was all darkness just beneath him, but off to the left was the glaring bluish light from the falling flares. Right on target, he thought as he calculated how many more seconds he had before hitting the ground.

He tried to pick out landmarks. Not only did memory serve him well, but the map and aerial photos of the Normandy coastline were burned into his mind, and along with them the intelligence briefings. He had been informed that an antiaircraft battery was still lodged in the church steeple, and trenches had been dug around and through the small town. "Rommel's Asparagus," the sharp pointed sticks that would spear a man when he landed from the air, peppered the fields. And there were the marshes.

"Watch the marshes," the intelligence officer had warned him. "The Germans built concrete dams to keep the fields flooded, and in some places they're flooded right to the treetops."

Men will drown there, Doug thought as he floated down, drown in the fields before they even fire a shot. And then thoughts fled his mind as he prepared himself to land.

As he hit the ground darkness enfolded him. He tugged at the parachute cables to pull in the billowing shroud while marveling at his luck in skirting a tall stand of trees that loomed to his right. As he worked at the cables he remembered having seen a ribbon of road. That would be National Highway 13, he thought, exactly what he was looking for.

In the dampness and light drizzle, he gathered the folds of green silk and stuffed the parachute into a tall, deep hedge, remembering the deadly hedgerows rimming the fields—havens for snipers. For several moments he crouched low in the hedge's shadowy protection. Finally he ventured from the hiding place and stole toward the road. Armand would be waiting for him at the home of Claude Gérard.

So far everything had gone as planned, the maps and papers were safe in the pouch at his side, and he was less than a quarter of a mile from Claude's house. The steady drone of planes was comforting. Those would be British Lancasters headed for the railroad yards near Paris. He pushed on, swallowed up by the night, his footsteps noiseless on the ground below.

The house was near the edge of the town, similar to all the others, of that dun-colored Normandy stone, square and shuttered, no light escaping. He stood deep in the shadows and watched it for several minutes. A dog barked not far away, then finally stopped. Drawing in his breath, he slipped across the road and tapped on the door, three short taps and one heavy knock. Suddenly he heard movement down the road and flattened himself hard against the wall. Just as heavy footsteps rounded the corner, he felt himself pulled inside and heard the door softly click shut, then a low familiar laugh.

"Welcome to France, my friend," the voice said as hands grasped his hard and drew him along a dark hallway, then into a room that glowed dimly from a single table lamp. Doug blinked for a moment, then laughed softly with relief and pleasure. Both Armand Moreau and Claude Gérard were smiling at him as they clasped his hands, then took the pouch he drew from beneath his black shirt.

"By God, you look the same as before," Doug exclaimed softly, clapping them on the back and remembering the Regensburg raid, the Fort shot down just minutes after they'd passed the French coast, Armand coming to the farmhouse where the farmer had taken him in and hidden him, then taking him away to this house in the night.

"And you look in better health," Claude joked, squeezing

his hands over and over. "Have no fear, we'll pare you down once more."

"I remember the sound of those boots too well," Doug said, indicating with a movement of his head the footsteps outside, "not to recognize them. Still strutting about, I see."

"Not for long." Armand laughed as he opened the pouch and drew out the maps and papers. "They are bewildered. They think the invasion will come in the Pas de Calais area, but they wonder at the leaflets that are being dropped and the increase in raids by your Fortresses and the British night callers."

"When will it be, Douglas?" Claude asked.

"Sunday, Monday, or Tuesday," Doug said, shrugging out of his heavy black sweater. "Depending on the weather conditions." He pointed to a spot on one of the maps Armand had spread out under the light. "You see where it is coming?"

Claude handed him a small glass of Calvados, his strong Norman face with its high cheekbones and pale blue eyes like granite in the dim light. Both Frenchmen nodded.

"And you understand the signals?"

"We heard on the BBC just before you arrived, the first line of Verlaine's '*Chanson d'Automne,*'" Armand said, his clever dark eyes excitedly aglow.

"The second line will come when General Eisenhower makes his decision." Doug's voice was thick with feeling. "'*Blessent mon coeur d'une langueur monotone.*' Then we wait, and in the next forty-eight hours . . ."

They nodded again.

Armand folded the maps and put them inside his black shirt, then clasped Doug's arms and said, "I will take these to Bayeux." He waved. "Good luck, my friend."

When Claude turned off the light, Armand slipped into the hallway and out the door, then Claude turned the light on once more. He poured more Calvados and handed a glass to Doug. "You will be safe here."

"There are going to be other messages," Doug said. "To tell us when to cut telephone lines, foul up the railroad tracks, and mark the drop zones for the airborne troops who will be dropping near here. Paratroops and glider men. We have to make contact with them, then move on when they do. Until then I'll work with you, Claude."

"Yes, as we said before, Douglas, you look enough like a Frenchman to pass for one. But a Frenchman from Paris, perhaps, yes?" He laughed. "Not one who grows apples for the Calvados in Normandy."

The second line of the Verlaine poem came from the BBC in a crackling, static-filled announcement during the evening of June 5.

Although radios had been confiscated by the Germans in April—the Vichy government directing owners to deliver them to their town halls—Claude had hidden his in a small room up under the eaves of the house. They spelled each other, one listening for messages while the other slept, and through the long hours of wakefulness Doug thought of Jenny, images of her laughing eyes and sudden smile flashing through his mind. Remembering the supple, satiny feeling of her flesh or the softness of her mouth on his, he would suddenly get up and pace around the low attic room. Each day or night, when it was his turn, he crawled up through a trap door in a cupboard and listened for hours to the dozens of meaningless messages that the BBC scattered through its programming to confuse the Germans. At last, almost a week later, he heard the one he had been waiting for.

"This is the night when *neither* of us sleep," he said to Claude as he pulled a black turtleneck sweater over his head. For hours they listened to the little radio; then, when the final message came, they nodded to each other and came down from the attic. Claude clasped Doug's hand for a long moment.

"I will not get as far as you, to Paris, my friend. Only as far as Saint-Lô." He smiled at Doug. "Come back to Sainte Mère Église to see us when this war is over."

Doug nodded. "Tell Armand we'll drink a bottle of Calvados."

Claude slipped out the door as Doug heard a low droning sound, growing louder, then the deep-throated roar of engines coming closer and closer, and the booming of antiaircraft guns in the Place de L'Église and from batteries farther away. He silently let himself out the door. A cloth sack slung at his side was filled with flares and fluorescent materials for marking drop zones. A long sheathed knife and pistol were at his other side.

He ran low, skirting the square. But as he ran he could see that the square was lit up as though by daylight, a great fire blazing in a house at the opposite side and the townspeople passing canvas buckets of water from hand to hand. Many of them had stopped and were staring upward at the heavy bombers overhead that were heading for railway lines, marshaling yards, and ammunition dumps.

Doug paused to watch another wave of planes—huge transports, coming in low, engines throbbing in an ear-splitting roar. Figures began to spill from the bellies of the planes. These men would be the Pathfinders, he knew, coming in to mark the drop zones for the airborne troops that would follow—his signal to move.

He raced along a hedge, headed for Highway 13 at the northern edge of town, where paratroops would converge after landing to cut the main highway through the Cotentin Peninsula, repelling any German attack from the south.

As he ran something white fluttering above the treetops ahead caught his eye. He crouched even lower and ran alongside a narrow road bordered by hedges, then suddenly stopped. As the planes droned on overhead he watched as a parachute, ghostly in the half darkness, collapsed into the branches of a tree ahead of him, a figure dangling on the cables and twisting frantically about in the eerie light of the moon.

Then he saw a second figure running along the ground, the moon glinting on the steel helmet. The barrel of the raised gun told him it was a German. Doug hesitated only a moment. He had never killed a man before. Flying at thousands of feet and dropping bombs had somehow seemed impersonal, detached. But now he moved swiftly, pulled his knife from the sheath, and plunged it into the soldier's back with a terrible force. Then he heard something . . . a bubbling from the man's throat as the body fell back, then crumpled slowly to the ground.

He quickly dragged the body into the underbrush and then ran forward to where the other figure thrashed wildly about just a few feet off the ground as he dangled on his parachute ropes.

"Jesus," he heard a voice mutter, and almost laughed aloud as he reached the paratrooper. "Jesus, now what!"

"Shut up," Doug hissed. "This place is crawling with Krauts." He quickly sliced through the ropes, then helped the soldier out of the chute as he dropped easily to the ground. They gathered up the silk and ropes and pushed it all into nearby bushes.

"Jesus, where did you come from?" the paratrooper asked in a strained whisper.

"Same place you came from, only a few days earlier," Doug answered. "Come on. I'm headed for the main highway. Maybe you'd better stick with me. I've been here before."

They began to run, hunched low, but hadn't gone one hundred feet before a voice rang out, ordering them in broken English to put their hands in the air and not move. Slowly they lifted their arms and waited as a German came up behind them.

Above the sound of the wind in the treetops, sweeping the rain away in its path, Jenny heard the steady drone of planes. They had started at midnight, continuing with no let-up, an awesome sound that signaled the movement of power and might. At three o'clock she finally dressed and rode her bicycle out to the airfield. Zeke was on the control tower deck, leaning over the railing and shouting down at her as she pulled up and parked her bike.

"Call Joe Bernstein. He's been trying to reach you!"

She placed the call in Lieutenant Parker's office but was told by the operator that all trunk lines were tied up. Finally at six a.m. she had him on the line.

"Come down to London!" he shouted. "The first wave of infantry is going in. My God, Jenny, the Channel is filled with ships, solid from here to the coast of France. Never has the world seen anything like it, the greatest invasion force that's ever happened. We're getting reports that the airborne troops went in before dawn, and now thousands and thousands of ships from battlewagons down to small landing craft. Maybe one hundred—no, one hundred and fifty thousand Americans, British, and Canadians are landing. Good God, it's what we've been waiting for. Nothing like it has ever been attempted before. Eisenhower's gamble, and by God, I think it's—"

"Can I go, Joe?" she shouted over his wild ramblings.

"Get down here and we'll talk about it. It's time we put your lousy French to some practice!"

Kate and Liz gathered close to the radio in the library at Finisterre as news of the invasion poured out of the speaker. Liz had tried to phone Dan in Washington all morning long to share the exciting news with him. She had been unable to get a call through, so she had gathered Julie up and rushed to Grand Central, where she caught a train to Brookton.

"I wanted to be with you, listening to it," she said to Kate when they were sitting in the library in front of the radio.

"Martin can bring our lunch to us in here," Kate said as the sound from the radio poured into the room. Looking at each other, startled, they froze. Behind the soft voice that plowed relentlessly on, they heard the deafening explosions of naval bombardment, then the sound of the ship's whistle through the static and shriek of planes and firing.

"We're getting a warning whistle here aboard our own ship," the voice said. "And we can see flak now, coming up in the sky . . ."

"Oh, God!" Kate cried out. "Listen."

"You can probably hear the planes overhead . . . German planes, coming and going. And bombs . . ." A thundering explosion rocked through the speaker. With the shattering noise, Kate grabbed Liz's hand and held it. "Hear it?" the voice shouted. "That was a hit. A bomb. Another one. That was a tracer line. You can see it, curving up into the darkness . . . still dark here. I'm recording this aboard one of our naval ships at five-thirty in the morning. Daylight's on the horizon, but up where the fiery bursts are, it's still darkness . . ." There were more deafening explosions, drowning his voice out for the moment. ". . . but it's dying down again. Here's another plane, low . . . low and coming right at us . . . but the antiaircraft fire in toward the shore is taking it up, forcing it up . . . the Nazis are attacking low. Their planes are right off our stern now . . ." His voice streaked up to a hoarse shout. "And I can see the streamer fire, close to the water."

They heard more ear-splitting sounds in the background, a sharp rapping, in bursts and spurts, then such a clamorous roar that Kate, somewhere in a corner of her mind, thought of Fourth of July when she was a child and the sounds through the windows of the San Francisco house when the boys of the neighborhood set off hundreds of firecrackers all at once in a terrifying clatter.

They listened through most of the afternoon. But at four o'clock Martin came to the door to tell Liz that Nelson was waiting with the car to drive her in to Manhattan. "I'm sure we'll have a performance tonight," she said, hugging Kate, then crossing to the door. She paused and said softly, "I only wish that Bill and Philip could be here and know what's happening there today," she said softly.

Kate smiled at her as she stood up and walked a few steps

toward her. "I'm somehow sure they know, Liz." There were tears in her wide green eyes. "Give an especially marvelous performance tonight. Dan says so many things in this play that have tremendous meaning on a day like this."

On D-Day plus one Jenny caught a train to London after tearful good-byes to Mrs. Barrington and many of the men on the base. For several days she and Joyce waited for word that they could proceed to the Channel coast, where they would wait to cross to France. Alone one late afternoon she went to St. Paul's Cathedral and sat in the back of the dim church, only vaguely aware of the softly echoing footsteps of worshippers and whispering voices. She sat there, piecing together thoughts about Doug. Fighting back panic, she told herself over and over that he was safe and would be waiting for her in Paris, whenever they both reached there.

She remembered how she had started to tell him about the baby that night in Portsmouth but had stopped herself. He was too preoccupied. It wasn't the right time. She would tell him when they reached Paris.

Finally she stood and walked out of the cathedral, feeling comforted, even closer to him. His disappearance had something to do with the invasion. Of that she felt sure. And because of it, she knew—just knew he was safe.

The following morning she and Joyce and Zeke and several others were driven to Weymouth, where they were billeted in a small hotel near the harbor and told to stay on twenty-four-hour alert for their departure. The port city was swarming with soldiers and sailors and military vehicles of every description, but there was a kind of orderly chaos as troops poured onto the transports that were shuttling back and forth between the English and French coasts.

Jenny had dinner the first night with Zeke and Joyce, then tried to avoid the couple. She not only felt that they wanted to be alone, but couldn't bear to watch them in their bittersweet hours of knowing they might soon be separated. It was all too reminiscent of her last hours with Doug.

She pounded out her stories on her small portable typewriter in her room high above the harbor, then phoned them to London each night. Each morning she returned to the dock area for more first-person accounts from Navy personnel returning from the beaches of Normandy. Late into the night she listened to the static-filled broadcasts from those beaches, the roar of the naval bombardment and drone of planes half drowning out the voices of the radio correspondents.

On D-Day plus six, and with no more than half an hour's notice, Zeke grabbed his gear and left, leaving Joyce and Jenny to roam day after day just outside the restricted areas, waiting for their orders and permission to proceed to France.

Chapter 26

JENNY RODE INTO Paris in a jeep on a Friday morning. It was August 25, and she rode in through the Porte d'Orleans with two other correspondents, Robert McGillicuddy of San Francisco and Charlie Stone of Boston, on the tail of a small group from the Fourth Infantry Division. They had been trailing General George Patton's Third Army across France from Avranches, traveling at Patton's famed breakneck speed, until almost reaching Troyes, the great railway center, when they heard that Paris was about to be liberated.

"I have to get to Paris!" she suddenly began to shout as she banged her fist on the hood of the jeep, which they had found abandoned on a road outside of Bayeux and which had come to life under the tinkering but talented hands of Charlie Stone. "Can't you jokers understand?" They were parked outside of an inn at Sens, near the Cathedral of Saint Etienne.

"All right, all right, all right," Robert calmed her, "and don't keep hitting the hood. The damned jeep is pasted together with chewing gum and bobby pins as it is." But he was smiling, his round, pleasant face and blue eyes telling her he understood. "Okay, kiddo, we'll help you find this guy Gilbert."

She had first met them on the transport coming from Weymouth. They separated on debarking at Omaha Beach after transferring to a small landing craft. She found an inn that would rent her a room in Carentan, less than fifty miles from Cherbourg, and had filed dispatches on the day-to-day attacks launched by General Lawton Collins' Seventh Corps on the big port city at the tip of the Contentin Peninsula. McGillicuddy and Stone had gone with the Canadian Third Infantry to follow its move toward Caen and the taking of Carpiquet Airfield. Then they had met again just inside of Avranches at the end of July. The Fourth Armored Division had entered the town on the retreating Germans' heels.

Robert spotted Jenny standing in a doorway just as a column of German vehicles came along the road. They bore huge red crosses on the sides, indicating that they were carrying wounded. He hurried over to her with a big smile of greeting on his face and quickly pulled her to the ground as gunfire suddenly burst from the trucks. Her chin rubbing in the rubble and dirt on the ground, she peered over Robert's arm as an American tank demolished the lead vehicles. Slowly getting to their feet, they watched Germans with their hands raised pile from the trucks that followed.

"You'd better stick with us," Charlie said that evening as they hungrily ate cheese and bread in a small café with half of its roof and walls missing. He raised his tin cup of wine to her, his hazel eyes twinkling behind horn-rimmed glasses. "You could get yourself killed, y'know."

"Well, only because I need a ride," she agreed grudgingly. "And because you've found this disabled jeep." As they began the move eastward Charlie and Robert heard a kind of desperation growing in her voice as she asked people she chanced to meet if they had met or seen an American pilot named Douglas Gilbert. Soon Charlie, who had a wife and children back in the States, began to suspect that she was pregnant.

"She looks a little green around the gills sometimes," he said in a low voice to Robert. "And a little plump in the middle, wouldn't you say?" And though they never mentioned it, knowing she was trying desperately to conceal it, they admired her pluck. "She has guts," Robert muttered on the morning they prepared to leave Avranches to follow Patton's Third Army.

In their race toward Paris they saw a new kind of hope flood her face. She even began talking to them about Doug as they skidded around bomb craters in the roads, drove through villages that had been leveled or half destroyed by Allied planes and artillery, and became bogged down in the crowds of refugees streaming their way back to Paris, most of them walking or pushing wagons or baby carriages filled with possessions.

But most of the time she sat quietly in the rear of the jeep, thinking of Doug . . . or of Christopher, her eyes somber and sad. Christopher was always at the back of her mind, but it was like a murky dream, his face still the face of the baby she had last seen, contorted in whimpering cries as Mary hurried through the living room and out the door with him . . . or

247

standing in his crib the day she went to Craddock Corners, the tiny quick glimpse she had of him, his little hand outstretched as though to reach for her . . . and then Fred's hands like steel bands on her arms, leading her away.

Quickly blinking back the tears, she would force herself to watch the refugees or walk along with them part of the time, asking them questions, giving them some of her K-rations or water from her canteen.

The three of them were completely unprepared for the roaring celebration that had overtaken Paris, even in the sectors where gunfire still reverberated. Maneuvering past barricades of overturned vehicles, furniture, and sandbags, they were continually swamped with joyous crowds who threw flowers at them, sang the "Marseillaise," and shouted "Vive l'Américain!" men leaning over the side of the jeep and kissing Jenny while women hugged Robert and Charlie. The townspeople hung garlands of flowers over their jeep, poured them wine, and showered them with kisses. The streets were filled with song and the roar of voices while guns of the Resistance still sounded in the distance as they fought on against the retreating Germans. White bedsheets that hung from windows indicated the surrender of Germans who lived inside those apartments or hotels. And festooning the buildings were hastily painted signs welcoming the French, British, and American troops. There were flags everywhere, from all three countries, and the names of General De Gaulle and General Leclerc were scrawled or hand-lettered on walls and shop windows. Blobs of paint had been smeared over German-language signs that had replaced the French signposts four years before, expressing in a haphazard way the joy-filled release from the painful humiliation that the people of Paris had suffered for so long.

They watched in speechless awe as hysterical joy enveloped them wherever they moved. There was singing and laughter everywhere, but still the sound of guns.

They let Jenny off at the Rue de Seine.

"We'll be at the Hotel Scribe," Robert said.

"And if you come looking for us," Charlie grinned, "we'll probably be in the bar. Just in case you need a room tonight."

"Day after tomorrow, Jen," Robert warned as she climbed from the jeep, pulling her gear with her and gazing up at the shuttered windows above a shop that had a *tabac* sign jutting from the wall. "We'll be here at 0700. Unless, of course, we see you tonight."

She watched them for a brief moment as they drove on, past the Hotel de Seine, a tall narrow building that jutted out in an L-shape along the narrow sidewalk.

The concierge pointed the way up the narrow stairs to flat number twelve. Jenny found the door and knocked with trembling fingers. When no one answered, her heart sank. Of course, she thought, why would anyone be at home? They would both be out celebrating. But as she turned and started back toward the stairway, she heard a latch turn in the door and stopped. All she heard was the voice, low and silvery, the darkness of the hallway casting the half-opened door in shadow. She hurried back, her heart in her mouth again, her hands trembling as she clutched her purse and knapsack and typewriter. *"Qui est là?"* the voice said.

"Excuse me," she said hurriedly. "My French is very bad and at this moment I can't remember a word of it. Do you by any chance speak—"

"But yes," the silvery voice said. "What is it you want?"

"Are you Solange Leroux?"

"Oui." The door opened a bit wider, and Jenny saw a pale but lovely face, thin with high cheekbones, brilliant dark eyes, and a clinging cap of black hair. She was staring at Jenny's uniform.

"Doug Gilbert told me to come here when I reached Paris—" she started to say as the door swung even wider, and she looked beyond for a moment to a large room filled with Oriental screens and long graceful windows, shining floors, and delicate tables. Huge gleaming armoires stood against walls filled with paintings. A music stand hovered near a window, and flowers and books were everywhere.

"Douglas Gilbert? But of course. An old and dear friend of François'. Please come in."

"Thank you." Jenny stepped into the apartment, past the tiny foyer and just beyond the door, where she turned and looked at the tall, slim young woman in the pale green dress. "My name is Jenny MacKenzie." Biting her lower lip with anxiety, she tried to smile.

"You are with the American Army?"

"War correspondent." Jenny showed her the patch on her left sleeve. "I'm a newspaper reporter. Madame Leroux—"

"Please sit down," the woman said, gesturing to a chair, but Jenny appeared not to have heard her, and, gripping her hands on the typewriter handle, she bent forward a little.

"Doug said he would be here or would leave word." The

woman looked puzzled. "He's a pilot," Jenny quickly explained, "with the American Air Force, and he left southern England just before the first of June. But I don't think he was flying. I mean, I think it was something else, some kind of mission he was on, something very secret, but just before he left he gave me your address and told me to come to see you for word of him."

Solange Leroux slowly shook her head, in a matter of seconds understanding the situation. She took the typewriter and knapsack and purse from Jenny and led her to a chair. Jenny had become deathly white and her lips were trembling. She was only half aware of Solange as she crossed to a table and poured a glass of brandy. Jenny sipped at it for a moment, then put it down on the table next to her and whispered, "Thank you." He wasn't here. They hadn't had any word.

"We haven't heard from Douglas," Solange said carefully, "not since before the Germans came. And now François is gone. He just left this morning."

"Left?" she asked blankly, feeling her heart plummet deeper and deeper. Doug wasn't in Paris. He hadn't reached here. The realization stunned her.

"He has left to join Colonel Raoul's French Forces of the Interior," Solange explained as she gently pulled Jenny's jacket off. "Until the Germans began to leave a few days ago, he was fighting with the Resistance." Suddenly she threw her hands wide and a soft laugh spilled from her lips. "You will have to forgive me, but until this moment I had not said that word aloud. Resistance." She seemed to taste the word, test it in her mouth, and repeated it. "Resistance!" she cried out, glorying in it.

For a moment Jenny forgot her own bitter disappointment and fears. "It's almost unbelievable, what you people have gone through here. You and the British! How I admire you!"

"It's almost unbelievable that you people are here, and that we are free again," Solange said, her eyes misting. On a sudden impulse she clasped Jenny's shoulders and kissed her on both cheeks. "You will stay here with me, and perhaps Douglas will come, now that the city is open and ours again."

But though they waited, never leaving Solange's flat, there was no word of Doug, and two mornings later Jenny stood down on the narrow sidewalk, waving and throwing a kiss to Solange as the jeep skidded around the corner toward her.

"Come back when you are ready, when you need help,"

Solange called down to her from the small balcony as the two men looked up and waved and smiled at her. She had guessed after a few hours that Jenny was going to have a baby, and excitedly said, "You must come back to Paris soon. This is where you will have the baby."

Jenny waved at her until she could no longer see her, then she huddled in the corner of the rear seat and quietly wept. In the short time she had spent in the flat on the Rue de Seine, she and Solange had become close friends, drawn together by the awesome moment in history they had shared and by their mutual sadness over the men in their lives.

"They are adventurers," Solange had told her in solemn tones. "They will always be gone on some bold and perilous mission. They are men of action, who will never be content with ordinary, routine lives."

"But he said he would meet me here or leave word," Jenny said stubbornly.

"They mean what they say when they say it, Jenny," Solange tried to comfort her. "But I am thankful for my music. You must be thankful for your life as a writer."

But all across the miles, as the Third Army hurled toward Metz and the German border, Jenny found herself wondering how anyone, even Douglas Gilbert, had been able to take the place of the stubborn independence she had once possessed, of the fierce and consuming desire to be a newspaper reporter before anything else. Aware that the loss of Christopher had pried open the door to feeling, she discovered she was like everyone else, vulnerable to pain and suffering.

As they raced through the countryside and villages that had been laid waste, she felt as exposed and raw as the land that had been plundered, the ancient houses that had crumbled into shards and dust. Only the sky remained untouched. Bombs had fallen through it, men had died among its clouds, and yet nothing marked the place where it had been violated. With her face buried in the pile of knapsacks tossed on the jeep's rear seat, she wept, cursing Douglas Gilbert, yet loving him no less . . . but only more, and feeling the pain cut deeper into her earthbound soul.

They had caught up with Patton and the Third Army halfway to Verdun, taking turns driving. "We're going straight through to the Rhine, I hear!" Charlie shouted. "That's what the old man keeps saying."

By September 5 they had crossed the Moselle River, driven on beyond Nancy, and were heading toward Metz. Field

Marshal Bernard Montgomery's armies had entered Antwerp, and General Hodges' First Army was approaching the Siegfried Line to start the battle for Aachen, but because of the serious problems of maintenance, communications, and supply for the hundreds of thousands of troops, and the necessary extension of lines to secure the port of Antwerp, the drive toward the German borders slowed to a crawl in many areas.

In early November, Patton's Third Army was south of the Ardennes Forest, engaged in an offensive against the Saar region, and after establishing bridgeheads across the Moselle north of the city of Metz, the city was taken and surrendered before the end of November. And by this time both Robert and Charlie were determined that Jenny had to return to Paris. But she was stubborn.

"The baby's not due until the middle of January," she protested. "And I feel fine." But she didn't feel fine, and on reaching Metz and the relative comforts of rooms in an inn, they refused to let her accompany them even on short runs beyond the city where pockets of resistance were still being fought. She did some of her best writing there, catching up with many of the first-person interviews she had done along the way and sending them off to be sent over the wire service that the *World-Dispatch* had hooked into. But she had begun to feel heavy and had sharp pains in her back. She was sleeping only an hour or two at a time and felt listless, sometimes even nauseated, and suddenly desperately lonely. Especially when Charlie and Robert left her for a week. With the Third Army spread in a wide arc from just below the Ardennes and Luxembourg to as far south as Nancy, they left for a week-long sweep of the front, first making arrangements for her to return on a transport supply plane that was going back to the Paris area.

But two letters from Solange had finally caught up with her, reporting still no word from Doug. With that she sank into lethargy, and when news came that the Germans had mounted a major attack to the northwest in the Ardennes, the two men rushed back, shocked to find her still there. They stopped only long enough to gather their gear and then headed northwest with her to a point near Luxembourg where General Omar Bradley had his headquarters. From there, they said, she would have to return to Paris.

"You can hitch a ride there," Robert said, glancing worriedly around at her and then peering back through the windshield at the snow as he drove. "Maybe one of the transport planes."

"Nothing's flying in this weather," Charlie said, looking through the isinglass on the side flaps up at the sky.

"Well, then one of our supply trucks. She can ride back with them." He glanced back at her quickly and smiled. "Not that we want to get rid of you, kid. But Charlie's no midwife, and I know even less than he does. Besides, you've got somebody else to start worrying about now."

Slipping her hands beneath the heavy coat and touching her stomach, she smiled. Part of Douglas was here with her. She stared at the backs of their heads and smiled again. In a way she loved them. She had only known them for a few months, but she felt as though she had known them always.

At a brief stopover near a town called Longuyon, they spotted a long column of halted vehicles, a military convoy pulled off to the side of the road. They sped along its length until they came to a mobile communications truck and stopped just as a sergeant jumped out of a jeep and hurried toward them.

"You'll have to go back or detour west of here," the sergeant called out. "We hear the Germans have busted through just above Arlon, and they've encircled Bastogne, another twenty or so miles up the line. We're waiting for any change in orders."

"You know of any supply outfits going back toward Paris?" Charlie asked him, stepping out on the road for a moment.

The sergeant was pointing back to an intersection they had just passed. "A group just turned off from this road and headed west. They just came down from the Bastogne area. Mostly ambulance corps."

Robert circled the jeep in a U-turn and then roared west as Jenny held her breath for long minutes at a time. She felt a strange, crawling kind of tightening in her abdomen and knew that she was beginning the long approach to her child's birth. The signs were almost imperceptible, signs she would probably never have noticed this soon if she hadn't been where she was, here almost on the eve of Christmas and one hundred and fifty miles from Paris.

They caught up with the convoy in about twenty minutes. It was traveling at a fast clip, but Robert gunned the jeep, pulled alongside the lead vehicle, and managed to flag it down. As the small convoy pulled to a stop Charlie jumped out and spoke to the lone driver of the first ambulance.

"We have a young woman here who has to get back to Paris fast," he said as she climbed out, her big winter coat bundled close and hiding any signs of pregnancy.

She looked back at Robert and, roughly rubbing the tears from her eyes as he leaned over to kiss her cheek, she said in a husky voice, "Come to Paris to see me."

"Damn right," Robert said, smiling. In the middle of the snow- and windswept road she hugged Charlie; then, as he handed her gear up to the driver, she hurried around to the other side and climbed up into the seat next to the driver. She heard the heavy sound of gears shifting and felt the vehicle move, but for a moment she kept her eyes shut tight, forcing back the tears.

"The name's Jack," the driver said, looking over at her with a quick smile. "Jack Wright. I'm from Altoona, Pennsylvania."

"Hi," she managed. "Jenny MacKenzie. From New York."

"Hey, I gotta cousin who lives in New York. Bert Behrens is his name."

"Never met him," she said, looking straight ahead. Then, as they glanced at each other, they both burst out laughing.

He told her about Altoona, about Ginny, his girl, about playing on the high school football team and Sunday dinner at one o'clock sharp when his father always delivered a lecture to his brother and sister and himself, and his mother cooked fricasseed chicken and dumplings. He had curly blond hair and gray-blue eyes and he was twenty years old. "I want to go to medical school when I get out of this blasted army." He gestured with his head toward the back of the ambulance. "Those poor guys back there. One of them may not make it, the doc said, and one of the other ones will probably lose his leg."

She saw the plane and remembered later wondering why she could see it, then realized the snow had stopped and the sky had cleared to a dull high gray. The plane seemed to loop lazily far off above the horizon, then suddenly it turned and, diving in a steep run, screamed toward them like a deadly arrow. She felt the ambulance lurch to a stop and heard the shriek of the plane as it shot past them just overhead, heard the clatter of gunfire and threw herself down onto the vehicle's floor. At a cry she looked up, saw blood spurting from Jack's left arm through the cloth of his coat, and reached up and pulled him down as she heard the plane come back. Four times the plane made the run, each time miraculously missing them. Then, with another lazy loop on the far horizon, it became a dot against the sky and disappeared.

She pulled herself back up on the seat, jumped out of the ambulance, and ran to the back, but the doors were already open and a medic from the second vehicle was just climbing down.

"They're okay!" he shouted. "Tell Jack to get this crate the hell out of here!" He was sprinting back to the other vehicle.

She stared after him, then ran and jumped into the front of the ambulance. "I'll fix you up, then I'd better drive," she said to Jack.

He grinned weakly. "The day I let a pregnant lady drive *me* to the hospital will be a zero day in hell."

She grinned back. "Bandages?"

"Footlocker in back of the seat. I think it's just a flesh wound."

"Try to pull your coat and shirt off," she ordered him as she scrambled her hands down into the footlocker and came up with bandages. "I'll do a tourniquet and a fast bandaging job. We have to get out of here."

In five minutes he shoved the ambulance into gear and they began to move. As she slumped back against the seat he smiled weakly and said, "And my mother warned me about picking up hitchhikers."

She smiled at him, then glanced back at the road as the ambulance rasped into high gear. Suddenly she gasped a little and held her breath. The first pain, starting in her back, slowly unfolded and began to grind downward. Gritting her teeth, then feeling the perspiration on her face, she looked at her wristwatch. Three fifteen.

"All I can say at this point, my unborn child," she muttered through clenched teeth, "is that this had better be a long labor."

Chapter 27

PACKAGES IN HER arms, Kate hurried along Brookton's main street toward her car, which was parked near the post office. It was midafternoon and she was tired. She had been rolling bandages for six straight hours at the Red Cross headquarters, one of the few volunteers to do the work on Saturdays, and her back muscles were sore from leaning over the table.

"Here, let me carry those for you," a voice said at her elbow and she turned. It was Mike McCauley, Edwinna McCauley's brother. He took the packages from her, then strode along beside her.

"Thanks," she said with a little laugh. "They *were* getting heavy. Books I'd ordered for the children, and I forgot I'd asked for that many. Of course, Jon's are just those little picture books. He's still too small for anything except illustrations of cows and horses and goats. But Joanna's getting into the read-me-a-story stage."

Mike nodded as he looked down at her with a smile. "Every night before she goes to bed, I suppose?"

Kate nodded as she stopped beside the long Packard and opened the door. "Here's my car. And thank you so much."

Just as she took the books from him and put the packages down on the front seat, he touched her arm. "How about a late afternoon drink?" He gestured toward the Brookton Inn, a small restaurant and cocktail lounge next to the post office. "Coffee, cocktail, anything you want."

"Thanks, but I *do* have to get back," Kate said, starting around to the driver's side of the car, but only half conscious of the curious stares of people walking in and out of the post office. Everyone in Brookton knew Kate, and everyone knew Mike McCauley.

"Please," he said, detaining her with another touch on the arm. "I'd like to talk to you. There's never time at the mills, even when I *do* see you there." As she hesitated, then started to walk around the car again, he said, "I could say that I have a couple of business matters I'd like to discuss with you, but—" His eyes were smiling and candid. "I'd just like to get to know you better, that's all."

Kate looked up at him for a moment, then nodded and smiled. "All right." She glanced at her tiny diamond wristwatch. "Just so I'm on my way by four thirty."

Their conversation, she discovered, came easily. Avoiding any talk about Adam, she found herself telling Mike about her years in California when she was growing up, the years at the beach house before her mother's death and then those at the big somber house in San Francisco, her father's remarriage, and finally how she had come to New York.

Mike hung on her every word, asked questions and offered comments, smiled in all the right places, but never took his eyes from her. And yet, strangely, she felt no discomfort. Quite to the contrary, she immediately felt at home with him, completely at ease. So much so that as he finished telling her about his growing years in Brookton and his first job at the mills at the age of sixteen, she looked at her watch and exclaimed, "But it's after five!" As she gathered up her gloves and looked around the half-darkened lounge while Mike called for the check, she realized it was the pleasantest two hours she had spent in a long time. And as they rose to leave, she felt a small glow inside and felt the flush on her cheeks as he helped her into her car and watched her drive away.

Halfway to Finisterre she turned on her headlights, and it was as though a light snapped on in her mind. She shook her head a little, as if clearing away disturbing thoughts. They *were* disturbing thoughts. What am I *thinking?* she asked herself silently as she eased her foot on the accelerator. She was driving way over the speed limit.

Quickly, almost angrily, she put a cigarette between her lips and pushed the lighter in on the dashboard. *I* know what I'm thinking, she thought. I'm thinking like some sex-starved spinster who finds every presentable man she meets a potential bed partner. She laughed then, throwing her head back a little, the laughter spilling softly from her lips.

Well, not *every* presentable man, she told herself. It was just because he was so very likable, so positive, so straight-from-the-shoulder, and—yes, attractive.

Now you're being ridiculous, Kate Barnfield, she told

herself with a short little laugh, and pressed her foot down on the accelerator again. She was running late for dinner, and Marianne and Reed were coming.

As the houseman put the silver coffee service down in front of her, she smiled, then picked up a cup and saucer and poured. "Thank you, Martin," she said. "We won't need you any longer." As Martin let the door to the butler's pantry swing silently behind him, she looked past the flickering candelabra at Jonathan. "Coffee, Jonathan?"

"I think not, my dear," he said heavily. "Dr. Newhouse says I must give that up too. First cigarettes, then red meat, sweets, and starches, and now coffee." He shook his head and grumbled, "There's nothing left. Nothing but my grandchildren, a short walk in the sun once in a while, the radio, and the newspapers. And at least the news there is good," he nodded. "I see that Patton has gotten across the Rhine and our planes are flattening the industrial towns in the Ruhr."

"To say nothing of the taking of Iwo Jima in the Pacific." Reed lounged back in his chair and lit a cigarette, then nodded at Kate as she handed him his coffee. "Looks as though we're in the final stretch, doesn't it?"

But Marianne was rapping her fingertips on the table with impatience. Stirring cream into her coffee, she looked at Jonathan. "You said you wanted to talk to us, Father."

As Kate gazed down the table she thought again how tired and gray Jonathan looked, how deeply lined his face had become. Since Adam's death he had steadily declined, a decline that had culminated in February with a mild heart attack.

"Yes, that's right," he said, looking first at Marianne and then at Kate and finally Reed. Reed sat up a bit, seeming suddenly startled at Jonathan's piercing gaze. "Dr. Newhouse has also said that I must curtail my working day," he said, a certain amount of sarcasm in his voice. "Which is utter nonsense, of course. However, I will take it easy for a while, until I begin to feel better." Slowly he looked around at Kate. "But I'm pleased to say I *can* relax a little. Kate has been an apt, sometimes even brilliant pupil, these past six or eight months."

Kate glanced quickly at Reed and saw the sudden anger in his face.

"And she has revealed an uncanny sense for business, our business in particular. And so, on the strength of her performance in these past months, I decided to give her a boost up the ladder to the post of vice-president in charge of production. We signed the contracts this morning. Of course, I'll be breathing over your shoulder, Kate." He smiled.

Reed stared at Jonathan, his face flushing in anger, as Marianne turned to Kate with sparkling eyes. "Kate, how wonderful," she said, stretching her hand along the table to clasp Kate's.

But suddenly Reed was standing, his chair shoved back. He was leaning on the table toward Jonathan. "Wait a minute—" He glanced angrily at Marianne, then back to Jonathan again. "It's not wonderful at all!"

"You will continue as secretary of the company, Reed," Jonathan said, his voice rising as Reed began to shout.

"Damn it!" Reed brought his fist down on the table. "First Adam, and now Kate! You told me when I came into the company that—"

"I told you a lot of things when you came into the company, Reed." Jonathan had risen; his face had paled and his hands were trembling. Kate and Marianne both stood up. "And among them was the clear expression that simply because you had become a member of the family did not mean that it was a free ride. It did not mean an empty title with afternoons on the polo field or at the tiller of a sailboat or in the bar of the Yale Club."

"Hold on now," Reed raged, "those War Production Board contracts didn't just walk in the door, Jonathan!"

"Those War Production Board contracts were more of Marianne's maneuvering than yours, Reed; people that you met through her, the father of a girl she went to school with, and—" He suddenly leaned down on the table, and his mouth seemed to go slack.

"But who do you think *talked* Billington into those contracts? Marianne?" Reed was still shouting, hearing and seeing nothing in his fury. "Not on your life. It was Reed Shaw, that's who it was! I spent a lot of hours—"

"Shut up, Reed!" Marianne screamed as she and Kate ran around the table to Jonathan, who had fallen into his chair and slumped back, his eyes stretched wide, incoherent sounds coming from his mouth.

Kate hurried to the butler's pantry door and swung it open, shouting, "Martin! Call Dr. Newhouse, quickly! No! No, get an ambulance. Call the hospital. For God's sake, hurry."

259

"Oh, dear God, Kate! Look at his face." Marianne was crying.

Kate knelt beside Jonathan and took his pulse. "Let's not wait," she said, looking up at Marianne. Then, turning to Reed, she said in low-voiced urgency, "Call Nelson on the house phone. Tell him to bring the Rolls around." And as Reed ran to the house phone, she looked at Marianne. "Tell Martin to get that wheelchair we used for Amanda out of the storeroom. We'll take him to the hospital ourselves."

As Marianne ran through the butler's pantry door Kate spoke to Jonathan, whose eyes rolled in terror as odd little gasping sounds came from his mouth.

"Just hold on, Jonathan," she soothed him, her heart pounding hard in her throat. "Hold on. We'll get you to the hospital in no time at all." She looked up at Marianne coming back from the kitchen area.

"Kate—Marianne—" he gasped, one hand clutching feebly at the air, his eyes still rolling.

"No, Jonathan!" Kate almost shouted, as though willing it. "You're going to be all right. Do you hear me?" She leaned down close to his ear. "Do you hear me?"

Slowly he nodded his head.

Chapter 28

By the spring of 1945 everyone, except perhaps Adolf Hitler, knew the war in Europe was coming to an end.

Liz, like most Americans, kept a radio turned on wherever she happened to be to hear the constant news bulletins and bought three and four editions of the newspapers each day to read the latest word on the war in both Europe and the Pacific.

But there was a sliver of unreality to it all for her. No matter how close the end of the war came, Dan never relented in his persistence to serve in an active capacity in some way before everything came to a halt.

She felt as though she were still walking along the edge of a precipice. A day never passed that he didn't speak about it, and he phoned people of influence in Washington at regular intervals and paid frequent visits to the OSS office of Colonel Donovan whenever he was in the nation's capital working at the OWI.

And yet, when it happened, she was completely unprepared. It came suddenly and unexpectedly as she sat halfway up the rows of seats in the theater where they were rehearsing Dan's newest play. She didn't come on again until the second act, and they were going over the last scene of the first act for the fourth time that afternoon.

Just one bare bulb illuminated the huge stage, which had been set with odds and ends of backstage chairs and tables to simulate the setting of an artist's studio in Greenwich Village. Liz sat off by herself, studying her lines with a small flashlight and making pencil marks on the script. At a tapping on her shoulder, she turned around, saw Dan in the row of seats behind her, and at a silent gesture from him, followed him out to the empty lobby, where he sat her down on a small upholstered bench. When she saw the expression in his eyes, the excitement there, the eagerness in his darkly handsome face, her heart stopped for a moment. Clasping her hands to her mouth, she said, "Oh, no!"

"Honey, it's not what you think," he insisted. "And it's something you've never even dreamed could happen."

"What, Dan?" she asked, her hands still clasped tight and held to her mouth. "Oh, God, what?" she cried. Quickly he sat beside her and grasped her hands.

"*Report Magazine*. They're sending me on a special assignment to Europe. They want me to be there for the ending of the war, for the Armistice signing, whatever happens, the ratification of Germany's surrender—whatever I can get before the whole thing rolls up for the finale."

She was shaking her head back and forth. "But it's not over—they're still fighting—"

"It can't go much longer. Our First Army's at the Rhine at Remagen. The Russians are getting ready to go into Austria."

"But the play—" She knew she sounded on the verge of hysteria and tried to control it. "And the work on your newest one—"

"You'll all be better off without me around to pick at you or rage when something goes wrong. Playwrights should keep away from their plays when they're in rehearsal—"

She stood up suddenly. "How long have you been working on this, trying to get this assignment?" she asked, all at once sounding very calm, almost toneless.

"I had lunch with the editor-in-chief and some other people about five weeks ago. At the time I told him I'd been trying to get over there ever since the damned war started. He phoned me this morning."

She simply nodded her head and reached up to touch his face. "I'd better get back. They'll be looking for me for the second act." As she walked back into the darkened theater he slowly followed her.

Liz had succeeded so far in not showing Dan any tears. She had dressed carefully for their farewell, in a close-fitting black and white silk suit and large black straw hat, a sable scarf over one shoulder and her golden blonde hair pulled back into a smart chignon.

As they came through Pennsylvania Station a woman stopped her for her autograph. "I saw you in your last play

262

and just thought you were so wonderful," she said as Liz handed her back the piece of paper.

"Thank you," Liz murmured, dropping her eyes so the woman wouldn't see the hint of tears. Then Dan had taken her arm again and led her through the crowds, his hand pressing warmly, telling her she was his, for always and always.

The night before he had held her all through the night. His lovemaking, as always, had started with a very special gentleness and concern, then it had swept her onward in a storm of murmurs and the touch of hands, their bodies pressed closely until she cried out in exquisite joy. But sadness, too, for she would miss him terribly, would lie awake nights in fear for his safety.

And as she lay in his arms, she heard his breathing become steady and knew he was sleeping. But long before he had slept, although he held her close, she knew he was already far away from her.

"What would you like to have, Liz?" Dan was asking as the white-jacketed waiter stood beside their table.

"Nothing. Oh—" she sounded distracted "—a whiskey sour, maybe." While pulling off her white gloves, she tried to smile. But Dan was ordering their drinks. She looked around the club car. They were sitting on the Congressional Limited, with half an hour before it was scheduled to leave. It was crowded and noisy and hot for April. She tried not to stare, but two women sitting across and down a little distance were crying. A man sitting with them was holding one of the women by her shoulders as though to comfort her.

"Look, honey," Dan was saying, his hand closing over hers on the small table, "I know it was sudden, and I know you're upset, but please try to understand." He was pleading, his face near as he leaned across the table to her. "It's what I've dreamed of, prayed for, even though it's coming close to the end."

She reached up and touched his cheek softly. "It's just that I'll miss you so terribly. And your new play. You won't even see the opening of your new play. Can't you wait just three days, then leave? And I'll be so nervous without you on opening night."

"Darling, they're working on my passport right now. I have to pick it up in the morning, right at the State Department;

263

then they're reserving me space on this military transport plane that leaves tomorrow night."

She looked frightened as she slowly pushed the dark lock of hair from his forehead. He grasped her hand and held it tight.

"You'll be right where the fighting is. Oh, Dan, I'm so afraid."

"Liz, you've been reading the newspapers. Those armies are moving so fast across Germany, I'll be lucky if I catch up with the rear guard. Why, this morning's newspaper said that sections of the Ninth Army were just fifty miles from Berlin last night. I've got to get there fast. The magazine's war desk wants me there when the Americans enter Berlin. They also want a report on the meeting of the Eastern and Western allies. The Red Army is at the Oder River right now, and this meeting isn't far off."

"If only you had told me, Dan, I could have been better prepared."

"Darling," he said, holding her hand tighter, "if I'd told you I was working on this assignment, trying to get it, you'd have started talking me out of it." A new sound came into his voice. "I have to go, Liz! I have to have a part somewhere in all of this. It's important to me, more important than you'll ever know."

She looked at him for a long moment, then nodded her head. "I know," she said softly, "and I understand, darling, I honestly—" A loud outcry across from them made her stop and look around. Another woman was crying. She had thrown her head back and was wailing, "Oh, God, no, no!" Just then their waiter put their drinks down in front of them, and Liz stared first at the woman, then at their waiter, who stood beside them, a distressed expression on his face.

"What's wrong?" she asked, bewildered.

"Our President, ma'am. It just came over the radio. President Roosevelt just died of a cerebral hemorrhage at the summer White House in Warm Springs."

Chapter 29

THE BABY HAD been born in December 1944 at the American Hospital in Paris, a healthy six-pound girl that Jenny named Susan. As she lay in the hospital bed, she couldn't help but remember how she had rejected Christopher when he was born. How miserably unhappy she had been, she thought. How much she hadn't wanted him. She turned her face to the pillow and wept.

"I tried to get him back," she explained to Solange. "But I had everything against me, and each time I went to court, the losing became worse. It was like something eating away at me, and finally I knew it was hopeless. But someday . . . someday . . ." Her eyes glittered as her fists clenched the coverlet.

Whenever the nurses brought Susan in to be nursed, Jenny's longing for Christopher became almost unbearable. Once the war was over, she promised herself, she would go back into court and fight for him again. By that time she and Doug would be together, and with Susan and Christopher it would be a whole new life for all of them.

She had written Henry Fremont, asking him for the Paris bureau job, at least temporarily, and he had responded in the affirmative, wishing her luck, congratulating her on a job well done, and wishing her happiness with the arrival of Susan.

"But take it easy for a couple of months," he wrote. "You've more than earned the rest. If, when your young man shows up in Paris, you decide you want to come back to New York, well, we'll work it out. Alison sends her love, and you have my best. Henry."

From the moment she walked out of the American Hospital in Neuilly with Susan in her arms, she knew that before anything she must find Douglas Gilbert. Solange took her home with her, saying that Jenny and the baby would keep

her from going mad worrying about François. He was somewhere with the French First Army, pushing up from southern
France into the Alsatian area at the German border.

But Paris was free of Germans for the first time in five
years. With Susan in a backpack, Jenny wandered through
the spring sunshine, haunting the Quartier, sitting in cafés,
her eyes darting from face to face. The city was filled with
American soldiers on twenty-four or forty-eight-hour passes
from the front, and whenever she saw the shoulder patch of
the Eighth Air Force, she walked up to the man and asked
him questions.

Newspaper headlines in the kiosks were a blur—President
Roosevelt's death, Patton's crossing of the Rhine, the taking
of Okinawa in the Pacific, and finally in May the end of the
war in Europe, with Parisians marching through the sunshine,
arms linked, singing and chanting and crying in joy.

When François returned, limping with a leg wound but
grateful to be alive, Jenny moved to a nearby flat. Before the
war François had been a rising young poet and writer in
France, and in the postwar gaiety and freedom the city was
filled once more with artists and writers, and life became
interesting again. At François and Solange's Sunday evening
soirees, Jenny met Janet Flanner, known as Genêt and André
Breton. She listened to the songs of Juliette Greco in the
Rose-Rouge and Dixieland music at Saint-Columbier in
Saint-Germain. But each place she went, every experience
she had, was diminished by the absence of Doug, and each
morning when she scooped Susan from her crib and held her
close, she yearned to see Christopher, to bring him home to
her, wherever "home" might be.

"Jenny has a son in America," François explained to Paul
Louvier, a lawyer friend of his, on a Sunday evening as
friends gathered in the Leroux flat. After briefly explaining
the circumstances that led up to her losing Christopher and
the court battles she had fought, François said, "And she
wants to go to New York and file a suit again."

Paul shook his head slowly. He had met Jenny before. His
wife, Janette, had become her friend. He knew about Doug
and her search for him.

"If she goes before the court, she will have to explain many
points. The court will want to know about her child Susan; it
will ask about her marital status, and having a child out of
wedlock. Her situation will perhaps be even more question-
able than before."

"I can't just sit here doing nothing," Jenny insisted. "I've got to do something!"

"Find this Douglas and marry him," Paul advised. "You must go before the court in America as a responsible young married woman."

Jenny went back to work, first covering Paris and the environs when stories broke; but as the months tumbled past she went farther afield. She traveled to Marseilles and did a long piece on the reassembling of the French fleet. She went to Nuremberg for the trials, reported in short pungent pieces the political crises that plagued France, and in longer, more detailed stories the launching and merits of the Marshall Plan's European Recovery Program. Burying herself in work and the spare hours she had with Susan, she stopped counting the months and years. To her it seemed the war had just happened yesterday. She still watched faces on the street for Doug. Though pure and simple logic should have told her to stop looking for him, she closed that part of her mind and lived on the fantasy that anything was possible.

The memory of Del Wheeler remained so clear and fresh in Kate's mind that as the next few years passed, she pushed the thought of Mike McCauley from her consciousness each time there were any other chance meetings in Brookton. She rarely saw him at the mills. Since he was a foreman, his path seldom crossed hers. Occasionally he came to Finisterre to report some matter of business to Jonathan, who still held the reins on the mills but did much of his work from his bed or a wheelchair in the library. Even at these times Kate usually exchanged only a few words with Mike. Only one other time, in Brookton, did she accept his invitation for a cup of coffee.

But Jonathan's announcement at the dinner table one night still came as a surprise to her.

"Mike McCauley's left us," he said without looking up as he cut a piece of white meat chicken and slowly lifted it to his mouth.

"Left us? For where?" Kate asked, surprised at the sudden lurch of her heartbeat.

"A mill in Massachusetts," Jonathan said, chewing slowly, his face gaunt in the candlelight, but the silvery head still imperious and handsome. "Didn't give any reason. Just said he wanted to move on. It's a smaller operation, so he'll be general manager in charge of production there."

"Well then, of course," Kate said, almost too quickly. "It's an advancement for him."

"Rubbish!" Jonathan said with a scowl. "In a mill one-tenth the size of the Barnfield Mills? What kind of advancement is that?" He was disgustedly pushing the chicken around his plate, and suddenly he put his knife and fork down. "Chicken," he grumbled. "That's all I find on my plate these days. Chicken."

"I'm sorry, but you know it's doctor's orders," Kate said, then quickly asked, "Then what do you think his reason was?"

"Haven't the faintest idea," Jonathan said, thinking hard. "Unless what Hamilton told me is true. Andrew Hamilton claims Mike's in love with some woman here who can't see him for dust."

Kate lifted her cup quickly and sipped her coffee just as Nelson came to the door.

"If you're going to get to the theater in time for the first-act curtain, Mrs. Barnfield, we'll have to leave in fifteen minutes."

"Thank you, Nelson." She rose quickly and hurried to the door, where she paused to say good night to Jonathan.

"Sorry I have to leave so abruptly, Jonathan, but it's the final night of Liz's play before she takes it on tour, and I haven't seen it yet."

"Go along and enjoy yourself," he said from the head of the long table as he waved her off. "You can tell me all about it tomorrow."

"I'll have Mrs. Harrison bring the children in to say good night, Jonathan." She turned at the door.

"Never mind, never mind," Jonathan said with another wave of his hand. "I'll have Martin wheel me down to the playroom to see them."

"Then good night," she said and was gone. For several moments he stared at the doorway where she had stood, as beautiful as ever in her long dinner gown and creamy pearls. Well, maybe *she* was blind, he thought with a small, tight smile, but he, Jonathan Barnfield, certainly wasn't. Of course, Mike McCauley had never been one for hiding what he was thinking, whether it was union business, mill business, or monkey business. But Jonathan's eyes were gleaming, and with that small, tight smile he shook his head slowly just as Martin came in from the butler's pantry. He had to admire Mike's style, getting out before the situation got out of hand.

"But, damnit, Martin, I'm losing a good man there, with Mike McCauley going up to Strummond," he said as Martin started wheeling the chair toward the door.

"Yes, sir," Martin said, agreeing as he always did with anything Jonathan Barnfield had to say.

As the house lights dimmed several times, Kate pushed through the lobby crowds back toward her seat, still caught in the spell of the play and Liz's performance. It was the best of Dan's work so far, she thought, a powerful piece that would have the critics raving in all or most of the newspapers, and with equal acclaim for Liz's performance in the starring role.

How Mike McCauley would have loved this play, she thought as she walked down the aisle, slowly edging past people to her seat—the brutal portrait of New York sweat-shop owners victimizing their employees, preying on their illiteracy and wretched living conditions, but underneath it all the hopeful theme of one person fighting back, in this instance a physically frail young woman who can't bear to watch the inhuman treatment inflicted on the very old and very young. "Theatricality, overzealous propaganda" is undoubtedly what the more conservative newspapers will say, she thought as she settled into her seat for the third act.

At that moment a young man in a dark suit walked out from between the folds of the closed curtain onto the apron of the stage and held his hand up until the audience settled down into program-rustling silence.

"Thank you," he said solemnly. "With great regret the management must inform you that Miss Elizabeth Lowndes has been taken ill and will not be able to complete the performance—" He raised his hand again to still the sudden outburst from the audience. "However, her understudy, Miss Charlotte Murdock, will take over the role—"

Kate heard no more. She immediately hurried up the aisle and around to the stage door, where she identified herself and asked the way to Liz's dressing room, aware of the sound of a siren off in the distance. Oh God, she thought, an ambulance.

Liz was stretched out on a chaise, her eyes closed, one hand in a fist and pressed to her mouth, the other clutching her abdomen. Hack Crawford was at the phone barking into it, obviously talking to the hospital, and Evelyn Crawford was sitting on a small chair pulled up next to the chaise, her hand on Liz's shoulder. When she saw Kate, she said, "Kate!

Thank God! I'm so glad you're here. Dan's in Los Angeles, but Hack couldn't reach him at his hotel."

"What is it?" Kate asked in alarm as she knelt down on the other side of the chaise.

At the sound of Kate's voice, Liz opened her eyes and grasped Kate's hand, then half whispered, "I . . . think it might be appendicitis. Please go with me, Kate."

"Of course," Kate said, clenching her hand just as Hack hung up the phone and two white-coated men hurried in with a stretcher.

"We'll follow in the car," Hack called out to Kate as she ran alongside the stretcher, through the backstage area, and out to the street where the ambulance waited, its red light still flashing. In moments they were racing uptown, the siren screaming. Kate watched the lights flash by and traffic move to the curbs as the ambulance shrieked past, then looked down at Liz, who was slowly opening her eyes and shaking her head as she looked at Kate.

"It's not appendicitis," she whispered. "It's a miscarriage." And tears began to roll down her face and onto the pillow beneath her head.

"Oh, Liz honey," Kate said, putting her cheek down against Liz's and clasping her hand tightly.

"No one knew," Liz went on. "I hadn't even told Dan. I was going to wait until the end of the New York run of this play, then ask him . . . ask him to replace me for the tour." She turned her head slowly and looked up at the ambulance window. "The last time, when Julie was born, the doctor told me this might happen. There's always the chance of it happening again." She looked back at Kate. "I wanted it so, Kate. And I thought everything was all right. I felt wonderful. Then tonight, just before the first curtain, I felt a dull ache, a cramp, like the beginning of menstrual cramps. But I was sure it was nothing, and went on—" She began to sob. "Oh, Kate . . ."

"Shhhh," Kate soothed her. "It's all right, honey. After some time has passed, you'll try again."

Liz slowly shook her head. "I wanted this one so badly, Kate. So badly. But I didn't tell Dan, because he still wanted me to wait." She clutched Kate's hand. "I don't want him ever to know. Promise me, Kate. Promise me!"

Kate, the doctor, and the Crawfords all kept their word and told Dan that Liz had had some kind of serious food poisoning. By the time he returned from the coast, she was home from the hospital and a week later was back in the play.

As the seasons rolled past, Kate found herself shouldering more and more of the responsibilities at the mills as Jonathan's health deteriorated. But it was too much, she knew. She simply didn't have the years of experience and knowledge required to take on the kind of load she found herself with. And when Andrew Hamilton, the elderly plant manager, gave notice that he wanted to retire, Kate, with Jonathan's permission, sat down and wrote Mike McCauley to ask him to return, but this time as general manager in charge of production.

Jonathan knew that Mike was undoubtedly still very much in love with Kate, but he also knew that he was the best man for the job.

"Could we stop over at the Brookton Inn for a drink when we're through here?" Mike asked Kate at the end of his first day back at the mills. "I have some things I want to talk over with you."

Kate looked at him for a moment, then slowly slipped her coat on. "Better still, Mike, come for dinner. We can talk over cocktails in the library, and Jonathan would love to see you at dinner, I'm sure."

He hesitated, then grinned as he walked out of her office. "I'll be there." He added softly, "It's been a long, long time."

"Six thirty," she called out, and he waved, then disappeared. She watched the door for a moment and, in that one fleeting second, wondered where Del was, what he was doing. It's almost midnight in England, she thought, and whispered softly into the silence, "Do you ever think about me? Or am I just someone who belongs only to the past, the far past? Oh God, will I ever be able to think of you in that way too?"

Chapter 30

"FRANÇOIS!" THE MAN stood next to their table, a slender, tall outline against the afternoon sun. Jenny squinted upward, then started to rise to leave but felt Solange's hand firmly on her arm, holding her in her chair. François was pumping the man's hand and people at the nearby café tables smiled at their exuberance and joy in seeing each other.

"But you remember Solange," François was saying as the stranger bent over and kissed Solange on both cheeks. "And this is our good friend Jenny MacKenzie, from the United States, a *journaliste,* like you. Ian writes for newspapers in England, Jenny. This is Ian Chase, a friend from long ago, a very close friend from my London University days." He laughed. "That was before my New York University days." His dark eyes were alight with pleasure.

"And we haven't seen each other in a donkey's age." Chase was smiling down at her and appraising her with frankly appreciative gray eyes. "Since before the war, actually."

Jenny smiled politely, then let her eyes wander back to the sidewalk where, from habit as much as anything after eight years, she studied each passing face.

She's still looking for him, Solange thought sadly, wondering when she would finally realize that Doug was gone for good.

"—and bring Susan," François was saying.

"What?" she asked. She hadn't been listening.

"For dinner," he laughed, chucking her under the chin as Ian sat down at the table. "And you can listen while Ian and I—how you say?—regale you with our escapades of our student days in London."

Jenny smiled again as she stood up.

"I must go," she said, "to pick up Susan at school. Then I have to get back to the office to finish the story on the ministers' meeting."

"For the European Defense Force?" Chase asked.

She nodded, then started off through the crowds. "Nice meeting you, Mr. Chase."

He looked after her, smiling, as Solange called out, "Seven, Jenny." Jenny smiled and waved, a pretty figure in a hurry. Solange called out again, "We will be expecting you, yes?"

Jenny simply nodded and hurried toward the Rue Racine, her eyes darting from face to face as people pushed past her going in the opposite direction. She glanced at her watch and slowed down. She would be early for Susan. As she walked on she shook her head a little. She had left Solange and François earlier than necessary. But—Ian Chase's direct gaze had disturbed her.

Solange and François were deeply in love, and because they thought love so wonderful, they constantly invited men to their apartment to meet Jenny.

"Please!" she had begged François. "No more matchmaking."

"Maman, Maman," Susan shouted as she ran toward Jenny, pulling her back into the present. Susan had Jenny's brown eyes but Doug's features: his high cheekbones, arched brows, and flawless skin. Where his features had been strong and finely chiseled, hers were delicate and exquisitely molded. Her face had never had the roundness or fullness of an infant or small child, but always this mature kind of beauty that caused older people to exclaim and children to turn to her for leadership. She was a strong child, strong in personality and convictions, strong in likes and dislikes, in her joy and small sorrows, in loyalties and decisions. She had become the core of Jenny's life, and when she asked just once about her father, Jenny told her the truth. He had never been mentioned between them again. Her name was MacKenzie, and it was because of her that Jenny stayed on in Paris.

"The French are more forgiving and accepting of an illegitimate child," she had written Henry Fremont in New York when telling him she wanted to stay on with the Paris bureau. "Especially one born during the war."

She left Susan with Helene, the young woman she had brought to live with them to take care of Susan, and hurried to her office just off the Champs-Élysées. Always, when walking through the streets of Paris, she thought of Douglas. Long before she had seen the city, she had known she would

273

fall in love with it. Doug had talked about Paris and its ancient gray stones, telling her of its strange and wonderful light and the Latin Quarter, its restaurants and cafés and boulevards and tiny, narrow, winding streets. She had never tired of listening to him talk about it, and found it even more than he had promised. And she had never tired of walking through its boulevards and streets; but as she did she ceaselessly glanced at every face, always in the hope of suddenly seeing Doug.

She crossed the Rue de Berri and ran up the stairs to the office she shared with correspondents from two other stateside newspapers. She pulled her notebook from her purse, then quickly ran some paper into her typewriter and sat down and began to pound the keys. It was a cut-and-dried story, straight facts on the signing by eight Western countries of a treaty forming a European defense force. "May 27, 1952," she typed at the top of the first take just as the phone rang.

"New York *Daily World-Dispatch*," she said, cradling the phone under her chin as she kept on typing.

"Jenny?"

She stopped, her fingers in midair, her heart lurching, then suddenly leaping wildly and beating hard against her chest.

"Doug!" Her voice was a husky, stunned rasp.

"I've been phoning all afternoon," he said.

"I was over at the Foreign Office," she said, trying to keep her voice from shaking, grasping the phone with both hands to keep it from falling to the floor. She strained to hear over the loud pounding of her heart in her eardrums. She wanted to cry, shriek, scream, lunge through the phone, but instead she asked, "Where are you? Are you in Paris?"

"About twenty minutes from your office," he said. "How about meeting me?"

"Yes," she said, still stunned. Then, "My God, it's really you!"

"How about Harry's Bar on the Rue Daunou?"

"As soon as I can get there. I'll fly, darling!"

She stopped outside on the Rue Daunou for a moment and, leaning against the building, closed her eyes, trying to catch her breath. It had been eight years. Eight long and lonely years, wondering what had happened to him, wondering if he was dead, but never giving up hope, never ending her search for him. For the first few years after the war ended, whenever she saw flyers from the American Army Air Corps, she rushed up to them and asked them questions. But of the hundreds she talked to over the years, she never met anyone who had known or heard of Doug. She had written to the Air Corps, but because she was not a wife or a blood relation, she was advised that they could not investigate further.

She had also written the local newspaper in Plainfield, New Jersey, only to receive information that the elder Gilbert had died and his wife had moved west, somewhere in California. But one morning she had looked across the Boulevard St.-Michel. Bud Corwin was walking along in the sunshine, limping a little and holding the arm of a pretty young woman, a camera dangling from his neck like any other tourist. She had dashed across the street, and as she leaped in front of him he threw his arms around her, then introduced her to his wife, Sally, excitedly explaining that Jenny had been at Chipping Epworth when he was there.

"I wanted to show Sally Paris," he laughed as they sat and sipped drinks in the Café de Cluny, "but a Paris that I never really saw, under the circumstances of my last visit." But when she asked him about Doug, he simply shook his head. "I never saw him again, Jen. None of us did. And never heard anything."

She told them then about Susan, showed them snapshots of her, and left them, feeling sadder and lonelier than before.

Now, standing in front of Harry's Bar, she felt a sudden shyness. Her legs were trembling, and for a brief second she wanted to turn and run. But she pushed the door open, stood for a moment adjusting her eyes to the light, then slowly walked toward him. He had risen from a small table in a corner, and she caught her breath, almost stopped. He looked the same—the dark narrow mustache and handsome face, the nonchalance as he smiled and raised his hand in greeting, the flashing teeth and graceful tilt of his head. And the eyes. That intense blue.

She stood for a moment, just looking at him; then she put her hands out and he quickly took them, drew her to him, and kissed her on the cheek. She wanted to throw herself in his arms, but there was a chair between them and he was pulling it out for her.

"Doug," she half whispered as she slowly sat down, never taking her eyes from him. "You see, I didn't know what happened, and I thought I'd never see you again."

He was signaling the waiter and asking her what she wanted. "Café," she told him, and he gave the waiter the order, then took her hands and turned back to her. "I was captured near Sainte Mère Église," he said, "along with a paratrooper whose feet had just barely touched the ground when they came up behind us. We had only moved on about one hundred yards from where he landed, when they came out from a clump of trees and that was it."

"Then you were in a prisoner-of-war camp?"

"They took us all the way to Germany."

"I tried to find you, wrote all kinds of letters, asked flyers I saw on the street, and—"

"Jenny." Something in his voice made her stop. Everything turned stiff and cold inside, and she found herself clutching her purse in her lap for something to hold on to. He looked at her for a long moment, then waited while the waiter put their drinks down on the table. As the waiter retreated he turned to her again. "I'm married, Jenny."

There was a long pause as she just stared at him. "Married?" Her voice was filled with disbelief, anguish, filling her throat and twisting the word, breaking it in half so that the last of it was lost in a gasping of breath.

"Jenny . . ." His voice was gentle. "I never said—"

"Don't say that!" she said. She looked away, tears hurting her throat, blurring her vision. "Who is she?" She tried to laugh. "That's the question they always ask in the movies, isn't it? Who is she?"

His voice was quiet, and he was looking down at the package of matches in his hand, slowly tearing them to little pieces. "She's a girl I met when I was stationed at Sheppard Field in Texas. Before I went to England I lived in a small town near there. We dated. Heavily. Then, just before I shipped out, she told me she was going to have a baby. So the day before I left, we got married. I wasn't in love with her. I knew that. But I thought—well, I thought maybe after the war, when I got back, we'd both agree it was a mistake." He kept looking at the torn matches as Jenny's eyes burned into his face. "I met you. You were the first woman I'd ever really cared about. But I knew I'd have to get home and settle the situation with Dorothy before—"

Her name was Dorothy. Jenny held her breath, caught her lip between her teeth.

"I was in pretty bad shape when the war finally ended. Two other men and myself, we'd tried to escape, and they really worked us over. The Allies, when they arrived at the POW camp shipped me right back to the States and a military hospital. She—she was waiting there for me. But not my son.

Robbie would have been two years old. I never saw him, you see. He'd died of leukemia just a month before I got home."

Jenny waited, unable to speak, emotionally torn, confused.

"All she could talk about then was having another baby, but she was afraid. Her sister had died of leukemia, too, and the doctors couldn't promise anything. They didn't know. It could be somewhere in the genes." He paused for a moment. "By that time I couldn't leave her. I didn't know what to do. I wanted to come back here, find you. But she was so sad, so lost, would hardly let me out of her sight. Finally I was released from the hospital, and I got a job as an airline pilot. Started flying the international route about a month ago. This is the first time I've gotten to Paris." He was silent again. "We adopted a little boy a year ago."

They sat quietly for several minutes, and in that passage of moments Jenny finally knew it was over. Doug was hopelessly enmeshed in a marriage that was built on mistakes and sorrow and death and fear, caught as so many young men were in loveless wartime marriages.

"Why are you here?" she asked, carefully controlling her voice. "Telling me . . . all of this?"

"I—" He looked down again. "I want to see our little girl."

"Susan?" she cried out. "What do you know about Susan?"

"I bumped into Bud Corwin about two weeks ago in Radio City. He and his wife were on a trip in New York. He told me he had seen you and that you had shown him pictures of a very beautiful little girl."

She looked at him for a long and searching moment, then asked softly, "Did you ever really love me, Doug?"

He raised his eyes. "Yes," he said in a low voice. "You were the most exciting and lovely creature I'd ever seen."

She felt as though she were drowning in the soft murmur of voices and the rise and fall of laughter all around them.

"Do you love her?" she asked, knowing the question was cruel, making her voice hard.

He thought for a long moment, then slowly shook his head. "No." He looked at Jenny pleadingly. "If you knew her, you'd understand. Understand why it's the way it is . . . has to be."

They were silent again.

"Jenny," he said, "I want to take our little girl back with me."

She stared at him, stunned. "What . . . did you say?"

"I want to take her back with me."

There was a terrible roaring in her ears. She tried to swallow but couldn't. Her mouth felt dry, as though it were filled with cotton, and she shivered, even in the warmth of the room. "Just . . . like that, you arrive in Paris, call me on the telephone, where . . . where you've always known you could find me, and say, 'I want to take Susan back with me.'"

"Jenny—" He had put his hand gently over hers but she snatched it away. "Dorothy and I can give her the kind of home and life she should have—"

"How do you know what kind of home and life she should have?" Her voice sounded as though it belonged to someone else, some stranger. She looked around and then back at him. This was the man she had touched and kissed and mourned for, the man who had made love to her in all the nights of that magical winter and spring, who had told her to wait in Paris for him, who had made her feel passion and pain and terrible deep loneliness. She started to push her chair back, but he grasped her wrist and held it hard. She tried to twist away, but his hand was like a vise. She looked into eyes she had never seen before.

"I'm prepared to take it into court, Jenny."

Now they were two strangers talking to each other. This voice of his was one she had never heard. With a strong, swift movement she pulled her wrist loose and stood up.

"You'd have to prove she was yours." She took a few steps. "And if you tried, I'd kill you first, Doug." She left the restaurant. Suddenly she started running. The sound of horns and traffic was very far away. She plunged ahead, running. Someone shouted. There was the screeching of brakes. As she ran into the traffic she felt nothing, heard nothing, was only half conscious of the cars and taxis all around her as she crossed to the other side.

An hour later, with Susan and Helene beside her, she rang the bell to François and Solange's flat. "Can we stay here for a few days, Solange?" she asked, distraught, whispering so that Susan wouldn't hear. "Until I find another place for us to live?"

"Of course," Solange said quickly, only her eyes asking questions.

"It's Doug. He's here in Paris." She pushed Susan gently toward the bedrooms. "He's married and wants to take Susan back to the States."

Solange simply nodded and closed the door.

Chapter 31

"I'M GOING TO have lunch here with Mrs. Coleman, Nelson," Kate said as the chauffeur held the limousine door open for her and Liz. She handed him a slip of paper as she stepped onto the sidewalk, while Liz quickly went up the brownstone steps. "Here's the address where you pick Joanna up at three o'clock." She laughed. "She'll probably give me an argument, saying she wants to stay over at Lydia's for another night. But it's an absolute *no.* Lydia's parents are always off to Sun Valley or Europe or Bermuda or someplace, and there isn't much supervision there. Besides, remind Joanna that it's her grandfather's birthday tomorrow, and I want her there the whole day. Not just for his dinner party."

Nelson smiled, taking the slip of paper, and said, "Well, she'll give me an argument, all right. She knows her own mind."

He watched her as she joined Liz on the steps, still smiling. He liked Mrs. Barnfield. All of the staff at Finisterre liked her. Fair, she was. And cared about people. Bonuses and gifts for everyone at Christmas, helping with bills when there was illness, paying for camp for staff members' children. A nice lady, he always reminded his wife. Beautiful too. He was proud to drive her, proud to have people see her sitting there in the rear seat. Looking at the slip of paper as he climbed back behind the wheel, he smiled again. That Joanna too. Only ten years old, but just like her mother, caring about people, always asking him how he felt.

As Liz and Kate walked into the cool, tile-floored foyer, Mrs. Hamilton, the housekeeper, closed the door. "Mr. Coleman's upstairs, Mrs. Coleman," she said quickly.

Liz turned, looking surprised. "Oh? For lunch?"

"No, ma'am," the housekeeper said as she walked toward the back of the house. "He's packing. Says he has to catch a

279

plane to London." She disappeared into the area of the kitchen.

Liz started up the stairway, then stopped as Dan rounded the curved landing and came down into the foyer, carrying two heavy suitcases. Hands spread in bewilderment, Liz said, "Isn't this terribly sudden? Why a plane to London in the middle of a Saturday afternoon?"

Kate watched them, slowly pulling off her gloves.

Dan put the suitcases down by the door, took her arm, and gestured to Kate, leading them into the library. "Let's have a drink." He spoke rapidly and seemed keyed up.

"Look, if you two want to talk, I can—" Kate said, starting toward the living room.

"No, please join us," he said warmly as they went into the small book-lined room. While he made drinks for them at the bar, the two young women sat on the sofa. "I'm going over to talk to some people about opening *The Last Dawn* in London."

"In London?" Liz seemed shocked. "But—"

"It's not the time for it here," Dan said quickly as he handed them their drinks. "Both Hack and I agree on that."

Kate nodded knowingly. "I gather this play, like the others, is controversial, carries what the blacklisters like to call a 'dangerous social message'?"

"It's more than that," Liz said, alarm in her voice. "Hack found out that Dan is on at least two blacklists, including the attorney general's. It's only a matter of time before he'll be called by the House Un-American Activities Committee. We know many people in the theater and film business who have already been served with subpoenas."

"And some of them are selling out," Kate said drily, disgust in her tone. "Naming names to save themselves."

"It's not a great time to be working in the theater," Dan said, his dryness matching Kate's. Then he looked at his watch and quickly downed half of his drink.

"Let's just say it's not a great time," she added.

"I hear you're having problems at the Barnfield Mills?" he said as he crossed to Liz and put his arms around her looking at Kate over her head.

"Labor problems," Kate admitted. "Jonathan and I lock horns nightly at dinner over the solutions. He's not at all well. The heart attack took its toll. But he manages to interfere, and we still argue."

"Good for you," Dan said softly, admiringly. "Is the old boy sorry he made you his v-p?"

"I don't think so," she said, shaking her head slowly. "He's very aware the world is changing and changing fast, and that his ideas for solving labor problems are doomed." She quickly crossed to him and lightly kissed his cheek, then said, "I want to go upstairs and freshen up a bit. Have a good trip, Dan."

They watched her as she left the room; then Liz looked up at him, fear in her eyes. "You *are* coming back?"

"Of course," he said, then tried to laugh. "McCarthy and his goons can't scare me."

With their arms around each other, they walked out of the library and toward the front door. As they stood there he held her close and kissed her; then, looking down at her, he pulled an envelope from his inner pocket and handed it to her. She looked at it, puzzled.

"I talked to Hack this morning, and he said he'll have your understudy walk through the rehearsals for you week after next, so you can come over to London for seven or eight days. That's your ticket."

She looked alarmed. "But, Dan—"

"I *will* be coming back, Liz, but I won't lie to you, honey. Hack has asked me to look into the possibility of his opening a production office over there. He thinks we're really going to be in for it here with the McCarthy investigations. For a while at least. And I have to be in a place where I can work, say what I want to say, what has to be said. You understand that, don't you?" He tipped her chin up and looked into her eyes.

"Then . . . you'll be staying on . . ."

"I want to meet a lot of people. Quentin Millhouse has shown some interest in *The Last Dawn*. Hack wants me to talk to him about coproducing with him, and the possibility then of Millhouse representing us there and coproducing other things in the future, including my plays. It just may mean that I'll be back and forth a lot, between here and London."

But Liz knew. In her heart she knew. Dan was leaving his options open, establishing a base in London, so that he could simply stay on there if matters worsened in the States with the McCarthy hearings and the House Un-American Activities Committee. At the sound of taxi horn outside, she put her arms around him and, squeezing back the tears, held him tightly to her.

After a moment Dan gently pried her hands loose and leaned down to kiss her. "Be on that plane," he said softly, tapping the envelope. "By that time I'll be half crazy, wanting you with me."

She smiled through a blur of tears and, reaching up to cup his face, whispered, "So will I, darling."

When the taxi honked again, he picked up his bags and left. She watched as the taxicab pulled away, then closed the door and started back toward the dining room.

Her week in London became a confused and exciting montage of sights and sounds and parties and the theater and long nights in Dan's hotel room in the Dorchester overlooking the park. She felt as she had when they were first married, thrilling with anticipation of the long hours of lovemaking that lay ahead each night. She watched from her pillow as he walked about the room, turned off the softly lit lamps, then slipped into the bed beside her. Then began the long and tantalizing ascent to that moment when their bodies were almost like one, caught in the sweep of passion and slowly drifting toward sleep as the passion ebbed and waited again for the early morning.

When the week came to an end, she clung to him just moments before they were to leave for the airport.

"Honey, I'll be back in New York before you know it," he said, stroking her face as he held her.

"A month?" she asked, and when he didn't answer, "Longer than a month, Dan?"

"I just don't know, Liz," he said gently. "It depends." Then suddenly he stood away from her a small distance and held her shoulders tightly. "Look, it's better to face it here, while we're together, rather than later on in a letter. I'll be back, honey, but it will have to be on a visit basis. I can't work in New York. I can't write the kind of plays there that I want to write. When the attorney general of the United States can order six detention camps to be set up to imprison *saboteurs* and so-called *spies,* well, it's no time for me to be there, working at what I have to work at."

She nodded, her shoulders heaving with a kind of hopelessness.

"It was in the newspapers this morning," he said grimly. "Even Truman seems to be believing this madman." He held her to him again. "But I'll be in New York often, and you'll come here between plays. It can't last long, honey. The American people won't let it go on like this."

She nodded again and turned as he quickly glanced at his watch and said, "We'll have to hurry. We've less than an hour before your plane leaves."

At the airport he went with her as far as he was allowed, then reluctantly let her go. He watched her as she walked away from him, turning just once to tearfully wave, then disappear beyond the high row of ticket desks. Then, shoving his hands into his pockets and feeling lonelier than he had ever felt in his life, he walked out of the terminal building and flagged down a taxi.

It was spring vacation for ten-year-old Joanna and eight-year-old Jon, and though they were driven daily by Nelson to private schools in Manhattan, Kate felt as though she hadn't seen them for weeks. By the time they reached home late each afternoon, had their supper in the playroom, and then did their homework, it was time for them to go to bed. It was only on weekends that she saw much of them, but Saturdays were taken up by dancing lessons and riding along the bridle paths with George Dennehy, the groom, and on Sundays there was Sunday school and long drives with their grandfather.

We're all too busy, she thought one sunny Saturday morning as she dropped them off at Miss Nolan's in Brookton for their piano lessons, then had Nelson leave her on Main Street near the stores where she had to do some shopping.

"Pick me up in an hour at Della Markham's, Nelson," she said. "She's doing some alterations for me." She waved him off with a smile, then set off down the sidewalk, nodding every now and then at townspeople she recognized. She heard the screech of brakes, but was looking at a display of books in Calder's shop window and didn't turn around.

"Kate!" she heard a voice call out and turned her head. Mike McCauley, in a bright plaid lumberjacket, was climbing out of his car and walking toward her. "Come take a ride with me. I'd like to show you something." He had a broad smile on his face and in several long strides he had crossed the sidewalk and was grasping her arm and pulling her toward the car.

"I can't, Mike," she said, laughing and pulling her arm free. She felt a faint flush in her cheeks, felt her pulse

283

quicken. "I have too many errands—medicine for Jonathan, socks for the children, two or three other things."

"They'll all wait," he said, taking her arm again, his face suddenly serious. "I really want you to see this. It's important. I was going to ask you to take a look on Monday, but this is much better."

"Really, Mike, I only have an hour before Nelson gets back, then we have to pick up Joanna and Jon."

"This won't take more than half an hour," he pleaded; then, seeing her relent a little, he pulled her toward the car and helped her in. "It's about two minutes from here."

"Half an hour then. No more," Kate said, laughing again as he ran to the other side of the car and slid behind the wheel.

When the car suddenly swung onto the main road leading to the Barnfield Mills, she looked at him questioningly, but he was talking about the new heating system that was being installed in Building Three. As the car slid up in front of an end house on one of the long rows of cottages that stretched endlessly along the road across from the mills, she sat forward and tensed a little. It was where he and Edwinna lived, where they had grown up when their father had worked in the mills, and where they still lived, by choice.

Why is he bringing me here? she wondered, then noticed that the trim around the windows had been freshly painted and framed by white shutters, the newly refinished door had a bright brass knocker on it, and the tiny patch of dirt in front showed fresh green shoots of grass bordered by a newly dug flowerbed that would bloom later in the spring.

"You have to see what we've done inside," he said excitedly, running around the car and opening her door. She started to protest but at that moment saw Edwinna throw open the door and wave at her to come in.

As they led her through the small house she stared about her, dumbfounded. They had completely redone the inside, installed a new kitchen, cut through extra windows to turn it from a dingy, dark hole into a brightly shining room with new cupboards and a gleaming stove and refrigerator. He had put in a tiny but perfectly adequate bathroom on the second floor, and the two small bedrooms had been repapered and painted and furnished with taste. The living room below had a charming country look about it, with a small coal stove in one corner, flowery chintzes, and crisp curtains. One wall was lined to the ceiling with bookcases, and the floors shone around the edges of the colorful braided rug.

"It's lovely," Kate exclaimed, breathless with the wonder of it all.

"We could do this to the rest of them, Kate, and at really very little cost," Edwinna said. "Mike has talked to most of the men who rent the houses, and they all say they'd be more than willing to do some of the work, if the materials were supplied."

"No," Kate said bluntly. They stared at her, suddenly filled with disappointment. She walked about in silence for a moment, looking up the stairway, then into the kitchen and tiny dining room. Then she looked at them again. "No. Why *should* they? Oh, maybe the painting and wallpapering, if they want to. But not the bathrooms and kitchens. We'll pay men to come in and do that work."

With a loud shout Mike and Edwinna grabbed her hands and whirled her around.

"Do you have any idea what this will do for the morale of this place?" Mike asked, delightedly pounding his fist on a table.

"Oh, my God!" Edwinna said, sitting down with a thump, unable to believe how easy it had been to convince Kate.

"Give me some cost sheets on it, Mike," Kate said, walking to the door as she glanced at her watch. "Let's get some bids on the work, and round figures on the cost of the other materials. And I want *all* of the houses done. Not just some of them."

"What's Jonathan going to say when . . . ?" Mike said, looking worried.

"Let *me* worry about Jonathan, Mike," she said softly as she opened the door. "And now, I *do* have to get back." She kissed Edwinna on the cheek, then hurried down the short walk to Mike's car as he followed her.

As they drove away from the mills and back toward the center of town, Mike looked over at her. They had been silent, Kate thinking hard about the project ahead, her eyes gleaming. He watched her for several minutes, admiring her beauty, the way the sun caught the gold in her darkening hair, the chiseled profile and softly smiling mouth.

She was wearing a dark pleated skirt and bright sweater, a casual polo coat and knee socks and loafers, and her long hair was caught back with a knotted silk scarf. When he pulled up to the curb in front of the alterations shop, where Kate had asked him to drop her off, he turned the engine off and for several moments they just sat there, Kate quietly thinking.

"Do you have any idea how absolutely marvelous you are?" Mike asked in a soft voice. His arm was stretched along the back of the seat, and as he spoke his hand lightly touched her shoulder.

She moved almost imperceptibly, but his touch disturbed her, made her pulse flutter, her heart beat fast in her throat, her cheeks flushed a soft pink. He saw and sensed it all and touched her again, this time on the cheek.

"You know how I feel, don't you?" he asked, his voice low.

She sat perfectly still; then at last she turned and looked at him and nodded. "But . . . I'm not ready for anything, Mike," she said, looking down at her hands in her lap and slowly shaking her head.

Again they were silent.

"It's all right," he said, his voice still low and soft. "I can wait. Just as long as you want me to wait."

She looked at him then and slowly smiled. Then without a word she opened the door and climbed out and, without looking back, walked into the alterations shop.

Chapter 32

"ANYTHING WORTH READING?"

Jenny put her newspaper down and looked up. Ian Chase was standing near her table, leaning on a long black furled umbrella, tall and lean, his gray eyes smiling down into hers.

"Did anyone ever tell you that you look like Leslie Howard?" she asked, squinting in the summer sunlight flooding the sidewalk café as he sat down in a chair next to her.

"Oh, but I *am* Leslie Howard," he said, hooking his umbrella over the back of the chair on the other side, then glancing out at the honking traffic along the Champs-Élysées. "The 'Ian Chase' is simply a disguise. And did anyone ever tell you that you look a bit like Ruby Keeler? Do you also tap dance?"

"Of course," she smiled. "And do Englishmen always carry furled umbrellas with them, even when it's not raining?"

"*Especially* when it's not raining. For it might always rain, you see. Even in Paris."

As he ordered coffee for them, she studied his face. Narrow with a high forehead, it had an esthetic look about it, and yet it was a strong face, with pale brows and lashes; an intelligent face, the gray eyes rimmed with a dark line at the edge of the iris, giving them a penetrating look.

"If it weren't that you always had a terribly important sounding excuse each time you've left Solange and François' flat when I've come in, I would say you've been trying to avoid me."

She watched the traffic and the people passing by for a moment, then turned to him. "Is that a question or an observation?"

"Both, I rather think."

She paused again. "You're right on both counts," she said, starting to pick up her purse.

"Oh, no, not again," he said, quickly reaching over and lightly holding her by the wrist. "At least wait for the coffee I ordered."

"But I have to gather up Susan and Helene. They're at the guignol, the puppet show just around the corner."

He held her wrist firmly as the waiter put their coffee down. "The puppets continue all afternoon," he assured her, then smiled. "Please. Although I detest coffee, I'm drinking it with you just to show you what a friendly chap I really am."

She laughed. "All right. Just to show you that I'm not a complete beast, I'll stay. For a few minutes at least."

As the summer of 1952 wore on she met Ian Chase often in the same café in the late afternoons. She knew it wasn't by chance, even though his cubbyhole of an office was near *Le Figaro*. It was a café she passed on her way from her office to her flat, but not one of the more popular places frequented by the writers and artists and musicians they both knew.

Jenny avoided these places, knowing that she might accidentally bump into Doug Gilbert again on one of his airline layovers. That was all behind her now. Forever.

Slowly the pain had worked itself into just bittersweet memories. The Douglas Gilbert she had met that day in Harry's Bar was not the Doug of Chipping Epworth and Cambridge and Portsmouth, of those languid nights in the Swan and laughing evenings in the smoke-filled, noisy Dove.

She never heard from him again—no letters, no phone calls, nothing. And finally she realized that she was relieved.

"I much prefer this nondescript, un-chic little place," she laughingly told Ian one early evening as they settled at a table in the café near her office. "Brasserie Lipp is too crowded for me."

"Some of its original charm has worn off," he said, "since the tourists started arriving in such large numbers after the war." But his eyes kept telling her that none of her charm had worn off for him, in spite of her lack of encouragement. She had simply accepted him as a warm friend, and that was all.

"Have you ever been married, engaged, attached, anything?" she asked him bluntly as they strolled along the Quai de la Mégisserie, watching the lights across the way on the Île de la Cité and a boat as it slid under the bridge. They had just had dinner with François and Solange and some other friends and were lagging far behind them.

"Married. Once," he said with a cheerful smile. "To an

Australian woman. But she didn't like the gypsy life of a roving correspondent. She's married again, with two children, and supremely happy."

"After being married to you?" Jenny demanded. "Hardly."

"I say, Jenny," he said, stopping to look down at her. "That's sporting of you, you know." But she quickly walked on.

Ian would be gone for weeks, sometimes months at a time, off on assignment to some far corner of the earth. In July he went to Buenos Aires to cover the funeral of Eva Perón, then from there went on to Cairo to report on the abdication of King Farouk.

She found that she missed him—missed their hours of talk about writers and writing at the café on the Champs-Élysées, their strolls along the riverbank, their Sunday evenings at Solange and François' flat, when musician and writer friends gathered for hours of music and poetry.

"Ian's writing a book, you know," Solange said to her as they put wine glasses and bowls of fruit on trays in her kitchen one Sunday evening.

"No, I didn't know," Jenny said, turning in surprise.

"He's very talented, and will probably be quite famous someday. But all of these assignments take him away from it. It goes very slowly."

When he returned from a second extended series of assignments that November of 1952, she suddenly realized, when she first saw him, how much she had missed him. He simply walked up to her and sat down at her café table one sunny and crisp afternoon, as though he had never been away at all. For a moment he just looked at her in her bright tweeds, her cheeks and eyes glowing, her little beret over one eye.

"Two coffees," he said to the waiter. He was carrying his furled umbrella and a copy of Apollinaire's *La Femme Assise* and was wearing a blue sweater under his heavy tweed jacket that turned his gray eyes to a pale blue. "You look very beautiful. I had almost forgotten how really beautiful you are." Jenny made a face.

"You never told me you were writing a book," she said, suddenly leaning toward him.

"Is that all you can say after my being away for six weeks?" he laughed.

"What's it about?" she persisted.

He thought for a moment, as though listening to the chorus of taxi horns on the broad boulevard. "About war," he said. "Useless death. About grace and valor and cowardice. And how it never seems to solve anything." He smiled. "Women should run the world, you know. There'd never be any wars. Until, of course, they began acting like men."

He and Susan had become fast friends, and when Jenny brought him back to her flat that afternoon, Susan threw herself into his arms and begged him to go to América with them. Jenny turned quickly away, pulling off her jacket.

He looked at her with raised eyebrows as Susan skipped off to her bedroom to put her spelling book away. Then he followed Jenny to the kitchen, where she took over the preparation of dinner from Helene, whose thin little dark-eyed face lit up when she saw him. The fragrance of roasting meat, cooking apples, cinnamon, and coffee filled the room. He sniffed appreciatively, idly stirred a pot of vegetables, playing for time, while Jenny washed fruit.

"You're going back to America?" He touched her arm. "Why, Jenny?"

Her back stiffened. "Not to stay, Ian," she said. But her voice sounded odd, strangely evasive. She stood at the sink for a long time, her back to the room. Slowly she turned to him. "I have a son in the States. His name is Christopher, and I haven't seen him since he was a very small baby. He was taken away from me then. I told Susan about him a month ago, and she said, 'I think we should go get him and bring him back with us, Mama.'" She turned away and started drying the fruit. "Sometime—someday, I'll explain it all—that is, if you want to know."

"I want to know, if you want to tell me, Jenny."

She nodded and went on with her tasks. "He'll be eleven years old in December. I want to see him. I want to bring him to Paris to live with us."

He took hold of her shoulders gently and made her face him.

"When you bring him back, will you come back to me?" He had said the words so softly that she wasn't certain she had heard them. But then she knew she had, caught her breath, and let it out slowly. "Yes, Ian." She looked up at him, and he put his arms around her and held her close. "Yes, I'll come back to you."

It's not the way it was with Doug, she thought, feeling the rough tweed of his coat against her face, the comfort and strength of his arms, the calm and stillness, as she breathed the fragrance of his pipe, his skin. Doug was like thunder and earthquake and storm, while Ian was like summer heat lightning, arcing on the horizon in silence, the light spreading softly against the sky and lasting into the night.

As they lingered at the table, Ian with his tea, Jenny with her coffee, he nodded with a sudden thought. "Yes, this is something you might be interested in. And you could do it while you're in New York."

"Do what?"

"A friend of mine, Dennis Bayles, has been appointed the head of an international study group that will prepare a report at the end of a three-year study on the long-lasting effects of the baby boom, actually the effects on children born during and just after the war years, whose fathers served in the military. This study, with the various governments under-writing it, will be made available to demographic experts, urban planners, sociologists, newspapers, and foundations. They need good reporters, like yourself, Jen, to help them with the study. Good reporters who are in touch with children, who know firsthand and who experienced just what happened in those ten years. You could see Dennis when you're in New York. He's gone there from London to set up his headquarters. If you're at all interested, of course."

She sipped her coffee, thinking about it, then took an apple from the bowl in the center of the table and sliced it and handed Ian a piece. "It sounds fascinating," she said slowly. "Perhaps I could. When I come back, perhaps I could do it between assignments here. The children of Paris would make an interesting study."

Far off in the other end of the apartment they heard Susan's little windup Victrola. She was playing her favorite record. Jenny tipped her head, listening and humming the tune under her breath. "Tina, the ballerina . . ."

"I wrote Christopher a letter," she said, toying with a spoon. "I didn't say too much. Just that I want to see him." She began to weep, the tears sliding slowly down her face, and as she wept and he held her hand, she told him the story of how she had lost Christopher. And when she had finished, he picked her up and carried her to a large chair in the small green and white salon at the front of her flat. He held her for a long time, stroking her hair and kissing her face. Then, long after she had become quiet, he spoke.

"You've said you'll marry me, Jenny. Why wait until you come back?" She started in his arms, but he held her close and she relaxed again. "Perhaps it would work in your favor, if there's a problem in bringing the boy back."

He had spoken quietly, and as his words echoed and re-echoed in her mind, she saw their wisdom. She nodded slowly and buried her face in his neck, and he felt her tears. But this time they were tears of relief and happiness. She felt for the first time in her life as though she had come home—back to a home she had never really had.

They were married in a quiet civil ceremony, with just Solange and François as witnesses and Susan and Helene as the only other guests. They took a train first to Milan and then to Venice.

"I've dreamed of seeing it," she begged. "I don't care if it's rainy and cold." Their room in the Danielli overlooked the Canale San Marco, but it was dark when they arrived, and she had to be content to wait for daylight. She had caught only glimpses of the canals and the astonishing houses that rose up straight out of the water, tall and lovely in their peeling, shabby splendor, their walls echoing with song and voices and the lapping of the boats in the narrow waterways. She heard snatches of music, saw tiny cafés and small piazzas, spires of churches and graceful bridges that arched over the canals, and watched the pigeons swirl through the reaches of Saint Mark's Square.

Ian made love to her as she had known he would, with quiet patience and infinite tenderness. In the beginning she felt her own impatience grow, but as he kissed and stroked her with unhurried grace and flickering, whispering touches of his fingers, she felt herself fall into the gentle rhythm and discovered the beauty of its pace. It teased her with promise, led her on with maddening anticipation, until at last he was above her and she opened herself to him. As he pressed into her hard, she heard his soft moan but knew, even as he moaned and she completely abandoned herself into his keeping, that it would be a long and exquisite climb to the moment of ecstasy, in a way that she had never known. And it was. In the darkness they lay in each other's arms. The doors to the balcony were open and they could hear the murmurs of the water, the sounds of footsteps, the call of a gondolier. "I love you," he whispered.

"And I love you," she whispered back. She had finally, really come home.

A week before Jenny and Susan were leaving for the States, Jenny picked up a letter from the pile of mail Helene had left on the small foyer table. She handled it gingerly, turning it over and over, as though studying the air mail stamps. It was in a handwriting she didn't recognize, but it was postmarked from Craddock Corners, Massachusetts. Slowly she tore the flap.

"Christopher doesn't want to see you," the handwriting scrawled across the page. "He will add his own note at the end of this letter, so that you can see this is his own decision. But even if he hadn't read your letter, and I was making the decision myself, I would keep you from seeing him. You seem to forget the court has turned you down three times. So stay out of our lives." It was signed "Fred Baldwin." Beneath his signature were six tiny, painfully stiff words. "I don't want to see you." And underneath those six words was the name "Christopher MacKenzie."

The flat was empty. Helene and Susan were shopping for clothes for Susan to take to the States, and Ian was in Greece covering the elections. She stared at the short message and signature at the bottom of the page. Softly she ran her fingers over it, as though if she touched it, she could find the real meaning beneath it. And then she couldn't see it. Tears had blurred her eyes and clung to her lashes. Clutching the letter to her, she walked to the salon windows and looked down into the narrow street. A little boy, just about Christopher's age, was running along the street, a long loaf of bread under his arm, and he was kicking a stone ahead of him along the narrow sidewalk.

She wouldn't tell anyone. No one need know about the letter. Ian wasn't returning from Athens before going to London, where his father had been hospitalized. She would probably not see him before she and Susan left for the States the following day. She hurried to the bedroom and buried the letter beneath the clothing she had already packed in the suitcase open on the bed.

Kate and Liz met them at Idlewild Airport with Joanna and Julie, who were curious about the woman war correspondent they had heard so much about. Jenny, pretty and trim in her camel's-hair coat, walked across the tarmac toward them with Susan by the hand. The three women simply stopped and looked at one another in the gray December day.

They look older, she thought, but more beautiful than ever. Both wore silky dark fur coats. They look *rich,* she thought, very very rich, and with a sudden burst of laughter she ran toward them and threw her arms around them. For a moment, in the confusion of laughter and tears and the rush of voices, Joanna and Julie and Susan stood on the perimeter, watching the reunion with tentatively smiling faces. Then Joanna, her wide gray-green eyes looking gravely down at Susan, said, "Come along, Susan. We'll wait in the car for them. They'll probably stand here for hours making all these crazy noises." And with Julie on one side of her and Susan by the hand on the other side, she marched them through the terminal and out to the roadway, where Nelson waited with the limousine.

Slowly Jenny and Kate and Liz pulled apart and simply stood there smiling at each other. But then Liz reached out and touched Jenny's cheek. "You still look like a child. About eighteen," she smiled. "But something's wrong, Jen. You look tired, drawn."

"The trip—" She tried to toss it off and started to walk.

"No," Kate said, her gloved hand under Jenny's chin. "It's something else."

Jenny looked back at the gleaming airliner, then up at the American flag above the air terminal, flapping madly in the cold wind. Anywhere to avoid their eyes, to keep them from seeing the quick surge of tears. "Fred Baldwin won't let me see Christopher," she said in a low, trembling voice. "But I have to see him. I have to!" Quickly brushing the tears away, she started to walk toward the terminal entrance. "And I think I've figured out a way."

Kate looked at Liz; then, after pulling the sable collar around her throat against the bitter cold, whipping wind, she took hold of Liz's hand and called out, "For heaven's sake, wait, Jenny!"

Chapter 33

JENNY AND SUSAN spent the first two weeks of that December in 1952 with Liz in her Washington Square house. They all planned to go to Finisterre for the holidays. Ian and Dan were coming from London. But until then Jenny spent much of her time taking Susan to see the sights in New York; the huge Christmas tree and ice skating at Radio City, the Christmas show at the Music Hall, the Museum of Natural History, a performance of *The King and I.* She also took Susan and Julie to a children's theater down in Greenwich Village and for dinner up to the Rainbow Grill, where she could look out over the city glittering beneath her in all of its postwar excitement and beauty.

Julie hurried home from school each day to go with them wherever she could. She was fascinated by Jenny, her life in Paris, her work and her friends and her experiences during the war. She asked Jenny endless questions, following her around the tall old brownstone house, bringing her milk and crackers and cookies at the end of the evening, and coffee early in the morning. Jenny was amused and touched at first, but then began to wonder and worry about the child and decided to talk to Liz about her.

"You're unbelievable!" she shouted at Liz as she ran into her dressing room at the theater. "Oh, Liz, I knew you were *good,* but I didn't realize *how* good. And the play is marvelous."

"Yes, it is, isn't it? Kenneth is a very talented playwright," Liz said as she creamed her face in front of the mirror. "And we'll probably have a long run. The critics gave it wonderful reviews."

Jenny glanced at her quickly in the mirror, then wandered about the dressing room, sniffing a vase of red roses, reading the card, examining Liz's third act costume, picking up a new script that lay on a table and reading the first few lines, then

295

putting it down again. "But it isn't a play by Dan. Is that what your voice is saying?" When there wasn't an answer, she pulled a chair up next to her and sat down.

"What's wrong, Liz?" she asked. "What happened with Dan? Why is he in London and you're here?"

Liz's fingers worked rapidly as she wiped off the cream with tissue, then began to apply her street makeup. Even without *any* makeup she was exquisite, Jenny thought, and yet there was a tightness around her mouth that hadn't been there before, a different, almost guarded look to her lovely blue eyes.

"Why, you know the theater, Jenny," she said, a chattering tone in her voice. "I have my career here. I'm taking this play on tour for four months right after January first. And Dan is doing well in London—"

"That's not true," Jenny said bluntly.

Liz turned and stared at her; then, slowly looking back at the mirror, she put her hands at each side of her face as though to hold it together. Tears filled her eyes. She took a tissue from the box and pressed it to her eyelids.

"I've heard, Liz. He's doing some radio things. That's about it." There was a long pause.

"His plays were controversial, as you know, Jen," Liz finally said. "And right after the war that was all right. In fact, he was on top of the world here with his first two plays. They were a tremendous success." She laughed with bitterness. "But plays with any political or social message have suddenly become unpopular. Hack was wonderful. He was worried about the third one but did it anyway."

She seemed bewildered. "Everything has changed so—the Cold War, the way people seem to be afraid to talk, to say anything. You've been out of the country for so long—"

"I read the papers," Jenny said grimly. "The Red Baiters."

"The McCarthy investigations and the hearings by the House Un-American Activities Committee—" Liz turned to Jenny. "It's unbelievable—friends turning against each other, making wild accusations at these hearings, exaggerations, actually lying."

"All right, where does Dan come into all this?"

"He went to London in May of 1945, before coming home. He had been in Rheims to cover the signing of the surrender at General Eisenhower's headquarters, then in London he closed a deal on a production there for *The Shining Gates*.

When he finally got back to New York, he was on top of it all. Producers were coming through the walls trying to do his plays. He even went out to Hollywood for several months to do the screen version of *Light Under the Door.*" She was quickly dressing as she talked, straightening the seams on her stockings, then slipping on the white silk blouse and slim black skirt of her suit. "He had finished the third play—Hack had it in rehearsal—and was halfway through his fourth play already. Oh, Jenny, there was just no stopping him."

"Or you." Jenny smiled briefly. "I've read most of your reviews. Kate has sent them to me."

Liz turned back to the mirror and combed her hair. "Then you've seen that my last four plays were not Dan's." Jenny nodded. "During the war he had joined countless organizations, mostly writer-affiliated groups." She smiled ruefully. "Dan's a joiner. I'm not, I'm afraid. Equity's about my speed. But these were mainly organizations that made it easier for government and military agencies to find writers for wartime activities, the USO shows and bond drive tours that performers made, for radio shows and the Red Cross programs, anything that helped the war effort." She sighed.

"And, of course, these organizations were the vanguard of the liberals," Jenny said, understanding it all.

"None of them were Communist-front organizations, Jenny."

"I didn't say that, Liz. They don't have to be with the political climate that has spread across this country. McCarthy's a monster. And most of his little mob around him. And the House Un-American Activities Committee is seeing traitors under every stone and bush. This is not a good time to have a social conscience, Liz. Conservatives equate moral obligation and intellectual tolerance with Stalinism."

"It's crazy! Horrible!"

"And so we have the attorney general's list, the blacklists with the names of anybody and everybody who ever even just casually flirted with left or liberal political activities during the late thirties and into the forties. And Dan's name is on those lists, I would imagine?"

"Each time the doorbell rings I'm afraid it's someone with a subpoena for him."

"He'd come back from London if he was served with one?"

"I think so. He said he'd feel he had to. There are those, like Lillian Hellman, Arthur Miller, others, who are refusing

297

to name names to the House Un-American Committee. They'll talk about themselves, but not anyone else. But they're risking going to prison. Dan says he would have to do the same, talk about himself and his own affiliations, but no one else."

Jenny nodded. "And so he stays in England."

"It's been like starting all over again. But the time in New York isn't right for Dan just now. Perhaps someday—maybe all of this terrible fear and hysteria will go away."

"And you stay on here?" Jenny asked the question quietly.

"My work is here, Jenny. Dan's income right now is hardly enough to keep him going."

"But Julie, Liz? She's lonely with you on tour so much of the time. And she misses Dan. Terribly. She told me so."

"She loves Dan, and—" Liz turned to slip her coat on, but held it over her arm as she thought over very carefully what she was going to say. "Even though she's only eleven years old, she thinks in the most astonishing way. She feels I should give all this up and go to London, that we should be with Dan, that it's the only really important thing." She put her coat on. "But I'm not at all known there. Not yet. So it would be completely unrealistic, of course. But Julie doesn't understand that."

Jenny smiled as she pulled her own coat on. "Liz, I love you. Me? I'd be in London in a cold-water flat, cursing my luck and kicking the wall. But you! You're so beautifully rational."

As they walked to the door she took Liz by the shoulders and turned her to face her, saying softly, "And you never did get that second baby, did you? Odd. Of the three of us, you're the one that Kate and I always felt would be the perfect mother."

"I will," Liz said with a stubborn set to her jaw as they walked out. "As soon as Dan comes back to stay."

Jenny watched Dennis Bayles as he talked. His office windows looked off to the west, where she could see the shores of New Jersey. A large white ship was steaming up the Hudson River, blackish furls streaming from its smokestacks.

"Listening to you makes me homesick." She smiled, and as she said it she suddenly realized that anywhere that Ian was would be home to her from now on. "I miss Ian."

"I miss Ian too." He smiled; his ruddy round face and

pinkish-blond hair, which stood somewhat on end, gave him a constantly pleased look. "Entertaining sort of bloke with his endless stories about all the corners of the globe. We were in the North African thing together, y'know."

"No, I didn't know. I knew he'd served with Montgomery's Eighth Army."

"Got a bellyful at Médenine, but pulled through it all right he did." He offered her a cigarette, then lit hers and his and settled back in his chair. "Well then, it looks as though we're all set with you, Jenny. You have an excellent grasp of the study. Your orientation results have been absolutely top-notch. And you have that natural reporter and researcher gift, which is so necessary in a job like this. Your employer has no objection to your working on this when you return to Paris?"

She smiled. She had had lunch with Henry Fremont, then dinner at his and Alison's apartment just the evening before. When she told him about the postwar study of children born in the 1940s, he had patted her shoulder and said, "Go to it, kiddo. Anything you can do to help make this lousy world a better place is okay with me. After what you've told me about Dan Coleman, I have even less hope for the future."

"He thinks it's a wonderful project," she said to Bayles. "And gave me his blessing."

As she rose to leave, Dennis Bayles rose, too, and walked around the massive walnut desk. He took her hand in his and held it for a moment. "When you go back, tell Ian I think he's a very lucky fellow."

"You can tell him yourself." She laughed. "He's coming for Christmas and arrives tomorrow night."

As she started for the door, pulling the fur collar of her coat close around her face, he called out to her and she stopped.

"For the comparative study before you leave the States, Jenny. You said on the phone the other day that you thought you'd found an excellent place?"

"Yes, I have," she said. "I selected a town up in Massachusetts, just a typical small American town, exactly the size of a small town not far from Paris that I expect to use for the study when I return. It's called—Craddock Corners."

"Fine," he said. "How long do you plan to be there?"

"Oh, perhaps ten days. I wrote Ian a week ago that I'd like him to take Susan back to Paris right after the holidays."

* * *

Christmas Eve and the following day gave them all memories they would carry for years and years afterward. Finisterre looked more beautiful than ever. The low pines all across the front of the mansion were like a fairyland with hundreds and hundreds of tiny white lights, and the huge spruce tree in the great hall blazed with tinsel and silver roping and colored lights. There was a smaller tree in the library, boughs of pine and mistletoe everywhere, and fires crackling in all of the fireplaces. At nine o'clock on Christmas Eve about twenty-five children spilled off a bus at the beginning of the long circular driveway and lined up in twos. With shielded candles in their hands, they walked slowly along the driveway singing Christmas carols as Kate and her family and guests stood on the terrace in the cold, frosty air and listened. When they had finished, Joanna and Jamie and Brenda, Marianne's twins and now tall and handsome teenagers, herded the children into the solarium, where they were given cider and doughnuts and gifts.

"Your Ian is a delight," Kate said softly to Jenny as Christmas day wound down to a weary but happy end in the late afternoon. They were sitting before the fire in the library, watching Ian as he performed some card tricks for Jon, now a fair-haired, tall nine-year-old. Carolyn Harrison and Julie sat at the piano playing duets of Christmas music, and Joanna and Susan leaned against the piano singing. Liz and Dan had gone to the theater, and Marianne and Reed had driven over to Windward Hills to see Sarah Wheeler, who was now bedridden.

Jenny nodded, looking into the fire. She sat with her legs and feet tucked beneath her, the firelight flickering in her wide brown eyes. "I'm happy—really, truly happy—for the first time in my life, I think." She looked around at Kate sitting at the other end of the long deep couch. "And you, Kate?"

Kate shrugged, then laughed a small laugh. "I'm fascinated with what I'm doing, if that's happiness. And I guess it is. Jonathan had to turn over much of his own work to me, the expediting of it, mainly." She laughed again. "He sits up there in that bed still dictating letters to secretaries, making phone calls, issuing orders. But I'm learning, oh, Jenny, how I'm learning. And he's actually letting me make a lot of the decisions—"

"Excuse me, Mrs. Barnfield." Martin was at the library door. A broad-shouldered, ruddy-faced man with a shock of curly black hair walked past him and halfway into the room. "Mr. McCauley is—"

"Mike," Kate said, getting to her feet and shaking his hand as he shifted a large manila envelope to the other hand.

"I told Jonathan I'd drop in for a few minutes this evening, Kate," he said after she introduced him to Jenny and Ian. "He wanted to look over these new contracts with the Workers' Association."

"Well, join us for a drink first," Kate said, starting toward the bar.

"Raincheck." He smiled, his eyes locking with hers until she looked away. "I promised my mother and sister I'd take them to the Association's Christmas party. I just dropped in to say hello and wish you all a Merry Christmas." He was smiling at everyone and heading for the door again. "Good night." And he was gone as quickly as he had arrived.

There was a long silence. Then the piano music resumed and Ian was onto another card trick.

"Well!" Jenny said in a rather breathless tone. "Does he always take you by little storms like that one?"

Kate smiled as she sat down, the flush on her cheeks still there. "He *is* rather brash, isn't he?"

"And *who* exactly is he?"

"The manager of the mills. He was the top foreman, and the one who came to Jonathan several years ago to warn him that unless he did something to improve conditions at the mills, he'd have the union moving in. He suggested the formation of this Workers' Association, giving the mill workers a voice to air their requests and grievances. Jonathan didn't want to—"

"I know," Jenny said. "I heard Reed complaining to Ian about it." She looked across the room to Ian as he shuffled the deck of cards, and smiled. "Poor darling, he didn't want to listen, I could tell, and only did it out of politeness. Reed was saying you're the one who convinced Jonathan that he should encourage the formation of the Association, and also make Mike McCauley the manager of the mills."

"Well, something had to be done."

"And what about this Mike McCauley?" Jenny asked with a sly grin. "Seems to me I caught him looking at you with something more interesting than just friendliness."

"Don't be ridiculous." Kate tried to laugh as she suddenly attacked the fire with a poker and sent sparks flying.

"Well, neither one of you may be admitting anything." Jenny nodded. "Even to yourselves. But it's there, my friend, it's there. And I must say he looks terribly exciting and sexy."

Kate laughed in spite of herself. "You're impossible, Jenny. So reserved in your opinions."

"Especially about men," Jenny said, grinning. "Well, a person would have to be blind not to see how he feels about you."

"That's ridiculous," Kate said, her green eyes snapping.

"Admit you find him attractive," Jenny persisted.

"I never thought of you as the incurable romantic," Kate said, looking at Jenny with curiosity and some annoyance.

"It's still Del, isn't it?" Jenny asked softly.

Kate turned sharply, then away again, and quickly lit a cigarette, with a silver lighter from the coffee table. "You're being even more ridiculous." Her voice stiffened. "Del is married and living in England."

"Why didn't he bring her back here?" Jenny probed, her voice even softer. A long silence fell between them, then Kate put her hand to her eyes.

"I . . . I don't know."

"I know why. Because he's probably still in love with you."

Kate put her cigarette out. Then she walked to the fireplace, took the poker, and stirred the embers. "That's over," she said, so quietly that Jenny had to strain to hear her. "It ended . . . before it could even begin, and wasn't meant to be, I guess." She half knelt before the fire, her long green jersey dress falling in folds on the floor. "Thank God, what I have to do at the mills keeps me from thinking too much." She looked up at Jenny, tears on her lashes.

Jenny put her hand out and touched Kate's softly. Whispering, she said, "It wouldn't be wrong, Kate dear. You don't just *watch* life as it passes you by. You have to *live* it too. And Mike McCauley is a very attractive man."

Kate rose again and stood looking down into the fire. "I can't think of much else but the difficulties we're having at the mills," she said, and Jenny knew the other subject was closed. "Nor can Mike. There's so much unrest, and Jonathan is difficult, hard to convince that more changes must be made."

"Your brother-in-law, Reed, feels you're exaggerating the problems."

Kate made a slight face at the mention of his name. "Reed doesn't understand. He never did. Nor did he want to. And he understands even less now that he and Marianne live in

302

New York. He spends even less time at the mills than he did before and understands less and less as time goes on. He thinks that everything should stay the same as it was when Jonathan's father ran the mills. People just won't work for those kinds of wages and under those conditions anymore, and they shouldn't have to."

"Well, I gather that Reed seems to feel the mills will fail with the new liberal policies that you want to establish, and that in the long run the workers wouldn't thank you for your liberal views." She then tread carefully. "He also suggested that Mike is a ruthless opportunist, and that he's still—and he actually used that dumb word—still the *proletariat*. That you're naive, and he's using you."

Kate's face hardened. "Mike McCauley is one of the most decent human beings I've ever known. He's been completely honest with me right from the start. He wants to see the mills survive, because thousands of lives are at stake. The town of Brookton would be destroyed if the mills failed, and because of that he has to work from both sides. I've always felt there's a middle ground somewhere, with decent wages and working conditions, the Association instead of some huge parent union, and a fair profit for management so that moderniza-tion can proceed for the buildings and machinery."

"Does Mike agree with that?"

"Yes." Kate's gaze was direct. "In the beginning he didn't. He felt the union was the only answer. But now, from this side, he's seen the books and knows what the alternatives are. If the union comes in, Jenny, the mills will have to be closed or sold. The machinery is old; the buildings need updating. But with a union contract we'd be finished. Mike and I honestly believe that if the Association would work with us, trust us, we could gradually bring the workers' wages up to a level in five years that would give them as much, if not more, than a union would. They're beginning to trust me, as a woman, because I've told them with new machinery, new production methods and modernization of the plant, we could increase production to a point that would make it possible for us to give them what they want and deserve. Jonathan had a long-range plan to move the mills, over a period of time, to the South where wages are cheap, much lower than in the North. This is what Reed has been fighting for. I've managed to put a stop to it, because I think it would destroy Brookton and most of the people who live here. The mills are the life-blood of Brookton."

303

"He has a very apt pupil in Jon, I noticed."

"You're even more observant than I remembered," Kate said worriedly. "I'm afraid the absence of a strong male hand in the house has made Jon turn to Reed."

"Well, perhaps if you play your cards right, Katie my friend," Jenny said with soft love in her eyes, "he'll turn to Mike McCauley for that strong male hand."

Jenny saw Ian and Susan off at Idlewild on New Year's night.

"Don't worry," he said, kissing her and holding her close. "Solange is looking forward to taking care of her, and I'll be there much of the time." Holding her away from him for a moment, he looked her directly in the eye. "You're sure you're doing the right thing?"

"Certain, Ian."

"Write to me."

"Every single night."

"Oh, dear God!" Ian said as he glanced up and looked over her shoulder. Jenny turned, then burst into laughter. Susan was standing before a cigarette machine mirror, watching herself as she blew huge bubbles with her gum. "Is this what we call one half of a cultural exchange?" She turned and grinned at them.

"Travel and learn, darling. That's what the travel posters say."

"Yes, but I don't think they were talking about bubble gum."

She waved to them as they walked across the tarmac toward the lighted plane, then watched as the plane taxied off from the terminal and disappeared in the darkness heading toward a far runway where it would take off for the trip to France.

"If you're interested," Meredith Ballard said, stamping a tall pile of library books with a Craddock Corners Public Library stamp as she talked, "I have two rooms in my house that I rent out to teachers. One of them has been vacant since November, so if you'd like to move from the tourist court into this room, I'd be glad to have you."

"Oh, thank you, Meredith," said Jenny. "I'd love it. The mattress in that tourist cabin is full of bricks, I think."

Meredith was the librarian at the public library, Jenny's liaison from the very start when she first wrote and asked if the library would be interested in helping her conduct her study. A letter had come back almost immediately with the signature "Meredith Ballard" and two enthusiastic pages of agreement and suggestions for expediting the project in the month each year for three years that Jenny said she would allot to it.

"I would like to help you," Meredith had written. Jenny had liked her immediately, without even seeing or meeting her. "It sounds like a fascinating project. If you want to send the questionnaires on to me for the children to fill out so that they'll be all ready for you to interview when you arrive, I'll be glad to get it started for you."

Jenny drove along the main street of Craddock Corners in her rented car the day she arrived. She was glad to see that Taylor House had burned to the ground sometime in the intervening years, but not with any loss of life, she hoped. A new two-story brick office building stood in its place. She was also glad to see that Tim Lucas no longer drove the only taxi in town as she glanced at Cheney's Garage when passing, but that a much younger man lounged against the fender of the taxi and that Cheney's Garage wasn't even Cheney's Garage anymore, but a brand-new gleaming gasoline station.

Meredith's house was a tiny cottage on the opposite side of town from the Baldwin house, a one-story Victorian cottage with long windows, her family antiques, and lots of plants. Jenny spent only one night in the tourist court and moved in with Meredith the next evening. And that night, with her bedroom door shut, she quickly went through the pile of questionnaires as she sat on her bed, a cigarette hanging from the corner of her mouth. Suddenly she stopped, slowly put the cigarette in the ashtray, and pulled a sheet of paper from the pile.

"Christopher MacKenzie," it said at the top of the sheet. "Age eleven. Father: Alan R. MacKenzie. Army Air Corps. Captain. Killed in action, December 7, 1941, Pearl Harbor."

There was more. She read it quickly. Then again, more slowly. There was no mention of her. Just details about where he was born, his interests, his hobbies, his likes and dislikes. She smiled through tears, tried to read between words, pounced on others. He was interested in drawing and books. He particularly liked Mark Twain. He liked to write stories. English was his favorite subject in school. He liked poetry, tried to write it. He liked ice skating and baseball, but always the recurrent theme in the list of answers was his love for writing and reading. As tears slid down her face, she hugged the piece of paper to her, then carefully smoothed it out on the bed.

"I want to interview the children, starting Monday," she said to Meredith at dinner the following night as they ate on a small table before the cheerily burning fireplace.

"I'll arrange it," Meredith said, pouring their tea. Jenny looked at her with fondness. She was engaged to a young man, a sergeant in the Army fighting in the Korean conflict. She was only twenty-three, a pretty young woman with hazel eyes and dark hair that she pulled back into a ribbon at the nape of her neck. "You're staring at me," she said, smiling as she stirred her tea.

"I was remembering what I was like when I was just twenty-three," Jenny said softly. She had been twenty-three when she and Alan had run through the leaves in Washington Square, danced slowly and sensuously to the music of Carmen Cavallaro on the Astor Roof, when Henry Fremont had given her a bonus for the series she'd written on the abortion ring, twenty-three when the child she had thought she didn't want had been born.

"Who are you really, Jenny?"

Jenny looked up at her, startled.

"Oh, I know, I know. You're Mrs. Ian Chase. You live in Paris, you have a daughter named Susan, you were born in New York, and you're thirty-four years old. There's more than that."

Jenny stirred her tea and, holding the cup in both hands, slowly sipped it. "More?"

"Why did you pick Craddock Corners to do your study?"

"Well, I took out a map, closed my eyes, and brought down my finger like this—"

Meredith slowly shook her head. "I saw your face yesterday when we drove past Hawthorne Avenue School. It wasn't just an interested or even a curious look. It was something more; there was something in your face, something . . . almost haunted. What are you *really* doing here?"

Jenny slowly put her cup down. "You're very observant. And . . . you're right. There is something more. I have a son in that school."

"A son?" She looked confused. "I don't understand."

"He was taken away from me when he was still just a baby by my husband's sister and her husband. My husband was killed at Pearl Harbor." She looked into the flickering firelight.

Meredith stared at her. "Taken away? But why?"

Jenny shook her head and smiled sadly. "I wasn't a very good mother then, Meredith. Not a good mother at all."

Jenny straightened the pile of questionnaires on the table in front of her, then straightened them again. Her hands were trembling, and she quietly cleared her throat. The sounds of the library, subdued and rustling, flowed around her in whispers and quiet footsteps and the turning of pages. She watched the little girl she had just interviewed—Marjorie Madison? was that her name?—as she walked away from her along the bookshelves and then turned the corner toward the main desk. Meredith had put Jenny at a table back in the corner where there was very little traffic. She leaned over and glanced at the questionnaire on top. Yes. MacKenzie. Christopher MacKenzie. She looked up. Her heart was pounding in her throat. She caught her breath and held it, hearing soft footsteps. And suddenly he was there . . . standing at the far aisle looking in both directions. Then, seeing her, he walked toward her.

She filled her eyes with him—his curly brown hair and the sprinkling of golden freckles over his nose and cheeks, the cleft in his chin, his long, sweeping black lashes. He was wearing a heavy dark blue jacket and carried a stocking cap in his hand.

"Hi," he said as he looked around, then pointed at the chair opposite her. "Shall I sit here?"

"Yes," she said, nodding rapidly. "Please do, Chris. Oh, is that what people call you? Chris?"

He nodded. "Most do. Except my mother."

She was startled. "Your mother?" Of course. That would be Mary. He'd call her his mother.

"Well, she's really my aunt." He smiled. "She calls me Chrissy."

"And your . . . mother?"

He looked around again and wiggled a little on the chair, then slipped his jacket off. "What?"

"Your . . . mother?"

"Oh. Well, she . . . she went away when I was little. Disappeared."

Her heart seemed to stop, then raced on, beating hard, pounding. She wanted to run around the table and kneel down and hold him in her arms and say, "No, no, no, Christopher, I'm here, I didn't go away and I'm here." But she knew she'd frighten him, knew he would get up and run away, out the door of the library, across the street, and never come back.

Pulling the long legal pad of paper in front of her, she picked up her pencil and forced herself to start her work. "Did Miss Ballard explain this to you?" she asked, looking at him. His eyes were the same as hers, as were his slightly snubbed nose and the cleft in his chin, but the rest was Alan. "What the study is for, and how I'm going to ask you questions?"

He nodded, actually looked interested. Most of the other children she had already interviewed had shown different degrees of interest, some none at all, squirming impatiently in their chairs, looking around, making faces.

"Did she tell you that this will go on for three years? That I'll come back next year at this time, and the year afterward, and that I'm also going to talk to children just like you in both France and England?"

He nodded again, then smiled a small smile. "That would be interesting. I'd like to have your job and go to England and France."

"Well . . . I live in France, Chris. In Paris."

"Someday I'd like to go there. And to Hawaii. That's where my dad was killed."

"I know," she said, carefully studying his face. He had said it very matter-of-factly. "In fact, that's one of the things I want to talk about, ask you questions about for the study."

"Okay," he said with the small smile again.

"Do you . . . mind talking about your father?"

He shook his head.

"Good," she said, dragging her eyes from his face and back to the legal pad.

For an hour she asked him questions and listened as he talked, making quick little notes on the legal pad and checkmarks on the long questionnaire. He talked about Alan as one might about a character in a book, painting him as larger-than-life, in gallant, heroic proportions.

"Would you like to be a pilot someday?" she asked.

He thought about it for a long moment, tipping his head to one side so that she could see the little cowlick that stood out from the back of his hair. Then he shook his head. "No. I don't think so," he said.

"What would you like to be?"

He thought again. "I'm not sure."

"Well, what do you like to do best of all the things you do?"

"I like to write stories," he said, and she caught her breath.

"Would you show me some that you've written, Christopher?" she asked.

"I don't know," he said shyly. "You might not like them. You might not think they were good."

"But if I don't like them, I'll tell you *why* I don't like them, what I think is wrong with them, so you can go back and write them so they're better the next time."

"I'll bring you some tomorrow," he said, standing up and pulling his stocking cap on.

She watched him as he walked away from her, then got up and hurried to the window, pressing her face close to the glass until she saw him run down the broad library steps, climb on his bicycle, and pedal off down the street.

She stood at the window for fully five minutes. It was like an image that lingers after closing one's eyes. She could still see him in his stocking cap just as his bicycle turned the corner and disappeared.

She watched the traffic pass on the street, not really seeing it. She could still hear his voice, see the bright smile, the little cowlick at the back of his head.

She calls me Chrissy. Mary's affection spilling out to him, always wanting a child of her own, never able to have one, and finally Christopher. It was obvious he loved Mary. *She calls me Chrissy.* When he said that, his voice had changed, become warm, filled with love.

Turning, she drew up, startled. A little girl was sitting at the table, quietly watching her.

"Hi," Jenny said, quickly sitting down and riffling through the questionnaires, hiding her eyes, blinking back the tears. "Now, let me see—yes, you must be Esther O'Brien."

Chapter 34

"NELSON WILL COME with the car to New York to pick you up, Liz," Kate said into the phone. "We're going to miss you terribly at Christmas. It really won't be the same without you here. But at least we'll have you for this coming week."

Liz had just returned from a four-month tour with her play, closing it in Chicago after a month's run at the Erlanger Theater. "I'm flying to London on the eighteenth with Julie," she told Kate. "We're going to spend the holidays with Dan. But a week first at Finisterre is just what I need. This tour has been an exhausting one."

That November of 1954 had been a blustery and bitterly cold one in Chicago. It seemed to drag on interminably. The play had run for fourteen months and the cast was bored with the play, tired of the one set, of each other, tired of the lines, the costumes, the green room conversation, the peeling walls in the dressing rooms, and even the view of the frozen lake out of their Congress Hotel windows.

But when Liz picked up her morning newspaper from the room service cart, then unfolded it and looked at the headlines that December third morning, she quickly put down her orange juice. "67 TO 22 VOTE IN SENATE CONDEMNS MCCARTHY," the headlines read. She looked off at the lakefront. Somehow she knew that a cruel and shameful era had come to an end. For more than four years she and Dan had lived in the shadow of this awesome terror, an ocean between them, the endless months of loneliness and living with the fear broken only by occasional visits by one or the other to London or New York. The subpoena had never come to the Washington Square house, but its threat hung over her head day in and day out.

Liz put a call in to London. It took most of the day to get the call through, and when she reached Dan, he sleepily said that he had just begun to doze off in bed over a book.

310

"Sorry, darling, but it's past midnight here, you know, and I was half asleep."

"Dan! The Senate has condemned Senator McCarthy. In a vote, sixty-seven to twenty-two." There was dead silence at the other end of the line, and all Liz could hear was the crackling of static.

"Good God!" Dan finally said, his voice husky.

"I've been trying to call you all day."

"I've been holed up here working, honey. Are you sure?" Suddenly he sounded uncertain. "Liz, are you sure?"

"Of course I'm sure," she laughed. "Darling, darling, now we can live like normal people again. I can't wait to see you, and I have reservations for us for December eighteenth. I'm going up to Finisterre to spend a week with Kate, just resting, then we'll drive up to Massachusetts to pick up Julie and Joanna at school for the holidays." She tried to hear his answer, but as the connection went bad, she hung up, still hearing his last words: ". . . and see you here on the eighteenth."

Arriving at Finisterre on the seventh, she joined Kate in the library after she had freshened up. Kate was on the phone and turned to her. "Just calling the girls to wish them happy birthday," she said, then quickly spoke into the phone. "Joanna? Yes, darling. Yes, Julie's mother is here too. Well, of course we will, we'll have a lovely birthday celebration dinner for you both the night we bring you home. No, I'm afraid not. Jon won't be home for the holidays until Christmas Eve. He's going skiing with Reed and Jamie in Vermont." Liz heard the slight pause at Reed's name. "Yes. Please put Julie on so she can talk to her mother."

At dinner Liz sat listening to the others as a pleasant indolence stole through her. She liked these McCauleys, the sister and brother. She liked their outspokenness and dark good looks. They had a certain charm and vitality about them that picked up the tempo of a room or charged any conversation they were involved in with a vibrant kind of electricity. She liked the musical lilt of Edwinna's voice.

"Amanda Barnfield's trust fund established the child center and guarantees certain funds each year," Edwinna was explaining to Liz, "but it's Kate who has kept it going with extra funds."

"No," Kate said with a quiet smile. "It's you, Winnie, who has kept it going. Without you, there'd be no child center."

"I'm thinking it's both of you," Mike said with a soft laugh as he lapsed into the rhythmic brogue of his forefathers. Watching him, Liz saw why he was a leader and why women were attracted to him. There was a strength and hardness in his face, a face that was kept from handsomeness by an irregularity of his nose, obviously broken at some point in his life, and a scar that ran at an angle across one cheek. But his eyes were as blue as the sea and startling in their frankness and steady gaze, and there was a deceptive gentleness about him, in the way he spoke, in his smile that flashed widely and with warmth. She saw his head turn before she heard Martin, the houseman, speak.

"Mr. McCauley, sir. It's Mr. Barnfield wanting to see you upstairs, sir. He would like to see you and Mrs. Barnfield."

As Kate rose and turned with a quick expression of apology, Liz smiled and waved her on as she stood up. "Go on along, Kate. Winnie and I will finish our coffee and chat until you come down."

Jonathan was half sitting up in the massive canopied bed, several piles of paper next to him and a letter in his hand. He was white and drawn. His cheeks had hollowed and his eyes seemed sunken in the sockets. When he saw Kate, he held up the letter and smiled.

"From Joanna," he said, his eyes showing sudden life as he spoke her name. "She says she will be home in a week. I miss her, Kate. I wish you hadn't sent her off to boarding school this year."

"Well, with Jon still home, Jonathan, that should be quite enough excitement here for you."

"Jon," he scowled. "He has no time for an old man." Then he picked up a sheaf of papers and handed them to Kate. "Here you are, the Palmer Hotel Chain contracts, all signed, and I congratulate you. You made an excellent deal. And your productivity figures for the coming year interest me. Let's talk further about them." He turned his head slowly. "And Mike," Jonathan said, his breathing becoming labored as he picked up another sheaf of papers from beside him. "This across-the-board wage increase demanded by the Workers' Association is one I reject. Cut it by half, you tell them, and I might talk business with them."

"They won't go for it, Mr. Barnfield," Mike warned. "They've heard rumors about the Palmer contract."

"Take it to them, Mike," Jonathan said, his voice fading,

his hand waving feebly as Mike took the papers. Mike started to speak again, his jaw hardening, but as Jonathan's eyes closed in great weariness, Mike looked at Kate, who shook her head slowly, and he followed her from the big shadowy room.

In the library Winnie sat down at the piano and idly let her fingers rove over the keys as Liz curled up at the end of the couch and listened. But after a while she walked away from the piano and crossed to the fireplace, where she sat down on the floor in front of it while Liz watched her. She was wearing a flowing, shapeless sort of dress in some dark material, and yet there was something arresting about her, Liz thought, an unusual kind of beauty in the dark hair that flowed down her back, the strong features and intelligent eyes. "Joanna adores her," Kate had said earlier, "and rushes to help her at the child center the moment she gets back from school each time."

"If it weren't for Kate, you know, this town would be through." Winnie looked at Liz. "The mills would have been moved south months ago. And if it weren't for Kate, the child care center would have been closed. Mr. Barnfield doesn't agree with her. But he admires her."

"She's amazing," Liz said, shaking her head slowly.

"Her child doesn't think so," Winnie said bluntly. Liz turned and looked at her in surprise. "Her son. Jon. He's only eleven, but he thinks Reed Shaw should be running the mills, and that everything should be moved to Mississippi. He's already talking about when he graduates from Harvard Business School and takes over the mills. Did you know that families like the Barnfields register their children in these schools when they're born? But only the sons, as a rule." She laughed scornfully. Suddenly she pulled a package of cigarettes from a pocket in the folds of her skirt and lit one, then threw the match into the fire. "Mike's terribly in love with Kate, you know," she said, then added quickly, "But he'd go into a black rage if he knew I'd said anything to you. So please. That's between us."

Liz watched her for a moment. "I'm so glad Kate has someone like you. And your brother. Warm, good friends, the way you are. Everyone needs someone like that. She and Jenny and I are such close friends. But Jenny's in Paris, and I'm on tour so much of the time—"

At that moment Kate and Mike walked into the room, and

in one graceful unfolding motion Edwinna rose from the hearth.

"Have to run," she said, smiling as she walked toward them and lightly kissed Kate on the cheek. "The children start arriving at six thirty, you know." She looked at Liz, explaining. "Kate insists that the children have breakfast there, and the mothers, too, those who want to."

"Kate insists on a lot of things," Mike said with a fond smile as they all walked slowly toward the door of the library. Then his mouth grew grim. "But a lot of them won't mean a damned thing if the union faction pushes hard enough." His expression softened as he looked over at Kate, a look that wasn't lost on Liz as they reached the door. "But we can thank God for the Kates in this world. If it weren't for them, we wouldn't get very far."

About an hour later Kate tapped on Liz's door and went in.

Liz was sitting at the dressing table in a pale blue velvet robe, doing her nails. "Oh, good!" she said, eyes shining. "I don't feel a bit sleepy."

As Kate crossed to the chaise, she pulled a package of cigarettes from the pocket of her yellow robe and lit one, then curled up on the chaise. "Just like the old days." She smiled. "Now if Jenny were only here." For a moment there was just the sound of the file on Liz's nails, then she looked up.

"Tell me," she said softly, smiling.

Kate laughed a little. "You always know, don't you, just exactly what I'm thinking?" She rose and walked restlessly to the window. "I'm not in love with him. But I'm terribly attracted to him, Liz. And I don't know if that's enough."

"Enough for . . . what, Kate?"

"For—for anything more than just a business relationship, or a casual friendship." She turned and leaned over the back of a chair. "I don't think I can only be friends with Mike McCauley. I think there has to be something more."

"Marriage?"

Kate shook her head. "No. At least not yet. I think I'd have to be in love with him for it to be marriage."

Liz nodded, understanding.

"You don't approve, do you?"

Liz thought for a long time. "Only because I don't want you to be hurt, Kate. Please, oh please, think about it very

314

carefully before you take any final steps. I just can't bear thinking you might be hurt by it."

Kate was never able to have a further discussion with her father-in-law about the new productivity figures she had given him.

Six days later Jonathan Barnfield was rushed to Barnfield Memorial Hospital with a massive coronary. He died in the ambulance enroute, with Kate holding his hand. Several hours later, when she returned to Finisterre in midafternoon, she found Liz in the solarium cutting flowers for a table centerpiece.

"He's gone," Kate said sorrowfully as she sat down in one of the white wicker chairs and stared out at the lake, covered with ice now beneath a wintry gray sky. Liz knelt down beside her and took her hand and held it.

"I'm sorry, Kate. I'm so sorry."

"It's funny," Kate said after a moment. "He was so much of what I despised in a human being—arrogant and manipulative, oblivious to the needs and wants of everyone except those closest to him, wielding power and influence as though it were his God-given right. And yet—there was something about him that I admired, even liked at times, that fierce, protective love he had for his family, his strength, his refusal to compromise on what he believed in." She smiled, forcing back the tears. "You have to admire someone like that."

"What can I do?" Liz asked. "What can I do to help?"

"Would you drive with Nelson to Massachusetts tomorrow to get Joanna and Julie and bring them back? And then, just be here with us until you leave for London?" She sighed wearily. "Joanna will be devastated, you know. She and Jonathan were so close. Loving enemies." She smiled. "They argued constantly about social issues, about the way the mills were run, about their differences in perception of values. He had such elitist ideas, and she hated most of them. But beneath it all she loved him deeply."

Liz nodded. "I'll leave first thing in the morning."

As she crossed the campus to Julie and Joanna's dormitory, Liz smiled at the pretty students who passed going in the opposite direction, some in twos and threes, others with their parents, carrying suitcases. She stopped for a moment in the wide corridor, seeing a group of people standing near Julie's room. But after Joanna ran toward her and flung herself, crying, into Liz's arms, she walked on slowly, holding the weeping girl. Julie was just coming out of the room carrying a suitcase, which she put down by the door, as a small redheaded girl turned to two older women standing nearby and exclaimed, "Oh, Mother, this is Julie's mother, Elizabeth Lowndes!"

The two women broke into effusive greetings, one of them saying, "Of course, Julie's mother. DeeDee told me at the beginning of the year that Elizabeth Lowndes' daughter lived in the room next to her." Liz tried to smile politely as she caught a quick glimpse of Julie's face. "I'm terribly sorry," she said to the women, edging past them with Joanna and Julie following. "But there's been a death in the family, and we must hurry."

Julie was sitting sideways on one of the little jump seats in the limousine, reaching back and holding on to Joanna's hand.

"It's okay, Jo," she said over and over in a soft, comforting voice. "You cry just as much as you want." Her golden head in the little navy blue school beanie bobbed in sympathy as Liz, from the corner of the limousine seat, watched with a soft smile on her lips.

"I'm sorry," Joanna said, looking around at Liz as she dabbed at her eyes with a hanky and tried to smile. "Granddad would be really upset if he saw me. He thought tears were sappy and a waste of time. He'd hate it if he thought I was sitting here crying over him." Sadly she looked off at the passing wintry countryside.

"You loved him very much, didn't you?" Liz asked softly as she reached out and patted Joanna's other hand.

"Well, he was kind of like my father really, instead of my grandfather. I was only two, you know, when my father died."

Liz stared at her for a moment, startled, then quickly looked out the window. Of course. She'd almost forgotten. Joanna had always thought Adam was her real father. She had never known about Philip Gray or that the three women had met in the hospital. The children had been told their mothers met right after the bombing of Pearl Harbor while working on a war bonds campaign.

"Mother!" Julie was nudging her. "You're not listening. Could we please stop someplace and get something to eat? I'm starved! Jo must be too."

"Sorry, darling." Liz smiled. "Kate's waiting dinner for us at Finisterre, and we'll be there in another half hour."

Following the burial services at the cemetery, Kate stood on the snowy ground and looked up at the Barnfield vault arching against the bare trees and winter sky, its polished stone facade gleaming dully in the gray light. Her eyes moved slowly across each letter of the name Barnfield, etched deeply into the stone above the entrance.

She couldn't accept Jonathan's death. Not yet. He had been too large a force, too strong a figure in all their lives. Turning, she walked through the crowd of mourners just as Justin Wheeler took her arm on one side and Margaret's arm on the other. But suddenly seeing Liz standing just behind Joanna, she excused herself and hurried over.

"Thank you for keeping an eye on her," she half whispered. They watched Joanna, who was staring at the grilled door of the vault, now closed. "Could you take her back to New York with you for a day or two, Liz? She's taking it so hard."

"Of course," Liz said, clasping Kate's hands. "We'll go this afternoon. I'll keep her with us until Julie and I leave for London day after tomorrow."

Kate shook her head sadly. "She takes everything so hard. Poor baby. Life won't be easy for her."

As everyone began to move down the hill toward the limousines, Kate saw Mike. He was talking to some people. Then he turned and looked up. He stood there as though waiting for her, and she crossed to him in the barren, windswept cemetery, whispering to him, "Please come back to the house, Mike. I must talk to you later. Henry Bishop will be there, probably to read the will to the family. He said Jonathan had told him several weeks before his death that he wanted all legal matters taken care of immediately."

"I'll be there," Mike said, looking down at her and holding her hand for a moment. He led her down to the limousine and helped her in, then walked over to Edwinna, who took his arm. Slowly they crossed to his car as the procession of limousines pulled out of the cemetery.

Marianne looked slowly around the lamplit room. Everyone seemed stunned. In a silence that was almost oppressive, no one moved or spoke. Even she was shocked. She knew her father had known how desperately she wanted a divorce. But she hadn't realized his dislike for Reed had gone as deeply as it had. It was all far more than she had bargained for.

"Well," Reed said in a tight, constricted voice. "That pretty much settles it, I guess." Jonathan's instructions had read that on the termination of Reed's contract with the Barnfield Mills, which was January 1, 1955—less than two weeks away—he was to be given a settlement of one hundred thousand dollars, but no renewal of his contract. Marianne rose and walked to the window, where she slowly lit a cigarette, then turned and watched Reed as he suddenly downed his drink where he stood at the bar. For a long moment he looked at Marianne; then, without another word, his face white with anger, he walked out of the room.

Kate started forward as though to rise and follow him, but Marianne stopped her. "Don't, Katy," she said softly, seeing the stricken look on her face. "He brought it on himself."

But Kate was thinking about how Jon would react. This was a matter of serious concern with her. Jon looked to Reed for guidance and approval and male companionship. There had always been a clashing of wills between Jonathan and his grandson, Jon. Reed, knowing this, had taken advantage and made himself a pal to Jon. Where Jonathan had never exerted discipline with his son, Adam, he had tried with Jon, and it had backfired on him.

Too late, Kate silently mourned, all of it had come too late. Jonathan had grieved deeply over Adam's death, then set about trying to avoid all the old mistakes he had made with his son as his grandson grew. But Jon's will had been as strong and stubborn as his own, and he had turned to Reed.

Kate looked back at Henry Bishop who sonorously read on, his glasses perched precariously at the end of his nose. Trust funds of two million dollars each were left to Jon, Joanna, Brenda, and Jamie. A larger one was left to Marianne, as well as forty-nine percent of the shares of the Barnfield Mills, and the estate in Palm Beach.

Finisterre was left outright to Kate. Jonathan also bequeathed fifty-one percent of the shares of the Barnfield Mills to her. As Henry Bishop handed Kate a sealed envelope with her name written on it in Jonathan's handwriting, he touched her arm and smiled.

"You can open it later," he said. "It's a personal message, I think. At least that's what he told me when he gave it to me for you."

"Thank you, Henry." She smiled, then turned. "If you'll

excuse me. I have some business I have to discuss with Mike McCauley, and I asked him to wait for me in the music room."

Henry watched her as she crossed the room, a tall, slim, graceful woman who had taken on the immense burden and responsibility of running the Barnfield Mills with an ease and grasp that he found staggering. "She won't do things the way I would have, Henry," Jonathan had told him three weeks earlier, "but she'll do her damnedest, whatever road she chooses to take."

Mike stood at the window of the music room, waiting for Kate. He watched Reed, dapper in his black Chesterfield and homburg, as he angrily stalked along the curved driveway to his car. Just minutes earlier he had started past the music room door, then, seeing Mike, he had stopped.

"Well, McCauley," he had said with a slight twist to his mouth. "I have to hand it to you. You really managed to pull it off."

Mike was on his guard. "Pull it off?"

"Oh, you'll find out." Reed smiled nastily. As he slapped his gray suede gloves against the palm of his other hand, he said, "Funny. I knew Kate had the old man pretty well buffaloed. But I never thought it would go this far." He started to leave, then stopped again. "Tell me something, McCauley. Do you plan to marry her?"

Mike took a quick step toward him, then stopped with clenched hands. "Wait a minute, Shaw!"

Reed took a step back, but he was still smiling. "And tell me something else. Did you at least get a high school diploma?" And he was gone before Mike could make another move.

When Kate finally found him in the music room, he was composed again. In spite of her grief, she was beautiful, her face pale above the simple high-necked black dress and the single strand of long pearls. She walked to the window and stood there staring out into the growing twilight.

He wanted to take her in his arms, hold her. Something intuitive told him she might, at this moment, turn to him, lean on him. But he couldn't be certain. And the memory of Reed's accusations stung deeply. Mike was proud, proud of his heritage, of coming up the hard way, and especially proud that he *had* finished high school, going to classes at night so that he could work during the day and take care of his family.

319

His father, an invalid, had been injured in a mill accident and was practically bedridden until his death just the year before. His mother's death four years earlier had meant Winnie had had to take over the nursing care of his father. None of it had been easy. Two younger brothers and a sister to get through school and on their way in life. Things were better now . . .

"I'm sorry, Mike," Kate said with a sigh, turning from the window and walking about turning lamps on, then slowly facing him. "Reed is out. Jonathan left a settlement for him in his will. Forty-nine percent of the mills' shares went to Marianne, and the remainder to me." He simply nodded, knowing that words were inappropriate. "I want you to help me run the mills, Mike, as general manager in charge of all production and sales." He stared at her, stunned, then watched as she ripped open an envelope. "Jonathan's lawyer gave me this. In his handwriting." She read a few words silently, then said aloud:

"My Dear Kate,
I have never believed that a hand should reach from the grave, which may seem strange to you, with all of my resistance to your proposals for what you feel is the well-being of both the Barnfield Mills and the townspeople of Brookton. I feel that a person should try to accomplish in a lifetime whatever he or she believes in, and push to the limit for those goals, for as long as there is breath left to do so. But once that breath is gone, then that effort must end. I don't believe in what it is you say you want to accomplish, but then I rather expect that with my passing, so passes an era. Do what you feel you must with whatever determination and will and stubbornness you can summon. You have my blessing, if not my approval. I have long admired you. And now I leave it in your hands.
                                                                Jonathan."

Slowly she folded the sheet of paper and slipped it back into the envelope. She smiled. "It sounds like Jonathan, doesn't it?" she said with a trace of tears in her voice.

He laughed softly. "It sounds like Jonathan."

"Everyone is staying for dinner, Mike. Please stay. I have something I want to tell everyone." She reached out as though to lead him by the hand, and he caught it. Slowly, in the half darkness, she moved to him and lifted her face. He felt her against him, the lovely long length of her body as she

320

pressed close, smelled the fragrance of her perfume, and turned her a little. One hand touched her throat, and he heard her catch her breath, then slowly he let his hand slip down over the softly clinging gown as he kissed her, a long and lingering kiss. His hand cupped her breast, then slipped farther down, caressing as it moved. Then he pulled her against him, and she felt his hardness and her breath caught on his lips as the kiss grew deeper. "I've loved you from the very first moment I saw you," he said.

"Yes," she whispered. "Yes, Mike."

He was shaking his head. "Never—I never believed this could happen to me."

After Martin had finally served the coffee and liqueurs and ice cream molds for the children, Kate looked around the table. The candles flickered brightly as everyone waited, knowing she had something she wanted to say. Jon watched her warily, his glance darting now and then with hidden anger to Mike McCauley, then back to his mother as his pink ice cream rooster melted before him. Kate reached over and softly touched his cheek.

"I don't want to wait to say this," she said, glancing at Marianne, who gazed at her with affection, but with open curiosity too. "You will probably think it was hasty and in bad taste, but I don't feel it can wait." She paused for a long moment, then drew a deep breath and went on, encouraged by the smile on Mike's face. "We need a large capital investment for the mills over the next five years, for modernization of the buildings and new machinery. I won't bore you with details, but costs have been rising since the war, especially with reconversion from wartime production, and profits have been shrinking. There's growing unrest among the mill workers, and to keep all of them at work, we must push our production up. We can't do that without new high-speed, high-efficiency machinery and equipment. There had been a long-range plan to move the mills south. Jonathan felt that was the solution. I did not. And so I presented a plan to him for modernization of the existing mill buildings and the purchase of new equipment." She held up the envelope. "This letter was given to me this afternoon by Henry." She nodded to the white-headed lawyer sitting to her right. "In the letter Jonathan has instructed me to do what I feel is right concerning the mills."

Marianne and Justin Wheeler were nodding their approval.

"And I agree with you, Kate, on every count except from a purely practical point of view," Justin said. "And that's a point I feel I can't ignore." He smiled. "Just last-minute warnings."

"Of course, Justin." Kate nodded at him and smiled. "But this is something we have discussed at length before. I'm fully aware that in moving the mills to Mississippi, we could avoid many of the dangers that face us by staying here. However, I've decided to go ahead with a full program of revitalization. Marianne and I are in full agreement: we would rather see the town of Brookton not only survive, but prosper and grow in the years ahead."

"As long as Kate does all the work," Marianne said in a teasing tone, and everyone at the table laughed.

"A second alternative came to us that we are also rejecting," Kate said, watching eyebrows rise around the table. "We have had an offer to sell. Cane-Lees Amalgamated, a large midwestern firm, would like to buy us out. But they would reduce the employment rolls by at least one half. Marianne and I decided last night that that also is not the answer. Which means, of course, that we're going ahead with the modernization of the buildings and the purchase of new equipment." She looked around the table. "How?" she asked softly. "Finisterre is going to give us the capital investment that we need."

"Finisterre?" Justin leaned forward.

Kate smiled. "For months now I have been carefully studying the growth pattern into and beyond the suburban areas of large cities since the war, particularly around New York City. My friend Jenny MacKenzie's study of the postwar baby boom gave me the idea. We are going through drastic changes, and one of them is the flood from the cities to suburban towns and settlements. As the years go on, people who work in the cities will travel farther and farther into the country to homes where they will live. With Brookton less than forty miles from New York City, Finisterre is an ideal location for a beautiful suburban settlement. We have already found a development corporation who will take the land and turn it into a model community, with the house and this section of the lake area for a country club, and the remainder of the land for two- and three-acre homesites."

"Incredible," Justin said with a wide smile. "What an idea!"

"The children and I will move to the gatehouse," Kate

said, "now that Marianne has taken an apartment in Manhattan, and the money from the sale of the estate will go into the modernization of the mills." She looked at Mike. "Mike and I have worked out a tentative plan that will take four to five years to put into full effect. We're bringing in an efficiency expert who will show us how to increase the productivity of the workers. With new machinery and equipment and a general overhaul of the buildings—why, in five years production should be at an all-time peak, wages will be equal to union wages, and the Barnfield Mills should be well on the road to total recovery. And that's not just simplistic pap. It's something that can actually happen."

"My congratulations, Kate," Justin said, raising his liqueur.

From the corner of her eye Kate saw Martin enter, a worried expression on his face. As he crossed to her she said, "What is it, Martin?"

"It's Mr. Gennaro, ma'am. He's in the entrance hall, waiting. He wants to talk to you and Mr. McCauley. He says he's sorry to disturb your dinner but—"

Both Kate and Mike were on their feet, hurrying from the room. "Please, Marianne," Kate said as she left. "Take everyone into the library. We'll only be a few moments, I'm sure."

Tom Gennaro was standing in the main entrance hall near the door, twisting his hat in his hand, his rather worn overcoat still buttoned to the top button, his gray hair mussed as though he had distractedly been running his hands through it.

"What's wrong, Tom?" Mike asked as they walked toward him.

"Wait a minute," Kate said, leading them to the small sitting room. "We'll talk in here." She gestured him to a chair, but he shook his head.

"Well, it's happened," Tom said, and his face seemed to collapse. "I don't know what triggered it. Mr. Barnfield's death, I guess."

"You'd better explain, Tom," Mike told the foreman.

"Some men from the union arrived in town late this afternoon. They've put up at the Anderson House over in Lesterville, and they've got Murphy and Ariente and Polk and . . . let's see"—he scratched his head—"and Pastore and Grumbach, the top guys from the Association. They're over there talkin' to them."

"Hmm," Mike said, walking to a window and looking out.

323

Kate sat down on the arm of a wing chair and waited, watching Mike. Then she looked at Tom Gennaro again.

"Do you think Mr. Shaw called them?"

"He might have," Tom said. "I don't want to talk outa turn, Mrs. Barnfield. But Mr. Shaw'd like to see the mills go to Mississippi."

"Mr. Shaw is no longer with the Barnfield Mills, Tom," Kate said quietly. Tom looked at her in surprise. He seemed to notice her for the first time. He had only seen her at the mills before, always dressed in tailored tweed suits or severe black or gray dresses. In her green velvet dinner gown, with the deep golden hair pulled back behind her ears, a single long strand of pearls and tiny pearl buttons on her earlobes, he thought she was the most beautiful woman he had ever seen.

"Well, Mike, the battle has begun." Her face was sad. "Even before we got a chance to fight."

Mike nodded, his eyes hardening to a flinty dark blue as he slowly lit a cigarette and blew the smoke toward the ceiling. Finally he spoke. "What do you think, Tom?"

"Well, soon's they're through with the union guys, they'll come back to Brookton and go to Dennehy's Bar and Grill. To talk it over. But they'll go alone, without the union guys."

"All right," Mike said. "Then maybe we'd better be there waiting for them."

"That's what I thought you'd say," Tom said, smiling as he walked toward the door. "Maybe we can talk some sense into 'em."

"You go ahead, Tom. I'll take my own car and meet you there. Wait outside for me."

"I'll do that." Tom turned at the door and smiled at Kate, who had risen and was standing next to Mike. "Good night, Mrs. Barnfield."

"Good night, Tom," she said as he walked out the door.

For several moments they stood in silence, close and facing each other. "I feel as though time has run out, Mike, as though they've stopped listening to us."

"No, they're listening," Mike said slowly, shaking his head. "But they're afraid of what they're hearing."

"Afraid?" Kate looked puzzled.

"They hear us talking about change, about new equipment and machinery, modernization of the buildings. But they hear other voices talking about automation, about new, more efficient, high-speed machinery bringing about something that's called *technological unemployment*. They see a new machine reducing the manual labor needed to run that machine, one or two workers able to do the work formerly done by four or five. They see the employment roll of eight thousand shrinking to perhaps five, even four thousand—"

"But we have a contract with them. The Workers' Association!" Kate protested. "We've assured them that our plan calls for increased production, not reduced employment."

"Fancy words to them. They believed it at first. Or wanted to. But now, with new voices talking to them—"

"But the contract, Mike!"

"Kate," he said, reaching out and ruffling her hair, watching it fall from behind her ears in soft, shining waves, "other companies have given worker groups contracts. And they've been written in good faith. Each side trusting the other. But sometimes when a company falls on hard times, management simply ignores the contract. Big powerful unions mean protection against that kind of management. They give the worker clout, insurance. They let him sleep nights, and collect his paycheck every week. And with so many of the textile mills still going south, they may feel they have to leap now. If they can get a union contract and tie you up for three or four years, you'd be powerless to effect a move in time—"

"Mike!" she exclaimed, throwing her hands wide. "We've got to buy time from them. They have to give us a chance."

He took her hands, then slowly pulled her into his arms and held her. "Tom and I will see what we can do, talk to them." As she pressed against him, then turned her face up to his, he kissed her. "You're lovely," he murmured against her mouth, "and I don't want to leave you. I want to come back to you, Kate. Tonight."

"I'll wait for you," she whispered. "At the gatehouse." He nodded and kissed her again, feeling the soft curving contours of her body beneath the clinging gown as she pressed close to him. "I'll go there at eleven o'clock." She watched him as he left, a part of her going with him. Then slowly she walked back to the library. No, not love, she thought. But something so strong, she couldn't fight it.

By ten that evening everyone had left. Kate threw a fur coat over her dinner gown and drove to the gate house. She was waiting for him in half darkness when he tapped on the garden door to the sunroom, where a single low lamp burned. He shook the snow from his coat and hat, took them off and threw them onto a wicker chair, and followed her to the small, cozy den where a fire burned in the fireplace.

"Tell me," she said impatiently as she poured them each a brandy, then crossed to the fire where he stood warming his hands and watching her, her hair a coppery gold in the firelight.

"Our contract with them has two years to run, Kate. They'll honor that contract, they say—"

"Thank God," she said, sinking down into a chair by the fire.

"—but they'll want to see marked progress in that two years."

"Of course," she said, thinking hard as she sipped the brandy. "As long as Joanna and Jon are protected financially, the risk is unimportant." She looked up, almost pleading. "You have to understand."

Mike looked down at her golden head and smiled, then said softly, "I understand completely. Taking care of your own first is a justifiable response, even an admirable one. Even Gordy Murphy, as fiery and as much of a rabble-rouser as he is, would agree with that. And tonight at Dennehy's he was forced to admit you're heading in the right direction, Kate."

"Mike—" There was a tentative, almost trembling sound in her voice. "Marianne and I have talked about it, and we agree. It will take time, but we want the Barnfield Mills to become a partnership with the employees; we want them to feel they have as much a stake in it as we do, more perhaps. We want—"

"Your son is a keen youngster for only eleven," Mike said sharply, rolling the brandy glass in his hands. "He's already pretty sore about what's been going on, and when he hears about this he won't like it or understand it."

"Someday he'll understand, Mike," she said with a quiet firmness he hadn't heard in her voice before when she spoke of Jon. "He'll have to, because he's my son . . . and Jonathan Barnfield's grandson. Jonathan, you see, was wise enough to know that we will have to change as circumstances change. Much as he despised it. His grandson will have to see that as well."

He took the glass from her hands, and slowly pulled her to her feet. For a moment they simply looked into each other's eyes; then, taking his hand, she led him through the darkened house and up the stairs, their feet sinking silently into the deeply carpeted floors and staircase. In a room with wide casement windows all across one end, they stood for several moments looking out on the rolling hills of Finisterre, bathed eerily in milky white moonlight. Then they slowly began to undress each other, their fingers somehow sure, as though they had known each other this way always. He pulled her dress from her shoulders, and she let it fall into a shimmering pool of pale green around her feet. In moments they stood naked, the moonlight touching their bodies with the whiteness of marble and shadowy mystery where the light fell away into darkness. She was even more beautiful than he had imagined, and he caught his breath and held it as she stood back a little and looked at him, seeing the broad, powerful shoulders tapering down to narrow hips and long, muscular legs. She held out her arms and he carried her to the wide bed. It all happened in silence, just the quickening of their breath softly breaking through the quiet mantle that enfolded them. Only the December wind moaned in a muffled wailing beyond the windows as his hands touched her everywhere, trailing like fire across her silken skin, finding hidden corners and lingering there with a maddening, persistent awareness. She stroked him, gently at first, his face and then down his chest in a lightly wondering search, then stronger as he writhed beneath her touch and her fingers slipped down his groin, caressing and holding him there until they could bear it no longer. With a swift and direct sureness he entered her, and all reason fled as she clasped him closer and closer. The moaning wind rose to a wintry wailing pitch, but they heard only each other, their wildly beating hearts, the incoherence of murmured words as the gathering storm of passion swept them along and carried them beyond reason, beyond heartbeat, beyond all touch with reality. It held them there in timeless, glowing space, floating on a mist that held only the two of them, locked in close embrace and motionless—until finally they looked at each other in the milky half light of moonlight and knew that they were finally whole and like one, inseparable from that moment on.

Chapter 35

DAN COLEMAN HAD taken a flat behind Park Lane, near Grosvenor Square where the American Embassy was located. It was there that he brought Liz and Julie after meeting them at the airport. He caught them both in a laughing embrace as they walked into the terminal from the plane, oblivious to the shouted greetings and laughter all around them.

"What a sight for sore, tired eyes!" he exclaimed. "The thought of facing the holidays without you was too much, and I'm right at a point in production of *At His Heels a Stone* where I can't leave London."

"But you knew we were coming," Liz cried happily.

"I was afraid they might extend your tour."

"I wouldn't have allowed it," Liz said, holding on to him as she loosened her furs and enfolded him in her perfume.

"And if they had, I would have kidnapped her," Julie crowed as she grasped Dan's arm, her tiny Scots tam askew over one eye.

"Two beauties," he marveled, looking at them. "Two raving beauties, and all mine."

"For two whole weeks," Liz said as he took their arms and led them toward the baggage pickup.

"That's all?" Dan asked in disappointment, pausing for a moment, then pushing on through the crowds. "Well, we'll talk about it later."

"Julie has to get back to school, and I start rehearsals in January."

"Honey, let's discuss it later," Dan said, turning to her and brushing his lips against her cheek as Julie clung to his other arm.

"But I have to be back by the sixth. I wrote you about that. Hack didn't have the contracts ready before I left, and I promised I'd sign them on the sixth."

Dan suddenly stopped. "You haven't signed them yet?"

When Liz shook her head, he said, "I was hoping you'd say that and that you'd dump the rest of this season and stay here with me." He glanced quickly at Julie. "Julie could transfer to a school here. And not a boarding school. I've already inquired, and there'd be no problem."

Julie was hopping up and down with excitement, her blue eyes dancing. "Oh, please, Mother, please! And I could live at home!"

"She wrote me that her marks are tip-top, so there'd be no problem there and—"

"You two have been writing back and forth about this?" Liz demanded, surprised.

"Well, you know how much I've wanted you here with me, Liz," Dan pleaded, "but it just wasn't possible until now. Everything is beginning to look good for me here, though, and—"

Liz suddenly turned to the baggage pickup, more to hide the hurt in her eyes than anything. "You should have written to me, Dan, before involving Julie in this."

"It wasn't him, it was me," Julie said, babbling excitedly. "I'd written to him and told him about how I was taking courses in filmmaking and how much I love it, and how I want to do this someday as my career, go to a college where I can study film production. And—"

"And I wrote back and told her that I'd begun to make all kinds of contacts in the film business here." Dan picked it up hurriedly, if somewhat sheepishly, as they moved aside to let a laughing group of young people pass by. "It isn't like New York here, you know, with films three thousand miles away on the West Coast and theater in New York. Everything's pretty much concentrated in one place. And when Julie's through high school, well, the film schools here are marvelous. And in Paris very exciting things are happening in film."

Liz pressed her lips together and started to turn away.

"Oh, please, Mother!" Julie grabbed her by the arm to turn her around as Dan took the baggage tickets from her hand. Liz felt a panic rise in her throat. "I was the one who wrote him," Julie insisted.

"Not now, Julie," she said with finality. "This isn't the place to discuss it. We'll talk about it later."

Dan took them to dinner at the Savoy. They stayed just long enough, to Julie's delight, for him to dance with them each once. In the taxi he sat between them, impulsively reaching out now and then to hug them as Julie chattered excitedly about the sights they were passing, recognizing Trafalgar Square, then Piccadilly Circus with its huge statue of Eros, and finally the embassy as they passed through Grosvenor Square.

"Tomorrow," Liz said to a sleepy Julie when they reached the flat. "It's too late and you're too tired to talk about anything serious right now." She kissed Julie good night, then watched as she wandered off to her bedroom. Liz walked about the room, touching things as she passed them, her fingers resting on a lamp, a vase, adjusting a print on the wall.

"The flat is lovely, Dan," she said. "You've done wonderful things with it. It's attractive and warm and . . . and home."

"Well, it was about time I got out of those hotel rooms and furnished flats and into something halfway decent." He smiled as he lit a cigarette, then walked to the small portable bar in the corner and poured them each a cognac. She turned and looked at his back. He seemed to be avoiding her eyes.

"But it . . . seems so permanent," she said.

For a long moment he didn't say anything, then he slowly turned and walked toward her, the two brandy snifters in his hands.

"Darling, I was serious today when I talked about you and Julie coming here. And I meant . . . to stay."

Liz looked at him as she took the glass. Dan would never change, she thought, not for a long, long time. The wayward lock of dark hair still hung down on his forehead, and his eyes still burned with some unsolved passion. They were sometimes dark gray, sometimes hazel with deep flecks of brown. His face had lost little of the spare, sensitive contours of sheer youth. He looked to be in his mid-twenties, and yet he had just turned thirty-eight in the autumn.

"To stay?" She sounded bewildered. "But I couldn't stay. Hack is doing Ainsley's new play next fall and wants me for it. And this next production of *A Doll's House*. We're going to tour it to four cities—Chicago, San Francisco, Washington, then close it in Boston—playing it for a month in each city—"

"But you haven't signed the contracts on it yet."

"Dan, you know how I feel about Nora. I've always wanted to do it." She was wringing her hands. "It's been my dream."

"Every time we've talked about this, over the years, all through the bad times, Liz," he argued, quickly putting his glass down and taking her hands in his, "we've said we were apart only because we had no choice. God knows we didn't

330

choose this kind of life. If the McCarthy thing hadn't happened, my career in New York would have gone on unbroken, with no interruptions. I'd have come back from Europe after the few months I was there for the end of the war and picked up everything just as I'd left it. My two plays were still running and we were on top of the world." Suddenly he turned and slammed a fist down on the table. And when he spoke again, it was in a low, hard voice. "But everything *did* change. I didn't plan it that way. That's just the way it happened. Until then we knew where we were going, and it was good, it was right. We both had careers. And we were together. But think back, Liz. That was when you always said you wanted us to have a baby. That was when things were right for us, when my career in the New York theater was well enough established, you'd stop and we'd have a baby. Well, I want you to stop now and—"

"Dan, I'm thirty-six years old!" she cried.

"We'll get the best doctors, talk to them, see what they have to say." He was excited, holding her arms. "Meanwhile, we'll find you a play here."

"No," she said. "I'm not known here. Why should any producer risk his play with an American actress that no one has ever heard of in London?" She sounded frightened, confused.

"But you always said that it didn't really matter, darling," he pleaded. "You said that Julie and our marriage always came first, and your career second. If something should happen and a play comes along for you, then that's wonderful. But meanwhile, this is where I've finally managed to make it all work for me, for us, darling. Please don't say no. I want you here with me, Liz. I need you. I'm only half a person without you."

Suddenly she was in his arms and they were holding each other, her cries mingling with his pleas. At first the situation seemed insoluble. For hours they tried to forget it, and he made long and hungry love to her. But then it was there again, facing them, and finally, in utter exhaustion, they fell asleep. Whenever they had a few moments or hours alone, they went over and over it again, agonizing, trying to find an answer, but only seeming to drift farther away from a solution. It loomed like a gray shadow over their holidays, never leaving Liz's mind, always a silent plea in Dan's eyes.

Liz took Julie Christmas shopping at Harrods and Fortnum and Mason, and between finding a tree for them to trim and all the other errands for their Christmas celebration, she managed to take Julie to some of the more famous sights in London. Jenny and Ian and Susan came for Christmas from Paris, laden with gaily wrapped gifts and enough luggage for Jenny to continue on to the States. Liz and a shining-eyed Julie met them at the airport.

"I'll go back with you, Liz," Jenny said that evening as she helped Liz make glittery cotton balls to hang on the tree. "This will be my final session with the children in Craddock Corners." Slowly she pulled a large piece of cotton from the box and rolled it lightly between her hands. Off in the distance they could hear Christmas music from the record player and the murmur of voices or the sudden spill of laughter from Susan and Julie. "It's hardest at Christmastime," she said. "That's when I miss him the most. And when I see him, I want so badly to just reach over and touch him, ruffle his hair, hug him, kiss those freckles. But I can't, of course. He'd just think I was some crazy lady."

Liz glanced up at her now and then as she carefully dipped a cotton ball into a bowl of glitter. "He might not."

"Yes he would," Jenny said. "He's a very reserved little boy, shy and quiet. Oh, but, Liz, he's so talented. He writes, you know. And sometimes he sends me the stories he's written, so that I can read them. I send them back to him with suggestions and sometimes just a 'Bravo' written in the margin, or just corrections in the spelling and grammar." She laughed, but it had an empty sound. "Once Mary wrote me a note and he enclosed it in his envelope. It said, 'Dear Mrs. Chase: Thank you for the interest you've taken in Christopher's writing. We all appreciate it very much.' If she only knew!"

Ian and Jenny were staying with Ian's sister, who lived in Belgravia, but between Christmas Day and New Year's, Liz and Jenny took Julie and Susan about, to the theater and shopping and to Eventide services at St. Paul's, a favorite of Jenny's. Joe Bernstein had gone back to the States, but one day Jenny took the train to Chipping Epworth. She found Mrs. Barrington and the small village almost exactly as she had left them, Mrs. Barrington just a bit more bent and slightly hard of hearing. But the bicycle was still there, and with tears pressing at her eyelids Jenny pedaled along the road that led to the air station.

She was alone. Only two automobiles passed her, and she

pedaled hard to keep warm as a cold wind drove along and sang mournfully in the topmost tree branches. Suddenly she came to the familiar opening in the road, where she had always turned into the air station. She stopped and slowly put one foot to the ground. Some of the low buildings were still there. But they were empty, and the windows gaped darkly, the glass missing in most of them. She walked the bicycle along the road, overgrown now with weeds, until she stood below the control tower deck, looking out over the deserted field, now a pasture. And she waited, listening. For a long while all she could hear was the wind. Then she tipped her head and strained forward. She heard the sound, so familiar and far off, the drone of motors, hundreds of them, the Flying Fortresses, heading toward the Channel, the sound far overhead, then growing farther and farther away, fainter and fainter, until she could hear it no longer.

Slowly she circled the bicycle around and walked it back to the main road. She stopped there and started to turn around to look once more. But instead she climbed on the bike and pedaled hard toward Chipping Epworth, never looking back, only once roughly wiping at the tears on her face with the back of her gloved hand. And when Ian met her train that evening, she rushed into his arms and buried her face against his coat.

"Home to stay, little one?" he asked her.

"Home to stay, Ian," she said, lifting her face to him. Bending, he kissed her tears away, and she whispered, "How did you know I wanted you here to meet me?"

Jenny, Liz, and Julie left on New Year's Day for the States, with Ian and Susan and Dan waving them off at the airport. Ian was staying on in London for several days to sign the contracts for the publishing of his book. Then he was taking Susan back to Paris.

"As soon as *A Doll's House* closes and Julie is out of school, we'll come back," Liz had finally said. Something weighed heavily inside.

"To stay?" Dan had asked, gently tipping her chin up.

"To stay," she said, a certain sadness in her voice, and he had held her close. "But I have to do this one last play, Dan. I have to."

They walked across the windswept tarmac to the plane and mounted the long flight of steps, and she turned and brightly smiled and waved back to him. But on the plane, as it winged its way out across the Atlantic, she pressed her hot forehead against the small window glass.

Jenny watched her worriedly, then put her hand on hers and said in a half whisper, "What is it, Liz?" Liz just shook her head back and forth for several moments. But Jenny persisted. "Hey, come on. This is when it matters, having a friend to talk to." There was a long pause.

"I'm afraid, Jenny," she said, and her voice sounded strange, frightened. "Afraid to have a baby."

"A baby?" Jenny said in surprise.

"Dan . . . we talked about it . . . I've always wanted another baby. But it was never the right time. And now, now that Dan wants me to have one, I'm afraid. I'm thirty-six, too old . . ." She was shivering, and Jenny quickly pulled out a blanket from the upper compartment and tucked it around her. In a low, almost conspiratorial voice Liz said, "Dan wants me to move to London for good, give up everything in New York. He said I can do a play in London. That's suicide. They've never heard of me there."

"They'll hear of you once you open in that play, honey," Jenny said soothingly.

"I'm afraid, oh, Jenny, I'm so afraid. I feel as though everything is beginning to unravel."

"You're tired, Liz honey, that's all. Just tired." She reached up into the compartment again, pulled down a small pillow, and put it behind Liz's head. "There. Close your eyes and try to get some sleep."

With a long sigh Liz put her head back and closed her eyes. For several minutes Jenny watched her, then turned, feeling a soft tapping on her arm. Julie was leaning into the aisle from her seat across from Jenny. There was an empty seat next to her and she pointed to it.

"Come sit with me, Aunt Jenny," she said. "I want to finish telling you about the film courses I'm taking."

Jenny put her finger to her lips in a hushing signal, then whispered, "In a while, Julie." But she was watching Julie and didn't see the look of pain that crossed Liz's face.

Jenny spent one night at Finisterre with Kate and her children, then took the train to Craddock Corners, where Meredith Ballard met her at the little station and drove her to the small Victorian house.

"You look wonderful, Jen," she said warmly as she helped Jenny unpack. "How long are you staying?"

"Just a week," Jenny said, looking up at her with affection, then back to the lingerie she was placing in a dresser drawer. "Have you seen him?" she asked eagerly.

"He comes to the library at least once a week," Meredith said, sitting down on the pretty flowered bedspread. "He loves to read, and sometimes he sits there for hours, writing."

Jenny smiled and nodded. "His stories are wonderful. He's a real weaver of tales." She looked down at the drawer to hide the tears. "Hey, how about a movie tonight, and dinner out? The treat's on me. But over in Wrentham. I don't want to take a chance on meeting Fred Baldwin."

It was all she could do, as she sat across the table from Christopher, to keep from reaching over and ruffling his hair or just touching his cheek. But she simply watched him as he talked, a bit shyly at first, but then the shyness disappeared as he told her all about everything he had been doing since he had last seen her—the camping trips with his scout troop, how he had tried out for the school orchestra and won a seat, his new dog, a collie named MacDuff, the ice skates he had gotten for Christmas, his first plane trip when the family had gone to Washington for a vacation, the summer cottage they had bought the spring before near Plymouth.

Jenny smiled secretly as she thought of the money order she sent to Mary—not Fred—each month, sent through Henry Fremont, never acknowledged, but never returned either. "Your life sounds very full and very happy, Christopher," she said, and he nodded with a small smile. What did she expect? Tales of cruelty and deprivation? Unhappiness? Alan's sister Mary was a decent, caring kind of woman. She probably loved Christopher very much. At least, Jenny thought, I've always known he was well taken care of the past thirteen years, and probably loved, and she looked away to hide the tears for all the years she had missed, and all of those ahead without him.

"Do you have any children?" he suddenly asked her, looking at her wedding ring.

"Yes," she finally answered softly. "I have a little girl named Susan. She's just ten years old. Her birthday is the same month as yours."

He looked at her in surprise. "You know when my birthday is?"

Slightly flustered, Jenny looked down at the information sheet in front of her. "Ye-es. It says right here, December seventh, 1941."

He nodded. "That was the day Pearl Harbor was bombed. The day he was killed." He looked out the window. "I've decided when I'm eighteen, I want to learn to fly a plane, like my dad did." He added softly, "I just want to see what it was like for him, and maybe know what he was thinking when he was way up there all alone in the sky."

Jenny silently caught her breath and squeezed the tears back. Oh, Christopher, she thought, I could tell you so much, so much that you'd want to hear, so many, many things that you'll never know.

She kept him there as long as she dared, then watched him as he walked toward the library entrance and went out into the cold afternoon. With a little gasp she ran to the window. He and his bicycle were just disappearing around the corner.

All through the spring and summer and on into the fall, Kate watched Finisterre as it was transformed into a community of luxury homes in a country club setting, with the beautiful old mansion the centerpiece, a clubhouse. Her relationship with Mike McCauley was one of long days in their work at the mills and discreetly stolen hours at the gatehouse when the servants were away, passion-filled hours that she cherished and he prayed would never come to an end.

Liz visited fairly often, except when she was on tour. With the closing of *A Doll's House* in June, she had taken Julie to London for a two-month stay with Dan, insisting that she had to postpone the permanent move until Julie was through secondary school. She also had to admit that Hack had begged her to do the new Peter Jameson play, convinced her, in fact, that it had been written with her in mind for the role.

But when Julie's graduation had come and gone, Liz was still entangled in a run-of-the-play contract on the new Ainsley work and was signed to do two important television dramas in the autumn.

"Send Julie to me," Jenny had written, "and we'll enroll her at the Conservatoire d'Art Dramatique here." And Liz stayed on in New York.

Finally in 1959 Liz shipped the furniture to London and boarded a plane, feeling a terrible sense of displacement already, a loss of self, a yearning, as the plane soared over the

Atlantic, for the beloved familiarity of the sunny Washington Square apartment. She was no longer the revered Broadway actress, Elizabeth Lowndes. She was Liz Coleman, wife and mother and new resident of London. The applause had been sweet. But now it was gone.

As the plane droned through the night she thought of Jenny—Jenny whose life was exciting and hectic. She and Ian were often at opposite ends of the planet, with joyous reunions in Paris, Helene there running the flat and caring for Susan and Julie. Jenny found her life in almost perfect balance, the excitement of her work and the pleasure of her home, attending the Big Four Conference in Geneva or surviving the harrowing days and nights in Budapest during the 1956 uprising against the Soviet troops, seeing and hearing Van Cliburn win the piano competition in Moscow, waiting in St. Peter's Square as the College of Cardinals chose a new pope after the death of Pius XII. Only the loss of Christopher cast a shadow.

Liz looked back at all the rich and rewarding years as the plane winged onward. And then she looked ahead and silently turned her face to the tiny window and wept.

Chapter 36

"You and Jon can go without me this summer," Joanna was saying as they stood on the Brookton platform and looked down the track for the first glimpse of the train where it would round the bend beneath snowy Conamasset Hill. Suddenly turning, she grasped Kate's hands. "Oh, please, Mom, I want this so badly. And you and Jon will be having so much fun in Europe, you won't even miss me."

"If you want it so much," Kate said reluctantly as she looked at her daughter, on her way back to college after the Christmas holidays, tall and slim and serious-faced in her gray squirrel coat and white knitted cap, her gray-green eyes wide with grave concern. Why, she's just like Philip, Kate thought, surprised at the sudden thought. Philip seemed like a faraway dream to her now, like an elusive thread of song that one strains to hear, returning only in fleeting touches of memory, like distant notes of music lost on the winds of time. But Joanna had his utopian sense of values, his never-ending search for humane effort. She even had his same fine features, but with Kate's high cheekbones, wide mouth, and gold-burnished hair. And as she watched down the track for the train, her gray-green eyes leaped with an urgency and inner fire.

"You say you'll get the training for the program this spring at Radcliffe?" Kate said, pulling her fur collar up against the wind.

"Well, in Boston." Then she added hurriedly, "And don't worry. I can handle it with my classes."

"United Nations Children's Fund!" Jon said with disgust as he picked up a stone and skipped it across the tracks, snapping his fingers in triumph as he heard it bounce on the rail. Kate looked at him in his Hotchkiss jacket, his short curly brown hair and large blue eyes helping to soften the arrogance of the thin, slightly curved mouth. At sixteen Jon already revealed a reedy slimness and rather hunched shoulders. Not like Del, she thought in absent study, remembering the broad, sloping shoulders, and how he was just two or three inches taller than she. Jon already towered over her. Like my father, she thought, and smiled softly. There was a lot in Jon from the male side, a lot altogether that would eventually bring him through. It was just that Reed had had so much influence over him, a strange sort of effect that never seemed to have taken hold of his own children, Jamie or Brenda. They were fun-loving, uncomplicated, like Marianne.

"Field worker!" he said again as he skipped another stone. "Holy Toledo! What a dumb thing to do. Where? In Transylvania?"

"Shut up, Jon!" Joanna said without changing expression or taking her eyes from the track.

"Please, Joanna," Kate said, suppressing a smile. "I hate it when you children use that expression."

"And how dopey can you get, taking the train back to school instead of driving your own car!" he said, leaping over her suitcase.

"I don't want a car at school!" Joanna said through tight lips, still not looking at him and simply shrugging away as he tweaked her cap and then tried to tickle her in the ribs through her furry coat. "God, what a bore, having a dimwitted little brother like you."

"Joanna—" Kate protested gently.

"God, what a bore—" Jon minced around her in a circle imitating her; then, with an irresistible grin, he grabbed her and danced her around on the platform. "Fuddy-duddy Joanna," he sang.

"Stop it, Jon," Joanna protested, laughing in spite of herself.

"That's enough, Jon," Kate said, suppressing a smile.

She's fair with *us*, Joanna thought as she heard a whistle in the distance and looked down the track. Why can't she be the same with the mill workers? "If only you'd realize that the plantation system in American mills has long since ended," she had told her mother, "that your Association is just a patronizing gesture. Mike McCauley and his opportunism!" But her mother had only smiled and said, "Darling, someday you'll understand. Sociology courses are one thing, bookkeeping figures something else."

Kate sighed as she watched down the track, the thundering

sound of the train coming closer. She took her children's arms and pulled them back from the track a few feet as the train roared past, then looked at Joanna's set face as she picked up her suitcase. Just like I once was, she thought, uncompromising, fiercely idealistic. Then things had changed. Oh, she was still fighting, but the goals weren't quite as high. She'd discovered accommodation. But she still cared. Oh, God, how she cared.

"Don't look so upset, Mom," Joanna said, throwing her arms around her. "I'm hoping they'll send me to India, but with my luck I'll probably be stuck in New York expediting supply shipments." She suddenly grasped Jon and hugged him tearily. "'Bye, dopey."

"So long, Jo," he said, swallowing. "I'm going to miss you."

With a wave she ran and hopped up the steps of the train and disappeared into the Pullman car as the train began to move.

"Boy!" Jon muttered, his voice cracking a little. "United Nations Children's Fund! What a dumb thing to do."

"Come on, Jon," Kate said softly, ruffling his hair as he hid his eyes from her and kicked at a pebble. Then she linked her arm through his as the train gained speed and disappeared down the track. "We have to get you packed for school too." She stood for a moment looking up at the gray sky, sniffed as though testing the air for snow, then opened the door and got into the long convertible while Jon climbed in on the other side. "When you two leave for school, I know the holidays are really over." Before starting the motor, she reached out and gently touched his cheek. "Have fun this year?"

"I'd have liked it better with just family," he said, looking out the window, his voice tight with resentment.

Kate started the motor and let it idle for a moment, then drove out of the station parking lot and headed for Finisterre. He meant the McCauleys, she thought. Mike in particular. Jon was openly hostile to Mike while Joanna politely ignored him.

Kate almost laughed aloud as she drove through Brookton. Jon fully blamed Mike McCauley for the mills not being moved to Mississippi, while Joanna believed Mike was responsible for her mother refusing to allow the union into the mills.

Her children were at the opposite ends of the poles, philosophically, and Mike was caught somewhere in the middle. She sighed. Mike had been offered a job in Roanoke, Virginia. Maybe he should take it, she thought.

"Hey, Mom," she heard Jon say, and smiled, recognizing the almost shyly offered note of conciliation. "I'll treat you to a hot fudge sundae if you'll stop at Wilson's."

Reaching out and clasping his hand, she said, "That's a deal."

Mike and Kate were just finishing a late dinner at Perrin's, a former roadhouse at the edge of Brookton, when Mike spotted Tom Gennaro at the entrance, looking around, trying to find them. As he worked his way through the tiny lamplit tables toward them, Kate looked back in alarm to Mike. The six o'clock Workers' Association meeting hadn't gone well. Both Mike and Kate had sensed a tension and a reticence. Even Gordy Murphy, the Association leader, who was never at a loss for words, seemed reluctant to speak out, except to constantly repeat the new wage demands that were far in excess of what the long-range plan had called for. Kate and Mike had taken a hard line, then by the evening's end had compromised with an offer that halfway met what the Association was demanding.

"We'll come back with an answer by midnight," Gordy Murphy had promised, his dark heavy brows drawn down in an angry scowl. "But I can't promise you much." Mike had nodded, saying he would be waiting in the mill offices at midnight for him.

"Just remember this one thing, Mr. Murphy," Kate had said quietly. "A little over four years ago the Association agreed to give us six years to complete this revitalization plan. By that time, we promised you, wages would be even with union scale and no worker would have lost his job because of automation. We promised you that modernization of the mill housing would be completed, that two more child centers would be opened, and the thirty-seven-and-one-half hour week would be put into effect. This was our agreement, but your demands earlier this evening are the goal we have set for two years from now. Please remember all of this before you return tonight at midnight." Murphy had just nodded and walked out.

Kate spoke quickly to Mike while Tom Gennaro was still halfway across the crowded restaurant. "I hadn't told you, Mike, because I saw no need to. I had another offer two weeks ago to sell the Barnfield Mills. The same company,

Cane-Lees. But I turned it down. Everything seemed to have been going so well. Our timetable was current, and I saw no need. But if there's going to be trouble—"

"Let's hear what Tom has to tell us," Mike said as Gennaro reached the table. Quickly pulling out a chair for him, Mike asked, "How about a drink?"

Tom simply shook his head, and Kate's heart sank. She could see the deep agitation reflected in his face, hear it in his voice as he twisted his hat in his hands. "There's a mob at the mills and growing bigger by the minute. Hundreds and hundreds, maybe thousands by now. Gordy Murphy tried to stop it. I have to give him credit for that. But it's that clique we've been worried about, Mike, and—"

"Clique?" Kate asked, looking at Mike.

"A small group from the dye house. We've been worried because they've been growing, agitating, spreading their poison—a bunch of malcontents who would be miserable regardless of who management was and with or without the union. Right now they think the union looks like the answer. If they got it, they'd probably change their minds and want the Association back."

"Well, they're pulling workers in by droves, Mike, and they're marching around with torches in the mill yard, yelling and shouting and chanting. It looks like the damned French Revolution, with only the guillotine missing. I called the town and state police, then came here."

Mike was signaling for the waiter as Kate slipped into her coat. As he gave the waiter some bills, he said, "You go home, Kate. As soon as I know anything I'll—"

"No!" she said. He stopped for a moment beside the table and looked at her as Tom hurried toward the door. "All right," he said slowly. "But if there's trouble I want you to leave."

She nodded and they walked quickly to the parking lot and climbed into Mike's car. As they roared along Conamasset Road toward the far side of town, she glanced at Mike's profile in the faint light from the dashboard. His mouth was set in a tight line as he bent over the wheel and peered through the windshield. She looked ahead again and suddenly gasped. They were approaching the main mill area, having skirted the town and the long row of small brown houses that nestled at the edge of Millhouse Road, and plunged into the center of the sprawling buildings where the big mill yard was.

She saw the hundreds of weaving torches before she saw anything else, then the solid sea of people as they shouted and swayed in the eerie light while a group of men harangued them with raised fists and shouting voices from the end of a long truck that had been backed into the yard. Several black and white police cars rimmed the area, and they could see the police standing by the cars.

"It doesn't look good, Kate," Mike said grimly as he slowed the car to a crawl and switched the headlights off. "I'd rather take you home first, then—"

"No, Mike!" She saw Tom Gennaro waiting for him.

"Then I want you to stay by the police cars." He looked down at her. "Otherwise I'm driving you home."

"All right," she said.

"That's a promise?" She nodded, and they got out of the car and walked toward a police car, where Mike pulled her into the deep shadow of a huge elm tree and held her close for a moment. She could feel his heart pounding and knew that hers was too. "I just wanted you to know, Katy, that I'm not leaving. I'm not taking that job at Roanoke."

"Oh, Mike," she said with a half cry of relief.

"And no matter what happens here tonight with this mob, I'm staying in Brookton, Kate. Because whatever it is that you and I have between us, it's more, so much more than I'd have there without you. God, how I love you, girl!" He was stroking her hair.

"Someday, Mike—" she started to say, but he quickly kissed her, then raised his head and looked at her in the flickering light. "No . . ." He spoke slowly, his voice low. "No, Katy, you'll never marry me. That's a wish I'll never be having." He pulled her close again and murmured in her hair. "But as long as I can hold you like this, as long as we have the nights, the wonderful hours alone, I can live with it. You've become my whole life, Kate."

She shivered, feeling the gentle strength of his hands as they slipped beneath her coat. He kissed her again, a long and softly searching kiss; then, still holding her, he led her toward the police car and called out, "Officer?" his breath fogging in the cold.

The policeman turned as they approached. "Mr. McCauley!" he shouted. "Am I glad to see you. The chief is lookin' for you."

"Please do me a favor." Mike leaned close to the officer's

ear so that he could hear him above the thunderous roar of voices. "Keep your eye on Mrs. Barnfield here. I'll come back for her as soon as I see what's happening and we get these people to leave."

"Sure thing. And if she gets cold, she can sit inside the car."

As Mike walked away from her toward Tom Gennaro, who waited at the edge of the closely packed mob, she listened to the rumbling clamor and the hoarse shouts of the speakers. Then she saw Mike and Tom push their way through and disappear, the seething crowd seeming to swallow them. She waited and watched as the torches flamed high in the blackness and the roar of voices rose and reverberated against the walls of the tall grim red buildings.

Mike was right, she thought. She would never marry him. She'd never marry anyone. Not after the loss of Del. Del was the only one she would ever have wanted to marry.

But she admired Mike and needed him in some supportive way, needed his strength, felt it flow into her when the going became hard. And then . . . there was this strong attraction she felt for him. Something primal in her responded keenly to the almost primitive maleness of him. She was a woman of strongly sensual desires, and he aroused these desires in her.

And there was so much more. More than the admiration, the desires, the close working relationship, the same goals. They genuinely enjoyed each other's company. She taught him how to have fun, took him on his first picnic, to his first stage play, bought him skis for Christmas and introduced him to the pleasures of horseback riding.

"You'll make a gentleman out of me yet," he had teased her one early morning as they rode through the forest. Then suddenly he had pulled to a stop, gently lifted her down from her horse, and led her into a heavy thicket of trees. In a small bowerlike opening, fragrant with pine and honeysuckle and the rich moist earth, he made long and intoxicating love to her. There was a richly voluptuous base to their relationship, tempered by the realities of the mill problems and her children's disapproval of him. And although she knew she would never marry him, she also knew he satisfied a deep and hungry need in her.

Mike, she thought with a long, heavy sigh as she stood in the cold near the police car. If need and desire were love . . .

Something caught her attention, and she suddenly stood on

344

her toes and strained her eyes through the dark. She saw a man clamber up onto the back of the flatbed truck and turn to the crowd, waving his arms above his head. It looked like Mike. Yes, it had to be Mike! There was a sudden roar above the uneven rumble, and hundreds—no, thousands of arms shot upward and waved wildly as he shouted at them. She could just faintly hear his voice, not the words, only the voice, but she knew he was reaching them. Mike was popular and trusted. The workers believed him when he told them something. Just seeing him there on the end of the flatbed truck would be enough for most of them. They were listening. *Listening!*

A wave of relief flooded through her, making her almost weak, and she shouted to the policeman, "Thank God!" hearing the relieved hysteria in her voice. She pushed her hand in her pocket and pulled out a package of cigarettes, her hands shaking with the sudden release of tension as she lit one. As she leaned back against the police car, she felt the cold for the first time and pulled her coat collar tighter about her throat, then dragged deeply on the cigarette. She closed her eyes for a moment and simply listened. Even though she couldn't sort out the words, she heard the power flow from his voice, the confidence and strength, and then she heard them answer in a deep, prolonged cry, their arms raised high against the moving light. The torchlight seemed friendly now, and the roar of voices warmed her heart.

"Yes! Yes! Yes!" they were shouting with one mighty voice, repeating it over and over as he asked the questions again and again. She smiled into the darkness. When she had first seen the surging crowd, the bizarre spectacle of bobbing torches and waving arms, she was sure the long uphill fight was lost. Just two years short of their goal. And in that split second, as she heard the angry roar of voices, she had decided to return to the house and, in spite of the hour, phone Stephen Henneshaw of Cane-Lees to tell him that she and Marianne would sell the Barnfield Mills. Now, as she heard the joyous shouts, she knew she would not.

Mike had jumped back down into the crowd. She dropped her cigarette to the ground and stepped on it, then suddenly stopped, her blood freezing. There was a crackling sound, sharp, whipping the air. An abrupt silence followed. Then she heard it again, a sound of shots, and a woman screamed. She held her breath, measuring the silence. As piercing police

345

whistles shattered the night and a crescendo of voices rose in terror, she plunged past the police car and started to run, but the officer grasped her arm and pushed her back.

"No, Mrs. Barnfield. You stay here." He started running, shouting back over his shoulder, "You wait here!"

Beneath the wildly waving torches she saw the crowd as it heaved out of control, surging in all directions from the center, figures leaping and running and stumbling as they fought toward the surrounding darkness. As a stream of people fled past her she pushed back against the car. She wanted to run, too, but toward the flatbed truck. Instead she clung to the door handle for support and heard herself sobbing, over and over, "Please God, please God, please God . . ."

The sound was fragmented now. Shouts and cries came from the darkness as figures hurried past, the women weeping, the men in groups with waving torches that they flung to the ground.

In the distance she could hear approaching sirens and the shrill whistles of the police. Her heart pounded wildly, hurting her chest, and she heard someone screaming Mike's name, then realized it was her own voice she heard and clamped her hands over her mouth.

That was when she saw Tom Gennaro loom out of the darkness. He was holding Edwinna McCauley by the arm, almost dragging her it seemed, as she stumbled along, her face chalky white, her hands hanging limp at her sides. They were coming toward her, and she whispered, "No." She took a step toward them, then said it again. "No!" This time it was louder, tearing from her throat in a long fluted sound, like the wounded cry of an animal. Then they were standing in front of her, the eerie light of the waving torches hollowing their eyes, making their mouths grotesque.

"He's dead, Kate," Winnie said. "He was winning them back, convincing them to talk across a table. But when he jumped down from the truck, someone—someone in the crowd pulled a gun and shot him."

Kate just shook her head. Back and forth. No sound came from her mouth as the torches flickered across her face. Silently they clutched and held on to one another for a long, long moment. Then, still not speaking, as figures streamed past them in the half darkness and shouts split the brittle, cold air, they walked toward Tom Gennaro's car standing next to Mike's in the lightly falling snow.

Chapter 37

"WELL? WHAT DO you think of your daughter Julie now?" Jenny asked, flicking off the movie projector and sitting back as Ian turned on a lamp.

"She's quite talented, you know," Ian said.

Liz simply shook her head back and forth and said softly, "It was beautiful. Such a moving little film. I just can't believe it."

"Amazing," Dan said, "even with all the limitations of the eight-millimeter camera. And the way she created the whole thing, right from scratch, and brought out the loneliness of that young girl."

"Now do you agree it was a good move to let her come here to study again this year?" Jenny said.

"Well, I—" Liz looked away, trying to hide her immediate reaction. She heard Ian asking Dan to come with him to help make some drinks, and she watched them as they left the room, watched as Jenny busied herself putting the projector away. "—she could have done the same thing in London."

"Not true," Jenny said as she wound the cord around the machine. "This is an experimental group that François is working with, in affiliation with the university, and now that he's not only writing but also directing his own films, it's a wonderful opportunity for Julie."

"I miss her, Jen," Liz said, her voice trembling with hurt. "I miss her so terribly. And with Dan so tied up days and evenings too—he has two plays running in the West End right now, you know—the flat seems like a big empty barn without her."

Jenny suddenly turned and sat down beside her. "Why don't you go to New York to do that play Hack wants you for?"

"No, Jenny, I can't. I'd have to be there by the first week in August for rehearsals, and I've already signed the lease on

347

the villa at Amalfi. Besides, don't forget Kate and Jon will be coming there for a visit after they've left you here in Paris."

"To hell with the villa in Amalfi! And Kate will understand."

"No," Liz said quickly. "Dan has promised he'll spend a whole month there. He needs the rest, needs to get away from everything. And Julie will be close by in Positano, where she'll be working with Elena Cefari. You remember what happened last Christmas. Dan took her to meet Signora Cefari when she was in London."

"The woman film director. Of course. François says it's a marvelous opportunity for Julie. Is Cefari making a film there?"

"Yes, with headquarters in Positano. So she'll only be a few miles away." She laughed a little. She sounded slightly hysterical, even to her own ears. "Julie says she'll be terribly busy most of the time, but I'm sure she'll find weekends when she'll bring new friends for parties or when she'll want to come and just lie on the beach and swim and sail. Dan loves to sail, you know, so we'll rent a little boat for . . ." The words trailed off.

For a moment there was silence. "Don't you miss it, Liz honey?" Jenny asked softly. "The stage?"

Liz rose slowly and walked over to a window, pushed the long velvet drapery back a little, and looked down into the narrow Paris street. "Yes," she said. "I miss it. And . . . sometime I'll do what Hack has suggested. Open a play in New York, then perhaps take it to London. Joel Ainsley is beginning work on a play right now, part of a trilogy that would also have an English actor in it. That would be perfect, of course, because then we could bring it to London if it was successful in New York, and—"

"Liz, two years ago you were saying the same thing," Jenny said gently, "and right after you first went to London you insisted you were going to go back to New York every two years to do a play, but you never have." She waited for a moment, but Liz didn't speak, didn't move. Softly she asked, "What is it, Liz?"

Finally Liz turned away from the window. It was open, and the soft spring Paris night flowed in, muted sounds of traffic from the faraway boulevards, some music from another flat, laughter and voices down in the street. "Where did you say Julie and Susan went?" She sounded vaguely distracted.

"Solange and François took them to a poetry reading." She

laughed. "Susan will be terribly bored. But last night they saw the ballet, and that made her happy. She's happiest when she's dancing or watching the ballet." She waited again. "Tell me."

Liz wandered around the pretty room almost aimlessly as Jenny watched. Then, far from the soft lamplight, she stopped, leaned against a table, and spoke so softly that Jenny had to strain to hear.

"Do you remember when I went back to New York from London that Christmas holiday in 1954? You and I flew over together, Jenny. I just went back to do that one production, *A Doll's House*. Only four months of touring it, and then I planned to move us out of the Washington Square house and come to London to stay, put Julie in school there . . ."

"I remember," Jenny said. There was a long pause. "Go on."

"It was when I was in Washington with the play that I first heard it, read about it in a gossip column. I didn't pay too much attention to it at first. Most of those gossip items are trumped-up stories or gross exaggerations of the truth. But in less than a week I read about it several times. She was an English actress. She had a role in his play." She walked back to the window again. "It—it ended before I moved to London. I don't know exactly when. I asked him then if it was true. He said that all the separations . . ." Still looking down into the street, she gestured in a helpless kind of way. "He insisted it was finally over. But . . . I thought, how can it ever be the same between us again?" Her voice broke a little. "We had loved each other so much. I still loved him, *do* love him now so much. It . . . it places something between you. You can't see it, can't name it, but it's there, like a shadow that you can't reach across. I thought about it over and over, kept seeing it, how he had held her in his arms, touched her, made . . . love to her . . ." She shivered and wrapped her arms about herself, as though a cold wind had blown in the window. Her slim figure looked fragile in the soft, low light as she gazed out at nothing beyond the window. "It hurt so terribly, Jenny."

The last words were a cry, and Jenny's heart ached for her. She ran across the room and held her as Liz softly sobbed. Sorrows and sleepless nights, Jenny thought. Walking in the darkness, softly tiptoeing so no one will waken. Oh, how she knew! That shattering feeling of loss, as though a piece of your body were gone, and with it your trust and self-respect

349

and desire to go on living. But thank God for Ian, she thought, gentle, even-tempered, gifted Ian with his sardonic wit and easy elegance, his complete sense of who he was.

She felt Liz slowly pull away.

"I'll never know for sure if he still loves me," Liz whispered.

At a burst of laughter from the two men in the other room, Liz started forward a little, then listened to the low hum of their voices and heard them coming closer.

Liz and Dan's eyes caught in a fleeting glance as the two men came into the room carrying fresh drinks. Ian put a new record on the player that he had told Dan he wanted him to hear, and Dan crossed to Liz and softly kissed her brow as he held her to him for a moment. He had seen the pain again in her eyes and wondered what he could do or say to erase it. It was over. Over for good. And once it was over, he could wonder why it had ever started with Diane.

Loneliness for the most part, he supposed, with the long separations between himself and Liz. And then the difficulty of disentangling himself once he knew it was finished. Diane Cliverton was not one to disentangle oneself from that easily.

"You can't just say it's finished, my pet, and expect me to simply drop off the face of the earth," she had told him that final day. And suddenly her trumped-up British accent was a matter of great annoyance to him. She was an American from Palo Alto, California, who had gone to London in her teens to study at the Royal Academy of Dramatic Art and stayed on to build a substantial career as an actress in the West End theaters.

"Nothing so drastic, Diane," he had said as he ordered them another drink in the small pub where they usually met after her performance. This time it was late afternoon; he had called her that morning and asked her to meet him there. She looked as lovely and enticing as ever, as dark as Liz was blonde, tall where Liz reached just to his shoulder, handsome sharp features where Liz's were delicate and flowerlike, hazel eyes that had seemed seductive but now appeared hard and calculating, while he suddenly recalled the clear sapphire blue that deepened almost to violet whenever he had whispered to Liz that he loved her.

"We both knew when we went into this that it had an end, that it wasn't permanent," he said in a low voice, wishing he could steal a glance at his watch and finally, gracefully leave.

"Perhaps *you* did," she argued, her voice rising.

"No," he insisted with finality. "We talked about it, right from the beginning. In fact, we slid into it. I never expected it to go as far as it did. I had thought we were friends and could—"

"Men!" she said bitterly. "They always say they want friendships with women, then first thing you know, it's hop into bed, my love. Next thing you know, the little wife finds out and he comes running and wringing his hands and saying, 'I didn't mean it, I only meant for us to be friends!'"

"You're right," he said miserably. "Guilty on all counts, but—"

"But 'I love my wife!' Is that it, lovey?"

He looked at her in surprise, then nodded. "Yes. Yes, I do love her." He gazed across at the bar, packed with prosperous looking men and women, laughing and chattering. His voice was low when he spoke again. "I've tried to tell her. But of course she doesn't believe me. And why should she?"

For a long moment there was silence between them. Then, surprisingly, she reached over and touched his cheek with great gentleness. "Poor Danny. Poor Danny's wife. I really didn't set out to destroy you, to destroy a marriage, you know."

"I know," he said with a smile, taking her hand in his and holding it for a moment. "And you didn't. I did it all myself."

"Give her time," Diane counseled softly.

"Yes. Time," Dan had said, and in a few moments he left her there, kissing her on the cheek and wishing her well.

She had finally made it easy for him, easy to leave and settle with his conscience. But with Liz it would be harder. Lovely, loving, trusting Liz. Once you tampered with that trust, it shriveled and died.

He had walked back to the theater and the rehearsal that late afternoon, knowing that only with time would Liz ever begin to trust him again. Men are different, I guess, he thought miserably, or at least *this* man is. The affair with Diane had not in any way diminished his love for Liz. He found her as exciting and beautiful as ever. If it hadn't been for the separations . . . Rubbish, he thought, angrily stepping up his pace, then sighed as he neared the theater. Time would heal the hurt, he told himself again.

As he stood in Jenny and Ian's Paris flat and listened to Billie Holiday's recording of "Good Morning, Heartache," he remembered that afternoon with Diane in the pub. Appropriate, he thought with a wry smile, and looked over at

Liz, but her head was turned as she listened to something that Jenny was telling her.

Liz and Julie flew down to Rome at the beginning of that July of 1960, checking in at the Excelsior on the Via Veneto. They spent three days sightseeing, driving about in a chauffeured Mercedes, with Julie's nose against the car window as she stared in awe at the soaring columns, the forums of Caesar and Augustus, the yellow-gold light that seemed to have seeped into the city's ancient stones, the splashing fountains of Bernini and Salvi, all of the magnificent glories of the past and the treasures of the Renaissance rushing past her eyes.

On the fourth day they took the train to Naples, where they stopped overnight, went sightseeing at Pompeii and Herculaneum, the nearby ancient ruins, then were met by another chauffeured car and driven to the place at Amalfi.

It was a rambling white villa nestled among olive trees, bougainvillea, and fragrant lemon blossoms. It seemed to hang somewhere like a mirage between puffy white clouds in the serene blue sky and the Tyrrhenian Sea below.

There was an elevator down to the beach, and for a week Julie sunned and swam and cavorted with new young friends along the sand spreading down to the blue-green water. Within a few days she was almost as bronzed as the golden, slim-hipped young men with long lashes and bruised eyes who ran laughing with her on their shoulders down to the foaming surf. "Don't worry," her eyes seemed to say to Liz, who sometimes sat nearby in a large floppy leghorn hat, a book in her lap, trying to seem detached and casual as she watched the beautiful blonde nymph who was her daughter.

She'll be gone again soon, Liz kept thinking as she furtively watched Julie from beneath the shadowy brim, off with Elena Cefari.

"Please don't hover, Mom," Julie had pleaded the first day, and so Liz had their driver, Guiseppe, take her to Sorrento to idly shop the second morning and to Positano the third morning, where she climbed the steep village hills and looked over the shoulders of the toiling street artists. But by early afternoon each day she was back down on the beach, trying to concentrate on her book in the shade of the cabana, but glancing every few moments at the deliciously laughing Julie as she raced in and out of the water with her friends.

"You can't live her life for her," Dan had gently warned her before they left London, and even more gently added, "and you have to understand these attachments, first for Jenny these past two years, and now probably Cefari." Liz had turned away, the hurt jabbing deeply. Dan had held her by the shoulders, but she kept her face turned. "Liz, honey, Jenny came into Julie's teenage life at the exact moment when she was looking for something. She completely captured her imagination. After all, Jen lives a crazy, exciting kind of life with her job as a foreign correspondent. That's pretty big stuff she does, getting caught, for instance, during the Hungarian revolt in Budapest, or covering the armed rebellion in Lebanon two years ago. And just this year, going to Moscow with that cultural exchange group when they gave the concerts. Who was it? Isaac Stern and Jan Peerce? Ian, too, honey. Look at how he's covering this whole self-rule movement in Algeria, and following de Gaulle all over the place. They're writing history, Liz. And on top of it, there's François. She met François through them and got into the film thing. This is heady stuff for an eighteen-year-old."

And I thought I was protecting her, Liz thought dully as she looked up and caught a glimpse of Julie's bright blue slip of a bathing suit as she dove into a wave, her pale golden head a splash of sunlight on the sea—protecting her from my kind of life, keeping her at boarding school, then in summer camp when we were still in New York. But she had wanted Julie's life to be normal, she argued silently with herself, filled with sun and light and schoolbooks and plaid-skirted friends with knee socks and loafers, field hockey and the hills of Connecticut. Then, when it had all started slipping through her fingers, she had packed up and moved them to London. So we could be a family again, she thought, and for six months it had been perfection—until Julie had insisted on going to school in Paris.

Suddenly she had become almost a stranger, half child, half woman. Oh, there were moments when she was still her child, warm and wonderful moments, in a wistful smile or a quick embrace, in a sleepy morning greeting or soft "Good night, Mom." But mostly it was this exquisite stranger, this half woman, who studied film in Paris, who had visited the set of *Orphée* in Provence at Les Baux with François and Solange and talked to the great Cocteau, who haunted the museum and Cinémathèque at the Trocadero Gardens to watch the daily films, or who had become a devotee of the *nouvelle-vague* French films and the new young filmmakers who were causing such embarrassment to the de Gaulle regime.

"Cheap and shoddy, I hear," Liz had argued with Jenny and François as Solange and Ian and Dan listened one evening in the Café Select before leaving Paris. "Vadim's *Les Liaisons Dangereuses 1960* is said to be giving this new wave a bad name. Hack Crawford was here two months ago and stopped off in London on his way back to New York and told us all about it. Pure sleaze, he said."

"But that film was simply one of many new wave films, Liz," Jenny explained, "being made by a group of young and not too well known directors who have new techniques, new approaches and ideas."

"These are directors who must work—how you say?—on a shoestring," François insisted, "and so we have *les films des jeunes,* finding decors that cost absolutely nothing, the street, the café, the quay, and exposing the real, the intense and true life to the camera's eye. We had become tired of the big, the costly film, and so we have now the *nouvelle-vague,* with Chabrol and Resnais and Malle, yes, and Godard making films for the new young French filmgoer. Julie and other students from America are coming here to see what is happening with filmmaking and to learn from directors such as Godard and Truffaut, who was known only as the *Cahiers du Cinéma* film critic until his *Les Quatre Cents Coup*." He had spread his hands wide. "It is the new way of the world, Liz," he said, pronouncing it *Leez.* "The young—they are rebelling, wanting change, tired of the old, extravagant way of doing things."

Looking up again, she saw Julie run from the water with two lean bronzed young men, their smiles flashing down on her as she led them toward the beach elevator.

"We're going to Positano," she called out. "To see if Signora Cefari has arrived yet."

Liz waved, then looked off toward the waters of the wide Bay of Salerno. Julie couldn't wait to leave. Couldn't wait for her work with Cefari to start. And once she was gone, Liz would hardly see her again until the end of the summer, a day here, a weekend there. Sighing, she tried to go on reading, but finally gathered up her book and beach bag and slowly walked toward the elevator. Well, at least Kate and Jon and Susan were coming soon from Paris. Dan would come in August, then Jenny would arrive toward the end of the summer. Ian was leaving for Algeria again, where there were rumors of a coming referendum for self-rule.

A terrible loneliness swept through her as she gazed up at the steep Lattari hills, stark and beautiful against the cerulean sky and spilling down to the shimmering brilliance below. Dan had promised to follow them to Amalfi a week after they left Paris, but he had been delayed in London with rewrites in the second act of his new play, which would open in October. Vivienne Campson, the actress who was starring in *Dawn Without Light*, wasn't right for the role, but they had discovered it too late. And now he had to reshape the role and would be delayed at least three weeks.

As the elevator creaked upward and she stepped off into the cool, lemon-fragrant arbor leading to the house, she heard a small sports car start and race off down the Amalfi Drive toward Positano, and something silently cried out. Julie would return for a token hour or so, have dinner with Liz on the terrace overlooking the sea and ruggedly curving coastline, then bathe and dress for an evening out with her new young friends, leaving Liz in the growing dusk. Restless, she bathed and dressed in a summery frock and spent the afternoon in Ravello, visiting the vaulted cloisters at Villa Cimbrone and the rose-filled flower gardens at Villa Rufolo, where kings and popes had once lived and Wagner composed one act of *Parsifal*.

Later, following dinner on the terrace, as the table candles burned low, she sipped her espresso and sat looking down at the lights flickering on in the Moorish-style village that crept up the steep, jutting hillside. She listened to the coming sounds of night, then slowly put out her cigarette and walked inside.

Kate and Jon and Susan arrived the following Sunday. Julie came for a few hours in the afternoon and evening, filling the villa with friends and dinner talk and laughter, then left in a roar of noisy sports cars and buzzing Vespas. But by Monday their lives began to fall into a pleasant routine.

Kate and Liz spent most of their mornings sitting in front of the cabana down on the beach, sunning and chatting, going into the water for short swims, then lazing in front of the tentlike cabana again, catching up on each other's lives, delighting in each other and smiling at the way Susan and Jon had become inseparable. They watched the young couple, lithe and slim and turning golden from the sun, sitting close on the sand a discreet distance from Liz and Kate, or walking hand in hand, Jon protective and jealous of other eyes from young men older than he, Susan looking up into his face, smiling adoringly, but with that mature wisdom that had marked her from birth.

"She's lovely," Kate said with a catch in her throat. "But they're so young, just seventeen and almost sixteen, too young for this kind of relationship. It's so intense. And it started from the moment they met in Paris."

"Well, when you leave and go back to the States—"

"No," Kate said, slowly shaking her head. "You don't know Jon. He holds on to something with a stubbornness that's frightening, even when it's so wrong, Liz. He still hasn't forgiven me for selling the mills and for not moving them to Mississippi before all the trouble started."

"What about Joanna?" Liz asked, looking up from the pale green afghan square she was knitting.

Kate thought for a moment, watching Susan and Jon as they spread suntan oil on each other's backs. Joanna had rushed home from school when she read the statement that Kate had given to the newspaper reporters when they broke the story about Mike McCauley's murder.

"How can you do it?" Joanna's eyes had blazed as she stood in the door of the library at the gatehouse. Kate had been sitting at her desk going over some figures when her daughter burst in upon her. "You *know* what's going to happen now. The new owners will cut back on the number of workers in the thousands. Don't you see what's going to happen? The town of Brookton will—"

"Joanna," Kate had tried to interrupt her.

"—die. Thousands will be out of work and they'll have no place to turn for jobs. They'll have to go as far as Bridgeport trying to find work, and what kind of work will they be able to find with so many of the textile mills going south? How could—?"

"Stop it!" Kate had risen and slammed her fist down on the desk. Stepping back as though she had been slapped, Joanna stared at her mother. Then she slowly pulled her hat and coat off, threw them onto a chair, and crossed to Kate.

"I didn't mean to—" Sitting down next to the desk, she looked with steady eyes at Kate. "I'm sorry. And . . . I'm sorry about Mike. I know how much you liked him. But I still think he—"

"You know nothing at all about Mike McCauley," Kate

had said with cold, carefully controlled anger, her voice trembling. "Mike McCauley was one of the finest men I have ever known. He tried to save the mills for the workers. That was our plan, mine and Marianne's with Mike. We were going to make them partners, with Marianne and I retaining fifty-one percent of the stock and issuing the other forty-nine percent to the workers in equal shares. But they never gave us a chance. That night, one hour after Mike was killed, they voted to join the union. There was nothing more we could do for them. They made their choice. They weren't willing to wait—" She turned and began to pace the room, a slim and beautiful woman in somber black, the firelight catching in her hair and shining golden-bright. "Just two years more. Two years more and we would have reached the goal. Their wages would have been up to the level of union wages, and we would have begun to issue the stock. The modernization would have been completed, and—"

"Mother—" Joanna had tried to say, but Kate had suddenly turned to her, and all the anguish and hurt from years before was there.

"Mike and I—were more than friends, Joanna. You and Jon didn't know. I never wanted you to know. He wanted me to marry him, but I didn't think I was in love with him. I *should* have married him. I could have given him at least that much before he died for something as stupid and futile as a dream, like the one we had."

"Oh, Mother!" Joanna sobbed, throwing herself into Kate's arms. "Oh, Mother, I'm so sorry, so sorry."

Kate remembered how she had held her, stroking her hair, softly kissing her brow, until the sobbing stopped and the only sound in the room was the soft crackling of the logs as the fire burned on.

"What about Joanna, you asked?" Kate said, turning to Liz as she pulled her floppy-brimmed hat lower to shade her eyes from the hot sun. "Joanna finally understood. When we sold the mills, we kept two of the older buildings that hadn't been used in recent years and a two-hundred-acre tract at the north end of the mills property that I'm in the process of developing as one of these new shopping centers. Joanna now feels that somehow we're compensating. It has put hundreds to work on the construction of the center, and when we open it will put hundreds more to work."

Liz smiled as she shook her head admiringly. "A real estate tycoon on top of everything else, with Finisterre subdivided and all those beautiful homes built there, and now this. A shopping center. You always were an amazing woman, Kate. What are you going to do next?"

"Next?" Kate asked, lighting a cigarette. "Well, we still have a large amount of ground available, and we already have the plans for a new kind of community there. Condominiums, they call them. Like attached houses, where the units are owned separately, but with common lawns, and a swimming pool we'll install and a small clubhouse. Marianne's new husband, Cal Drummond, and I have formed a new company, the Barnfield Development Corporation. We've already acquired several other pieces of property in the New England area where we'll build these condominium communities, and in some cases adjoining shopping centers. It's the future, Liz. We've hired demographics experts, and the move from the cities to the suburbs is growing, but with former apartment dwellers not wanting to have to worry about lawns and maintenance." She looked off to the water as a long sleek white yacht, its name in brightly lettered gold on the prow, steamed along the gulf toward Capri. When she finally spoke again, her voice was low with bitterness. "It's something Mike and I could have done together, if I had sold the mills sooner, and before everything that happened that awful night two years ago."

Liz watched her for a moment. "But knowing you, Kate, you couldn't have done it any other way." They sat quietly for a while, then, rising, Liz put her hand out. "Come on. Let's go and dress. I want to take you to Positano. There's a dance festival there this week, and you'll buy a painting from one of the artists sitting at his easel right out on the cobblestones. Then we'll sit in a café and eat huge shrimp and drink wine beneath the oleander and eucalyptus trees."

Laughing, Kate rose, brushing the sand from her green bathing suit. But she stopped for a moment and clasped Liz's hand. "What would I do without you and Jen? It's always like coming home, seeing and talking to you again." As Liz smiled and picked up her book and beach bag, Kate watched her. "And what about you, Liz?" she asked softly. "Are things working out the way you wanted?"

Liz started to look away, but Kate had softly touched her cheek and turned her face back toward her. With a bright smile on her lips, Liz said, "Well, Dan says in his letters that the rewrite work on the Vivienne Campson role is going better than he expected and—"

Kate shook her head. "I was talking about you and Dan."

Liz looked off toward the water. She started to speak, then caught her lip between her teeth. "I love Dan," she said in a low voice. "I think I love him even more than I did before—before all this happened. It's always been that way with me. Each time I would see him again after a long separation, I'd realize that I loved him even more. And there never could have been anyone else for me. But when I found out about . . . about her, I felt as though he had twisted a knife in me."

"Liz, dear," Kate pleaded, taking hold of her hands, "Dan worships you. He's always adored you."

"Then why?" Liz spread her arms wide, and Kate heard the catch in her voice.

"I don't know why, Liz. Some people do stupid, destructive things when they're lonely. Try to meet him more than halfway, Liz, when he gets here. Try to forget what happened. You need him. Both you and Julie need him. All of you need each other."

Liz just shook her head in bewilderment, then smiled an odd smile. "Life for people like you and me just doesn't work out the way we want it to, does it, Kate?"

"Meaning?" Kate said as they began to walk slowly up the sloping beach, circling around a large laughing group of people sitting on the sand.

"Well, naturally I'd hoped that Julie would go to school in London. I took her out of boarding school in Connecticut and moved us to London with Dan, because I thought it was finally time the three of us were together, living as a family. But of course this film thing happened in Paris and—" Suddenly she stopped and turned and called out. "Susan and Jon, we're going to Positano. I'll send Guiseppe back with the car in case you two want to go somewhere." She headed up the beach, then paused and turned. "Did you ever try to mend a badly broken glass, Kate? For some reason it just never looks the same again." And she walked on up the beach.

Jon watched his mother and Liz as their slim figures grew smaller and smaller, then, turning and flopping on his stomach and resting his chin on his hands, he said, "I can't believe it. I just can't believe it!"

"Believe what?" Susan asked, flinging her long dark hair back over her shoulder and sliding down beside him, her cheek on her hand.

He raised his head and touched her face, wonderingly let his fingers trace her lips, then her brows, and pushed the tendrils of curls back from her face. "That I almost went white-water canoeing out west with some friends instead of coming to Paris and then here with my mother," he said softly. "You're all grown up."

Susan's laugh was open and direct as she dribbled sand on his arm. "Well, after all, I am almost sixteen. I was only about ten or eleven when we saw each other the last time at that big, *huge, tremendous* house you live in."

"We don't live there anymore," he said, looking away toward the water, a note of sulkiness creeping into his voice.

"Well, thank goodness!" she said, and he looked at her in surprise. "I can just imagine how awful it must be to live in a place like that, like a hotel or a museum."

"Well, it *was* pretty big," he said, his voice thoughtful as he turned on his back and, rolling a towel under his head, gazed out at the blue-green sea. He was thinking about it, actually *thinking* about it for the first time, and began to feel that Susan was right. That was what he liked about her, the way she seemed to think things out in such a simple, straightforward way. Well, that wasn't all he liked about her, he thought, turning his head and squinting his eyes against the sun as he watched her. She was just about the most beautiful girl he had ever seen, with that glossy dark hair, long and waving almost to her waist, her white skin, her cheeks faintly tinged with rose, the way her dark eyebrows arched, and the rest of her features, so delicate and perfect. She was tiny, hardly coming up to his shoulder, and when they'd danced on the terrace the night before at that hotel in Sorrento, it was as though they'd always danced together.

"Did you know that I'm illegitimate?"

Slowly he sat up and turned to stare at her. "You're what?" he asked, his face bewildered for a moment.

"Does it matter?" she asked, sitting up and rubbing suntan oil on her arms and the tops of her thighs.

"N-no," he said, and suddenly he knew it didn't. "Why should it matter?" He was still reeling, not so much from what she said as from how she had said it, with such simple, direct honesty.

"Well, it seems to make a difference to some people, although it doesn't matter in the slightest to me. I mean, Ian's my father, you see. And I love him dearly. I don't even know my real father's name. He was a pilot during World War Two,

360

and he just never came back to Paris after the war. When he finally did come back one day, my mother told him to disappear and never come back again."

"Are you—curious about him?" Jon asked carefully.

"Not really," Susan answered after a moment. "After all, he couldn't be much of a person. Anyone whose feelings are that shallow and thoughtless for someone else who was that close to him, as my mother was, well, he couldn't be very interesting."

Jon was dumbfounded. He looked away so she couldn't see his face while he recovered. "I—I guess you're right," he muttered. "He couldn't be that interesting." Then he smiled. "You remind me of Joanna."

"Where did you say Joanna went this summer?" she asked, and he looked around again. He started to laugh, make a sarcastic remark, then caught himself. Susan would think what Joanna was doing was wonderful.

"She's working with the United Nations Children's Fund in the Philippines," he said, suddenly hearing a new and certain note of pride in his voice.

"Oh Jon, I want to do something just as exciting with my life as Joanna's doing when I'm her age," she said, her eyes shining as she sat up and hugged her knees. He looked at her. It was all he could do to keep from touching her.

"Well, whatever it is," he said, feeling her excitement and responding, and wondering where the words were coming from that he heard spilling from his mouth, "I think I want to do it with you—swim the Channel, climb the Himalayas, cross the Atlantic in a sailboat, go to the moon. Hey"—he was on one knee and holding her hand—"if the Russians can put two dogs into orbit in space and have them come back to earth like they just did Sunday, well, we can go to the moon, Susan! Somebody's going to be heading for the moon one of these days, so why not us?" He pulled her to her feet and started to run with her toward the water. "Come on, let's swim to Capri!"

"No, Jon." She stopped him and pulled her watch from her beach bag. "We promised Julie we'd be there by two o'clock. No siesta on Elena Cefari's set, she said, so we'd better hurry."

Signora Cefari's party was shooting the film at a thirteenth-century palace on the edge of Ravello that day. The gray-haired, smiling Guiseppe dropped them off at the entrance on the road, promising to return to pick them up at four. Eagerly they sniffed the air, heavily perfumed from the surrounding lemon and orange groves, as hand in hand they walked into the high-walled entry courtyard. One of the inner walls was blanketed with brilliant red bougainvillea, and the shade and sun-dappled silence seemed untouched by passing time, as though it had lain quietly this way beneath the spreading palm trees for centuries.

But as they walked farther in, past flower gardens and through roofless corridors, they heard voices, then other sounds, a voice bawling through a megaphone, a loud cranking noise and the low hum of a motor. As they entered the large courtyard they could see why this site had been selected for a shooting location. It was a huge courtyard with pointed gothic arches, balconies, flowering vines, and stone buttresses topped by grotesque stone gargoyles. But in the center of the medieval setting was a long, low-slung, gleaming car surrounded by cameras, tall light stands, giant metal reflectors, and people rushing about shouting at one another beneath a yawning crane and cameras and mike booms. A generator truck hummed and another truck was filled with a costume wardrobe and other equipment.

Susan watched as Julie ran toward them in rumpled slacks, an unironed blue work shirt, and soiled white sneakers, a blue-billed cap pulled down over her shining head and a wide smile on her face.

"Hey, I'm glad you came," she said, hugging them and then leading them toward a group crowded around a woman sitting in a canvas-backed chair. In her mid-thirties, the woman had short dark curly hair and a large nose that was oddly attractive in the hawklike face that framed warm but darting brown eyes. She wore thong sandals and a black cotton dress that somehow seemed sensuous and inviting on her, and she leaned forward with an intensity as she talked, speaking rapidly.

"Susan and Jon are like my brother and sister," Julie said as she introduced them to Elena Cefari, holding their hands. "Our mothers have been close friends since we were babies, and even though we all live in different countries, we're very close."

"*Si. Vicino e affetuoso.* Loving friends, and such young beauties. Here. Sit. And you will watch as we work. Alonzo!" she called out, her voice strident but rich and warm from the Italy of the south, her gesture imperious. "Coca-Cola for our guests while they watch *scena di grande amore.*"

For the next hour they watched as a handsome couple, the young actress in flame-colored floating chiffon and the young man in dinner clothes, stood halfway up a wide stone staircase that jutted from the high wall of the palazzo. *"Silenzio!"* a man shouted as lights from the tall stands blazed on, a strange sight to Jon and Susan in the flooding sunlight. Then, as an odd silence fell over the courtyard, Elena Cefari gestured, and the action began. A rubber-wheeled camera carriage moved forward as the man swept the young woman up into his arms and carried her down to the waiting car. From the corner of her eye Susan saw Julie scribbling furiously on a clipboard over near the camera crew.

For two hours they watched as the same scene was shot again and again until the woman director was satisfied. At that moment Susan saw an odd expression on Julie's face as she stared across the courtyard, and Susan looked around to the entrance. Liz and Kate were standing there in their summery dresses and wide-brimmed hats, watching.

Disturbed by the expression on Julie's face, Susan suddenly grasped the director's hand on impulse and led her across the courtyard. "Signora Cefari, come and meet Jon and Julie's mothers." The three women met halfway just as Julie walked over to them and stopped, her face closed.

"Signora Cefari," Susan said, "this is Jon's mother, Mrs. Barnfield, and Julie's mother, Mrs. Coleman—"

"But I know you!" Elena Cefari exclaimed, grasping Liz's hands. "Ah yes, I *know* you. You are Elizabeth Lowndes, the American actress. Yes, I know you, signora. Oh, not personally, but I know who you are."

Liz suddenly smiled as Julie's expression became confused.

"I saw you many times on the stage in New York when I was there for a year, studying at the university. Five times I saw you." She put up five fingers as her eyes widened with excitement. "Five times in *A Doll's House*. It was magnificent. *You*, signora, were magnificent!"

"Why, thank you, Signora Cefari," Liz said, obviously pleased. "But it was a marvelous cast and a fine director—"

"Liz is always ridiculously modest about her work," Kate said to the Italian director, "but I've never seen her give anything but a marvelous performance." She cast a quick glance at Julie. "It's such a shame that she gave up the theater."

"You are no longer performing, signora?" Elena Cefari looked shocked.

"Well, we live in London now," Liz said confusedly.

"But certainly you should not stop, signora. Anyone as gifted as you must go on with your work." She turned quickly to Julie. "You didn't tell me your mother was Elizabeth Lowndes, Julie!"

"Well, I didn't know you'd ever lived in the States, signora," Julie said, suddenly looking at Liz. "So it never occurred to me you'd know who she was."

As Elena Cefari walked with Liz through the lush gardens and walkways toward the entry courtyard, where Guiseppe waited with the car, Kate and Susan and Jon followed after kissing Julie good-bye.

"Julie told me that Daniel Coleman, the playwright, was her father, but this is such a fine surprise," Elena said, linking her arm through Liz's as they walked. "Now I know where Julie gets all her talent—"

"No!" Liz stopped short in the path and faced her, a worried expression on her face. "You mustn't say that. I mean—please, Julie would be terribly upset if she heard that."

As they walked on, Elena glanced at her profile. "But yes," she said drily. "Young people, they think they invented the world. In particular, sex." She laughed heartily. "And the creative arts, of course."

"She's very talented in her own right," Liz insisted stubbornly.

"Yes, signora," Elena Cefari said softly. "I have seen her work. That is why I asked her to become the *apprendista,* serve the apprenticeship with this film. I met your husband once in London, and he sent me two of her small films." Stopping several yards from the gate, she took one of Liz's hands in hers. "You are two separate persons, madame, each with much to give. Don't stand in the shadow of such a young tree. It has much growing to do. But it will grow. It is a fine tree, a promising and beautiful tree, with strong roots, one that will do well on its own. Step back into the sunlight, signora, for that's where you belong. Just as Julie, if perhaps a bit clumsily, has tried to do."

"Thank you, Signora Cefari," Liz whispered, tears in her eyes. "You understand a great deal."

"I am honored," Elena Cefari said, stepping back and smiling as Liz walked to the car and climbed in, then waved slightly as Guiseppe pulled the car into the road and sped toward Amalfi.

Dan finally arrived for the final week in August.

"Darling, you look exhausted," Liz said, holding him tightly as he stepped from the car where Guiseppe had stopped it beneath the row of magnolia trees. She led him to the low, sprawling villa that spilled in levels down to the clifftop overlooking the sparkling waters of the bay.

"It's wonderful, Liz," he said as he stood and looked far down to the beach and the Moorish-style houses tucked into the steeply sloping hill, all bathed in that extraordinary, brilliant light of the Amalfi coastline. He walked back toward her and for a long moment held her close. "Now that I'm here, finally, I'll change all that. I'll sleep and eat and sleep and eat and"—he was laughing softly—"and hold you and love you, and sleep and eat, and hold you and love you some more."

"Oh, Dan," she whispered, tears clinging to her lashes. "I've missed you so. I'd thought we were going to have the whole month of August here together."

"I'm sorry, honey," he said as they walked inside, his arm around her and holding her close against his side. "But that reworking of the role of Marta was a devil of a job, and I'm still not happy with it. It was still better the way I originally wrote it, but Vivienne couldn't handle it the way it was."

Julie came for dinner, bringing Elena Cefari with her. She ran through the villa, shouting for Dan and finding him on the lower terrace pensively smoking and looking down at the lights of the village. Throwing herself into his arms, she shrieked delightedly, "I was afraid you weren't coming at all."

"Not on your life, little urchin. I'm here for a week, no matter what happens. Now if you'll get yourself a week off from that slave-driving film director, we can swim and sail for the next six days."

"Oh, Pop, I'd love to," Julie said, pulling out of his arms, "but we're running about ten days over on Elena's shooting schedule. Then Aunt Jen comes tomorrow, and I'm going back to Paris with her next Saturday." She took his hand. "But come up to the terrace," she said, leading him up the stone steps to the upper terrace, where he heard laughter and voices and saw candlelight on the big round table under the canopy.

"Daniel Coleman!" Elena Cefari called out. "You sent me a jewel, a precious gem in this Julie of yours."

Jenny came the following day. She had been in Moscow, interviewing Mrs. Francis Gary Powers, who was there to try and gain clemency for her husband, the American U-2 pilot who had been shot down near Sverdlovsk in May. As they all trooped down to the beach, Liz watched with a wistful kind of expression as Susan and Julie excitedly asked her questions about Russia.

"Hey you," Jenny asked Julie, having caught a glimpse of Liz's face, "shouldn't you be at work?"

"I took the afternoon off just to see you," Julie said as they walked from the elevator out into the blazing sunlight.

Dan laughed good-naturedly. "You only took the evening off for me, kiddo." He looked around at the almost deserted beach as they settled in front of their cabana. "What is it they say? Mad dogs and Englishmen? And Americans, I guess—go out in the midday sun."

"That's the nice thing about siesta time," Jon shouted as he grabbed Susan's and Julie's hands and raced them to the water. "We have the beach all to ourselves."

"Tell us about Ian, Jenny," Kate said, lighting a cigarette and squinting through the smoke as they watched the shore-line, where Jon was pulling the girls into the waves.

"Well, he's gone to Cairo first, to try to interview Ferhat Abbas," she said, a worried look in her eyes as she gazed at the calm sea. "He's the first premier of the Algerian government-in-exile there in Egypt. De Gaulle fooled every-one, you know," she said suddenly, and Dan nodded. "French civilians and army officers in Algeria who thought de Gaulle would prosecute the war against the nationalists forced his return to power two years ago, but when he expressed himself as favoring eventual self-rule in Algeria, why, all hell broke loose. It has even spilled over into France itself."

The tension she had brought with her partially disappeared in the next few days as she lay on the beach and soaked up the sun, turning a rich brown in her tiny white bikini.

"She still looks like a child," Liz said softly to Kate as they watched her run into the surf with Susan, "no older than Susan from this distance."

Kate nodded, a sad smile on her lips. "Last night, out on the terrace, she told me she wants to go back to the States to try and see Christopher. Maybe at Christmas. As Jenny Chase, of course, still as the woman who made the children-of-the-war study. He writes to her sometimes, you know."

"Yes, I know," Liz said softly.

"She said . . . his letters sound lonely. He works in a gas station and told her he's trying to save up enough money to get out of Craddock Corners. She's still afraid to write and tell him who she really is—afraid he'll turn against her completely. So she just keeps on sending him letters and encouraging him to write his poetry and short stories."

"If only—" Liz began, then stopped for a moment, her eyes sad as she watched Julie dive into the waves. "If only there were some magic word to make everything with your children all right."

Kate watched her for a moment, then turned her eyes to the water just as Jon shot upward out of a wave and plunged down again, pulling a shrieking Susan beneath the surf with him. "Yes, I know. If we could just find out what that word is."

Liz stood at the head of the road leading to the villa and waved as the Mercedes, with Guiseppe at the wheel and Dan beside him, sped toward the Amalfi Drive and headed for Naples. Jenny and Julie and Susan were sitting in the back seat, and without knowing why, just as the car turned a corner, Julie looked back and waved. She looks so alone, Julie thought, and for a moment she wanted to shout to Guiseppe to stop the car so she could run back and hold her mother and tell her she would see her at Christmas, that for days they would just shop and trim the flat, put up the Christmas tree and bake cookies and pies, spend hours and hours together, have fun together getting ready for the holidays.

"I wish she were coming with us," Julie said to Dan.

"Well, she insists on closing up the villa *after* we're all out from under her feet. And as we four are the last to go, she can really get everything done now and finish up by tomorrow."

"When will she get home?" Jenny asked. Something nagged at the back of her mind, eluding her. Liz's moods kept changing so.

"Guiseppe will drive her to Naples late tomorrow afternoon. She'll spend the night at the Excelsior, then take the train to Rome and catch an afternoon flight home."

"I was a little surprised," Jenny said, carefully feeling her way, "because she said she was going to ask Hack about doing a play in New York this coming winter. She said Hack is in London right now and—"

"I asked her to postpone it for a while," Dan said, looking out the window as the driver narrowly missed a donkey cart. "Once I get *Dawn Without Light* opened in early December, then the holidays over with, I want us to do some traveling—Hawaii, then on to Hong Kong, and get to Australia along about March. We're opening a second company of *Dawn* in Melbourne and plan to cast part of it there."

"Oh, I forgot to tell you." She said it casually. "I stopped in London on my way back from Moscow. Had lunch with Kevin McLain, the theater critic. He was awfully surprised that Vivienne Campson was doing *Dawn*."

"Really? Why?"

"Said he just couldn't see her in a Coleman play. I can't either. She'll probably do a belly-flopper."

"Thanks," Dan said drily, with a cutting look over his shoulder.

She was quiet for several moments, watching from the car window as they slowed to a walker's pace and passed through a small village with its narrow winding streets and ancient walls.

"I think Vivienne Campson is all wrong for that role, Dan," she said bravely. "Vivienne is marvelous with comedy. I've seen her before and admire her tremendously. But damnit, Dan, that part was tailor-made for Liz."

They had stopped for a funeral cortege that was passing.

"Julie, look!" Susan exclaimed, grabbing Julie's hand and pointing. A gleaming black carriage was being pulled by four brightly-plumed black horses, while mourners, dressed in black and carrying huge bouquets of flowers, followed. But Dan was preoccupied.

"For Liz?" He seemed surprised, and thought about it for a moment. "It's an Englishwoman the way it's written."

"The woman could be an American, with a little rewriting."

"That's right," Julie said, turning around to Jenny. "I read the script last week, and for some reason it occurred to me at the time that the criticism by his friends and relatives, when he tells all of them he wants to marry someone not in his social standing, could be even more pointed if she *weren't* English."

Jenny was nodding excitely. "Of course, you little old

filmmaker you," she said, grabbing Julie and hugging her, then looking at Dan. "When you go to Melbourne, you could have Liz ready for the London cast, and have Vivienne open in Melbourne."

Dan was slowly nodding his head. "Not a bad idea." He looked at them and softly laughed. "Pretty sly, you two, aren't you? But still, it's not a bad idea. We could start early giving her a big buildup." He was still nodding, thinking. "Let me see if Vivienne wants to go to Melbourne. New worlds for her to conquer."

He stood near the gate, eyes anxiously searching the last group of straggling passengers as they came through customs.

"I don't understand," Dan said to Hack Crawford, who was in London on business and had come to Heathrow Airport with him to meet Liz. "She specifically said she'd be on this plane."

"Well, maybe she missed it and will come in on the next one," Hack said.

"No. If she'd missed it, she would have phoned the office, and when I just called there, the secretary said they'd heard nothing at all."

They waited for several hours, watching the gates as each arrival was announced from Rome. Finally, in the late afternoon, they raced back to London in the hope of finding her at the flat, perhaps having arrived by another route and at another airport. But she wasn't there, nor was there any word. Mrs. Cummings, the housekeeper, padded back to the kitchen area, shaking her gray head worriedly and telling them she'd make them a sandwich before they went off to the airport again.

"The best thing to do," Hack said as Dan quickly poured them each a whiskey, "is to go back and trace her steps."

"I'll call the Excelsior Hotel in Naples," Dan said, picking up the phone and putting the call through. It took about ten minutes, and when the call went through, Dan barked her name into the phone and the fact that she was to have checked in the afternoon before. Hack stood near him watching and trying to interpret his terse answers as someone on the other end of the line talked.

Dan looked at his watch. It was six o'clock. "I'll take a plane tonight," he said, "and get to Naples as soon as possible. If you should hear anything in the meantime, please phone my office." He gave them his office phone number, hung up, and quickly downed his whiskey, his hands trembling. "She checked in late yesterday afternoon and went out this morning. But . . . she left her luggage in the room. And she hasn't come back since."

"I'm going with you," Hack said, starting to the door. "Just let me get over to my hotel and grab a bag, and I'll meet you at Heathrow."

"Wait a minute," Dan said, stopping him. "Just one more phone call. To Jenny and Julie. Liz might have gone to Paris for some reason."

But when he had the operator put the call through to Paris, Jenny knew nothing.

"Oh God, Dan, Julie will be terrified," she said in a low voice. She thought back quickly. Liz had been strangely quiet that morning they had left.

"Well, you'll have to tell her," Dan said heavily. "She'd never forgive us if something happened and she hadn't known anything. I'll phone you as soon as I know anything at all. We'll go straight to the Excelsior in Naples."

They changed planes at the Rome airport for a local flight to Naples and reached the hotel just before dawn. A man from the hotel security force met them and told them he had traced a driver who said she had hired him to take her back to Amalfi, saying that she had left her daughter there and was going back to find her where she was working with a motion picture crew.

Dan and Hack looked at each other ominously. He's just holding himself together, Hack thought, and gently gripped Dan's shoulder. "Look, fella, we'll find her, and she's going to be all right."

"Can you get us a car?" Hack asked the man.

Within moments they were speeding toward Amalfi with the hotel man, Carlo Renati, at the wheel. "I know the way," he said. "It will save you much valuable time, signore."

They stopped first at the villa. But it was tightly closed up. Driving on to the town, they made inquiries and were told that Elena Cefari had last been filming at the old thirteenth-century palace near Ravello that Julie had taken Dan to the week he was at the villa. They drove into the entry courtyard and, hearing sounds, hurried along the overgrown path to the rear courtyard, where three men were piling equipment into a truck. Carlo approached the men and told them who they were looking for. He described her, and one of them suddenly smiled.

"Ahhh, the Americana," he said. "The beautiful lady with the blonde hair. Yes, signore, she was here this morning. But she left again when we told her Signora Cefari was gone. She said she was going back to Naples to look for her daughter."

They climbed into the car and raced back to Naples, hardly speaking throughout the ride. When Carlo pulled up to the entrance, Dan started into the hotel, then saw Julie running toward him. Her face was white, and she threw herself into his arms.

"Don't worry, honey," he said, holding her and patting her shoulder. "We'll find her. We've *got* to find her. And when we do, we'll begin showing her how much we really care."

"She has to know we love her, Pop." Her face was stricken.

"Does she?" he asked, leading her to an upholstered bench by the wall and sitting her down. "We know it, Julie, but I guess we've had a funny way of showing it. Me by insisting that she stay with me in London, never really realizing how much she gave up to come to London. Putting my work before her and never encouraging her to go to New York at least once every year or two to do a play, or making it possible for her to do a play in London. And you?"

Julie looked at him fearfully, her tear-stained face raised and questioning.

"You, honey? Well, do you remember a time when your mother drove up to school to pick you and Joanna up, right after Joanna's grandfather died?"

Julie nodded, her eyes questioning beneath the tears.

"Liz told me, you see," he went on, stroking her hand, his voice gentle. "She'd never really realized how unhappy it made you when people talked to you about your mother, how beautiful she was, how talented and famous." Quickly Julie looked away, her eyes clouding. "That day at the school, she said, when somebody introduced her to the parents of two of the girls, she said she suddenly caught a glimpse of your face when the people began to talk about how they'd seen her in her latest play."

Julie was slowly nodding her head, far away with her thoughts, reliving that moment. "Amy Worthington's mother said to me, 'So that's where your talent comes from, Julie. We saw you in the Christmas play last year, and you were just so *sweet* in it.' I think . . . I think I almost hated Mom then, hated her for all the times I'd had girls ask me for auto-graphed pictures of her, for all the times the drama coach asked me why I couldn't be graceful like my mother, for all the times the teachers asked me if I could get matinee tickets for them during the holidays." Suddenly she buried her head against him. "Oh, Dan, she gave up everything for me, but I still turned against her, still kept running from her."

"No, baby," he said, smiling inwardly as he realized how she called him Pop when she was happy and Dan when she was sad or miserable. "She gave up a lot for both of us, but neither one of us really appreciated it. Not enough, Julie, not enough. She's pretty precious stuff, that mother of yours. So we'd better go and find her and take good care of her from now on." He took his handkerchief from his pocket and dried her eyes. "We went to Amalfi and found out she'd been there." He spoke carefully. "She went to the place where they'd been filming the movie. We talked to some of the cleanup men there. One of them said she'd come back . . . looking for her daughter."

He saw her suddenly clutch her handbag in her lap, but her eyes seemed very far away. Her brows were drawn together hard, as though she were trying to remember something, something that kept escaping her. Slowly she looked back at Dan.

"I think I know where she might be," she whispered.

"You what?" He grasped her wrists. "Where, Julie?"

"When we were here this summer at the beginning of July, before going to Amalfi, we spent two days sightseeing. The first day we went to Pompeii, but as we were driving back, Signore Russo, our driver, said we should go to another place, the ruins of a smaller town that was in a better state of preservation than Pompeii. Herculaneum, beneath the present town of Resina. Oh, it's wonderful," she said breathlessly, remembering. "It was discovered much later than Pompeii and was excavated with far better scientific means, so that the workers dug it out with more care. So we went. He took us there the next morning. You walk down a long long path around the edge, deep down into the ground past a long row of cypress trees, and as you walk down you look across the rooftops of all these houses that were buried for almost two thousand years. It's a strange, eerie place, but so beautiful. There was hardly anyone there, and we walked around for hours, going in and out of these houses where people had last lived thousands and thousands of years ago, some of the villas and shops without roofs, or walls, but some in almost perfect condition, buried under all that lava from Mount Vesuvius since the time of Christ." She paused for a long moment, watching but not really seeing hotel guests with their bags going by toward the elevators. "All of a sudden I realized I hadn't seen Mother for a long while. I could hear the distant sounds of the city of Resina high above and a long way away. There was just the buzzing of insects and that hot sun, and I could smell the sea and the dust under my feet and see the bright green of the cypress trees. Then I heard her call my name. I went into this house beyond a portico and found her standing near a wall, staring at a tiny etched portrait, no bigger than my hand, cut right into the wall. It was a profile of a girl, and beneath it was scratched the name 'Julia.' She stood so still, just staring at it. 'Look, Julie,' she said to me. 'It even looks like you.' I walked over to her and looked at it, and it . . . it did. It looked like me. Oh, Dan, it was so ghostly. As though maybe I'd lived there thousands of years ago. She looked at me with this strange look, then she never said another word, but just walked out of the villa and onto the narrow street."

For a moment Dan stared at her, his face filled with doubt. Then he took her hand and called to Hack and Carlo, who were standing by the concierge's desk. "It's worth a try," he said.

It was exactly the way Julie had described it, a still and ancient fabric of what was once life, houses standing side by side, many of them seeming to wait for their owners to return, inhabitants who had fled almost two thousand years before in a flight of panic from the flow of lava and the rain of fire and fumes and ash. Dan and Hack peered into the villas as they hurried past, following Julie who ran from house to house, looking inside, trying to remember which one had had the tiny fresco of a girl named Julia on its wall.

Suddenly they saw her stop at an open door beyond a columned portico. They waited, then slowly walked forward. Julie simply stood there looking into the shadowy villa. Over her shoulders they saw Liz, standing at the wall, softly touching the small etching. Her pale green linen suit was rumpled and she was ashen, but there was a small smile on her face.

Gently Dan walked past Julie, shaking his head. He walked over to Liz and touched her arm. She turned to him, as though he had always been standing there, and it was then that he saw how far away her eyes seemed, dreamy and vague and terribly sad.

"Julie's lost," she said softly. "I heard her crying, and I

tried to follow her, Dan. I tried to find her. But there was a terrible storm. And it was dark and everything was disappearing. I ran away. I left her because I couldn't find her in time. And now she's lost."

She began to cry, and Dan took her in his arms and held her, trying to comfort her.

"Mama?"

Liz lifted her head a little.

"Mama?" It was only a whisper. Liz looked up and gently touched Julie's cheek, wiping the tears with her hand. "Mama," Julie half cried.

"Oh, Julie," Liz said, so softly that only Julie and Dan could hear. "I thought you were lost, and that I would never find you again." She turned to Dan. "Both of you. I thought I'd lost you."

Dan leaned down and kissed her cheek, and they walked out of the villa, Liz holding their hands. They went along the narrow street and out of the deep and ancient shadows, up the path past the long row of cypress trees and into the sunshine.

Chapter 38

As THE FLAMING days of October drew to a close, Jenny's impatience and restlessness grew. Ian's letters arrived with regularity, three and four each week, but she missed him with a deep and painful longing. He had flown from Algeria to Madrid and on to the United States in mid-October to interview the two presidential candidates, first to Washington to see Vice-President Richard Nixon, and then up to Hyannis on Cape Cod where he spent half a day with the handsome young senator from Massachusetts, John Kennedy, who had just received the Democratic party nomination for President in July.

Her impatience to see Ian was evenly matched by her wish to see the weeks pass quickly to mid-December, when they planned to go to New York and then Connecticut to spend the Christmas holidays with Kate and her family. While there, she was going to Craddock Corners to try and see Christopher, still in the guise of checking on the children in her study, now in their late teens and early twenties. Meredith Ballard had written to her that she would arrange meetings with the young people, "those who are left in Craddock Corners," her letter had said, "and Christopher is still one of them."

She was working on a news release one morning when the phone rang. Cupping it between her shoulder and chin as she kept on typing, she barked, *"Daily World-Dispatch."* Her eyes widened as she heard his voice.

"Darling," Ian said, a smile coming through. "Just got in from London. And I have until eight tomorrow morning before I take off again, for Algiers. I'm out at Orly."

"Ian!" she shrieked, jumping up from her desk, her brown eyes filled with a childlike excitement.

"Meet me at home, darling," he said. "We'll gather up

Susan and Julie and celebrate with dinner at La Closerie des Lilas."

"Only until tomorrow morning?" she demanded. "Damn, damn, damn, I want you longer than that."

"Here now, old girl," he laughed, "we have to be grateful for what little amount of time the gods reward us."

"Look here, you old fuddy-duddy. You don't have to be so damned stiff-upper-lip about these inconveniences." She laughed.

"You're wasting time, m'dear. The sooner you get off the telephone, the sooner I'll be there." He grinned. "And try to act like a lady at dinner."

"You jolly well don't say?" she said, giving him the Bronx cheer and hanging up. Then with a loud whoop she ran from the office.

Susan and Julie smiled broadly as they looked about the restaurant at the paneled mirrors and shaded wall sconces and discreetly bustling waiters in their black tuxedoes.

"Thank you for including us, Uncle Ian," Julie said with a teasing but somehow shy smile. "I know that you two would like to be alone."

"Alone?" Ian laughed with a sly wink at Jenny, who made a face at him. "When I can be with three ravishing women?"

"Women!" Susan said with a big smile. "Somebody finally called me a woman."

"Not for long, my pet," Jenny laughed, chucking her under the chin. "When you flunk another test in school, I'll remind you of what a baby you are."

"No business at this celebration dinner," Ian said, softly rapping the table with a spoon. "Just pleasure. Purely pleasure. Which reminds me, Julie, I saw your parents in London."

"Where?" she squealed excitedly. "What were they doing?"

"They were rehearsing. At least your mother was."

A wide smile of relief flooded across Julie's face. "Then she finally agreed to do it."

"Dan said it took some doing. She was frightened, apparently, of a number of things. She'd been away from it for so long. Then the London audience. That can be quite forbidding, you know. Performing in another country for the first time."

"Darling," Jenny said, putting her hand over his on the

table's edge. "You couldn't have brought us more wonderful news."

"How . . . how was she in it, Uncle Ian?"

"She was absolutely magnificent," he said. "Even with a script in her hand. And even from the little I saw of it, I rather suspect this is Dan's best play to date."

"And you, darling?" Jenny asked. "Now you?"

"Me?" he teased. "Oh, not a great deal. Outside of the fact that I signed for the book in both New York and London." Jenny let out a little shriek as Julie and Susan began to laugh with excitement. "It will be published in the late spring."

"*That* calls for a celebration. Champagne and caviar!" Jenny exclaimed.

"Could I have a hamburger?" Susan asked in a small voice.

"At La Closerie?" Julie demanded.

"With truffles?" Susan said, and they all laughed.

Long after Julie and Susan had gone off to bed, Jenny and Ian sat on the wide window seat in the softly lit salon, sipping wine and holding hands, the windows open to the gentle winelike breeze of autumn, a low October moon hanging above the Paris rooftops.

"Come along, my darling," he said, taking her hand and leading her to their bedroom. Ian softly closed the door, and went to her in the center of the large room, and for a long moment they looked deeply into each other's eyes, seeing there the long slow building of passion that had flickered all through dinner each time their eyes met. As he began to unfasten her blouse with slow and deliberate motions, she gently placed her hands on his chest, then slipped her hands along the buttons. At last he picked her up and carried her to the bed. The sheets were cool and sweet, the fragrance of her perfume rising to tease him. Gently he kissed her, her eyes and then her mouth and down to her throat. She held her breath as his lips flickered downward across her breasts and circled her nipples.

"Ian," she whispered, "I love you so." And in the dark she waited for that voice that came only with his lovemaking, strangely harsh and without the chuckling laughter that was his other, normal voice. "Love?" he said. "Is that all, my darling? I worship and adore you. You've breathed life into these cold, lonely bones. You keep me alive with your beauty and laughter, wherever I go, with the memory of your mouth and eyes, and with . . . this."

377

He touched her low and she groaned softly, then rose to him as his fingers moved in a gentle, circling rhythm. With fluttering, quick motions one hand slid down his thigh and slipped with thrilling insistence into a warm and secret place that she knew so well. For what seemed like hours they felt the rush and ebb of passion, until at last with hoarse and panting breath, with fire leaping in their loins, they came together, Ian's body stretched and exalting above hers as he breathed life and exquisite pleasure into her soul.

"Ian!" A sharp cry of joy sprang from her lips and he crushed her mouth beneath his. For long, long moments they didn't move. Then slowly he slipped down next to her, his lips never leaving hers. At last they lay on their backs, watching the play of lights on the ceiling, hands clasped tightly. For a long while they were silent.

"This will have to last me until I come back," he said softly. "I'll only be gone a few weeks this time. De Gaulle has invited the leaders of Algeria's government-in-exile here for a conference, negotiations, but it was rejected. So he'll have to go to Algiers soon. It will probably be the referendum, and de Gaulle will urge everyone to vote yes on his policies of economic and social development. I think it will all soon come to an end there and Algeria will finally have its independence."

"Come back to me soon, Ian," she pleaded. "I'm just no damned good without you."

But the three weeks stretched into four, with Ian's letters promising he would be back in Paris soon. Each morning, after walking Susan to school, Jenny turned toward the office, stopping first at a café on the Rue de Lille for her morning coffee and a look at the daily headlines. In the chill of the November mornings, the café was almost deserted, with most patrons now inside. But she liked the crisp air and pale sunshine, sitting there reading the Paris *Herald,* glancing up now and then at the traffic and passersby, feeling the pulse and color of the old city, listening to its sounds, breathing its fragrance and cherishing its warmth even as a cold wind blew around the corner.

KENNEDY WINS BY NARROW MARGIN, she read in the headlines and smiled, grinding out her cigarette, then taking a sip of coffee. Ian had liked him, liked his quick wit and stylish, yes, elegant manner, his nimble mind. "It will be good for the world if he wins," he had said when he returned from the States in October.

She bent to the story again as she took another sip of her coffee.

"Is it . . . is it all right if I sit down?" a voice asked.

Jenny looked up sharply. For a moment she simply stared, bewildered. She shook her head a little and lifted a hand to her eyes as though to clear them, to clear a mist.

"Christopher!" she whispered, her voice deserting her. "My God!" Reaching over and grasping his hands, she drew him down next to her, still not believing what she was seeing. He had a strange expression on his face, a small, uncertain smile, and his gray eyes were wide with uncertainty, but with something else too. "Christopher!" Her voice was husky with shock. "What are you doing here?"

She wanted to grab him, hold him close and kiss him, but instead she let her eyes feast on him, trying not to let him see what was really there. Still holding his hands, she looked him up and down, from his longish dark hair ruffling silkily over the edges of his ears to the sensitive thin mouth and well-formed nose. He was wearing denim pants and a thick, fleece-lined jacket, and as he sat down he slipped a heavy knapsack off his back and let it slide to the ground. He was tall, so much taller than the last time she had seen him —six years. It had been six years since she had last seen him.

"Why, you were just a little boy," she said, hearing her voice break and catching it, forcing back the tears, feeling them ache in her throat. "Just a punky, funny little kid, with freckles and a hole in the knees of your pants, and some beautiful wonderful stories you'd written."

He was staring at her with that strange expression.

"How did you find me here?" she asked, touching his cheek, then grasping his hand again. "I mean, here in the café?"

"I—I've been following you," he said. "Ever since I got here three days ago. I'd wait each morning outside where you lived, standing down the street just a little, then I followed you here and saw how you stopped each morning for your coffee."

"And I never noticed," she laughed, hearing the tight hysteria in her voice. "How wonderful! How wonderful to see you. I was coming to Craddock Corners in December"— she felt she was babbling, but plunged on—"as a follow-up to the study. To ask more questions, as a follow-up. But here you are—" She stopped, sensing something, seeing it in his eyes, in the way his mouth worked a little, and she waited, holding his hands tightly.

"You're my mother, aren't you?"

For a long moment she didn't speak, didn't move. She felt frozen, lifeless. Her heart had stopped beating, then raced on, and she felt the blood pounding in her ears. She tried to speak, but when she opened her lips, no sound came out. It was like a small death. There would be nothing afterward, if she spoke, just a cold sudden hatred in his eyes, and then nothing. He would stand up and walk away and disappear in the rushing crowds that filled the sidewalks. And she would never see him again. At last she shook her head slowly, up and down, and he saw the pain in her eyes, the pain and the love and the wanting, and a small sob ripped from his mouth.

"Christopher," she whispered again and pulled his head down to her shoulder. "How did you know?" For a long time he didn't speak.

"Miss Ballard told me when I asked her," he said as he pulled his head away and looked at her. She saw tears in his eyes, but he was smiling, a tremulous smile that grew and grew. "Somehow I knew. I don't know how I knew, but I did. And one day it just came to me. I was reading one of your letters, and suddenly I just knew."

Her hands were framing his face, then softly touching his cheeks. She pulled his face to her and softly kissed him on each closed eyelid.

"What do you say we go home?" she said, her voice breaking, but with a smile on her lips. "I'll make you a great big breakfast, and we'll talk, then soon Susan will come home from school. Then we'll all go out and buy new curtains for your bedroom, and we'll put a call through to Ian in Algiers and tell him he has a new son, and"—she was bubbling over—"and we'll have Christmas here, instead of going to America, and you'll live here forever and ever and ever."

Over a huge breakfast of omelettes and croissants, he told her of how he had worked in a gasoline station and saved his money for the trip. Jenny hung on his every word and followed him as he walked about the apartment, pausing for a long time in the doorway to Susan's room, then going on silently, touching objects that he knew were treasures of Jenny's, standing for long minutes below the walls of books in the study, reading the titles, fingering the bindings.

"I like Hemingway," he said, pointing to one book, "but I like Morley Callaghan more."

"Oh, so do I," Jenny exclaimed, pulling down Callaghan's *The Loved and the Lost* and pushing it into Christopher's hands.

Finally he turned to her and said, "It doesn't matter why it happened. Aunt Mary told me a little. Not much. But enough that I—well, I understand, you see."

She didn't *see*, because she didn't know what Mary had told him, but it didn't matter to Jenny either, and she took his hands and drew him down on the couch. "Then we won't talk about it, Christopher, if it doesn't matter." Actually, she had dreaded talking about it and felt relieved.

"But I have to make you understand one thing," he said, and she knew he was finding it difficult to put these particular thoughts into words. "I love them. They were good to me—Aunt Mary and Uncle Fred. My grandmother, too, until she died last year. They . . . they treated me like I was their own son. But . . ." She hung on his words. "You're my mother," he said in a soft, quavering voice. "And I wanted to come and see you—" He looked around the handsome room, beyond to the spacious tall-ceilinged apartment, then up at the walls of books and back to Jenny. "—and maybe stay, if I could."

"Oh, Christopher!" Jenny put her arms around him, and for several moments they sat there as she cradled and rocked him back and forth. "I've dreamed of this, over and over. This is home now, darling. Home for you forever, even when you go off and do the wonderful things you're going to do with your life."

Later in the day, when Susan walked in the door and went past the study toward her room, she stopped and looked in.

Christopher was standing again at the wall of books, running his fingers over the titles on one shelf, and turned and looked at her. For a moment there was silence.

"You're Christopher, aren't you?" she said, then took several steps into the room and stopped again.

"How did you know?" he cautiously asked.

"I don't know," Susan said slowly. "I just knew." Then she walked toward him and stood looking up at him. "Would it embarrass you if I kissed you?" she asked tremulously, tears on her lashes.

He started shaking his head, unable to speak for a moment, but as she reached up and kissed his cheek, he grabbed her and swung her around with a loud whoop that brought Jenny running into the room from her bedroom where she was changing her clothes.

"And I was going to introduce you," Jenny said, laughing and crying at the same time as Christopher hugged Susan, lifted her off her feet, then carefully set her down again.

"I think I have to say this," Jenny said, wiping the tears from her cheeks. "I think it's very important I say this, right at this moment, that this is the happiest I have ever been in my life, I think. I have Ian, and I have both of you." She kissed them both softly on the cheek, then turned and hurried to the cloak closet off the foyer. "And now we're going to celebrate. We're going to walk to the Boulevard Saint-Germain, and along the way I'm going to shout at all the shopkeepers I know to come out and meet my son, and then we will go to Chez Lipp for a wonderful celebration meal. We may even see Sartre there." And at the door, as Christopher was pulling on his jacket, she turned and said, "Now we'll show you Paris!"

Ian rose early on the day de Gaulle was rumored to be arriving in Algiers. Dawn was just breaking, with pinkish streaks fingering up from the bay. He pulled on his shirt and walked onto the balcony of his hotel room, feeling refreshed from a shower, breathing deeply of the still, cool morning air. There was little traffic on the boulevard below, but as he looked off to the upper city, where ancient, winding, narrow streets twisted and turned through the dank and shadowy native quarter, his eyes narrowed. He was weary of this port city where Barbary pirates once preyed, weary of this troubled country with its fighting and bloodshed, weary of the Maghrib, this land of low plains and high plateaus, steep valleys and harrowing, narrow gorges, bounded by the blue Mediterranean on the north and the vast and forbidding Sahara Desert to the south. Then he remembered the plane ticket in his jacket pocket and smiled. Soon he would be gone from all this ancient sorrow and protest against French colonial policies, this rise of nationalism, talk of self-rule and referendums, rumors of the French Army elements who were forming a secret organization to strike at the National Liberation Front. Soon, the very next day, in fact, he would be gone. Arriving in the same wave of planes with de Gaulle was Ian's successor, a young and eager newspaperman from Birmingham who would take over his post. And by eight the next morning Ian would be on a plane heading for Paris. Paris and Jenny.

As he thought of her he walked back into the room, took a belt from the dresser top, and slipped it through the loops of his khaki trousers. A warm and tingling sensation flooded through him as he formed her name on his lips. He could almost see her, throwing her head back in soft morning laughter, then the laughter floating away as his hands touched her and her eyes turned a melting golden brown, the rich smile disappearing and her mouth coming close, the fragrance that clung to her skin and hair, the long dark lashes sweeping her cheeks, faintly rosy from sleep, her voice murmuring.

Quickly he jammed his wallet into his back pocket and walked out of the room, forcing his mind back to what lay immediately ahead of him. De Gaulle was due to arrive at about ten. He was coming to urge a "yes" vote on the referendum leading toward self-rule that was to take place in the following month of January. A new beginning, he thought, in 1961 for Algeria. He left the hotel and headed for a nearby restaurant for some breakfast. Two correspondents he knew were sitting at a table. He joined them and ordered tea and a croissant.

"De Gaulle's in Ain Témouchent," said Hal Baker, a graying news veteran from San Francisco. "There's talk he won't be coming here. The Ultras have spread rumors of one-way integration between the Arab and European communities." He looked around warily and sipped his coffee.

"Ain Témouchent?" Ian asked, crumbling his croissant.

"A village out on the desert," Geoffrey Waggoner, a Scotsman from Aberdeen, said. "And he would be wise to wait there." When Ian raised his eyebrows above his teacup, the Scotsman said, "There's trouble gathering here. The Arabs are streaming out of their casbahs, waving their rebel flags and shouting their bloody heads off."

Ian left the two men there and began to walk through the streets toward the heart of the lower city. And as the crushing crowds grew larger he sensed the feeling of unrest that seemed to roll like a gathering storm. He was walking along the route that was to have been de Gaulle's route of travel by a convoy of automobiles. The crowds had lined the streets, still expecting the French leader. They were chanting and shouting for the man they now thought of as their savior. Suddenly Ian heard shots. And with the sound the crowds broke loose and poured into the street, screaming, their voices a dissonant roar.

Pulled with them, he ran, fighting his way on a lateral angle, trying to break free and out of the center of the onrushing mob. A rumbling truck hurtled toward him, and with a leap and a superhuman thrust he managed to crash through the pushing bodies all around him and escape being crushed beneath the huge vehicle. He heard the grind of gears; then, as the truck passed, he saw soldiers leap from its rear, their carbines raised and firing.

He heard the shots again, an ear-splitting, crackling series of explosions, and was vaguely conscious of the screams as men and women fought past him, stumbling, clawing their way, mouths gaping in horror and fear.

Just as he felt the searing pain and went down on one knee, he grasped at his shirtfront, and in one flashing moment of utter clarity he remembered the dispatch he had filed the night before to London: ". . . and in a tour of the Algerian countryside, I saw burned-out villages and farms; cows lying stiffly with legs pointing straight at the sky; a woman, dead, face blown partly away, but a small bit of pretty colored ribbon in her hand, closed tightly and holding on to it with rigid fingers as though this were the answer to life, and if she were to let it go her life would ebb away even as the blood flowed from her face and—"

He knew he was falling. Everything was slipping away—the roar of voices, the jamming, grinding gears of the trucks, the sound of gunfire, all fading . . . fading so fast. He tried to see, but the light was going from the sky, and he felt her name on his lips, saw her eyes looking up and laughing at him, saw her mouth, moving in gentle, whispering words, felt her hands soft and cool on his face, touching the tears . . . touching the tears. "Men can cry, Ian," she was whispering, "men can cry, too. . . ."

She had gotten special permission to ride in the ambulance as it drove onto the airfield. She was standing between the two white-coated attendants, watching as the military plane rolled toward them. It seemed an eternity, waiting while it came to a stop, then waiting longer until the steps were pushed into place and the plane doors opened, and again another eternity until two men, hoisting a stretcher, eased their way down the steps. Pressing her fingers to her mouth, she forced back a sob. Suddenly she was beside him, just barely able to hold on to one of his hands as the attendants took over and hurried across the tarmac with the stretcher, placing it into the ambulance. She leaped in and knelt beside him just as the ambulance roared to life and streaked across the field.

"Ian," she cried softly, touching his face.

Slowly he opened one eye and looked at her with a wan but steady grin. "Sorry, old girl. You always did tell me not to cross the street against the lights."

"Oh, Ian," she gasped in relief and carefully put her head down next to his. "Thank God, you're all right. Your friend Geoffrey Waggoner got in touch with me, but he didn't know much except that you were alive." She was stroking and kissing his face. "I was so frightened, afraid that maybe he was wrong, or you had died after he had heard—"

"Well, actually I got it rather soundly, one in the chest and one through the shoulder, but fortunately nothing vital was hit." He looked up and winced at the sound of the screaming siren. "Really, old girl, I wish they wouldn't make quite such a fuss up there. This is most embarrassing, you know."

"Oh, my God!" Jenny said, then collapsed in a combination of laughter and long-held tears as he put one arm around her and pressed his lips to her hair. Against his cheek she murmured, "Ian, Ian. Thank God!"

"It struck me," he finally said softly, "that somehow I had to get back here. You see, my darling, we haven't even half finished our lives together yet."

Chapter 39

"A LADY TO see you, Mrs. Barnfield," Martin said from the door of the library. Kate looked up from the stack of papers on the desk before her and put her pen down. She appeared slightly annoyed at the interruption. A fire burned cheerily on the hearth and a Brahms piano concerto poured from the record player. "She wouldn't give me her name, but said she knew you'd want to talk to her."

With curiosity, Kate rose and followed him to the gatehouse sunroom. As Martin discreetly disappeared, she stood for a moment in the arched doorway and looked at the woman—about her own age, with blue eyes like cornflowers and lovely patrician features. Her shining soft brown hair was drawn back into a plain bun that was oddly attractive, and the high natural color on her cheeks made her eyebrows and lashes seem even lighter. The tweeds she was wearing simply accentuated her slim figure, and her only piece of jewelry was a small gold locket.

She had thrown her coat over the back of one of the white wicker chairs and was looking out into the winter-barren garden.

"Yes?" Kate said, walking slowly toward her. The woman turned and stared at her, not speaking, her eyes intense, as though trying in the short span of fifteen or twenty seconds to decide what kind of person Kate was. "You wanted to see me?"

"Oh, I'm frightfully sorry," the woman said, and Kate heard the British accent, saw the attempt at a smile. "This must seem awfully rude of me. I could have simply written you a letter. But I—well, I felt that I had to see you. Please forgive me for coming like this."

"I'm afraid I don't understand." Kate slowly shook her head.

"I suppose I wanted to see if I could tell exactly what kind of person you are." She laughed a small apologetic laugh, one with an undertone of sadness in it. "The kind of person that"—she paused—"a man can't stop loving."

Bewildered, Kate spread her hands and shook her head.

"My name is Meg Wheeler."

As recognition stole through Kate, she gasped and quickly gripped the back of a chair for support. "Please—please sit down."

"Del is in New York on business." The woman smiled and sat on the wicker settee. "His first trip back to the States since the war. And he wanted to see his grandmother."

"Did she recognize him?" Kate recovered enough to ask. "She's so very old, and her memory slips quite badly."

Meg smiled again, a sweet, understanding smile. "Yes, fortunately. She was terribly thrilled to see him." For a moment they were silent, then she spoke again. "He doesn't know I'm here, of course. But before I—" She looked down at her hands in her lap. "I wanted to see you, talk to you, see if I could discover what you're really like." She looked up with clear blue eyes. "He never told me about you. Not for years. But somehow a woman knows. If she lives with a man. And then, at last, I asked him. I didn't want to. For years I had convinced myself that he really cared, that there wasn't anyone else, not really. Although deep down inside, I knew. But one day I could stand it no longer. And I asked him. We never had children." She said it so simply that tears came to Kate's eyes. "And it seemed I had held him long enough."

"I'm so sorry," Kate whispered, crossing to her and sitting beside her.

"He told me everything. All about you, and something . . ." She looked off to the garden through the french doors. ". . . of what had been between you." She looked up again, and Kate saw the pain in her eyes. "Is your son his child? Del wonders, you see."

Kate looked away, then slowly nodded. "Yes,"

There was a long pause.

"Is he here?"

"No." Kate shook her head slowly. "He's away at school."

Again there was a long pause.

"I suppose it will seem strange to you, but I would like to have seen him."

"No." Kate smiled a little. "I think I can understand."

Meg rose and walked to one of the wide windows and looked out. "It's lovely here. Even at this time of the year."

She turned back once more. "I want to apologize again for coming here."

"Please don't," Kate said quickly, moving toward her, suddenly wanting to reach out and touch her, comfort her, tell her she knew how she was suffering, and that it had taken great courage to do what she was doing. "I can understand that too."

Meg smiled sadly. "I wish I could go away from here telling myself that you're not the right person for him, not worth all these years of loss. But I can't, you see." She laughed a little. "You seem quite like the kind of person I would like to have known, to have for a friend."

Kate walked to her and took her hand. "I was thinking the same thing," she said, smiling a tremulous smile.

Meg's clasp tightened on Kate's hand, then she picked up her coat. "I told the taxi driver to please wait for me." She crossed to the door, where she turned. "I shall tell Del that I want a divorce. That I want to go back to England alone."

She was smiling, but Kate saw the glint of tears as she slipped on her coat and disappeared. Moments later she heard the distant sound of Martin's voice as he saw her to the door, then the motor on the taxi starting up and finally driving away.

She stood at the window of the sunroom until the sky had grown dark. She felt numb, stunned by Meg Wheeler's visit. The sound of Meg's voice was still in the room, silvery and clear, and Kate kept seeing her eyes, filled with pain, but smiling, reaching out. She could see why Del had married her. There was a gentleness about her, a quick warmth, a straightforwardness that Del would have immediately responded to. Yes . . . she and Meg, in another life, could have been friends.

But as the numbness began to flow away, she felt a growing excitement. Del, she thought . . . in her wildest dreams she could never have believed this could happen. Perhaps seeing him again, feeling his arms around her, hearing his voice. After all these years her love was as strong for him as it had ever been. Stronger, she thought. She felt her heart beating hard, a tingling along her spine, almost a faintness, as she imagined him kissing her again, his hands against her flesh, whispering in her ear, telling her he loved her and wanted her. Wanted her. "Del," she whispered into the dusk, "are you coming back to me?"

Catching her breath in a little gasp, she walked about the

room, turning on lamps. How will I ever bear it, she wondered, waiting for him to call, waiting for him to come to me? By going back to the library and finishing the work on those figures, she told herself.

But instead she floated through the house and up the staircase. She would take a long, hot, scented bath, then have her dinner on a tray before the fire in her bedroom, and just . . . dream. Dream of how perhaps her whole life was going to be different from that moment on.

It was three days before Del phoned her.

Kate dressed carefully. She put on a sheer wool dress in gray that fell softly over her hips and her single strand of long pearls, then stood back and looked at herself in the full-length mirror. What would Del see? she wondered. Would he find her changed? And Del? Would he be changed, look different? She smiled softly. Nothing that she loved in Del could be changed. Older, yes. They were both eighteen years older. But the qualities in Del that had first drawn her to him and made her fall deeply in love with him, only to have that love grow stronger with the years—those qualities never change in a person, she thought. His quiet sense of purpose, his strength and strong principles, the way he made her feel protected, safe. And yes, his charm, his ability to laugh at foolish, unimportant things, his polished masculinity and quiet virility.

Obviously these were the qualities that had made Meg fall in love with him, too, Kate admitted, the qualities that had carried him through the long and terrible months of hiding in France from the Nazis, fighting his way to the coast and waiting there for rescue.

Slowly she turned and looked at her reflection in the mirror once more. The tiny lines at her eyes and near her mouth, the wide band of silver in her dark gold hair, would surprise him perhaps. A wildly romantic soul in spite of his good common sense and stability, he would expect her to be the same. All these years he would have thought of her as exactly the way she was the last moment they had seen each other, there in the lovely room above the cove.

"Oh, Del," she whispered softly, "I want to be exactly the same for you." And she felt tears come to her eyes as she thought of lost youth and shattered dreams.

She turned and walked out of her bedroom, down the stairs of the empty house, and into the sunroom. Martin and

Nelson and Carla had been given the day and the night off. She waited and waited until the sun slanted low in the west, sending long fingers of light through the wide arched windows and across the polished flagstone floor.

She heard the sound of a car and somehow knew it would be Del. At the crunch of wheels in the circular driveway, she ran through the house and flung open the door.

For several moments they simply looked at each other, Del halfway up the walk, Kate in the doorway, oblivious to the cold wind. Then he caught her in his arms on the steps. "Del!" she cried.

"Katy, Katy, Katy," he whispered against her hair. "I've dreamed over and over about this happening, but never believed that it would."

She felt her tears against the rough fabric of his coat, heard her voice, half in laughter, half in sobs. "Del," she kept saying, over and over.

Somehow they found themselves in the house with the door closed, and then in the library in front of the fire. She was in his arms, and they sank to the floor. For what seemed like forever, he stroked her face and searched each feature with his eyes, murmuring over and over, "As lovely as ever, Katy. Lovelier than when I last saw you."

"I was afraid you'd find me old," she whispered.

"Old!" he laughed. "You look exactly the same, only more beautiful than ever."

She looked into his face and understood what he meant. The lines had deepened, his face was thinner, the skin more tautly drawn over his cheekbones, and his hair was longer, the military cut gone. But he looked the same, strong and male and bronzed, just as she remembered him. Older, yes, but the same; the dear familiarity of his face, the feel of his arms as he held her, the great surge of longing she felt as he held her closer and closer.

"I have to say this, all of this, before we go any further," he said, still holding her to him and speaking softly, rapidly against her hair. And as he spoke she didn't move, simply let him talk and carefully listened. "I loved Meg—*love*, not loved—you have to understand that, Katy. She's thoroughly decent and lovely and good and intelligent, and no one could have been more fortunate than I to have met her when I did. And I—I would never have asked her to even consider a divorce. But . . . well, all this time, it seems, she suspected something. And finally she insisted that I tell her. Even then,

390

when I told her, nothing more was said. And much as I wanted you—" His arms tightened and his lips brushed her cheek. "I wouldn't have done anything. But then, two days ago, she told me she had been here, and how much she liked you—"

"Oh, Del," Kate said with a sob.

"No, my darling, no," he said softly, stroking her, rocking her in his arms. "Both she and I knew, in that moment, there was no going back. Meg is that kind of woman."

"I know," Kate said softly, nodding her head.

For a long, long moment they were silent. They heard the soft crackling of the fire and the wind soughing against the windows, and then he turned her face up to his and kissed her, and the fire of old blazed through her. And then they were quiet once more.

"It's funny," he said, "but you were never out of my mind, always there, lurking in the back, no matter where I was or what I was doing. And I remember one moment in particular, when I realized that always in my subconscious somewhere I had thought I would see you again, be with you again some day. They were smuggling us out of Paris to the coast, and they smuggled us right out in the open, gave us civilian clothes and phoney papers. We'd picked up enough French to get by, especially with the Germans whose French usually wasn't any better than ours."

He was speaking in a low, even monotone as he held her close.

"Then they finally took us to the railway station, the Gare Saint Lazare, about ten of us, and with just one Resistance member, my friend Michel Poussin, who told us to break up and mingle with the crowds until the train was announced, then merge immediately at the train gate and follow him onto the train. He warned us to keep an eye on one another, and we did."

Kate knew that he was far away, reliving every moment.

"Suddenly I heard the announcement and, looking around as I walked toward the gate, I saw some of the others pushing through the crowds too. There were German soldiers all around us, but we all pushed on, and everything seemed fine. I saw Michel at the gate and was almost there, when suddenly a voice from back near the stand where newspapers were sold shouted out, 'Hey, you guys, wait for me!' "

He stopped. And she felt the terror and shock he must have known.

"It was Ferguson, a Fortress tail gunner, who had forgotten to keep his eyes open, and was looking at the magazines on the stand, when suddenly he looked up and realized he didn't see any of us. I kept right on walking, knowing that the Germans would be alerted, and all at once I found myself, in a panic, thinking, 'They're going to begin shooting, and I'll never see Katy again!'" As she clutched him, his arms tightened again. "But nothing happened and we got to the train all right. Even Ferguson. And made it to the coast, and finally England." He stroked her face again and whispered, "So, you see, I never really gave up . . . always felt that . . . somehow this would happen."

"Marry me, Del, and come here to live with me."

"Here, and the house at the cove, Katy."

They rose and walked up the thickly carpeted stairway to her bedroom, where slowly they undressed each other in the firelight and lay back on the bed. A sleeting snow lashed the windows, but Kate felt the safeness and warmth of his arms as he simply held her for long minutes. Her heart was pounding and then she felt the wild beating of his heart, too, as he began to touch her body. She had forgotten—or had she?— the sweet drowning sensation, the familiarity of his hands as they roamed softly over her flesh. Every nerve ending had come alive, and with eagerness she touched him as well, felt him tense for a moment, then move against her in a maddening rhythm, his long smooth body and knowing hands possessing her, feeding her hunger. And as he pressed within her, she cried out, only his name and some incoherent cry of love. Caught in the plunging tide of passion, their bodies writhed in the golden firelight until the burst of release was followed by stillness, and they lay back, drowsily, hands still touching, but in soft, reassuring caresses, words coming in whispers.

Finally he rose. Kate watched him against the flickering light as he crossed and put another log on the hearth. Stretching languorously, she said, "Please, Del, just stand there for a moment, just a moment—so I can really believe this is real, that I'm not dreaming." He stood quietly, watching her, then crossed back and slipped down beside her. Wide green eyes watched him in the fragrant half darkness. He touched her, running his hands down the satiny skin, and she shivered, rising to his touch. They had made love, and would again, she knew, before the night was over, but for now she just wanted this exquisite awareness, the touching and murmuring and knowing that at last they were together once more.

With her fingertips she traced the fine lines at the corner of his eyes, touched the strands of silver at the edges of his hair.

"We *are* older, Del," she said with a thread of questioning in her voice.

"Thank God for that. Hopefully all the mistakes have been made."

The restaurant was packed with its usual lunchtime crowd. It was that time of day when voices and laughter were at a pitch and tables were at a premium. But John, the maitre d', was giving his two best waiters certain instructions.

"That party in the corner, Mrs. Barnfield's party. It's a very special luncheon, so I want you to pay particular attention. And Elizabeth Lowndes is in the party. She's opening in a new play and may have rehearsals this afternoon, so keep an eye on her in case she's in a hurry."

The waiters nodded, discreetly rushed to the table, and placed menus in front of each member of the party, then just as discreetly withdrew.

Jenny looked down the restaurant table to where Jon and Susan sat at the end, almost whispering as they talked and, with a certain shyness, tested their feelings. They hadn't seen each other since the summer at Amalfi three years before, and even letters and memories and the fantasy dreams of the young hadn't prepared them for this meeting. Usually brash and always in control, Jon could find nothing clever or amusing to say, while Susan, ordinarily a thoroughly poised young nineteen-year-old, seemed breathless and beyond sensible conversation, her lovely young face raised to his.

Turning to Kate sitting next to her, Jenny grinned. "Good Lord, do you remember what it was like to feel like that?"

"Yes," Kate said softly. "With Del back. But to be that young again?" She looked at them, and then at Jenny. "It was 1941."

Jenny's grin slowly turned to a wistful smile. "Just think . . . how we might never have been in that room together."

Kate nodded, her mood matching Jenny's. "So much has happened since we met on that dismal gray morning so many years ago."

They both looked at Liz, who sat across the table from them, listening. "Almost exactly twenty-two years ago," she said, shaking her head. "It doesn't seem possible."

393

For a moment they glanced about at the other three, Julie and Christopher and Joanna, deep in conversation at the other end of the table, suddenly bursting into laughter as Chris, sitting between the two girls, finished telling them a story. They were so beautiful and vibrant and young.

"Chris just came from a long morning meeting with Hack Crawford. Thanks to Liz," Jenny explained to Kate. "He's written several plays, one-acts, and Hack says he's talented. That's one reason Ian and I decided to come to New York to live, so Chris could work in the theater here. Hack put him on as an assistant stage manager for Liz's new play." She looked down the table at Susan and Jon again. "And of course Susan was delighted, for more reasons than one, among them a passionate desire to attend an American college, watch American television, and learn how to do some kind of wacky dances called the Bop and the Stroll."

They laughed comfortably, ordered cocktails and their lunch, often reached out and simply touched or clasped hands, listened to the lighthearted banter or earnest discussions of their children, then turned back to one another as they lingered over a final cup of coffee.

"All living here again," Liz said, looking up and smiling, her smile embracing them both. Then she glanced around the table and back to them. "I'm so glad you suggested this, Kate, with all the children here at this one moment, and you two both in town." She looked long and lovingly at Julie, who had flown in especially for the reunion from the West Coast, where she worked for Keith Widemeyer, the producer.

"Well, when Joanna wrote that the Peace Corps was transferring her from the training camp in Hawaii to her first post in Uganda, I knew we all had to get together. Who knows when she'll get back to the States again? And luckily it just coincided with Jon's Thanksgiving week from Harvard."

"And Susan's no problem," Jenny said, stirring a lump of sugar into her coffee. "Right here at New York University."

"Dan phoned last night. Said he wished he could be here," Liz said and smiled. "At least it's all in reverse now, working and living in New York and going to London occasionally on business, rather than the other way around."

She looked at Kate and Jenny, thinking how the passage of years had been kind to them, sadness and loss leaving a mark, but in a strong rather than hardening way. She suddenly reached out and held their hands.

"What *about* you and Del, Kate?"